# Around the Way Girls 9

# Around the Way Girls 9

*Ms. Michel Moore, La'Tonya West, and T.C. Littles*

www.urbanbooks.net

M oo

Urban Books, LLC
97 N 18th Street
Wyandanch, NY 11798

ISBN 13: 978-1-62286-909-1
ISBN 10: 1-62286-909-5

First Mass Market Printing June 2015
First Trade Paperback Printing July 2014
Printed in the United States of America

10 9 8 7 6 5 4 3 2 1

Distributed by Kensington Publishing Corp.
Submit Orders to:
Customer Service
400 Hahn Road
Westminster, MD 21157-4627
Phone: 1-800-733-3000
Fax: 1-800-659-2436

# Around the Way Girls 9

Ms. Michel Moore, La'Tonya West, and T.C. Littles

# Smooth as Butter

by

*Ms. Michel Moore*

# Chapter One

## *Shannon*

"Um, excuse the hell outta me, but since when did you start giving a fuck about me and my well-being, Ma?" Rolling my eyes with intensity, everything about this out-of-the-blue conversation was starting to aggravate me in the worst type of way known to mankind. "You know we ain't even like that with each other now don't you?"

"Shannon, enough is enough. You really need to let go of the past, sweetheart. If you haven't noticed from all your destructive behavior, look around, it's practically eating you alive. I've been telling you for years now I'm a changed person. For God's sake, can't you see that? I'm not that woman anymore."

Shannon knew her mother. She knew right about now her mom was tightly clutching her blue spiral notebook of handwritten faith prayers she kept nearby. It was common knowledge Fly Shawntay, as she'd once nicknamed herself in a former life, prayed her daughter would at least give their relationship a chance to heal. Wanting to try anything to make things right, Shannon knew, her mother figured that having her estranged daughter's cell phone number was at least a start.

"Oh, please stop it, Ma. For once try to keep it real with me and get off your soapbox. It's not enough days in the week or weeks in the years in the entire world to undo what the woman you allegedly are now," she snidely mocked, sucking her teeth, "used to do to me. So you can do me a favor and fall all the way back with that 'get over it and move on' routine you running. Me, trust, I'm straight on all that. Save your sob story of redemption for the Lord you all of sudden love so damn much more than the bottle, or some random stray-ass man you picked up from the gutter the night before; I've gotta go. I got real shit to do with real motherfuckers who care about me!" Hanging up the phone in her ear without so much as a second thought, I could only shake my head in regret of my childhood. See, there wasn't nothing Ms. Fly Shawntay could tell me about being a Christian woman that I'd go for. In my eyes, flat out, she'd always be that over-the-top alcoholic I learned my addictive behavior from, so for that, among a thousand or so countless other reasons I could easily name, she wasn't about to get treated with nothing more than a swift "Fuck you long and hard and good-the-hell-bye."

Taking a long look in the floor-length mirror propped in the far corner of my room, I hated myself more each passing day. Seeing a small but ever-present reflection of my mother in my eyes and my father in my skin tone, I pawed at my natural hair down the middle of my back. "Damn!" I fumed, angry at what most weave-wearing females walking the streets prayed for. "Why'd I have to be born like this? Why couldn't I just be as black as her or white as him? Not some 'stuck in the middle,' out-of-place mute everyone hates on!"

Taking a few sips of the Avión on ice I'd been slow nursing all morning, I was ready to guzzle the entire bottle down after listening to my mother front like she gave two sweet fucks about the way my life was turning out. That rotten-intentions bitch had figured out long ago how to get inside my head and mess it up. But after a few stiff drinks and a couple of "get right" pills, I'd be right back on track as if she'd never called. I ain't never been Shawntay's prized possession like most daughters would be to their mothers, so I knew the Clair Huxtable game she was trying to run on me was for the birds. As usual, Shawntay wanted something; that much was crystal clear. She might've been saved, or so she said, but I was still Butter, baby, and my shit was too smooth to fall for her old tricks.

Walking into the bathroom, I ignored my ringing cell knowing it was only her trying to recite

some scripture or beg for forgiveness; all part of
the scam she was probably running. *Damn, leave
me alone and drop dead!* Making a mental note
to get my number changed, I rolled my eyes with
disgust over who'd given it to her from jump. I
couldn't control how she was acting and I hated it.
This was nothing more than her dose of drama for
the month. Taking another sip of the eighty-proof
liquor that was getting my mind right for work, I
popped the rubber band from my long, wavy hair,
letting it cascade down my back. *Damn, I wish I
could catch a break in this cold-hearted-ass world.
Ain't shit ever been easy for me. Nothing like these
bitter hoes think*. Rubbing my temples trying to
relieve the throbbing and pressure, I couldn't wait
to totally transform from Shannon into Butter and
get my night started. Dancing had become more
than my crutch for living my upscale lifestyle, but
my escape as well.

With a lust for relaxation, I slid my pink robe
off. In a daze, I watched the floating mist rise from
the heated water. Letting my garment fall onto the
cold marble floor, I took another sip of my drink
before setting the long-stemmed glass down on
the window's edge. Taking a deep breath, I dipped
my freshly manicured toes into the Jacuzzi tub
of water, testing the temperature before happily
easing my entire down body inside. Turning the
jets on high, the bubbles started to engulf me as the

warmth soothed my aching muscles. *Oh yeah, this is exactly what a bitch like me needs!*

As much self-hate as I had stored up in me for this half-breed, moneymaking body of mine, men, young and old, black and white, completely adored it. They couldn't get enough of their mulatto baby doll. So, by nature of loving that almighty dollar I worked long hours to fulfill their every, sometimes extremely perverted, desire; every lap dance was a quick twenty a song. Not interested in the desperate life I once led, I wasn't trying to go back to broke. I'd made up my mind, long ago, that bullshit wasn't an option. I was true to the game of my craft and played my role to the fullest. There wasn't a center-stage pole I couldn't climb to the top of and do a few of my signature twist-and-turn moves on without being guaranteed a pile of money at the bottom once I seductively slid back down. As most men remarked, I had the total package. If it wasn't my green cat eyes inherited from my sperm donor father that lured them in, it was my curved black-girl body I most certainly got from Shawntay that kept them blessing me with tips. I might've ultimately hated her and James for my creation but if it weren't for them giving me the perfect blend of black and white, I wouldn't have the exotic look that kept the nameless cake customers consistently throwing cash my way.

I'd been headlining at Bare Faxxx for almost a solid two years, seeing both up and down days inside the dimly lit palace of seduction. But never before had it been cranking like this past weekend. The owner had been promising better days to come and it seemed like his half-good-ass word actually had some truth to it. The drinks were flowing and the dollars were raining. Stan Dilbert and his puppet-master mayor were in the midst of transforming downtown Detroit from a dilapidated, crack-infested haven into a white-businessman-money Mecca. Low-key, they'd been buying up property, successfully evicting the crud out of the heart of the city, taking it over one block at a time. The housing of heroin pushers and junkies that the area was notoriously known for had been replaced by the working class, suit and tie briefcase carriers, who were once afraid to drive into the D from suburbia let alone party after dark. Where did I fit in? Let's just say me and my girls were just good-looking trinkets to fulfill their freaking fantasies.

*Damn! Maybe I'm more like Shawntay than I think; she was Daddy's whore too.*

Grabbing the vanilla body wash, I poured a generous amount into the loofa before rubbing all over the top half of my body. As much as I tried to get lost in the soft, lingering scent, I couldn't push the echo of harsh voices and cruel images out of my mind that were starting to play out.

*"Scrub harder 'til that black comes off your little monkey body! Schultz genes gotta be stronger than that nigger blood."* As far back as I could remember, my so-called grandmother, my dad's mother, had been nothing but callous and cold to me my entire life. As a youth, on some days, I felt like she took pride in punishing me for my own conception. It was like living in pure hell on God's green earth. Come to think of it, that's why I have little faith and hope now in people. While seemingly forced, giving me baths as a child, Sally Schultz would put damn near a whole gallon of milk into the scalding water, hoping the mixture would miraculously soak into my skin to lighten my complexion up more. From bleaching creams shipped from third world countries to consulting every dermatologist her money could buy, she was on a mission to make me appear not such an embarrassment to her uppity, judgmental, prejudiced friends.

*"I can't believe he done made me a colored grandbaby. Your father is just downright disgraceful to our race, Shannon; well, mines anyway."* Grandmother Sally used to shake her head as I stared up at her with six-year-old innocent doe eyes. Confused, but eager to please, I'd sit in the same ice-cold tub of milk for hours waiting on it to "make a miracle" as she'd call it. But never once was I pure white enough to fully be her precious, unconditionally loved grandbaby.

Emotionally scarred from my trip back down memory lane, I shook off the constant flashback coming back to reality. Standing up, I shivered. Glancing into the steam-filled mirror, I instantly gasped. Seeing my body had turned beet red from me trying to scrub away the slight tan I'd gotten in the mild summer heat, I dropped the loofa, immediately jumping out of the water cooling down. "Shit, I am fucked up in the head. Maybe that bitch Shawntay is right for once and my past is eating me alive!"

## 1996: Shawntay

Running through the house spraying the cheap can of aerosol spray trying to mask the pungent smell of marijuana, the last thing I needed was for James to come up in here complaining about the way I lived. I didn't owe him much of nothing but this sweet black juice he loved to drink two times a week on the regular; but for some reason, like all white people, James felt entitled to run my life. As much as he claimed he was bored with Beth, running over here to me two to three times a week, James still wanted me to be just as dainty, prissy, and stiff as his white wife while being his black fetish freak in the bedroom.

The year was 1996 and BET was just premiering its music-oriented talk show *Planet Groove*. I was dancing through the unkempt, junky living room, tripping over trash, snack bags, and liquor bottles, trying to be just as sexy if not sexier than Foxy Brown. Her video with Blackstreet, "Get Me Home," was blasting through the television as I watched her hard, wishing I had at least a quarter of the confidence she was displaying for the world to see. Foxy was flossing in luxury cars with flamboyant clothes while I was stuck driving a beat-up Ford Tempo struggle buggy, rocking Dots' fanciest clearance sale apparel. Females like Foxy were my idols; I just could never get on their level. It damn sure wasn't from lack of trying though. Men found me attractive but I never made it further than the bed or sofa they were making me orgasm on. I finally came to the conclusion that's just how it was in Fly Shawntay Jenkins's life: I was the foolish forever dreamer.

Sounds of a horn rang out. Back to reality. Running to my dingy curtains, I peeked through them, seeing James's shiny white Mercedes-Benz pulling into the broken concrete driveway of my rented flat. He might've hated the hood, so he said, but he loved getting the attention poor black folks were known to give if they saw "the man" flossing. My neighbors were no different from the norm. They stayed gossiping about the blond-haired, green-eyed devil I welcomed into my home every time they'd blink.

"Hey, lover boy, long day golfing?" I swung the door open, cooing softly while smiling.

"As a matter of fact I did have a long day at the course. It was nothing but a relief to get a breather from that stuffy conference room to cater to some potential clients over tee time." Enunciating every single syllable with exactness and clarity, James' properness matched his swag: 100 percent straight-gate nerdish.

He was dressed in a pair of pleated khaki shorts that came right above his knees, a hard-pressed white Ralph Lauren Polo shirt and matching Polo boat shoes with no socks. I laughed on the inside because he was the perfect prototype for Barbie's Ken, only I wasn't Barbie. Ken was taking a walk on the dark side fucking Chrissy. "I guess I don't have to ask what you've been doing with your day." He snobbishly turned his nose up, waving away the smell I had tried to hide from his Inspector Gadget nostrils.

"Nope, you don't. I ain't trying to hear that shit today, James, so don't."

"Stop." He threw his hand up in front of my face as if he was a school crossing guard. "You know I'm not a fan of your bitching. So I won't say another word on the subject, I swear!" Sitting down onto my taped-together leather furniture, I could tell by his square jaw being locked tight that he was fighting off coming at me with another smart comment or insult, but held it back. "Here, make use of yourself. Fix me a stiff drink." He handed me the brown paper bag.

I didn't bother peeking inside. My Caucasian meal ticket stayed consistent. Every Monday, Wednesday, and sometimes on a good week Friday he'd come here with an unopened fifth of Absolut vodka, a half gallon of orange juice, and a tiny blue pill to get him just right. After about an hour of us drinking and me seductively dancing for him, I'd be posted down on my knees getting them bitches dirty or twisted in some crazed porno position, getting his less-than-meaty dick roughly rammed inside me. Jimmy wasn't the best fuck I'd ever experienced, but he no doubt was the most consistent. Besides him hitting it on the regular, I couldn't keep the black-ass weed man out of my hot pocket either.

After getting him comfortable with a drink and a hard on, I disappeared into the bedroom to get dressed for my hustle, which paid my bills. My everyday street-ready wardrobe might've been meager to say the least, but my silk, lace, and satin lingerie collection could easily shut any one department store's selection down. Once a week for sure I always knew James was going to walk through the door with a sexy pair of panties for me to model for him. That was "his thang." Now I wasn't judging him, because we all got some shit with us, and that sexy lingerie plastered on a hot black female body was his. Now I didn't know if he treated his wife like a sex kitten; but if he wasn't concerned about his supposed sacred marriage vows why should I have been? As for me, I played whatever role my "big daddy" wanted me to play, including his sex slave, because his dollars spent long and at the end of the day money was all that mattered.

Grabbing the dollar store container of Shea butter from my nightstand, I scooped out a half-dollar-sized amount, sliding it up and down my ashy legs, working the grease in. Making sure my whole body was smooth, I sprayed on the Elizabeth Taylor White Diamonds perfume he'd brought me during one of his many visits. I hated this loud-smelling white woman scent but he wouldn't touch me without smelling it on my dark skin. In that weird motherfucker's head, he probably wanted me to smell like Beth so he could fuck his fantasy while smelling his true love at the same time. Sliding on the red bustier set he'd brought me from Victoria's Secret, the thong disappeared into my forty-two-inch ass while my thirty-six C-cup tits set lovely. Damn, I was a fly bitch.

Coming out of the bedroom seeing James stripped down to his tighty-whitey Polo drawers and crisp white Hanes undershirt, the little bulge was a clear sign his pill had taken full effect. He seemed out of place in my scanty, stale-smelling house full of mismatched furniture and outdated electronics. But I wasn't the least bit embarrassed about the way I lived. He'd made it perfectly clear the first time we met through the call service I worked for that he had a fetish for thick black girls. I'd heard it all before: white guys loved our thick curves, fat asses, and the massive explosion they'd get from having our nappy hair wrapped in their hands. I didn't mind playing the stereotypical role. Once he became a regular client, it was easy for me to cut my madam out, allowing him to come straight to my house so I could keep the entire profit for myself. He didn't turn the proposition down because it allowed him to get more uninhibited.

"What are you over there hiding all of that fine chocolate sexiness for?" James looked up from his drink, already drooling. "I done already seen all of what you got. Bring that body over here." He sounded like a true redneck, like he always did once the liquor got into his system.

"I'm sorry for keeping you waiting, daddy," I purred. Modeling across the room, I kept my brown eyes glued to his while they eagerly lit up. Once I got in front of him, I started to sway sexily, trying to further arouse him. Turning around, I bent over, letting him smush his face into my round behind as I jiggled knowing it was turning him on. My juices were starting to flow. I loved getting down with this kinky white man. "You love this ass huh? Smack it up, massa!" I was getting all the way into my role and he was also feeling it.

James smacked my ass a few rough times making me jump and breathe hard. He loved taking control. Grabbing my waist, turning me around, he ran his tongue across my neck then to my ear. "You smell delicious, my little blackberry—almost good enough to eat." As much as "my Jimmy" loved my cunt and I begged for it, he'd never stick his tongue into this juicy peach. "Get on them knees, girl, and put that smart mouth of yours to use." Dropping down, seeing his hard pink cock staring me in the face, it was time to get to work and earn my revenue.

### James aka Jimmy

Shawntay was a fucking wet dream come to life. I was mesmerized by her dark beauty in every way. Her black body was thick, perfect, and available when I needed it to be. I'd had plenty of black girls service me growing up in a Confederate household, but none were grown up enough to take the degrading things I liked to do. Shawntay fulfilled every fantasy I dreamed of, mimicked every porn star I was in love with, and never once turned her face up when I asked for a rim job. She was the absolute best in bed, nothing like my wife. Beth had been threatening to leave me and end our marriage since finding out my fetish had been happening more regularly; but I wasn't getting ready to give up carrying on Schultz man tradition in any way. We lived dirty by doing filthy things to the help behind closed doors but our family motto was to take our unclean deeds to the grave.

Besides needing Shawntay to fulfill my sexual fantasies, I needed to release this nut because the tension of waiting on multiple investors to help me get my company even further off the ground was overbearing. Beth was pregnant, our bills were growing, and my mother was slowly running through the estate money my dad left to her. The burden was heavy on me to provide for my entire family; my father would've expected no less.

Shawntay was going to town on my pink pecker. I could feel the mixture of drool and my pre-cum running down to my ball sac but never once did she slow down or come up for air. *This bitch is the fucking best!* Moaning loudly, I was getting lost in how hot she looked gripping my white cock with her dark fingers. "Slurp it all up you little slut," I whispered through clenched teeth, grabbing her head. Feeling her tongue tickle my shaft, I gripped two handfuls of her kinky hair, using them as reins as I used all of my force to thrust my hips to meet her mouth. Her slurping sounds were turning me on even more. "Get down on the floor and spread 'em wide, tootsie." *I gotta give it to her good. I know she's accustomed to horse-hung black men.*

## Shawntay

I bet he couldn't fuck Beth like this; her flat booty and prude attitude probably couldn't take all of Jimmy's stamina. I allowed him to climb on top of me to do his business until he fell over drunk and sweaty. I worked hard for my dollar. "Damn, Jimmy, you're working this fat cat out. You're so big and good!" It was all part of the game, even though he wasn't half bad at this.

After twenty minutes of him panting, trying his best to be the best fuck of my life, his eyes rolled into the back of his head as he let out a loud scream. "I'm about to unload this thick cream up in you!" Within two seconds I could feel his hot sperm shooting up in me. "I love black pussy!" After Jimmy pulled out, letting his now-flaccid penis fall limp to the left, my vagina was leaking globs of his semen.

*I keep telling his Shawntay-loving ass I ain't on no birth control pill.*

# Chapter Two

## *Shannon aka Butter*

"What up, Butter baby? I see you came in early to take some of these bum bitches' money." Dazz, the DJ of Bare Faxxx, laughed when he saw me walk in.

"You already know it, my baby." I smiled, making my way to the bar. "I'm trying to get winning and stay that way."

"Don't I know it. Well, if you ain't too tired after mopping the club with these bitches, holla at ya mans for a private dance. I've got dollars." Dazz stayed flirting with me and every other dancer in the club. None of us took him serious but all of us took trips into the booth with him. He always made good on his word to fill our thongs with even more.

"We'll see how the night goes no doubt." I winked before turning to order my drink from the bar. I might've had no problem getting raunchy for some greenbacks but I had to have my liquor to do so. "Hey, Dolly, let me get a double shot of Patrón."

Dolly was the bartender who kept all of us extra fucked up while we got our jobs done. She'd always put a little extra in the dancers' drinks knowing we'd have to take any and every patron getting as frisky as they wanted. Frank, the manager, with his dark-haired, musty, Chaldean self didn't believe in giving his paying patrons rules—especially with so many of them owning business around this small dump.

"Afternoon, Butter." Dolly slid the shot glass across the bar. "Imagine seeing you up this early after last night."

"Girl, bye. You know this shit is like water to me; it's nothing." Tilting the glass back, taking the shot down halfway, I had to remember I'd be here for the long haul, probably 'til two o'clock. I was on a paper chase, hungry to feed my habits, so getting drunk straight in the door wasn't a good idea. Plus I had my own bottle stashed away in my duffel bag to keep the money I made pocketed.

"I would get hammered too if I had to deal with these petty-ass bitches." She rolled her eyes, running her hands through her long weave. Dolly was never part of the drama but always stayed in the drama. I knew these wannabe skeezers had it out for me so she didn't need to add her two cents. But it was all part of the club mentality.

"I ain't worried about them, Doll. If it ain't green with dead presidents on it, Butter ain't meltin'." It was a daily endeavor to deal with the amount of attitude these girls served up to me because of my natural beauty. I couldn't help that I could serve what my momma gave me.

"I feel that, honey. I wouldn't be slowing up either for these hating bitches. Make that money!" Reaching over, giving me a high five, we laughed for a moment 'til I caught Isis staring coldly from the sideline. She was the main mad-hating trick. Isis wasn't ugly in the face if you liked 'em extra black with thick lips and a big nose. If it wasn't for her DD chest, forty-inch ass, and pole climbing techniques, she would've been an alley cat for sure. I ain't give a fuck though 'cause her hustle wasn't slowing my grind.

"Here we go!" Taking a second thought then gulping my drink, it was time to get in rare form so I could handle Isis. "Is there something I can do for you, babe? Can I buy you a drink or something?" Turning toward my nemesis, I was taunting her on purpose. "I know shit around here has been slow for you lately."

"Bitch, you ain't in my pile. It's definitely straight over this way." She looked herself up and down, admiring her own body. "Every nigga who walk through this door ain't checking for your mix-breed ass. Believe that!"

"Again I ask then, Isis, why you all in my grill over here checking for me?" Rolling my eyes, snatching my bag up, I wasn't getting ready to entertain this li'l monkey any longer with the lunch doors getting ready to open. "Today ain't the day, Isis. Please do you and let me do me. It's money to be made." Turning my back on her and walking away, I wasn't the least bit intimidated or worried about her attacking me from the back. Not only was Dolly there to break us up if something popped off, Isis didn't have her homegirls to back her up. No one moved in the club solo-dolo but me.

"Yo' drunk ass probably gonna be passed out before dinnertime. Keep clutching that bottle."

I ignored Isis, letting the locker room door close out her still-irritating voice. She wasn't getting ready to say anything I hadn't already heard. Growing up in the hood with light eyes, long, soft hair, super light skin, and getting picked up in a Mercedes-Benz once a week made me stand out to be bullied by all the kids in the neighborhood. I'd been called everything from an Oreo to a wigger. It ain't shit these money-hungry heffas could call me that the cruel kids in the hood hadn't already run into the ground.

Unzipping my duffel bag, pulling my first custom-made outfit out, I was getting ready to stunt on these hoes big time. Stan Dilbert was hosting a Rebuild Detroit conference at Cobo Hall, so the tables were expected to be overflowing with associates paid out of their mind like him. I'd worked the Friday nightshift when all of his low-level employees partied hard, tipping me their checks. And if their hourly paychecks afforded to pay my car note, rent, and bills while accommodating my wardrobe and alcohol taste, I could only imagine what the real CEO/owner was working with. Signaling for the makeup artist so she could put me down for a spot, I slid my clothes off in preparation to transform.

"A'ight you filthy-rich bastards, get them cards out 'cause we're now accepting plastic. Coming to the stage for your lunch special delight is the infamous Butter!"

Bare Faxxx was packed with white faces all with loose-collared business shirts and hanging ties. With hunger in their eyes, they watched, drooling like dogs as I walked onto the stage. These men were craving to see my lustrous body bend over, twirl, and gyrate. Their wish was my command as I saw big bills, dollar bills, and credit cards fly up into the air. Dressed in an electric-blue sequin stretch leather set, the G-string itself had been swallowed by my two cheeks while the bra barely held my tits up. Stripping the tip off, I jiggled then played with my nipples, making even more dollars fly. *Yeah, Butter, let's take these white boys for a ride.* Moving across the stage, giving them all equal attention, I needed to milk their pockets just right so Butter could become more than just a household name. I was trying to be bigger than the game.

"Let me see that fat ass bounce, girl! Climb that pole! It's definitely Butter, baby!" Rolling my eyes, biting my lip, I fell right into line hip rolling then twerking for my fans. *G'on and take their money. You can drink, smoke, and snort hella good tonight.* It didn't take much for me to fall into my "get money by any means" trance. I could tell why the other dancers felt inferior when I came on the set; no matter how much I hated myself, my flawless beauty and curved physique couldn't be denied. These men were craving me like addicts but I was down to fulfill whatever dirty desires they had. Bending over, letting the cold pole slide up and down my chubby cheeks, I saw dollars flying onto the stage but I was just getting warmed up.

"You want some of this?" I ground my kitten while whispering to a few of the men who'd become brave enough to come front and center to the stage. "G'on and pay for it." I was more like Jimmy than I liked to admit. I loved the power and control I'd get over guys with my pussy. It was more than amazing! Feeling their clammy palms gripping on my legs, running across my inner thighs, and trying to steal feels on my twat, I pulled back a little all in the game of trying to tease them. Dropping to the floor, I cat-crawled across the stage toward the pole, getting ready to put on an all-star performance. I could see Isis standing to the side with her face curled up, knowing I was shutting any chances she had at making money today down.

"Come on, redbone! Don't keep us waiting; work that motherfucking pole!" These suited-up men were ready for me to get the party started, obviously. Scanning the club, I saw Dolly keeping the drinks flowing while Frank watched me back with a stern eye. He took his breadwinners very seriously. Seeing Isis griming me from the sideline, I winked then twerked a little harder just for her. *I know it's hard to see your money dwindle down, baby girl. I've been on the broke side of the tracks once before—wasn't shit nice about it!* "You can rock my shit any day. That ass is fat, light skin."

Feeding off of the cheers, rants, and whorish names they called me, I climbed the pole like the Energizer Bunny, ready to stunt from the rafters. Flipping upside down, spreading my legs wide, I popped my ass ferociously as dollar bills flew onto the stage. *That's what the fucks I'm talking about.* Sliding back down the pole into the splits, I was feeling a rush as more men flocked over onto the stage, ready to tip me swell. Up and at 'em, spreading my thong to the side, I exposed a peek at my bare cat, ready to get flooded with even more cash.

"Yeah, fellas, show Butter some love. It's time to get your private dances on. Twenty bucks a set!" Dazz started an uproar as I sashayed off stage heading for the locker room.

Frank had employees strictly in place to collect our piles of cash so I wasn't worried about coming up short. With a roomful of horny white men turned up ready to touch, pull, and grab, I needed my liquid courage to finish the job. Yeah, it was about to be a long day with an even longer night ahead.

# Chapter Three

## *Shawntay*

"That's our daughter, Jimmy, you've gotta do something."

"How in the hell did you get this number?" James growled into the phone. "I thought I'd left your ass back in the nineties."

Shawntay gripped her Bible, hoping this wouldn't be the night to push her over the edge. It had been almost a year of her being clean—no alcohol, drugs, or prostituting—but there were always triggers to make her lose her sobriety. "Trust me; I wouldn't be calling you if it wasn't an emergency. Our baby girl is working down at Bare Faxxx. And you know what comes with that."

"Aw, come on now, you can't be that surprised. The apple don't fall far from the tree, Tay." He laughed, finding humor in something not funny at all. "What did you want her to do? Become a doctor or lawyer?"

James was never a fan of me having his child but with me hiding the pregnancy 'til I was too far long for an abortion, I'd pulled a sneak move on his ass knowing if nothing else I'd be securing child support. Every female who uses her body for money knows that once you get played out the game is over. I was looking out for the best interest of my future. James and his family, however, didn't see a biracial girl in their future. Shannon was treated bold right out of the door, starting with the DNA test he forced me to get.

"You don't have to be so cold-hearted, James. I know you ain't never been a fan of Shannon but, wow, is it really like that? You and I both know she's your flesh and blood." I was being a hypocrite because I had been nothing but harsh and callous toward Shannon growing up.

"I've told you time and time again, woman, it's not Shannon I'm not a fan of; it's sneaky whores like you who try to ruin men like me."

"It's been over twenty years. I guess you're seriously sticking to the plan on taking your hatred for me to the grave."

"Yes, indeed. Please do us both a favor and not call again. I've spent far too much money changing my number to keep you out of contact." Hanging up the phone in my ear, James and Shannon truly shared the same disrespectful gene.

## 1996: Shawntay

I'd been working eight weeks straight without seeing a drop of blood fall from my coochie. I kept up with my menstrual like the disabled counted down days to the first, so I knew what was up before even making the clinic appointment: I was pregnant. My body wasn't gonna be worth more than shit once this load dropped. It was already obvious since already I was carrying almost five pounds more, plus the mood swings had kicked in. The only good thing about this whole "gift and a curse" ordeal was that I'd be guaranteed a monthly stipend. If it was the weed man's baby I could call him or her a black solider. If it was Jimmy's baby, I could consider him or her the oppressor. Either way they both had cash, so once the doctor confirmed what I already knew, I'd be a retired call girl turned mother.

"Shawntay Jenkins," the nurse of the free neighborhood clinic called out. Dressed in hot pink scrubs with a mangy wig mounted on her head, I hoped and prayed this was Jimmy's baby so I could get some real cash to do better. I was tired of this hood shit.

"Yeah, that's me." Jumping up and walking to the door, I followed her through, being led to the examination room. It was super crowded with patients even sitting in the hallway. No one in the hood had adequate insurance so everyone from around the way got serviced here.

"Here, pee in this cup, then bring it back in here with you. I'll be back to get your vitals." Handing over the plastic cup, she turned to tend to the nodding patient getting ready to fall into the wall. "Damn, it's gonna be a long day up in this joint." She smacked her lips. Then I watched as she switched away in the most unprofessional way possible. I took a deep breath before going to go give the sample of tainted pregnant urine.

It was a dreadful long hour wait for the doctor to examine me, test my urine, and talk to me about my options. Since I was only four weeks into nine months of carrying, if I needed to terminate the pregnancy I could. "Naw, Doc, I'll just take the prenatal vitamins. This one here is a keeper." Rubbing my stomach feeling like I'd hit the jackpot; Jimmy had fathered this child so it was about to be smooth sailing from here.

## 1996: James

"How much longer is this going to go on, Jim? I can't keep taking this treatment, especially carrying our child!" Waddling into the living room as I was coming in from Shawntay's house, Beth's usual makeup-beaten face was pale, covered in streamlines of tears.

I didn't feel like hearing this with the investors just leaving a message about going elsewhere with their investment, but what other choice would I have? A woman scorned would run through flames to be heard.

"You promised me you'd quit but you've been seeing this black bitch more and more." Beth was my wife and partner going on ten years. She was the one who'd orchestrated the meetings in the first place, knowing our son would take her away from being a fifty-fifty partner in our company. I knew the extra stress of me still not having a successful investor would send her into early labor definitely, so if nothing else as a man I had to find a way to ensure our future. Had it not been for her business brain and nurturing woman instincts, I would've never taken a leap of faith to start my own company so I owed her at least that. Beth had never made me lose trust in her, being faithful and loyal to the Schultz name since I placed the two-karat diamond ring on her finger. Had I not been addicted to the sweet smell of black pussy, I wouldn't be ruining my seemingly perfect marriage.

Kicking my shoes off, falling onto the couch, I was sloppy drunk from drinking the entire bottle of Absolut myself tonight. It had definitely been an occasion to get totally fucked up. Hearing Beth whine about my fetish when it had come back to bite me in the ass for sure wasn't high on my list. "Come on now, honey, the Schultz men have been the same for generations. You knew this, your mother knew this, hell, your mother's mom knew this. We like side pieces of black meat to accompany our perfect lives." As if Beth wasn't shocked enough with her jaw dropped to the floor, I kept going with my unbearable words. "If your prude ass weren't so stale to the idea, we'd move Shawntay in to help you cook, clean, and fuck me. It'd be like that *Sister Wives* bullshit on TV."

"Go to hell, Jim! A family full of sick bastards is what I've married into. And to think I'm having a son; I hope he doesn't get cursed with any Schultz DNA. You stay out here on the couch tonight; you're not allowed in our room or at the doctor's appointment in the morning." Stomping off, Beth thought she'd thrown a small dagger; but, no, I had to have the last word.

A drunk's tongue spoke an honest word because the liquor made it impossible for the mind to control the mouth's conversation. Simply put: a drunk ain't shit. "No problem, sweetheart. Sleep tight. I'll just call Shawntay up to let her know I'm free for our baby's appointment."

Hearing her heeled slippers stop clicking on the marbled floor, I knew she was probably fuming, reading to kill strike for blood. "What the fuck did you just say to me, James Theodore Schultz III? Did I hear correctly? The nigger mistress is pregnant?" Beth's words got louder and louder as the clicks from her heels got closer. Once she appeared in the living room again, Beth was holding a vase, ready to aim and toss my way. "Now is not the time for silence, James."

"You heard me, Beth, there's no need to repeat—"

"You're a sick, trifling, dirty, cheating bastard!" She threw the vase in my direction.

I dodged to the left just as it grazed my head then shattered to a million pieces onto the hardwood floor.

"I can't believe you're sleeping with her dirty black behind without a condom! How dare you expose me to all her filthiness and germs?" Running toward me like she wasn't eight months pregnant or a woman with the lighter hand, Beth saw nothing but red and wanted instant revenge. Out of all the affairs I'd had, she'd never reacted so out of control. But then, too, I'd never slipped up in such a way.

"Calm down, Beth, it can't be undone. Just accept it so we can move on from this," I slurred, grabbing her arms to keep her from hitting me.

"Calm down? Accept it? You having a baby with your nigger-loving mistress is not something I could just move on from, Jim! You don't love me or this family." Crying hysterically, Beth couldn't stop twisting her arms, trying to pull herself away from me. My grip was too strong. "You're hurting me; just stop it and let me go."

"Not until you quit fighting me back. Wrong or not, you will not be allowed to tear this house or me up. This horrid situation is not going to go away, Beth, I'm sorry."

"As God is my witness, Jim, you better make it. If not, that kid will never exist to me. It will never be allowed in this house, to know my son, or to carry the Schultz name. You created it in the streets, so that's right where it will stay." Beth didn't blink, stutter, or give an insinuation that she was to be taken lightly. "And for that rodent you let become an intrusion into this family's wealth, she's to be cut the fuck off. I didn't struggle with you to help her live a better life, believe it." No longer fighting but staring me straight in the eye, Beth's weakness turned to a vindictive bitterness. She'd seldom cursed, usually speaking in a soft, loving tone; but at this moment, my wife meant business.

"Beth—" I tried to speak but was cut off again. Snatching her hands away from me, I'd become the weak link to a woman scorned.

"You've said too much of nothing already. I'll be calling your mother plus the lawyer in the morning to secure my best interest. If you try any funny business continuing to go against the grain, I'll take everything you have; plus you'll never see my son."

# Chapter Four

## *Shannon*

My calves were aching, my behind had been smacked raw, and I'd consumed a bottle in shots of Patrón. Yes, indeed, I was feeling high on cloud nine. Bare Faxxx had been turning over men left and right. It was lovely for all of the girls on shift because each crowd came with even longer cash than the last. Frank's eyes were lit up with greed each time a dancer led a John Doe to the back. No doubt even Isis was gonna eat like a pig tonight. Wrapping up my last dance, I tossed the few dollars I'd made from freaking up on him into my bag then made a beeline for the bar. "It's been like a madhouse in here tonight. Dolly, let me get another shot."

"Damn, girl, you better slow down. I've been watching Isis and her girls stalk you out with the evil eye all night. I don't trust 'em." Setting a bottle of water down onto the bar instead, Dolly called herself being motherly but it was just pissing me off.

"I get you're trying to be helpful and all, Dolly, but I've got this. These bitches don't want none of what I've got stored up." Picking the bottle up, cracking the top open, I downed almost half of the hydrator before slamming it back down. "Now my shot, please!"

"That's on you. Don't say I ain't told ya little young ass nothing." Walking away to fill my order, she threw her hand up with brashness then mumbled some smart shit underneath her breath. Dolly was known for getting hostile when her word wasn't taken as gospel. We could be cool behind these walls all day long but I wasn't looking for an accomplice, comrade, or an ace boon coon. She ain't know my life or the type of shit I'd lived through, so I wasn't into backing down or taking advice easily. Me and friends have never mixed and Shawntay didn't play the motherly role often. Let's just say it was hard for me to recognize real; the barmaid actually had my back. Whatever the case, Isis could come for me if she wanted. I had something for their slick asses tonight.

As men trickled through the door in small groups, I worked the VIP sections for the rest of the night, only doing one additional stage show. The ballers who bought booths out made it rain enough for me to stay content. Turning the gold bottles of Moët up, guzzling the last drops then licking the rim, I imitated deep throating it seductively because I knew they secretly wanted head.

"I can unbuckle my pants to see if you've truly got skills."

"You're gonna have to pull the lint from your pockets first." Turning to face the man who had such nerve to talk so slickly without having at least a Benjamin in his hand, I was caught off-guard at how handsome he was. Usually not into white men, this one here was something different.

"Lint? What is that a joke? I've got more than a pocketful of money, little lady." He laughed, pulling a knot of cash from his denim jeans pocket. "Whatever you charge for your services, I can pay double." Lifting his fitted Detroit Tigers hat up so I could see his face, I was caught off-guard at how handsome he was.

"It's twenty-five dollars a song in the private room, which totals fifty dollars for you." Running my fingers through my long, curly hair, I batted my eyelashes trying to seductively seduce him.

"I'll need five hundred dollars' worth of your time." Standing up, peeling five crisp one hundred dollar bills from the knot, he waved them past my face awaiting an answer. "Do I pay you or that wannabe pimp houseman over there?" Casually pointing toward Frank, I saw him watching with a keen eye all in our conversation.

"Never mind him, baby, right this way." Wasting not another moment from taking my guaranteed car note and insurance from his pale fingers, I grabbed his hand in mine knowing I'd just hit a lick. Walking through the club with my sexy white boy close behind in tow, I could feel the hate from everyone including Dolly. *If these skeezers would focus more on getting money than my redbone fine ass, their bread game would be up*. The hallway of private rooms was in the back of the club monitored by one of Frank's workers. Right before the entrance we were flagged to hold off for a few minutes as a dancer and customer were finishing up. Letting the attendant know we were up next, I tipped him twenty dollars for the extra assurance we wouldn't be bothered. Normally the rooms only hit us five bucks but special favors never were free.

"Looks like you're gonna have to give me a quick dance right here, right now while we wait." Pulling me to the side, he forcefully bent me over rubbing his midsection into my cheeks. I had no other choice with him being so forceful but I really wanted to find another place to freak him with Isis working right next to where he picked. "I ain't gonna be able last long with this juicy booty bouncing like this."

*Looks like I was close to right. Feels like a big dick but from the sound of it, he's a quickie. This private session ain't gonna be about shit!* Jiggling, twerking, and pushing my fat ass farther back up on him I felt his big bulge—in both his pocket and crotch. Moving his hands from my waist, I soon saw dollars falling onto the floor then his hands rubbing the sides of my thighs. "That's right, baby, tell Butter how you like it." More dollars fell on top of me then to the floor.

"I like it rough and raw." He pulled me up from position to whisper even nastier things into my ear. I continued to work hard for the money but was enjoying every minute. Seeing the money pile on the floor growing, my pussy couldn't do nothing but get wet.

"Room's ready, Butter," the attendant yelled over, waving at us.

"Let's finish this dance up behind closed doors, baby." Bending down to pick up the money he'd paid me so far, I stuffed it into my wrist purse, ready to lead him toward the available room.

"Bitch, if you don't throw my motherfucking money back down, I'm gonna crack your pale face open." Isis grabbed my wrist in mid-swipe.

"Get your dirty hands up off me wit'cha Jigaboo ass!" Snatching my arm back, I twisted my face up in disgust. I was tired of Isis coming at me from far left field.

"Ladies, ladies, play nice!" Dazz announced over the loud system, seeing a scrap getting ready to take place. "Take ya separate corners!"

"I'll see ya ass later, Butter; you can't slick nothing this way, bitch," Isis spat, returning to her dance.

"Please believe I ain't worried." Making sure I hadn't dropped a bill during the lightweight struggle, I snatched the white boy's hand up again as he waited by the side patiently so I could get to work.

The private room consisted of a couch, two chairs, a lamp, a small table, a sink, and sheets Frank made sure were bleached daily. There were bottles of Lysol, air freshener, bars of soap, and clean linen for us and the customers to get back smelling fresh after whatever behind-the-scenes action took place. Many women went by the motto of having no rules once the door shut, me included.

Once all the way inside with the door closed, the white boy took his seat on the couch, spreading his legs, getting comfortable. Checking the digital clock above the wall door for the exact time, the bouncer would let us know when time was up but I always tried to stay a few minutes ahead of the game.

As the music played, I gyrated my hips from side to side as he sat in a trance captivated by everything that was Butter. Dropping my top, I smiled. Making sure I threw in a few of my "guaranteed to have a man gone" signature moves, I could easily tell he was more than feeling me by the huge grin on his face. It was obvious he was going to become a regular.

## Jay

"You have thirteen voicemail messages. To hear your messages press one."

Climbing into my Audi still smelling the sweet scent of Butter lingering on me, I couldn't wait to hook up with her tonight. I knew she'd never turn a man of my caliber down. No low-budget woman could. Pulling out of the parking garage into traffic, I headed back to the hotel/casino where me and a few other business partners were staying. Marie had been calling me nonstop all night. Unluckily for her I'd been drained completely, making me not want to be bothered with her, our twins, or any responsibility that came with our arranged marriage. Since birth we'd been groomed for one another. What started as just an investment into my father's business had spiraled into much more. If it weren't for me marrying my parents' business investor's daughter, our family would've been starved out a long time ago. I'd been groomed since birth to be the perfect man: educated, professional, and successful. And my wife has been groomed in the exact same way. It was called keeping it in the family.

Marie was okay with the arrangement, being able to plan the most lavish fairytale wedding since first reading "Cinderella," but the man in me had become bored having to stick to the routine. I was dying for excitement, desperate for a thrill, and tired of the mundane dullness that had become us. The only reason I'd knocked her up with the twins in the first place was to secure my position to always be around. I'd known since before the day we got married that I was a true Schultz man with the same disturbing desires.

# Chapter Five

Slamming then locking the steel security door, the bouncer signaled the club was clear and it was time for money countdown. I'd been dancing my ass off all night plus J.T. had tipped me hella cash so all of my pertinent bills could be paid. People frowned on the lives of dancers, but in one hard day's worth of work, I was about to afford what my living expenses were for the month. Fuck quitting, I was just getting started! Hopefully Mr. Moneybags had all intentions of using my cell number as promised so I could secure future financial strains. The knot in his pocket in addition to the charge cards I saw when he whipped out his leather wallet let me know he was a cash cow.

Frank was already running the money machine as his right-hand man rubber banded each hundred dollar stack. Every girl in here should've been eating steak and lobster from twerking tonight from the looks of it. Even Dolly was peeling back twenties from tips men left on top of their tabs. Looking up, giving me a half-ass nod, I rolled my eyes with the same "bitch, I don't give a fuck attitude," keeping it moving toward the DJ booth. I hadn't forgotten about Dazz's request, plus I had to make payout to him for the night. I didn't know what the other dancers did to stay right with the men who made the club run like a well-oiled machine, but I kept the bouncers, DJs, and even Frank in my back pocket by making money and tipping well.

"What up, my baby? What's the star dancer of Bare Faxxx about to get into?" Unplugging the mixers and subwoofers, Dazz was moving swiftly through the compacted space, packing up so he could get out of here.

"Not much of nothing. You already know I'm about to head to the crib to get fried." Pulling out the crisp fifty I was tipping him, he pushed it back toward me before I could drop it into his cup.

"Naw, Butter baby, you straight on that. What you can do is feed ya mans." Rubbing his stomach, staring at me with a smile, I knew he must've been drunk, high, or both thinking I got down in the kitchen. The only thing I knew how to make was a top-shelf alcoholic beverage. "Let's ride the isle, blow a blunt, and smash some Big Boy before you call it a night. I ain't seen you hit the kitchen all night!"

He must've read my mind about cooking and it was obvious he'd kept an eye on my moves, too. Feeling my stomach grumble right on cue, I figured the after-hours company would be nice. At least I'd have a backup plan already in motion if ol' boy didn't come thorugh. "As a matter of fact, I am starvin' like Marvin. Some bacon, cheesy eggs, and hash browns would set a sista up straight right about now!" Now the one rubbing my stomach, so caught up in the hustle I'd forgotten to get nourishment. I could almost taste the food!

"Sista my ass." He laughed. "You say shit like that and have the nerve to wonder why Isis and these other girls run around here ready to knock your head off. The only thing sista about you is those cheeks." Smacking me on the behind, I rolled my eyes hearing the same thing I've heard every day of my life. *I'm too white to be black but I've got too many black features to be just white.*

"So whose side are you on? Those tack-headed hoes or mine? I thought we were better than that!"

"I knew there was a softer side to Butter." He leaned back onto the many speakers. "Don't go getting all soft on me, girl, I was just playing."

"Emotional my ass! Don't play ya'self out of a free meal, nigga! See you in a few." Turning to go down the stairs, I threw my two fingers up letting him know we were still cool. I'd gained enough enemies tonight. Wasn't no sense in gaining another. "You know the routine; see you after payout."

Heading toward the locker room, it was time to throw my Victoria's Secret Pink sweats back on so I could get up out of here. It was well after two in the morning, my stomach was growling, and I was ready to get my late-night impromptu vamp session started with Dazz. He had an overprotective girl at the crib so I knew he wasn't trying to get an all-nighter popping. Regardless though, I was still planning on sliding through the twenty-four-hour Kush spot around my way before going in. My choke sessions never stopped so I had to get right before morning came since I was bone dry out. I didn't save my tails like budget smokers, so I didn't even have the emergency stash to hit up.

Opening the door to the sweaty-smelling locker room, almost every dancer was stripped down but booty naked getting changed for after parties or to go home to their snotty-nosed kids. Those who only made small piles that could fit in their wrist purses throughout the night were already dressed, heading for the door, while the headliners sat posted, counting cash, waiting on Frank. Opening my locker, I pulled out my Gucci purse, scrambling for my phone. If ol' boy texted as promised, I'd be cancelling with Dazz without a second thought. Seeing the envelope icon lit up in my notifications, I quickly entered my pass code, messing up twice out of anxiousness. *Damn, bitch, slow down; you actin' like one of these thirst buckets in here.*

Instantly annoyed seeing just a gang of messages from my mother, which were more like begs for me to come by, talk to her, or at least read the prayers she'd sent, I threw the phone back into my purse, picking up the canteen of Avión instead. Fucking with Shawntay kept the rim of any bottle glued to my lips. Tilting it back, feeling the warm liquor slide down my throat, by the time I made it to my bed I'd be too lit to remember the night. Screwing the lid back onto the container, I put it back into my purse then proceeded to slide off my outfit.

Smelling like smoke from head to foot, I needed a shower like a bum needed rehab, but wasn't trying to lurk around Bare Faxxx no longer than necessary. Grabbing a few baby wipes from my duffel bag, I started to wipe my body down, hoping the little bit of fresh scent and disinfectant it had in the small cloth would be enough to mask the sweaty smell. Dazz knew I'd just got done popping on a handstand but that wasn't no reason for me to go out smelling musty or not giving a fuck. I was a lady first, please believe!

"Hey yo, Butter bitch, you swiped some money up out my pile with your mutt dog sneak ass. I'm gonna need them bills back." Isis walked in with her tits hanging low. "I know you didn't think I forgot!"

*Here the fuck we go!* Isis wanted any reason to get at me. She knew like the Lord knew I wasn't a thief. "You better kill yo'self on that note. Butter don't steal, baby. I tend to charity cases like ya'self if nothing else!" Rolling my eyes, I played it off like I was getting some more wipes but I was really wrapping my fingers around the handle of my .380. If this hound dog wanted to bring heat to the table, she was gonna catch a hot one fa'sho. I wasn't taking no risks of getting cuts or scrapes to this pretty, moneymaking face.

"You better run my money, Butter, or it's gonna be a problem. I let you go earlier not to fuck up the flow but, bitch, I'm back on my worst behavior." Not backing down, she knew I hadn't been close to her pile but her intentions were always to start drama with me. Walking toward me, I tilted my head left then right, cracking my neck, pretty much ready to go to war.

"Bitch, bring it 'cause I'm about sick of your wild beast-looking ass throwing shade at me 'cause you on a drought!" Every conversation around us had ceased; each eye was on me and Isis as we battled it out in the center of the locker room. Deciding it wasn't the right time to pull out my pistol, I knew I could scrap her ass out anyway. I'd gotten in enough fights growing up with jealous females to be skilled at throwing jabs, so this wasn't anything new. Dropping my duffel bag back onto the floor, I discreetly picked up my lock, clutching it in the palm of my hand. If she tested me running up wanting to test the biggest wolf, I'd crack her water-swollen head to the white meat.

"Trust and believe ya pale-faced pussy ass can't hang!" Isis took two steps before lunging in my direction. I wasn't caught off-guard nor did I move two seconds too late. Exposing my right hand, letting Isis know the joke was truly on her, there was nothing she could do being already caught up in trying to throw the first blow. Screams, shrills, and gasps of disbelief were heard throughout the small locker room as my fist of steel (literally) slapped her in the face.

The sound echoed off the walls.

"All you heffas around here better take a lesson from this ass whopping!" Going to town beating Isis to a pulp, blood was dripping down her busted forehead and jaw, both places I'd split open, before mistakenly dropping the lock onto the floor. Boiling with anger I couldn't be contained. Isis had been the right one to fuck with me at the absolute wrong time. All of my pent-up aggression was taken out on her within a blink of everyone's eyes.

"Yo' what in the fuck! Break these broads up!" Hearing Frank screaming over all of the dancers cheering us on, I knew he was hotter than fish grease seeing total mayhem in his establishment. "Butter, Isis, break it up!" He pushed through the crowd of nudeness.

I heard his voice getting louder, but the body-guards he'd called out to probably hadn't even heard him with the normal routine of getting drunk at the bar with Dolly.

"G'on and tag that bitch a few more times before the guards come!" Not being able to recognize which dancer was serving orders, I tried whipping around with the quickness to catch whatever one was running up. I'd already been caught slipping with sneak attacks to my back.

Turning to catch a glimpse over my shoulder, the same lock I'd split Isis's cranium to the white meat with had knocked me in the ear.

"Ahh, fuck!" I shouted hearing my eardrums ringing loudly then simultaneously feeling my head throb. Dropping the handful of Isis's hair I was holding her still by, I grabbed the other dancer by her long weave, whipping her down onto the floor. Able to overpower her, we wrestled as I fought not to be embarrassed or whitewashed. *These mangy broads keep coming for me. Dumb hoes didn't even know I was cut from the same poor, insignificant cloth as them. Isn't no shame in my game.* Me and the less-than-attractive dancer exchanged a few blows before the guards pulled us off of one another. I was still going so crazy trying to attack both her and Isis that I fucked around and clawed Dazz's face.

"Yo Butter, chill out, my baby, damn!" Now bear-hugging me with one arm, holding me a few inches from the floor, my feet dangled as Dazz tried to keep control of me while touching on his face to check the damage.

Isis had since gotten up, tag-teamed with the scrawny, brazen chick, and was coming my and Dazz's way. "Let me down! I've got something for these puss-face hoes!" With my arms swinging, my legs kicking, and half-oiled body wiggling roughly in his arms, he had to drop me down to hold off the other girls. Jumping over the wooden stool to my locker, I swung my bag up with quickness ready to pull out my sweet baby. Enough was enough!

"I'll spray you bitches dead if y'all make another step!" Dazz stopped all of us dead in our tracks as he stood firm with his piece. "A nigga just trying to eat," he said more calmly, still waving the Smith & Wesson around. "I don't care where y'all handle part two at, but it ain't gonna be up here in Bare Faxxx."

Looking around the room to make sure everyone was on the same page in respecting him, I wondered how many of the dancers were itching to go for their pistols too. With CCWs given out like water in the D, everyone who was anyone was carrying. In the law of the land, he who pulled shooting precisely first was the winner.

"Frank, man, I ain't telling you how to run ya' shit, man, but come up off my girl Butter's payout so we can bounce. Butter baby, get dressed so we can be out."

I didn't flinch. Seeing Isis and the low-paid dancer I couldn't even call out by name griming me, I shook my head knowing their jaded asses. "Damn, Isis, was it worth getting your face split and rocked? Now you're really ugly!"

Isis made a sudden movement like she was about to run up.

Dazz swiftly turned, directly pointing his pistol at her. "Bitch, did I stutter?"

# Chapter Six

## 1997: Shawntay

"Oh my God! I ain't never felt a pain like this. Please get this baby the fuck up out of me!" Screaming to the high heavens, my coochie was being ripped to shreds as the doctor only could tell me to push, breathe, and stay calm. "Give me meds, knock me out, I can't take this shit anymore!"

"Ms. Jenkins, please take a deep breath then give me the biggest push you can. We must get past this crowning part." Sounding exasperated with my behavior, I dared this state-paid doctor to hop his cracker-jack ass up on this table to push another human being out.

Doing as I was told, I couldn't wait to light a joint up but especially sip on the fifth of alcohol I snuck into the hospital. I'd never stopped drinking this entire pregnancy, especially with Jimmy having his lawyer contact me demanding a paternity test before any further contact. I'd called his phone over and over 'til his number was changed, leaving me no further way to contact him. The only thing I had to fall back on was getting my food stamps and cash assistance increased from the government, plus the pitiful eye when I applied for emergency assistance when my lights and gas were set to be cut off. Thankfully I was able to keep up with my subsidized thirty-eight-dollar rent.

"You're doing great, Ms. Jenkins. Keep that up because we're almost there."

Pushing with all my force, I knew my vagina would never quite work the streets the same. The epidural they'd given me must've been a placebo. "This shit hurts! Ahh!" Yelling, totally spazzing out, I swore to God I'd never go through this so-called miracle of child birth again. Balling my face up, pushing with every bit of strength that was left, I felt the baby start to slide farther out, which made the pain slightly subside.

"You've got it! Now the next time a contraction comes, push harder than before okay?"

Nodding my head, I wiped beads of sweat from my face then fought hard to catch my breath. My contractions were coming left and right with no break, so I knew within seconds I would be back into the zone. "Okay, Doc," I managed to whisper, gripping the bedrail, feeling the contraction about to hit strong. "Fuuuuuckkkk!" Thirty seconds later the pressure in my abdomen subsided, sending a stream of relief through my body. My life had changed.

"Congratulations, Ms. Jenkins, it's a girl!"

## James

"Da, Da, Da, Da!"

"Daddy, yup, that's right, my boy!" Hearing my ten-month-old son coo, smile, giggle, and try to babble his first words, I continued to roll around on the floor, tossing him into the air. He was a spitting image of my wife with dark brown hair and big hazel eyes. Even the way his lips curled at the sides mimicked Beth's. I didn't know if she seriously prayed for J.T. not to resemble me but one thing was for sure: the Schultz once-dominant genes of blond hair and blue eyes didn't get passed down to my offspring. Locked in the nursery, I was trying hard to enjoy the subtle calm before the storm. Through the wooden door, all the way down a flight of stairs, I could hear my wife having a phone conversation with my mother. *Well I see my day is getting ready to be ruined. I should sneak out for a fake business meeting to my new little call girl's spot.* It would sure beat the verbal tag-team attack I was up for.

Ever since the drunken night of me mistakenly spilling the beans about Shawntay's pregnancy, Beth was like a madwoman trying to secure her

position while controlling my desires. With Sally
helping her lead the coalition of angry white wives,
I was in a double hell with the two most important
women in my life hating me. Since Beth made
it brutally clear Shawntay had to be cut off, I
didn't go against her wishes knowing black pussy
could be replaced. She'd even found a more-than-
wealthy investor to take the company we branded
to astronomical heights. But even for that business
relationship something had to be sacrificed. My
entire life could crumble if Beth exposed our family
secret so I took her threats to heart. After getting
my mother Sally involved, not only did I hear a
verbal thrashing about being just like my dead
father, God rest his soul, but how she would now be
the dictator with my matters concerning Shawntay.
My mother's hand wasn't gentle like a saint so I
knew turmoil would soon come.

Hearing Beth tap on the other side of the door,
I didn't want to answer because I knew drama
lingered on the other side. The triple mixture of
her hormones, postpartum depression, and the
fact that I had a baby during our marriage had her
coming at me with fury each time we interacted.

"Answer this door, James. I know you hear me."
She knocked harder. "Your mother is on the phone.
It's important."

"All right, all right!" Putting my son into his crib,
I hesitated but slowly walked to the door, swinging
it open for Beth to come in.

"Speaking of the devil." I took the phone from Beth's hand as she rolled her eyes, walking off. *What's her beef now?* "I was just thinking of you, Mother." Continuing to watch Beth move through the nursery gathering what seemed to be for J.T.'s bath time, I sat down in his rocking chair rubbing my piercing temples. She and I didn't have the best relationship because I reminded her so much of my father. No matter how much I tried, I couldn't please her, so I'd given up many years ago.

"You should've been busy thinking about how to clean up the mess you've created with this ratchet-looking disgrace of a woman you risked everything for," Sally spat out. "I've had more than enough of my share of turmoil to clean up in dealing with your penis-slinging father, God rest his soul." My mother walked a fine line when it came to loving and hating my father. Even though she chose to deal with the burdens he passed down just like my grandmother, he was the responsible one for turning her heart ice cold.

"Then why don't you try swinging by to spend some time with your grandson? It'll be a change from the dreadful life the men in your world have created for you." Taking J.T. from Beth's arms as she struggled to carry him plus the towel, sleeper, diaper, ointment, lotion, and so forth, I tried not letting my mother's bad mood rub off on me. I'd earned plus lived up to the title of being the ill-rotten child who thirsted for dirty fruit. My marriage was barely holding on by thin threads. J.T. had been a lifeline so in my mind he could definitely bring some light to my mother's world too.

"Get your head out of the clouds, Jimmy. Are you sleeping with so many whores you can't keep track of time? This is the ninth month; the bastard has been born. Leave to meet me at Henry Ford Hospital; I'll be in the main lobby."

Damn near dropping J.T., being completely overwhelmed by the news, my heart skipped a few beats as my chest seemed to cave in. It was D-Day; time for me to dance to the music I once loved stroking. Without getting swabbed, I was already 99.9 percent sure Shawntay's daughter was going to be mine.

## Shawntay

A bitch was surely out of it, believe that. *As God is my witness, I'll never push another baby up out of this once-tight coochie.* Scared to even clinch my pussy walls to see if there was even a chance of bringing them back to life, I lay still in the hospital bed wishing I'd gotten the abortion like Jimmy requested. But at the time, all I could see was dollar signs and how my pockets could get filled with his. Every man paid child support in America so having Shannon was my guaranteed piece of the pie. Trying hard to feel motherly and bond with my only daughter, I kept failing miserably, not even able to look into her green eyes. How some mothers adored their offspring, not being able to send them away to the nursery, I was pissed than a bitch they were making her stay in this room with me. Shannon was six pounds, six ounces, and twenty-one inches long. Even though she was just a few hours old, nothing about her resembled me. Having Jimmy's milky white skin, small button nose, and light-colored eyes, this little girl was a spitting image of her father. I might've been his most consistent whore but now I was his most recent baby momma. My mother, may she rest in peace, might've been the Queen of Hoeing but she would've never tied herself to the white man for life. If she was still living, even at sixty in age, it would've been nothing for her to butcher knife her grandchild from my womb without thinking twice.

"How are you feeling, Miss Jenkins?" The nurse knocked on then pushed the door open. "I hate to bother you but I've gotta take your vitals and make sure everything is still on the up and up." Being overly friendly, I knew that if I'd seen this working professional on the street she would look down on me. Me and her were cut from different cloths. Hell, for all I knew, she could be best friends with the woman whose husband's baby I was having. It's a small world and Detroit is even tinier.

"I'm still feeling quite a bit of pain in my back but the pressure in my abdomen has gone away. Can you give me another drip?" Keeping my eyes closed, I was making the situation be a tad bit worse since I was in the perfect place to get fed drugs. Everybody around the way knew Henry Ford Hospital served top-notch druggies to the supposed ailing around metro Detroit. So I was in the right place to get the best high. Fuck nursing li'l Shannon; she could sip on some Similac. Knowing I wasn't the type of woman always on time, I didn't dare set myself up for being on call to pop a titty out every time this kid got hungry. Naw, I wasn't banking on that! *Jimmy's child support better buy her a personal feeder.*

"Wow, your tolerance for pain is extremely low. On a scale from one to ten, where does yours fall?" Sounding like she didn't believe me, I didn't blame her nor did I care. Right about now all I wanted was more meds.

"I'm about at an eight."

"Okay, I'll report that to your doctor. I've given you the maximum amount of morphine already so he'll have to order the next drip. Besides, you might want to start fighting off the pain naturally so you can get to that beautiful baby of yours."

"She ain't that damn beautiful." I turned my nose up to the alleged bundle of joy who was responsible for the many struggling months I'd just lived through.

The nurse returned the same look of disgust I'd just dished to my daughter as she continued to check my vitals. "You can't mean that, Ms. Jenkins. Truly you mustn't. I'll send the social worker in here to have a talk with you. That's just the postpartum depression talking. I can't tell you how many young mothers I see get struck with it." The nurse was trying to make a positive spin out of something that sounded so horrible. I actually wondered how many mothers had let the words fall from their lips but actually meant it.

"Naw, I'm good on you having the social worker come by. Just like you said, it must be a young mother thang." Lying through my teeth, I instantly started backpeddling, not wanting anyone with authority to come in meddling with me. *Let that paper-pushing bitch stay wherever she's at. I don't need my stamps or cash tampered with.*

"Are you sure, Ms. Jenkins? I've seen Ms. Basheer help a lot of women get through the first few days; plus if you need a car seat, stroller, crib, some clothes, any of the essentials, she'll take care of that."

My eyes widened. "On second thought, send her by; there's a few things I need for baby Shannon before going home." No longer trying to keep the state-appointed hospital human service worker away, I decided to embrace her by running off a long list of things I needed for my newborn. I really didn't give two shits about caring for this kid but with Ms. Basheer's help, I wouldn't have to come out of my pocket for anything. Out of these whole nine months, I hadn't purchased not even a pack of diapers for the baby I was only twenty-four hours away from taking home.

"Not a problem. Once your visitors leave, I'll send Ms. Basheer up. And don't worry, those feelings of depression, uncertainty, and anxiety will soon start to fade. You truly have a beautiful daughter."

"Whoa, slow up! Who in the fuck is here to see me?" Caught off-guard, forgetting that I was supposed to be in a tremendous amount of pain, I shot up like a mentally disabled junkie on the first of the month.

I hadn't seen James face to face in months. I'd spent many hours and days stalking him, his wife Beth, and the little boy they had a few weeks after he cut me completely off. From the way he'd been acting, refusing my calls before finally changing his number altogether, it made it hard for me to believe our dynamic would change that much. Having this baby might've been playing myself.

"I can't believe you went through with this." Jimmy came in, shaking his head. "You've created so much drama by trying to force this bullshit on me and my family." Through gritted teeth, Jimmy was talking in a low tone, almost to a whisper. "I wish you would've taken the money."

"Fuck you, Jimmy. You should've been putting pocket condoms on that little dick of yours if you ain't want no more babies!" Ready to go to war, if he thought I was going to let him show up in my hospital room to talk shit after nine months of a hiatus, he was dead wrong!

"Your trifling ass should've never said you were on the pill. That's what I get for trusting a dirty black ho!" Jimmy's words were slicing me like a knife. It was obvious he didn't compassionately care about me but after all of the sexual hours I'd put in on his ass, you would've thought we were at least better than that.

"You, your wife, and that big bubble-headed son of yours can go to hell!" Screaming with nothing but rage and spite, I let the cat out of the bag that I'd been discretely watching his life. "You were all in love with this sweet black pussy a few months ago. Hence Shannon!" Screaming with tears falling from my eyes uncontrollably, I wasn't in the right mind frame for taking nor dishing out verbal abuse. The nurse had been right; my feelings were all over the place.

"As long as he gets to take this little bastard with him." Walking into the room looking like a fat koala bear, a pasty white woman who was an exact replica of Jimmy—which were now features of Shannon—came limping in with a cane. "Let me see this alleged kid of yours." She limped toward James, totally ignoring me.

"Uh, excuse me, and who in the fuck are you?" Ready to go all the way off, I wasn't stressing over her calling Shannon a bastard 'cause by definition that's what she was. But I wasn't into giving anyone a pass on blatantly disrespecting me.

"I'm your worst nightmare, chile." The woman turned to scowl at me. Pulling two long cotton-swapped sticks from her purse, she roughly swabbed Jimmy with one then handed it off to the nurse. Leaning over, sticking one in Shannon's mouth too, the little baby I had yet to bond with screamed at the top of her tiny lungs like this Lucifer lookalike stuck it too far down her throat.

"Get these IVs up out of me." I tried jumping out of the bed, feeling the needle piercing my arm. "I'm about to admit this bitch!"

"Ms. Jenkins!" the nurse yelled, running to my bedside. "Mrs. Schultz, I think you have enough of baby Jenkins's saliva for the sample. Please hand me the swab." Reaching for it, she made sure to stand in the middle of us to prevent me from having a clear shot.

"Oh, my dear, of course, you're right." Smiling devilishly, she handed the swab over to the nurse then winked at me. "Bring your nigger-loving ass on, James!"

# Chapter Seven

## *Shannon*

"That was a good look. I appreciate you for having my back," I thanked Dazz as soon as he answered. I couldn't get comfortable in my driver's seat before hitting his line. He was still in the locker room holding it down with the only two bouncers who were left while Frank made sure I made it to my car safely. Dazz had come through in a helluva way without me having to reveal I stayed strapped so I owed him more than a few strips of bacon and eggs.

"I got you, no doubt. But I'm gonna have to take a rain check on tonight. Frank asked me to stay and help lock down on account of your rowdy behind."

"I figured that much but I can't say I'm not disappointed. A bitch is in need of that session more than ever right about now. Do me another solid and make sure you don't let them wannabes get me fired. I already know Isis is in Frank's ear talking shit about me stealing out of her pile. You better let 'em know." Barking orders at Dazz, I swerved into traffic, out of the parking structure, heading up Griswold.

"Chill out, a'ight, need I keep getting my resume read? Ain't shit shady about to be done on my clock so be cool." Speaking with authority, Dazz had no reason to lie or half step at this point. He'd already come up out the holster on my behalf so why should I doubt him to finish the job or hold true to his word? At this point, Dazz was my only definite comrade at Bare Faxxx.

"My bad, boo." I took a cop. "I just want at those hoes so bad. One thing I do know is that Frank better be on the same page as you. It better not faze him if they get a strippers coalition to rally and picket my dismissal; he better know who the real breadwinner of that hellhole is!" Talking reckless as loud as I could, the liquor had definitely sunk in. Without me dancing or swinging to block right hooks, my buzz was starting to settle in a not-so-good way. "Like I told him when he escorted me to the car, Isis's big brick-head ass came for me. I was just gettin' back at her. And the other girl, I don't know where her skinny 'miss too many meals' ass even came from. These bitches be having undercover beefs." I couldn't control the tantrum spilling out of me. Getting turned up all over again, I wanted to bust a U-turn so I could go back to standing my ground. I didn't want to venture out to the suburbs because the white population who once filled them were now moving into the new lofts, renovated midtown gems, and luxurious apartments above financially booming storefronts. Detroit was where it was happening at so I needed to be right in the thick of it. Living in my subsidized apartment only a couple of miles from Bare Faxxx, I wasn't getting ready to uproot, relocate, or burn up tanks of gas on the strength of some hating hoes. Dancing at predominately black clubs in the hood was totally out of the question because they employed mostly unglammed hood rats with attitudes.

"Why are you still amped when I told you to be easy? White girls be smart as a whip but ain't got a lick of street sense." He threw a sneak diss my way. "Now for the last time, be cool. I'll hit you up when I'm out of here but I'll take my rain check for some grub in the morning." Hanging up abruptly, Dazz left me alone with my thoughts.

I didn't take offense to him disconnecting the call 'cause I knew he was still technically punched in. Even though he didn't serve on the security team, he'd been recruited for the emergency, having to make sure the chaos stayed under control. Since I was one of the parties involved with having him still on the clock, I didn't call back to nag or bite his head off for being so rude. Instead I pulled the half a blunt I was blowing on before going into work out from the ashtray, lighting it up. These tricks had gone way too far getting crunk with me tonight. My head was still pounding from getting grazed by the lock but at least Isis had to take a trip to the emergency room. With her being the aggressor and so much shady shit constantly going down within the club, I wasn't worried about her filing a police report or pressing charges against me. Every day of my life I'd been grinding against the grain to get a fair shake out here from bitches but they never wanted to give respect.

Too amped up but not having a choice other than to go home, I kept pulling on the non-hitting blunt wishing I would soon start to feel high. Hearing my phone ring, getting excited, I grabbed it out of my lap, realizing it was only Shawntay calling again. Sending her to voicemail, I rolled my eyes feeling my headache starting to get worse. "Why can't she get the point?" I screamed out in my empty car. Jesus Christ Himself was gonna have to come down here from heaven, tap me on the shoulder, and tell me to forgive my mother. As far as I was concerned, we were done.

Jefferson Avenue was humming with partiers. Commonly known as the strip in the D, everyone made sure to have their cars washed, waxed, and sound systems bumping. Every Friday and Saturday the parking lot at the hottest bars up and down the avenue would be flooded with wannabe pimps trying to score big after the club. People would be dressed in their freshest attire hanging from cars trying to get picked up for the night. The regular routine around these parts couldn't be easily broken. Wishing I could make a stop to join the festivities, I kept pushing my whip toward home, having to get my earnings locked up safely. With so much shady things going on to women in Detroit, I wasn't taking any chances by keeping so much cash on my person. Turning into the parking lot of my apartment complex, I pulled into my spot turning the radio low so I could finish hitting my blunt. It wasn't worth putting out then relighting; plus I hated smoking what tasted like ash.

I heard the sounds of the phone ringing.

*You can't be serious. I'm about to curse this chick out for real.* Looking at the caller ID on my phone, my attitude immediately calmed. "Hello." I answered the unknown out-of-state phone number without thinking twice. My hopes were high that it was Jay on the other end.

"Butter?"

"Yes?" The voice sounded too proper to be one of the thugs I usually crept with but I didn't jump the gun in calling him out.

"My pretty lady, you sound just as good as you look and feel. Did I catch you at a bad time?"

"No, not at all. I see you're truly a man of your word." I smiled into the phone, happy he'd called to spend some more money on me. With my fate uncertain at the bar, I needed to stack all of the money I could get my hands on.

"I'm a man who knows what he likes if nothing else. If I like what I see then I go for it."

"Oh okay, I like a man who knows what he wants. It takes the bullshit out of things." Keeping it real with him, I was speaking terminology he could understand. We both knew why he was calling so why waste time with word or mind games?

"Listen here, a few of my buddies and I are staying at the hotel for the night gambling, drinking, and trying to get into a little mischief." He laughed sounding like only a true white boy could. "At the club I had to pay five hundred fat ones plus an uncountable amount of dollar bills for a few R&B songs of your time. I was just wondering what your rates were for an after-hours call."

Jay was blunt and direct, something I grew to fear but had no other choice but to respect. For all my years I'd been handled with a long-handle spoon by those people closest to me; and my Grandma Sally, oh God, had she been the most brutally honest person I knew.

"Hello? Butter, are you still there? Was that too forward for you, hon?"

"Yeah, I'm here. Um, nope, it wasn't too forward. I guess you're into callin' 'em how you see 'em. I can feel you on that." Jay couldn't think more about me than I'd already put on display for him. The only thing left to imagination was how my twat and warm mouth actually felt without a tease.

"I actually call it paying it how I play. So what will be the ticket?"

After running down a price he didn't hesitate to pick up, I found out his location then ended the call. There was no way I was getting ready to miss out on any of this cash. We'd just agreed upon a definite grand upon arrival. I aimed high 'cause if I didn't put heavy stock into my pussy then who would? If I played my cards right he could end up being a sneak vacation to get away from the drama around here. But if nothing else he'd make one helluva sponsor. Locking his number I ensured he would just be one tap away.

Now moving with speed, I snatched the garbage bags of money from my trunk, running into the house hoping no one followed me here. Tossing them into the second bedroom of my apartment then locking the deadbolt back, I only had a few minutes to get scantily dressed to meet up with Jay at the casino. My cell was ringing nonstop but it was only Shawntay refusing to leave me alone. She'd been clicking in during my and Jay's conversation but I was too caught in his words to even care. But enough was enough. I wasn't interested in anything her jinx ass had to say, but me answering was the only way she'd stop bothering me.

"Yes, Ma, damn. What's up?" Fumbling through my drawers for a cute panty set, I snatched out a hot pink lace bra and matching thong, running into the bathroom to do a quick ho wash up.

"Oh, sweet Jesus, you're okay! Almighty Father, you do work miracles. I'm truly sorry I ever doubted you." My mother started in with talking to the God who'd abandoned me along with my father's side of the family.

"Hello, Shawntay. I'm kinda busy, what's up?" Rolling my eyes to the back of my head, I couldn't stand hearing her play the sanctified role. Putting the phone on speaker, I set the phone down onto the bathroom sink, running the water to soap up my rag.

"I'm just glad you're okay. I don't rest at all with you dancing at the bar. I know a pretty girl like yourself has made enough money to quit. Maybe you can go back to school for art. You were always running around the house drawing pictures."

"I know this is a joke. You can't be serious. The only reason I was drawing pictures is 'cause the school therapist said it was the best way to get my feelings out 'cause you were too busy to deal with my 'ugly, frog-looking ass.'" I repeated the harsh words I heard her call me as a child. In my world there weren't second chances, just consequences. I'd seen that with Dazz. "Don't come judging me now when you made me this way." Rubbing the rag back, forth, then around my vagina, I even made sure my asshole was fresh and clean just in case the white boy was one of those kink freaks.

"I'm sorry, Shannon. But the Lord has forgiven me for my sins so I can't keep dwelling on the past. Please just take a step at seeing the new me. I know I haven't always been the best mother or role model but people do change." My mother was barking up the wrong tree.

"Me and God ain't cool, Ma." I laughed like she should've known. "You know how many nights I prayed for Him to feed us? To keep your punk-ass boyfriend's hands out of my panties? I used to hold my pee all day knowing he'd be creeping around with his pudgy fingers so I'd piss on him in attempts to keep him away. At five I was learning how to fend for myself 'cause you were too busy snorting lines. But you want me to let the past go? And I ain't even about to start no pity party about what went down at my grandmother's house. Let's just say I ain't never fit nowhere I done been at in all my life." Feeling my emotions starting to pour over, I had to hurry up and dry my hands to end the call. Digging up my past only meant trouble; and tonight with Jay I was anxious to get into something new. Finally a paid businessman was after Butter. Shawntay wasn't gonna have my mind too twisted to perform.

"Your soul is gonna be damned, Shannon, if you don't get right with your Lord. I don't want you to keep living how I lived 'cause that ain't gonna get you nowhere but to the grave."

"It's been damned since conception, bitch!" Finally able to hang up the phone, I'd had enough of the counterfeit Christian. How dare she judge me? Wasn't that a sin within itself? I didn't feel like having Shawntay ruin my night any longer. Going through my phone to the settings, I blocked her number so she wouldn't be able to get in contact with me until I felt like being bothered again. It was the next best thing next to having T-Mobile change my number. I'd given Shawntay all of my childhood years to ruin; for the rest of my life she'd have to take a back seat.

Dipping my hairbrush into the water, I brushed my hair until the waves bounced back fresh, then made sure my makeup was on point. The amount of liquor I was consuming was starting to take a toll on my beauty. A few months ago I only needed eye shadow and lip gloss to enhance my beauty. Now I needed foundation and concealer to hide where my skin had broken out. Thankfully tonight the dark circles that sometimes hung under my eyes were less than noticeable. I guessed I could thank Sally for finally giving me something I could use in my adulthood life besides resentment for being mixed. Sally used to say I had big raccoon eyes like my mother so she'd put cucumbers on them to make them less puffy. I followed suit a few days ago, seeing the combination of me smoking too much weed, drinking too much liquor, and not sleeping enough had my eyes touch my cheeks. It wasn't a good look at all. Sliding on a pair of low-rise denim ripped jeans, a white cropped top, and the only red bottoms I owned, I could thank Shawntay for this dynamic body. I had curves for days! Once I was completely ready with my keys in hand about to walk out the door, I sent Jay a text to let him know I was only ten minutes away.

## 2003: Shawntay

"Wake ya ass up, little girl." I shook Shannon's small fragile body. "Pull them pissy-ass panties back up so we can go!" Not the least bit concerned that the John Doe I tricked with last night also got off on little girls, I had no intentions of playing gentle with Shannon. She might've been my daughter but she wasn't all my blood. Each day of her existence has been a harsh reminder of my hatred for her father. Shannon's long, silky hair and high yellow complexion got her far too many compliments anyway. *She might as well get used to niggas using her for her looks now, 'cause that's all I've ever been worth.*

"Hurry up, trick. I ain't got all day for you and this whiny-ass brat."

"We're going, nigga, damn!" Snatching Shannon and the few Barbie dolls I let her bring so I could use them to demonstrate how ol' boy would touch her private parts, I was booking out of the door so I could get to chasing my high. He'd given me a hundred for the fuck plus an extra bill to rub on Shannon's baby twat. At first I called him a sick-minded fuck, cursing the day he was born, but after drinking a fifth of bumpy-face vodka, smoking a dime bag of loud Kush, and having him treat me to a line of coke, I might as well put his fingers into her panties myself.

"Mommy, he hurt me," Shannon cried out as we ran out the door down the flight of stairs.

"I know, just hush up. Plenty of men are gonna hurt you, girl. It's all part of being a woman. You want to be like Mommy right?" Bending down in my too-small micro miniskirt, I tried bonding with my little one.

"I guess. NaNa says you ain't shit though." Some might've assumed this was crazy but I let Shannon curse. It didn't make no difference to me if she learned to speak the proper King's English like her father's side 'cause growing up with me, she was doomed from the start.

"Fuck your NaNa, Shannon. She don't know nothing about me. Her ass is just a worker for the devil." I grabbed her face, making sure every word I said was clearly understood. I'd hated Sally with every pulse in my body since seeing her limp into my hospital room. The eight-hour visitations Sally and James spent with Shannon were full of bashing sessions about me. "If you don't remember nothing else in this cold world, Shannon, remember this: your value to a man don't go further than it takes for him to nut. It might've seemed like a lifetime last night, baby girl, but trust me, it'll get easier as you get older, trust me. Now keep up; Mommy's got some stops to make!"

Since I was scamming the system, getting childcare checks for a babysitter I'd never even met, wherever I went Shannon had to tag along too. Wasn't no need letting someone else collect almost $800 a month to ignore her; I was doing just fine with that part on my own. Walking through the cold streets, I pulled my hoodie closer together, wishing the zipper at least worked. It was a cold day for the end of September but I wasn't about to waste not a single dime on bus or cab fare. I had a habit to feed so every dollar was on reserve for just that. I only lived a few miles up Linwood from where we were so as long as Shannon didn't whine about her little legs being tired I was straight. I was a veteran of walking this strip; day in and out it was no thang!

"Mommy, can Daddy pick us up?" Shannon called from ten paces behind me.

"Have you ever seen his punk ass pick me up? Hell, he barely lets you in that fancy car of his." I rolled my eyes hollering at her over my shoulder.

"Well can we sit down then?" Her existence was starting to irritate the hell out of me. Why couldn't Jimmy's ass come get her more? Had I known I'd be stuck on twenty-four-seven, I would've taken a triple payout on top of the abortion money. It was too fucking late now.

"If you sit your ass down, you'll be getting left. Now I don't want to hear another word out of your good-for-nothing ass for the rest of the day! Keep up!"

"But, Mommy, my flip-flop broke and I'm hungry."

Turning around, running back to her, I slapped the right side of her face with fury. "Didn't you just hear me tell you to shut the fuck up? Don't let me tell you again."

Sniffling, trying not to cry, Shannon already knew I wasn't soft to tears. Matter of fact I wasn't a nurturing-type parent at all. Shannon could learn the hard way if she chose to. Whatever I said was the golden rule so the only way to survive in my household was to abide by all of them. Picking the dollar store flip-flop off of the cement, seeing it ripped in half, I shook my head, annoyed in the worst way. "Oh well, guess you gonna have to watch your step. I keep tellin' ya little young ass to take care of your things. I'm not about to keep spending the little pennies I get from your daddy on shoes and shit!" Shoving the flip-flop in her hand, I turned to start back on my stroll. "Bring ya ass!"

## 2001: James

"I'll be going to get that filthy child of yours this weekend, Jimmy," my mother reminded me. She'd been playing the middleman picking Shannon up from Shawntay for years so I wouldn't have to be bothered. I couldn't wait for that child to turn eighteen, getting out of my pocket for good. My son was all I needed in this life to be secure. "I know I said you shouldn't have anything to do with her, but seeing how poorly kempt that whore has been keeping her even saddens my cold heart."

I'd never heard my mother speak gently of Shannon. She was always too dark, too chunky, or her teeth were spaced apart too far. It had been a rough five years of me being able to balance my marriage with Beth while keeping Shannon at bay with one eight-hour visitation a week. It might've sounded pathetic but that's all she was worth.

"Is it that bad? Shawntay gets the one hundred dollars a week faithfully."

"My assumption is that she spends it on alcohol and drugs, 'cause that child reeks of both when she comes over here. She leaves a ring around my bath! And in my old age, I'm getting tired of driving all the way across town into the ghetto. You're just like how your father was: a trash prowler. I hope you teach that junior of yours something different." No matter what day of the week or when the conversation took place, Sally always found a way to tear my father's legacy down. I never once got a thank-you for taking over as her financial provider once she went bone dry. "Whatever the case, bring her some clothes for over here. Those holey, smelly, roach-infested rags her momma sends her with in a grocery store shopping bag gets left at the curb before even pulling off. You lucky you ain't brought no disease home to that poor Beth."

# Chapter Eight

## *Shannon*

Driving in circles around the parking structure looking for a spot closest to the door, I kept ringing Jay's cell, hoping he'd pick up.

"Butter baby, I'm in the middle of betting. Are you here?"

"Pulling into valet as we speak; can you meet me down here?" Tired of searching for the impossible, I swerved in front of a few other cars that were indecisively trying to figure out where to go and made sure anything of value was locked in my glove compartment so the valet attendant wouldn't get any bright ideas.

"I'll have an employee of the casino escort you up here." He hung up, not giving me a chance to contest.

You can never tell what time it is inside of a casino. Cigarette smoke, loud chatter, and the ringing of machines were sounding through the air as people tried their chances with Lady Luck. Walking through with a black jacket security guard, I peeped Jay across the room at a craps table with a hard, concentrating face.

"Right this way, ma'am." The guard lifted the rope for me to walk through.

"Thank you." I smiled at the guard, walking through as Jay took my hand. "All this for a little stripper," I joked, as he grabbed my waist, pulling me in for a hug.

"You're worth more and you'll get more. I'm glad that you could make it," he whispered, kissing my ear as each word slipped from his mouth. "Waitress, take the lady's drink order." Pulling back from me he diverted his attention back to the dice game. As my eyes traveled to the stacked winnings near him, I could see why he'd sent someone to get me in the first place, plus the reason he had so much clout. Jay was taking this casino for a ride. "Sorry for the holdup but now that I have Lady Luck on my side, we can continue."

The attendant opened the table back up for betting.

"A Patrón margarita please." It wasn't odd to be hanging with a John Doe from the club; this was how many dancers made their extra money on the side. But this white boy was balling on a level I'd never seen before. Pulling out bills left and right at the roped-off, reserved craps table, it was obvious he had longer cash than what I thought.

"Yeah, I'll take those too." He graciously accepted the double stacks of one-hundred dollar valued chips from the dealer as she nodded my way smiling. He'd been blazing this table up each time he threw the dice, stacking his winnings even higher. And I hadn't left his side since getting here. I was glued to Jay's side, refusing to let my potential money get away. My guardian angel had gotten away; my money man sure wasn't about to.

"So have you been milking these tables since you left the titty bar?" I asked, sipping seductively from my drink. "I must didn't do my job good enough in the private room."

"Indeed I have, but don't let that discredit your moves, Butter. I enjoyed you most certainly; that's why you're here. A man must have many hobbies though; gambling happens to be one of mine."

"What other hobbies do you have? Tell me what really interests you." Leaning over, whispering into his ear, I made sure to push my breasts into him so he could feel my hardened nipples. The thought of his money had me really turned on.

"Um, you're a bad girl, Butter." He grabbed my lower back, pulling me in closer. "And I like 'em bad." Kissing my neck gently, I felt my coochie starting to tingle. His Gucci Guilty cologne smelled like heaven and our attraction seemed inevitable.

"Show me you're more than just talk."

"In due time, pretty girl. Something's telling me I'm going to need more winnings to afford you." Leaning over, gently kissing my forehead, Jay was really turning into a charmer. He'd said the magical words to let me know I definitely wouldn't be walking away close to empty-handed. "Waitress, bring the lady another round!" Snapping his fingers, waving for the half-naked girl, everyone around here was scurrying like ants taking his orders. "Gotta have my Lady Luck feeling lovely." He winked, turning toward the game table.

He had it all wrong. Wasn't nothing about me lucky. My so-called family made sure I understood that from the day I was born.

"Bets are open," the table attendant spoke up, interrupting our intense conversation.

The few guys who mingled with Jay at the bar were now joining him at the craps table placing high bets. All were accompanied by women dressed as provocatively as me. I was the baddest mix breed in the crowd killing these hoes softly. Recognizing a new girl from Bare Faxxx eyeing me with hate, I figured she probably rolled with Isis or that other skinny bitch who tried to bum-rush me. It didn't matter though; I wasn't the least bit concerned. Not only was she looking hella laced, the casino's security would hammer her to the wall for coming at me sideways. As she moved her eyes from me, giving the John Doe her undivided attention, I made a mental note to keep an eye on her just in case. Enough slipups had occurred tonight.

Watching Jay get back into the game, each time he bet big, he won even bigger. Each hand he played was worth a hundred and each time the waitress brought shots of Patrón, his bet doubled. He was on fire and had people stopping left and right to scope his game.

"Bets are now closed." The dealer waved her hand across the table, signaling the gamblers to stop.

Jay blew on the dice, rolling them around in his hands, before putting them in front of my lips for me to kiss. I played the role hoping my bad luck wouldn't rub off on him. Once the dice were in perfect position to pay out, he gripped them tightly then tossed them across the table. Popping off the backside of the table then landing on his expected nine, he rubbed my hands together hungrily. "That bet was for you!"

I was gonna be wearing Jay before the night was over. We shared eye fucks, quick pecks, and naughty comments between each other that had me actually feeling him. I wasn't hiding my hand. I was flat-out flirting.

## Jay

Each hand I played was worth a stack. I had money to blow plus there was more in the room if

I bet too big for my pockets. But it was going to be a cold day in hell for that to happen. "Yeah, pass those winnings over, sweet lady. I'll be needing all of that money for my after party." I winked, smiling widely at Butter. By now, I'd hung my blazer over a chair and loosened up the few top buttons of my shirt. Staring at her before making my next few bets, I couldn't help but be intrigued by her features. She seemed familiar to me but I'd have remembered coming across someone so gorgeous before. I could tell she was mixed but I didn't know exactly with what. The only thing important was that she had black in her and that had been confirmed by the smartness of her tongue and that fat, chunky ass I couldn't wait to stuff. It's like I could smell black pussy from a mile away. And Butter's had the sweetest smell I'd ever had my nose so close to. I couldn't wait to get her up to the room to have my way with her. "I've got a few more rounds to clean up on, need another drink?"

"No, I'm good. I'd rather have you order us a bottle of expensive wine with strawberries when we get upstairs." She threw around more hints. Smiling at me with her eyes, I was undressing her with mine.

I was liking her style and had been intrigued by her since the titty bar. There was something out of the ordinary about Butter that made me want her close. Marie was the furthest thought from my mind. The next round of boring business meetings full of proposals to get companies like mine to invest in the rebuild of Detroit, which was more like a gentrification, wasn't 'til noon, so I had all night to party like my father taught me.

The night before he forced me to marry my wife Marie, my dad brought me down to this same casino I was now taking for a ride, getting me drunker than I'd ever been. Taking me to the motel up the street, he opened the door to the dirtiest room I'd ever been in with the prettiest black girl I'd ever laid eyes on. She was dark brown with baby soft skin, an amazing smile, and a fluffy ass unlike any of the white girls in my neighborhood or school. My dad was delivering me a legacy; I'd never forget his words:

*"Welcome to being a man, my boy. This has been the Schultz tradition stretching many generations back. Out of all the little pink pussies you've touched growing up, ain't nothing like the juice of a black woman. Keep Marie as the prize and your dirty work in the closet. Once you go black you ain't never gonna go back. Your granddaddy would be proud."*

My father thought he was creating a replica of himself and the men he followed with the demeaning tradition; but according to my father I would be an even bigger disgrace to my family than any of them had Sally found out. I adored black women.

Matter of fact, my attraction to them was stronger than to white women. To keep my hidden lusts as undercover as possible, I sought out beautiful mixed girls who could go either way. I'd never taken anyone but the purest white of white Beckys home to meet my mother and grandmother but my father knew the cold, hard truth. We were just alike in many ways.

"Excuse me, sir, but we have to shut the table down momentarily for shift change. It's been a pleasure being your dealer tonight. Good luck." The attendant smiled at both Butter and me before dismissing herself.

"Oh, I hate that you have to go. You've been so kind." I winked again. I wasn't a flirt but I considered myself a ladies' man. Women loved that extra touch in a conversation.

"Why thank you, sir, I'm just doing my job. Please enjoy a round on the house." The dealer smiled as the waitress showed up on time with another round of what we'd been ordering all night. As her replacement, the banker, and the manager started to break down the table in prep for shift change, I took that as my cue to retire to my room for the private after party.

"We'll take these to go. Please send room service up immediately with a bottle of the casino's finest champagne." Taking the two shots of Patrón from her platter, I was a firm believer in omens and the muscular, cut dealer on deck who resembled Wesley Snipes probably wasn't gonna bring me a drop of luck. "Come on, baby, so I can break all the way in." I grabbed Butter's hand, leading her toward the elevator as she followed like a dog in heat.

## Butter

I'd gambled at MGM casino before and even fucked in the hotel before, but never in a deluxe luxury suite. Since J.T. was playing like a high roller, I guessed he had to rest his head as one, too. Walking into the 1,000-square-foot luxury corner suite, for a brief moment I was speechless. As my red bottom heels clicked on the marble floor through the foyer on the way to the oversized wrap-around window, I couldn't help but to wish upon a star staring out at the sparkling lights illuminating the city of Detroit. This view was spectacular. Too bad my life wasn't close to this small fairytale I was experiencing.

There was a knock at the door. "Room Service."

"Make yourself comfortable, Butter." J.T. unbuttoned his shirt, leaving on just a crisp white wife beater. "Let me grab our bottle of champagne and get rid of the help."

"Oh, okay." *The help? Yeah, you're rich and white for real. My father's mother would love you. You're just her type.* Trying not to let the abnormal issues I had with my family ruin what was left of the night, I pushed everything about Shawntay and the Schultz to the back of my mind, deciding to take a quick tour of the room. There was a separate sitting area, a wet bar, and the most luxurious bathroom I'd ever seen. Between the forty-inch plasma flat screens in the bedroom and bathroom, I knew it would be hard to tear myself from this place. I could get drunk as a skunk in complete peace. *Oh yeah, this dude has got that old, long cash so I need to pull out some of my best stunts to keep him panting.*

"Your wish is my command, pretty lady; here's your drink." J.T. found me gawking at all of the high-tech amenities then handed me my glass of champagne with strawberries filled to the top. "What type of music would you like to listen to? I've got quite a range loaded up on my iPod."

"You pick, I can move to anything." Taking a gulp then a strawberry in my mouth, I sucked on it sexily while at the same time dropping hints.

After turning on a song from John Legend, he wasted no time in going for what he wanted. His hands wandered all over my curvaceous body just like they'd done at the club, but this time in a more seductive way. Sliding his hands down the back of my low-rise pants, he tickled my asshole gently making me breath lightly. *Good thing I paid extra attention to back there.* Starting to sway my hips and grind my crotch on his hands each time he slipped them between my thighs, he didn't have to be tipping right now for me to be turned on. Whatever he was working with, I wanted my taste. This man was making me feel so good.

"G'on and dance for daddy." He smacked my ass making it jump up and down. Pulling out the fat wad of winnings he'd collected downstairs, my eyes lit up as my pussy juices were now running down my leg, ready to work for every dollar.

"Is all that for me?" I couldn't help but questioning, sounding like an innocent child. Turning around bending it over while spreading 'em wide, I twerked 'til my cheeks ached from J.T. smacking them so hard.

"Show me why you deserve it." J.T. leaned back onto the couch with his drink in one hand and his other stroking his manhood. Not as hung as the black men I'd gotten rammed by, the width looked like it could do a little damage.

I put on the best show I could for him. From touching him, to myself, to masturbating 'til I came for his viewing pleasure, J.T. was having the time of his life calling himself turning me out. "I don't like all touch and no play." I wanted him to join in with the fun.

Not wasting a moment, taking full reign to my invitation, he started caressing my breasts while sucking on my nipples like a starved newborn. "Let me taste your honey, Butter; climb on top of my hungry mouth."

Within seconds I was sitting on top of his face as ordered. I was grinding on his mouth slowly as the feeling was making my whole body tingle. "Oh my God this feels so good!"

"I see you like that." He lifted his head up bringing all of my pleasure to an immediate halt. "Well I'm about to take your smooth body to new heights." Lifting my limp body up, I wrapped my legs tightly around his waist ready to experience pure sexual bliss. At this point it wasn't about the money; it was about chasing this nut.

"I'm so ready." Any type I could get from this fucked-up world was welcomed.

## Jay

Marie couldn't compete with Butter in any way imaginable. Her smooth skin, intoxicating smell, and mysterious attitude made me crave her in the worst way. Every time I snuck away from Marie, I ended up between the legs of another woman. Cheating on Marie wasn't hard; I didn't love her in the first place. Everything about my marriage was business; this right here with Butter was pleasure.

Sitting her body down into the water, I slid in with her instantly rubbing my hands all over her again. The more I touched her, the more she moaned and ground back. Our sexual chemistry was off the charts. Leaning down, kissing her stomach, she lifted her midsection up to my face letting me know she wanted me back kissing between her thighs. Sitting her up on the side of the Jacuzzi, I dined on her without remorse while hearing my cell phone ringing from my blazer jacket pocket.

## Butter

I screamed at how far he stuck his tongue inside of me. There was no holds barred. Jay was touching my G-spot with his tongue making me splash water all over the place but the feeling was sensational; I loved it. This white boy sure knew how to eat some pussy. "Oh shit, Jay, yes! I'm gonna cum!" The harder I ground myself on his face, the harder he grabbed my hips keeping me from lifting up. Jay was working like he wanted every last drop. He seemed hungry for this cat. Feeling my body tense up before cumming, I ran my fingers through his thick brown hair making sure he didn't tease me out of my moment.

Coming up for air, he took a handful of water, rinsing my juices from around his mouth before leaning in to kiss me hard and rough. Moving his mouth down to my neck sucking a hickey on me almost instantly, I felt my coochie starting to tingle again, ready to come back out for play. "Your pussy is so warm and sweet." He slid his finger back inside of me, finger fucked me roughly, and then slid it inside of my mouth. The water was splashing all over the place but neither one of us cared.

"Now let's switch so you can suck this nut out of me. I saw how you worked that bottle in your mouth at the club earlier." As I got down into the water, Jay pointed his stiff, hard dick into my face. Staring at the rounded mushroom, I licked it first then gobbled it down with the intentions of making him cum quick.

He literally fucked my face, grabbing the top of my head as he relentlessly rammed his manhood down my throat. I didn't lose a beat of rhythm. I could suck dick with the best of 'em, ya better believe it! The only sounds that filled the room were his moans, my slurping noises, and, annoyingly enough, both of our cells ringing off the hook. Mine was probably Shawntay. His was probably some wife or girlfriend highly irate that he was unreachable. As his body began jerking, the grips on my head got tighter. I knew what time it was so I created a vacuum suction with my mouth sucking every drop of nut out of him. *He gonna pay big for this head job.*

"Come on, let's retire to the bed." He pulled his now semi-limp dick from my mouth as I swallowed each drop. Climbing out of the water, leaving wet footprints across the room, I sprawled out on the bed as directed. "Turn over on your front," he commanded. Feeling oil dropping on my back, I started to feel his big hands massaging my neck, shoulder, back, and legs. Starting to grind my body into the bed, I was so turned on I was begging for more. Kissing all over my body, I lifted my booty in the air as he placed soft kisses on it too. I felt a vibe and connection with him that was unexplainable. My inner thighs were sticky as my body almost went limp from creaming all over the sheets.

Within seconds his hard dick entered my pussy. I arched my back to willingly accept the obvious pounding he'd worked up for me. As he smacked my ass while giving it to me doggie style, there was a thin line between pleasure and pain but I refused to back down as I wasn't a stranger to either of the two. Jay was paying close attention to my body; and I was more than loving it. I tried to look back but my face was pushed back down into the fluffy pillows. There was no limit; I'd never had anyone completely control me in the bedroom. This was the one place I could usually dominate someone. I'd been trained since a child to take hard dick like a pro, so I was gonna ride tonight 'til the wheels fell off.

"Flip me over," I called out, finally able to catch my wind. I wanted him to hit it from another way, dig my guts from a different angle.

Doing just that, this white boy had strength. Flipping me over by my leg, he wasted no time digging his tool back into my spot. "You liking this, Butter?"

"Oh my God yes, Jay! You feel so good." Panting, feeling another orgasm coming on, this man was sexing all of the tension out of me effortlessly. It's like he knew just what to do. I spread my legs wide as they would go and dug my nails into his back, pulling him deeper inside of me. The pressure was in my stomach and as soon as his bare dick nutted, his sperm would be there too. "Give it to me, daddy!" Squeezing my vagina muscles tightly, once his eyes rolled into the back of head, I knew he was whipped on the feeling of fucking something so juicy raw dog.

That was the wrong thing to say. He pushed me up against the headboard, ramming it all the way in. "Take this dick then. Open them legs up wider." Yelling, starting to turn into a madman, I wasn't fazed or scared 'cause most men went ballistic over good sex. The wider I opened my legs, the deeper he stroked me, making my body respond to him with back-to-back orgasms.

All night long he gave me the business. Position after position, porno after porno, fantasy after fantasy, we turned each other out. We had sex all over the bedroom, the sitting room, the marble foyer floor, and finished up in the shower. My head was a mess, my liquor buzz was still flowing, but I needed a Kush blunt badly for the icing on top of the cake. Sliding down under the sheets, my breasts brushed against Jay. "Can you hold me?" I usually made it a rule to never cuddle, get close or connected to John Does but I wasn't ready to leave Jay just yet. There was something special about this guy, something calming that made me want to be around him.

"Come here," he said, pulling me close. "I need to wake up to some of that good pussy to send me off right to my business meeting; stay." I allowed him to wrap me up tightly in his arms before drifting off to sleep.

"Butter. Wake up. Butter!"

Feeling Jay shake me, I was sleeping hard, caught up in a dream about my father. I'd been having more and more of him lately but didn't know what they meant.

One day, when I was a little girl, he'd come over my grandmother's house, his mother's, with bags and bags of clothes just for me. There were pink lace dresses, sailor boat outfits, barrettes, Barbie dolls, and even nail polish for me to play in. He'd seldom come but when he did, I never got this special treatment. I felt like a princess off of TV, all 'cause of my daddy.

*"Get up off the floor in your new pretty dress, child!"* My grandmother came in yelling with her milky white face balled up in a knot.

*"Sorry, ma'am."* I jumped to my feet, afraid of the switch.

*"What did I tell you about wallowing on the floor, Shannon?"* Her stern face dared me not to remember the line she made me recite one hundred times each time I messed up.

*"To act like a lady, not like a monkey."* I hung my head low realizing at a young age I could never please her.

*"Wow, Ma, that's what you're over here teaching her? She'll be part of this family more so than you think."* My father laughed, setting down his beer. *"Come here, Shannon, sit by me on the couch and play with your Barbie dolls."*

I looked toward my grandmother who was giving him the evil eye but wouldn't dare give up the chance to be close to my father. I always watched him walk into my grandmother's house in a suit and tie, set his briefcase on the table, and hand her a sealed white envelope before finally patting me on the head. I would always be sitting at the breakfast counter eating fruits waiting on my grandmother to give me my next calculated move. She never let me go anywhere or do anything in her house without standing by my side. She called me a thief; I never stole a thing. She called me a

*liar; I was never allowed to speak. She'd whip me*
*for being bad; I didn't have anyone around me*
*doing good.*

*"You're gonna send me to the grave early!" She*
*stormed out of the room cursing both of us to hell.*

After that my daddy became my knight in shining
armor. Not only did he make sure to have a present
each time he saw me, but his visits were regular so
I was seldom alone with my evil grandmother. She
would still pick me up in her big white Cadillac alone
but by the time she dunked me into the first bath
my dad would be walking in. I hated my mother and
Sally but would look forward to seeing my daddy. He
made my childhood so bearable. I couldn't take any
of my presents home but those few hours I played as
a princess at my grandmother's was worth it.

Every night I'd have the same dream then wake
up with a bittersweet smile on my face. This time I
was waking up to something different.

# Chapter Nine

## *Shawntay*

My daughter had every valid reason in the world to hate me. Hearing her curse me out then hang up every time I called was starting to take a toll on my recovery. Feeling my legs starting to shake, I began chewing my lips trying to fight the sudden hunger I had to quench my thirst. *Just one sip. It'll take the edge off.* I'd been clean for years but hearing Shannon tear me down taking me back down memory lane had me feeling weak. *You've come too far to go back. Don't let that devil's liquid touch your lips.* I was completely torn. Shannon said all of the triggers I needed to revert to my old ways of being a drunk, a druggie, and, most of all, a disgrace. I used to rush her off to her evil grandmother's house so I could have a few hours of peace with my drug of choice. It didn't matter if she came back with hours of horror stories, lash marks from getting disciplined, or pissing like a race horse because Sally tried to flush the black out of her; I wished Shannon gone twenty-four hours of the day.

*"Mommy, can we play? None of the kids will share their toys with me."* Shannon came in with a beet-red face from crying.

*"Naw, Momma busy. G'on in that room and just imagine yourself playing."* I shooed her from in front of the television screen not caring that another group of girls had bullied her. *"You might as well get used to these nappy-headed girls showing you their asses, Shannon. None of them have long hair, bright skin, or pretty eyes like you. So they ain't gonna never want you as their friend! Get used to it, girl."*

No matter how I dished reality to Shannon, she took it without blinking. Back then I was too far gone in the mind to realize I was truly poisoning her mind to the point of no return.

Tossing and turning, wishing she'd answer my calls, I couldn't sleep a wink throughout the night praying, wishing, and hoping God would give her the strength to forgive me. I'd been calling, texting, and leaving voicemails all night but I was sure she was more than busy following in my footsteps living fancy free and wild. Looking at the picture of her I kept inside of my Bible, I touched it gently, afraid that I might tarnish it too, then prayed for God to work a miracle.

Shannon's spitfire attitude came from my side of the family. She thought I was trying to judge her lifestyle when in reality my pleas were more so warnings. I knew firsthand what this lifestyle was gonna get my baby; and I was the main reason to blame for her choosing this way of life. This was how I trained her up to be. I was more than familiar with the path she's going down because it's the same one I traveled that ended me here. My walk with the Lord started because my decisions made me sick. I had no one else to turn to but Him and He forgave me like preachers always said He would.

I couldn't go to the grave without at least fighting tooth and nail for my daughter's forgiveness. My past had become her demon so I felt it was my duty to save her from the belly of the beast. Nothing I was doing was working. She'd turned her back on me the same way I'd done to her for so many years. The only person who could save her was the main person who wished me nothing but strife for her creation: her father. Getting up from my knees, closing my Bible from the book of Psalms, I grabbed my car keys, rushing out of the house toward the estate my child and I had been barred from.

## James

"Beth, calm down! I've been trying J.T.'s cell all night. He isn't answering for me either." Having a strong, tall glass of whiskey, I was going to lose my mind between my wife and daughter-in-law using me as a ploy to try to reach my son. If my gut served me right, he was laid up with some hot-tail colored girl getting served up. My boy was a Schultz man so I knew his desires ran thick. Beth knew the truth too but refused to be the bad guy in breaking Marie's poor little heart. Besides, if their marriage crumbled, I was sure our business collaboration with the Dilberts would too. "I know what you're thinking, Beth. I'll try again."

"You better! Marie is on a warpath and the last thing we need for her to do is call her father complaining about J.T. not coming home. Get a hold of your son, damn it! I know how that poor girl feels." Beth hadn't screamed this loud since seeing a picture of Shannon on my lap at Sally's. Back then she raised the dead; today's pitch might've brought down Jesus Christ Himself.

"What do you want me to do, Beth? He's not a little boy I can throw over my lap or threaten to hold a trust from anymore. That's a married man." The one part that went unspoken that was surely known was that I was the one who'd introduced J.T. to cheating in the first place. Just how my dad had done me.

"Exactly, James, hence the keyword 'married.' He must stay that way. You can play that innocent game with me like you don't have any influence over your son but we both know better. If you want to die a rich man like you've been living securely since he married our wealthy partner's daughter, I suggest you wheel your DNA back into the program."

The doorbell rang out.

"Call your son now, James. That should be Marie and the twins."

Shaking my head, hitting redial, I really didn't want to call my son to be a hypocrite but of course Beth had great points. Our company might've got invested in many years ago, but since then Stan had taken over more interest in our business plus a substantial amount of growing investments within the city. He was now far more valuable to us than we could ever be to him, which meant J.T. had to make Marie happily ever after.

"James! James Theodore Schultz III, hurry up down here now!"

"I'm coming, Beth!" I couldn't hang the phone up fast enough speeding down the stairs. J.T. hadn't answered anyway. Hopefully there wasn't nothing wrong with Marie or those precious grandbabies but from the way Beth had screamed something was terribly wrong. In my old age, my brightest moments were spending it with them when my pretty young brown thang was busy. Getting to the end of the stairwell, expecting to at least hear the little pitter-patter of Josh and Jill's feet, instead I was greeted by a cold, hard slap to the face.

"Well hello, James Theodore Schultz III." Shawntay Jenkins stood on the other side of my door clutching a King James Bible. I thought I was seeing a ghost.

"What in the hell is she doing at our house?" Beth went to smack me again but her arms were caught in mid-swing. "Have you been slumming again, James?"

"Beth, calm down. I don't know! Let me get to the bottom of this." Marching toward the door, I thought for sure I was getting ready to catch my first case. "Shawntay, I've told you never to come here. There's no reason for you to be on my doorstep, especially since Shannon is over eighteen. I have never owed you shit but definitely not now."

"Tell her ass to get on from here, James, or I'll call the police on her for trespassing!" Yelling like a madwoman with the phone in her hand, I knew Beth was serious but the phone call wouldn't harm me in no way. I'd paid my debt to Shawntay and Shannon, every cent of child support ordered.

"Tell your wife if she calls the police I'll be giving them a reason to come," Shawntay threatened. "I may be a woman of God now but I came to raise hell about my daughter, something I should've done over twenty years ago!" Taking a brief moment to take Shawntay in, no longer was she dressed like the cheapest streetwalker Detroit employed. Her once droopy red eyes, alcoholic breath, and horrid

weed smell had been replaced by bright, angry
eyes, a God-speaking tongue, and the will not to
back down. *I guess you can teach a dog new tricks*.

"Your time has come and gone, Shawntay. The
only leverage you had with me was Shannon and
she's grown now. Any responsibility I had to that
girl died the day she turned eighteen. I'm going to
ask you one final time: please leave and never bring
your ass back around here."

"NaNa, PawPaw!" Josh and Jill were running up
the walkway with Marie close behind.

"Wow, PawPaw, really? You ain't even play
father to one of your kids but now you're playing
granddad to two others!"

"What? He don't owe you or that Oreo kid of
yours nothing more!" Beth screamed at Shawntay.
"Yes, police, can you please send a squad car to
21766 Hummingbird Lane? There's a trespasser on
the property refusing to leave." By now Marie had
a twin in each arm running into the living room to
keep them from the unknown drama unfolding.

"I don't even know what I expected by coming
here," Shawntay mumbled under her breath. "Look,
Shannon is tough as nails out in these streets but
she's gonna need someone to turn to once everything
in her life comes tumbling down. And even though
your racist, ugly, low self-esteem having–ass wife is
against it, you're Shannon's father so it's your duty
to be that for the rest of her natural life. She told me

how you stuck up for her as a little girl when Sally was picking on her, so I figured that somewhere in that ice-cold heart of yours had to be some love for our baby."

I knew Beth was steaming hearing that I'd even been around Shannon. But when she was a little girl I was intrigued by the definite features of mine she had. I could tell she was a lot like me from her timid personality, wandering eyes, and how shaken she would be from my mother's voice. I was the same when I was a child; that's why I made it my duty to protect her from what ruined me at her age. But our father-daughter relationship went no further. "I don't think none of that will be happening, Shannon. You two have been dead to me. I am with my wife on this one; charges will be pressed if you don't get off of our property!" Trying to slam the door, I wanted Shawntay to crawl back under whatever rock she'd just crawled from under.

"Your wish will come true sooner than you think. The grave you've been digging for me since the nineties is almost six feet deep." Shawntay dropped her head, seeming weaker than I'd ever seen or heard her. Over all the years of her cursing me out, I'd never heard her voice so low. "I was diagnosed with HIV-AIDS a few years ago. I only came here to ask you to help patch up my and Shannon's relationship before I die."

# Chapter Ten

## *Jay*

"Hold on, Marie, slow down. What's going on? Who is there?" Butter was showering, it was just past seven in the morning, and I'd just gotten done going over the itinerary for today's schedule of meetings. I'd stroked her sleep then woke her up with my stiff pink penis in her mouth so of course until Marie's call I was gliding on cloud nine. My plan had been to hit Bare Faxxx for another afternoon of Butter's loving once the business part of my day had ended. But of course family drama was throwing daggers in all of my preconceived plans.

"I'm at your parents', they're arguing, no one will tell me much of anything. I just know me, Josh, and Jill walked up on your dad fussing with a black woman. Can you come home? Please! And where have you been? Why haven't you been answering any of my calls?"

"Why are you at my parents'? Get the twins and go home. I told you I was staying at the hotel to get some work done, Marie. You know your father has a slew of meetings planned all day and tomorrow. I can't come home just yet but stop worrying yourself over my parents' drama." In the back of my mind I knew the black woman Marie probably saw was a mistress of my father's. He liked to act like his temptation and dirty desires were repressed but me being just like him, I knew better.

"Please try to make time. I'll get the kids and head home."

"Don't worry, Marie; for you and those kids you know I'll try." Hanging up the phone I knew I'd just lied through my teeth. I didn't have any true intentions of going home maybe the whole weekend. If Butter would give me my way, she'd be laid up in this room all night playing a sex slave to me.

"Okay, Jay, don't forget you promised to call me after your slew of meetings." Butter appeared from the bathroom with the hotel's white fluffy robe on.

"Don't worry; you'll be seeing me after those meetings. Save a VIP room for me."

"Aren't we the big spender." She smiled, placing a kiss on my slender lips. "Even though you worked me over last night, my rates still stand."

Winning me over with her smile, I was falling hard for Butter in the worst way. I didn't care about how Marie felt, my father's disapproval, or my mother going bat-shit crazy because I was risking our family's financial stability for a stripper; this one seemed special enough to go on the wild ride with.

"So why are you rushing out of here?" I could've paid for any pussy I wanted to. I craved hers.

"I promised a friend we could meet up for breakfast." Grabbing the hotel lotion from my open suitcase, she started rubbing it all over her body, making my dick stand at attention.

"A friend at seven in the morning? Must be some special friend." I didn't like to be turned down, plus the prize I'd been paying into wasn't getting ready to be given to someone else. I'd paid enough cash into Butter to own her as far as I was concerned.

"It's not like that, sweetheart. He's the DJ at the club. We're just grabbing a bite to eat so he can fill me in on all the drama that went down at last night after I left. Nothing more, nothing less."

"I can't say that I'm not deflated to hear the news. I would've loved to come back to this room after those boring business meetings to find you stark naked ready for some wood. How much is he paying you to grab a bite to eat anyway?"

"Huh? What do you mean?" No longer moisturizing her skin, she stopped to look up at me, confused like she didn't charge me for my time. Money made the world go 'round as my father taught me, so Butter could be bought too.

"Whatever he's paying you for your time, I can pay you more. It's nothing." Money was of no object. Doing business with Marie's father secured my financial security so I blew money whenever I felt the urge.

Letting out a breath of air in exasperation, I could tell she was thinking twice on my proposition. "Wow, this is going to be harder than I thought." She sighed. "My friend and I had a crazy night so this breakfast meeting is a must. I promise it's nothing more than that, but I'll call you right when we're done, my word."

"Just make sure this pussy come back just how I left it." Pushing her back onto the bed, I opened the robe and made love to her sexy body until sending my seed deep inside of her. I knew I should've been strapped up or at least pulled out to jack my nut off onto her stomach, but I couldn't deny the love my dick had for her warmth. I was in sexual heaven.

## Butter

I heard Jay up talking on the phone to his wife, girlfriend, significant other, whoever—I didn't care. I had my hand deep in my pockets after really peeping what he was worth so ya better believe the chick on the phone's role was compromised already. He hadn't strapped up not one time of us fucking like rabbits so if my period came up late, I'd come up knocked up and keeping it. After getting sexed, paid, and sent out the door, I was climbing into my whip tipping the valet one of the tens I'd made last night.

Keeping it real with ol' boy, wasn't nothing about my story fabricated. I tried adding a cherry on top by letting him work me out before having to leave, so hopefully that helped not to sour his mood; but I had to hook up with Dazz so we could discuss what went down last night. He'd been one of the many calls from early this morning I couldn't answer but via text he let me know that we needed to hook up ASAP before I went into work.

"Thank you, and have a good day, ma'am." The attendant waved, happy that his day started off the right way.

"Oh no doubt. And you do the same." Pulling off toward Big Boy, I had to meet up with Dazz for breakfast. Jay was throwing major shade about me hooking up with another guy but he had some nerve having a girl with twins at home. Men weren't shit but at least Jay paid me enough to overlook it.

Riding down Jefferson, everything was much different than it was last night. All of the partiers were probably still knocked out as nothing but trash was left in the parking lots running over into the streets. Many business owners were out sweeping, cleaning up, and prepping for their Saturday morning patrons.

The phone rang. Reaching for my phone thinking it was Dazz, I answered without checking. Big mistake! "Hello."

"Hi, Shannon," a deep voice spoke back.

Pulling the phone back, looking at the number, I didn't know anyone from that area code prefix so it must've been a bill collector. "Yeah, who is this? I ain't got no job, money, or nothing; plus it's too early to be calling my phone about some bill shit."

"Your father."

I hadn't heard from this man since he'd told me to have a nice life on my eighteenth birthday handing my mother the final child support payment. I didn't know she faithfully received. He looked at me as his daughter then turned and walked away. Why in the hell was he calling me now? Absolutely speechless, I didn't know what to say. "The only father I know of wouldn't be calling me." What else could I say to the stranger who'd chosen to stay away?

"Your tongue is just as sharp as your mother's."

"Yeah, well, and so? I was raised by her." He'd woken me up with his criticism like I had any other choice but to be like the woman I hated to the core of my soul.

Dazz pulled up, blowing the horn. "Ay, yo, Butter baby, c'mon, girl!" Waving for me to jump in his ride, I was glad Dazz was there because I needed more of a reason to end this call. I wasn't interested in entertaining him or Shawntay. Why were they surfacing anyhow?

"Look, James, my friend just pulled up. Can we rush this conversation along?"

"I'll be free again around lunchtime. Please call me by then or I'll call you."

"How about you call me? We both know how it goes when it comes to me trying to reach out to you. I'm too old for that letdown shit." I looked over at Dazz who was holding up our morning breakfast: a plump swisher sweet.

"I'll be calling you around noon. Talk to you then."

Staring down at my phone's blinking call duration, a boatload of memories rushed into my mind. The whole life I'd steadily pushed down was starting to come back at me full force. I couldn't understand why, 'cause the people I pushed away were the same people who isolated me in the first place. I felt like everything around me was spinning. My heart was racing, I couldn't catch my breath, and for a moment I completely zoned out.

Dazz blew the horn once more.

"What up? You straight?" Dazz asked as I jumped in his Yukon still dazed from talking to my dad.

"I'm good. That phone call just shook me up a bit." Not wanting to get too deep into my personal business with Dazz, I kept my answer short and sweet hoping he got the point.

"I can tell. G'on and light this up. It'll get ya mind right. Let's get this wake and bake session started." Passing over the blunt I'd been eyeing since getting in, I grabbed the lighter from the cup holder, taking my orders with no reluctance.

"Don't mind if I do."

"So what you get into last night? You and white boy you did a private with hookup?" Dazz wasted no time cutting into me as soon as I hopped into his Yukon Denali.

"Damn, you must have a LoJack recording device hooked up to me somewhere," I joked, buckling up as he pulled off.

"Oh please believe I keep tabs on everything I have an interest in. And from the looks of it, you should be happy that I do. Them bitches were gunning for your head last night." Looking over to make sure I was listening, I had a feeling Dazz really wanted to say more.

"No doubt, no doubt! I'm more than apprecia-tive. Frank wouldn't have wasted a moment firing my ass had I pulled out my .380. You came out looking like a savior by keeping the peace between our wild asses. It was about to be a murder may-hem up in the club please believe me!" Taking a few puffs before passing the tightly wrapped packed cigarillo, I welcomed the calming buzz it brought over my overworked body. "So what's the word? What all went down last night? I'm pretty sure I've gotta walk around watching over my shoulder."

"Well as long as I'm around, you ain't never gotta worry." Reaching over me popping the glove compartment, he pulled out a Ziploc half full of marijuana tossing it onto my lap. "Roll up so we can get this real right and kick it before hitting Big Boy."

Catching a whiff of the loud green before even fully opening the bag, the funk spread throughout the truck like a wildfire once I opened it to sneak a whiff. "Damn this is some hella loud right here!" Picking up one of the many fliers that were spread throughout his truck, I broke down a few of the corned popcorn buds, making sure this would be a fat one. "I've gotta buy a few grams of this fire up off ya. This would save me the trouble from having to make a stop."

"You know I ain't about taking your money, Butter. A real nigga don't have his hand out. Take you a handful on me then roll up another fat one. You straight." Gripping the wheel turning the radio back up, I followed my commands not questioning his boss status.

Riding across the bridge to the park, I was feeling hella high already but that didn't stop me from pulling super hard. Between Kush and alcohol, that was the only time I had peace and comfort. I couldn't wait to get a drink up in me. Rolling down the window to let the thick smoke seep out into the air, my long, wavy hair flowed in the wind as I stared off into the sky. Something just wasn't sitting right in the pit of my stomach. With so much unraveling in my life at the same time, I couldn't pinpoint where the uneasy feeling was coming from. So much had gone down the last twenty-four hours. Deciding to keep quiet not to kill the vibe, I bobbed my head to the Jeezy song trying to shake the irking feeling. *Chill out, Shannon, you only tripping about your dad. Get it together so you can get faded the right way.*

Pulling into a parking space by the water, Dazz shut the ignition off then pulled a blanket from the back seat. "Bring that choke with you; we're going to sit by the water."

# Chapter Eleven

## *Marie*

Having a cup of coffee, listening to my mother-in-law vent, I couldn't believe J.T. had kept so many family secrets from me. I guessed had he told me the dark truths of the Schultz men I would've questioned his loyalty to me as his wife.

"Would you like another cup, Beth?" I held the mug up after filling my mug to the brim. I hadn't slept a wink and from the looks of it couldn't plan to catch any rest for hours to come. Luckily the twins were asleep.

"No, I'll be needing something stronger. I can't believe that home-wrecking whore showed up to my house! Pour me a glass of wine from that open bottle in the fridge." Beth was on a rampage. Since being introduced to her as a child, I always met the mild, sweet, docile, mothering woman who always took me and J.T. on play dates. Now she was shivering mad pouring every problem out that she and the second man I called dad had since before my time.

"I don't know what to say, Ma." Handing her the whole bottle, she poured her own sorrows as I sipped what I hoped would give me enough energy to deal with what she was about to lay on me.

"I do! His ass better not come back to this house after crossing me. All those years of sneak visits . . . What did he call himself doing? Bonding? I warned him."

Mrs. Schultz was speaking babble. The more she drank the more she went on and on about family secrets I could've never fathomed. My father-in-law had a daughter out of wedlock with a black woman and Beth refused to acknowledge the little girl. As the hurt feelings spilled out more, I pieced together that me and my father were just ploys to ensure the Schultz financial bottom didn't fall out. The woman who I thought was more passive than my mother uncovered her masked face of deception. She was the furthest thing from weak, resembling more of a mastermind than any of the money-hungry men I'd seen my father do business with.

"Does J.T. know he has a sister?" Too intrigued by the skeletons in their closet, I was nothing but all ears. Pouring my cup of coffee down the sink, joining Beth in drinking in the wee hours of the morning, the drama she was putting on the table was more than a reason to get lit.

"Of course not! What type of mother would I had been if I let my only son be raised with a black girl?

I did what any well-educated, respectable white woman would've done and got my husband back in line. I'd worked too hard at training my husband on how to provide. No nigger woman or her child was gonna reap my riches." The more Beth talked, the more scorned she sounded. Instead of controlling the situation and keeping the family she thought was so sacred to her, Beth had been pushing down resentment for James for over twenty years.

"I wonder what my mother would've done if dad put her in the same situation. And, hell, what would I do if J.T. followed in his father's footsteps?" Staring at Beth I really wanted to know what her honest response would be.

"Your mother would've kept her family together by any means. Your dad is a very prestigious man, he has women paying to suck his dick. So I'm sure your mother stands in her corner of the ring with a list of demands of her own. We as the wives of successful men must know how to play our part."

Mrs. Schultz was in rare form. I'd never heard her speak so brash.

### Shawntay

Speeding down the highway doing about a hundred mph, I was spitting bullets mad. All my life I'd been fighting against the odds, coming up short each time. I was tired of the struggle, I was tired of losing, and I was tired of never at least being the runner-up. Shawntay Jenkins ain't never been shit! Calling Shannon over and over again, each call was going straight to voicemail. My faith was starting to waver as I felt hopeless. "Oh, God, please stop punishing me. Can I have another chance at having a relationship with my only daughter?" Screaming out, hitting the steering wheel in anger, my frustration was boiling over. Nothing I was doing was enough. No path I was walking was getting me closer to forgiveness from Shannon. I might've been a demon in my earlier days but I was walking as a saint in my eyes today. When would my punishment end? Why me?

He and his racist wife slandered even the saved name I'd been diligently working on. I knew I was nothing more to Jimmy than a quick nut but I hadn't expected him to still be so cold even after telling him I was diagnosed to die. At some point in my life before it was all over, I guessed I was still expecting more than a cold shoulder.

There was no reason for me to hold on to hope anymore. Snatching from my nightstand drawer the bag of medications my doctor said would help prolong my life, or at least keep me out of pain while my immune system ate away at itself, I swallowed a mouthful of pills then drank a full glass of water. The rest I dumped down the toilet bowl then flushed. "I'm over this life! Ain't shit been happy about my ever after!" Walking with determination into the living room, I grabbed the bottle of Absolut I'd successfully walked past for three years and unscrewed the top. Drinking my first sip, I'd missed the hard, harsh taste, the burning sensation going down my throat, and the immediate buzz liquor brought me. "I'm sorry I ever left your side!"

Giving into my temptation, this was the only thing that ensured my mind didn't have to deal with how pitiful I actually was. Tilting it back, drinking the whole fifth down nonstop, I didn't care that my body was starting to negatively react from the mixture of alcohol and prescriptions. Once done with the first bottle, I grabbed another fifth then drank it straight down too. I was weak, wobbly, and barely breathing. They say a recovering alcoholic should get rid of all their liquor in their house to help lessen the chance of relapsing. I guessed my walk to recovery was just as much of a joke as my walk with the Lord. Feeling my chest starting to hurt then tighten up, I fell to the ground gasping for my last breath. This was it.

## James

I was finally about to do right by Shannon and Shawntay; well, at least until her final days. Neither one of them deserved to be shunned when I was the one who'd made them a reality in my life in the first place. All of these years of allowing Beth and Sally to dictate how Shannon was raised was the worst mistake of my life. No matter how many days I tried denying it, my heart had a place for Shannon and I didn't want to end up burying her like she was about to have to do her mother. Reaching down on my hip, grabbing my phone from the holster, I saw it was my mother calling again, probably on behalf of Beth. The puppet master games were over.

"Hello." I spoke calmly into the phone, turning down the street I last knew Shawntay's house to be on. "If you're calling to berate me, Mother, you've wasted your time."

"Are you out of your fucking mind? I called your house to speak to Beth but she's a drunken mess. She told me about that nigger lover you've called yourself running after. You need to turn that car around, get home to your wife, and pray to God you haven't ruined my opportunity to die a rich woman!" Screaming into the phone ol' Sally was still the same bitter old woman my dad grew to resent.

"Beth better prepare the guest room because I'll be bringing Shannon home to meet the family she should've grown up with. It'll be nice if you're there." I taunted her with my words knowing it was getting under her skin.

"Over my dead body, James Theodore Schultz III."

"Then I guess the first family function Shannon will attend will be your funeral." Hanging up, I was moments away from knocking on Shawntay's door. I owed her a few apologies and, from the looks of this shabby, half-standing house, a few dollars to upgrade herself. Over all the years of death wishes I'd begged God to curse Shawntay with was finally unfolding. I wouldn't say God was the one responsible for shortening her lifespan because I was the one busy praying against her existence and today I knew it was too late to wish all of those words away. All of that time and energy could've been put toward helping Shannon have at least half the life afforded to my son. Shawntay's only request of me was to help her and Shannon mend their relationship; that was the least I could do.

# Chapter Twelve

## *Shannon*

Me and Dazz had been sitting by the water blowing through blunt after blunt kicking it about all of the nonsense at the club. At first I'd gotten amped up with him telling me Isis and her group of flunkies was dropping innuendo Facebook statuses about getting at me after tonight's shift. But that energy was soon diverted to thinking of a plan to get at them first. I was tired of everyone marking me for weak so it was time to start biting bitches' heads off. I'd taken more strife than a little bit but was still standing strong. As much as I hated the women in my life, Sally and Shawntay, their trifling asses broke the soft spirit these chicks in the street thought they were testing in me.

After a while the calming scenery, sound of the waves, and loudness of the Kush we were blowing had me in a meditating zone not thinking about Isis or her posse but the whirlwind of unexpected events with Shawntay and now James. It was easy for me to diss my mother but my father was the one person I always wanted a relationship with. Now with him calling me I didn't know if that option was on the table. I was grown enough to know I was the ugly duckling child he couldn't claim but those few hours at my grandmother's were the only happy moments I ever had in my childhood. I couldn't help but pour my heart out as Dazz became my sounding board for all of the shit I'd been holding in about my growing up neglected, Shawntay, Sally, and my father. He was one helluva listener and, real talk, I needed the bootleg therapy session. Because most females were jealous of my looks, afraid that I would steal the attention they craved from their man, I rolled solo-dolo never having anyone to confide in. Even the chicks who had egos big enough to not be intimidated by me didn't want to roll with the peasant-looking girl. That's how Amsterdam, vodka, and Patrón became my best friends. They never tested a bitch's loyalty and always were loyal, listening to my woes.

"Damn, I ain't know it was like that, Butter. I could tell you came with a story, but I ain't know it was that deep." He ashed the blunt, reaching for the Naked fruit smoothie he was drinking. "Isis and them better come correct or not come at all. You're working with more than a few bolts loose up there."

"I ain't worried about that McGruff the Crime Dog—looking bitch or her clique, please believe me!"

"A'ight, A'ight, save all that 'go hard, scrap a bitch up' energy for your shift. We already know Isis won't be on deck until afterward 'cause her face is fucked up but her girls will be lurking all night. I know you ain't worried but them project chicks be on some gritty shit," he warned. "But you can't be tough every day of your life, baby. You're smooth like Butter, not tough as nails. So when you need a break from being a gangster in the streets, you can come be the soft ass I know you really are." He passed the blunt, giving me a nudge. Dazz got up, straightening his clothes then holding his hand out for me to grab.

High as hell feeling more relaxed than I'd ever been, Dazz had gotten me together most definitely. I might've been floating off THC but my stomach still fluttered with butterflies. Dazz knew we had to take yet another rain check on going to eat but he seemed to be just as satisfied with us kicking it on some one-on-one shit. "Can you stop at the gas station so I can get a Red Bull and a few blunts for my charity case weed?" I joked with him but was serious about needing to make the stop.

"I got you. Since we ain't grabbing nothing to eat, I'm gonna need another smoothie and some junk food to hold me over." He rubbed his stomach.

Driving across the bridge then crossing over Jefferson, we pulled directly into the Speedway gas station, which had just been renamed after the Isle. Stan Dilbert left no major landmark in the city alone. Everything had to undergo a major renovation for his cracker-ass billionaire friends to even think about investing in Deadly Detroit. No matter how hard he tried to clear out the black folks, the diehards weren't going anywhere. The gas station was fairly empty except for early morning risers, workers, and kids running errands for their mom.

"G'on and run in, baby girl, throw fifty dollars in the tank, grab my smoothie and some healthy-looking shit, and whatever you was buying." He handed me a hundred dollar bill. I might've had stacks of cash in my purse but I was never quick to spend my own. Unlocking the doors, sliding out, he walked around to the passenger side, popping the gas door plus opening mine.

Blushing from ear to ear, it felt good having someone who was honestly all the way on my team. Running into the convenience store of the station, I hurried through the aisles grabbing more than a few snacks for him to choose from plus the stuff I wanted to nibble on. Making it to the cashier, I tossed him the one hundred spot for the gas, Dazz's stuff, and my Red Bull, pop, chewing gum, potato chips, and a few packs of White Owls. Waiting on the cashier to hand over my change, I stood back looking out of the window, scoping the scene. "Dazz, oh my God! Watch out!"

Swerving into the Belle Isle gas station on two wheels, it was my nemesis Isis driving a minivan filled with goons. "Dazz, it's Isis!" Nothing about this seemed right. Dropping everything I was holding onto the floor, I ran toward the door never once hushing my screams trying to warn him. But it was too late. The entire east side of Detroit was awakened by an explosion of AK-47 gunshots. As bullets ripped through the Yukon truck, I stood in horror crying like a newborn baby watching the only nigga who had my back get murked. Not having my purse I wasn't strapped to shoot back. *Damn!* "Dazz! Please, God, don't say he's dead!"

"There's that crossbreed bitch right there! Blast her ass!"

Hearing the call made on my life, I dove to the right into the chip rack in an attempt to dodge the bullets now spraying the gas station up.

## James

Shawntay's body was sprawled across the same living room floor I once used to bang her back out on. Scared to touch her, not wanting to contract the virus, I waited on the ambulance I'd called once peeking through the window seeing her like this. They wanted me to feel for a pulse once bursting through the window but I wasn't having that. I could tell she was still slightly breathing from placing nothing but a small fingertip on her back. Looking around the tiny house, much had changed since being here drinking on her dusty couch. Not smelling the lingering scent of marijuana anymore, from the numerous amounts of scriptures, quotes, and certificates praising her continued sobriety, I hung my head low once I saw the two bottles of fifth completely bone dry. Me and Beth were probably the responsible ones for making her relapse, possibly drinking herself dead.

Help finally arrived.

"Emergency!" The paramedics rushed into her house as I backed away from her body.

"She just told me about an hour ago she was HIV-positive. I just found her like this." I spat out a warning, looking in horror as they rolled Shawntay over onto her back prepping her for CPR.

"We've got this, sir, thank you. Are you her next of kin? Will you be trailing the ambulance or riding with her?" As they fought to keep Shawntay from dying, I was selfish trying to use that as my one time to beg God to have mercy on her soul. I didn't want her death hanging over my head any longer than it had to.

"No, I'm not her next of kin but I can try getting in touch with her daughter for you. And yes, I'll be trailing you to the hospital," I finally responded as they stabilized her breathing then strapped her down onto the stretcher.

"Okay, put your hazards on and stay close behind. We'll be going to Henry Ford Hospital. If you get too far behind, please abide by the traffic laws as we cannot be liable for any tickets or accidents." The paramedic ran down the rules as Shawntay was rolled up into the ambulance. As they closed the doors and hit the sirens, my heart dropped not knowing Shawntay's fate. Just like that, the emergency vehicle rolled up the street heading toward the hospital my firstborn was birthed at. Digging my phone from my blazer, I saw both Sally and Beth had called but I dismissed them both to dial Shannon's to deliver some bad news.

## Shannon

As I heard the minivan swerve off, I climbed off the floor dusting debris off of myself. With a face full of tears coming from my eyes, I was too afraid to face what was outside.

The cashier could barely keep a steady-paced voice trying to report the drive-by shooting. "It was a dark-colored van, maybe black, and there's a man drooped over dead still pumping gas into his car."

Running through the doors like a madwoman over shattered glass not wanting this whole ordeal to be true, I fell to my knees onto the rocked cement once my eyes locked in on Dazz's lifeless body. His eyes were bugged out wide, his spunk had been murdered, and his hard head had been splattered with his brain oozing down onto his once-fresh outfit. "Turn the motherfucking pump off you greedy-ass bastard!" Hollering to the attendant, seeing gas spilling out all over the bullet-punctured Yukon, Dazz's hand was caught on the pump of the handle, meaning the gas was spurting out onto him too. "Turn the fucking pump off you 'rab-ass monkey!" He wasn't doing shit but milking every dollar of this sale as Dazz's body hung like a rag doll. "Damn, my baby, I'm so sorry." Shaking my head, letting the tears fall uncontrollably, my heavy heart told me this wasn't a horrendous nightmare I'd soon wake up from.

Hearing tires burn rubber from a close distance, there was no time to mourn my homeboy 'cause I feared Isis was doubling back. Climbing up off my knees, I ran around to the other side of the truck, stepping up so I could snatch my purse from the passenger seat. Grabbing my loaded pistol from my bag, if it was Isis trying to bring more heat, I wasn't going down without at least busting a bullet her way. I slid my shoes off, throwing them in my purse instead. I wasn't a stranger to walking barefoot from my li'l tike days with Shawntay. "Protect me from these bitches. Dazz, you were right, I am smooth as butter. This gangsta shit ain't for me!"

Tossing my purse over my shoulder, I said a prayer to God for the only dude who had my back to rest in peace before breaking camp on two heels away from the crime scene.

Getting back to my car after running barefoot more than probably four blocks, I couldn't stop my hands from shaking uncontrollably as I tried to dig my car keys from my oversized purse. I'd almost gotten hit trying to cross at a flashing light but being moments away from solidarity within this car eased my anxiety. This shit was all my fault! You couldn't tell me anything different! Had I not made him stop on a dummy mission for my own needs, none of this never would've happened! He told me they were out for my head; why weren't we being more careful? Finally finding my keys then hitting the alarm, I jumped in, immediately scanning the perimeter to see if Isis and her crew were creeping around to finish the job. I was almost sure they knew I hadn't been hit; and from the looks of it she wasn't trying to handle our beef without bullets. *Damn, Dazz, this shit is all bad! Can you promise to watch out for ya' girl from heaven?*

The eerie feeling I had going onto the Isle in the first place had been right. Hearing sirens then seeing cops floating up Jefferson one behind the other, I started my car, getting the fuck out of dodge. Coasting up the side streets trying to stay clear of any more problems, I dialed Jay's number, needing to take him up on the offer to crash at the hotel. With Dazz a few miles back in a puddle of blood on account of Isis and her goons, no way was I about to go home. I was bad luck to everyone I met. Hopefully my bad fortune wouldn't pass off on Jay too.

"Did I catch you at a bad time?" I was trying not to breathe heavily into the phone.

"Just a little bit, but nothing I can't pause for you. What's up?"

"I'm not going into the club today; wanted to know if the offer still stood. I kinda need a get-away." Not wanting to tell him what had just gone down, for sure the white boy would be scared away.

"On one condition: you perform all of the tricks you would've done at work."

"Oh that's nothing, baby; I've got you for sure. I'm on the way." Dressed in the same clothes, I wasn't even about to take a chance stopping to even buy something new. I wasn't letting up on this gas pedal 'til I was surrounded by hotel security and Jay.

# Chapter Thirteen

## *Shawntay*

"Code blue coming through! This patient was found unresponsive on her living room floor with two fifths of alcohol near her body. A gentleman reported she's HIV-positive. We haven't been able to keep her vitals stable, Doc."

My hearing was going in and out. I was not dead but I wanted to be.

As my body fought to hold on, my broken heart was fighting to die. If my daughter wished me dead, who else did I have to live for? I could hear the doctors working over me, sticking me with needles, and taking my vitals. I didn't want them to save my life but I was too weak to fight back. Last I knew I was alone in my living room; how'd they get to me anyway? I was hoping the overdose and alcohol poisoning I kept hearing them speak of was enough to take this pitiful life I hadn't done much of shit with. I was almost sure I'd heard Jimmy talking over me but I was sure that was just a flashback of some horrid night of my life with him. For sure he hadn't left his perfect life to answer my pleas. I ain't never been that important to him.

"We're losing her! Nurse, please hurry, grab the crash cart!"

I knew no one would care about Shawntay Jenkins being dead 'cause no one cared when I was living. God knew my heart was changing but it wasn't enough to get peace from people whose lives I ruined. I didn't know if my soul would be traveling to hell, but if God didn't want me in the afterlife, I didn't think I could blame Him. *Please, God, please make me one of your angels. I'm tired of Satan having his hands on me.*

"Doctor, her heart rate keeps dropping!"

Then it was over; everything around me went quiet.

# Chapter Fourteen

## *Marie*

I'd left Beth at home a drunken mess and both the twins in their cribs screaming mad. My mother was on her way to their house to save the day 'cause I was speeding down the highway toward the hotel J.T. was staying at. If Beth thought I was going to be the type of wife who allowed her husband to cheat and fuck around with floozies, she'd pegged me all wrong. I wasn't about to keep sitting at home pouring my sorrows; naw, my dad was a go-getter and I was more like him than anyone could ever know. After letting Beth tell too much of the Schultz family secrets, I put two and two together knowing without a doubt Jay was cheating too, and had been since before the day we got married. And, I wasn't having that! I didn't need Jay, he needed me. Matter of fact, the entire Schultz family needed the Dilbert family in order to thrive. My father had the power to have them wiped out completely and if I caught Jay in the act like my gut told me I was getting ready to, he could kiss me, the kids, and his small fortune away.

"Yes, I'm Marie Dilbert. My father called you on the way over." I approached the manager with a calm but devious smile.

"Oh yes, madam, here you are. Would you like an escort?"

My father made everyone in the city dance like a puppet. I didn't know why Jay thought he was gonna be able to get away with this.

"No, thank you." Heading toward the elevator, I thought, *James Theodore Schultz IV had better be on his best behavior, for his sake.*

## James

"I'm sorry, sir; we weren't able to save your friend. The consumption of alcohol mixed with the medications caused her already-weak organs to shut down. We did everything we could do."

"I'm sure, I'm sure." I nodded, wanting to cry for Shawntay but really feeling horrible for myself. I'd dug a grave for her that might not be too far from me filling myself.

"Were you able to get in contact with her next of kin, her daughter? The hospital has a social worker who can help with bereavement issues, counseling, anything that might aid both of you in recovery." The nurse tried being more compassionate. She probably didn't remember me but she was the same lady who swabbed me and Shannon over twenty years ago.

"No, I've been calling but not getting a response. I'll take the social worker's number." I graciously accepted her offer. I didn't know the true extent or severity of Shannon and Shawntay's relationship but I was sure she was gonna break down once finding out her mother had died.

As the nurse scurried off to get me the social worker's card and a few pamphlets, I took a seat staring out into the heavens trying to piece together the start of this morning. Beth was scorching pissed, along with Sally, but what was different?

My cell rang, interrupting my train of thought. "Hey, son, it's about time you called me back. Marie called your mother and me; she's livid."

"Tell me something I don't know. She's on the other side of my hotel room and the stripper I just started fucking is locked in the bathroom."

"Aw shit, son!" Jumping up, running out of the hospital, I didn't have time to double back to get the information the nurse was yelling behind me with. My son was in trouble and needed his father to have his back.

## Shannon

This was some straight bullshit! Locked in this bathroom pacing back and forth, there was no way out of this drama white boy had me in. I would've been better off taking my chances going home. At least I knew the territory and what Isis was working with.

"Marie, take your ass home with the twins! Get from down here!" I heard Jay screaming. "I'm going to have hotel security escort you downstairs."

"You cheating son of a bitch! Open this door. I am hotel security!"

I didn't blame her and would've done the same thing if I ever got a man. I guessed my run with him had come to an end but that was the name of the game.

There were five maybe six knocks at the door.

"Butter baby, it's me. I'm sorry about all of this; here's your clothes. I can't leave her out there forever and something tells me she won't be leaving without a fight. I'll try holding her down so you can make a run for it. Can I call you when this all blows over?"

"You just better. You've been busting nuts in me all night and morning; I might just have some news to share." I kept it real then held my hand out.

Rolling his eyes but smiling, he reached into his wallet, handing out a few hundred for all this trouble. Jay wasn't a stranger to tricking; he wasn't new to the game. "I'll be in touch. Now hurry up and get dressed."

Pulling the door back closed, I regretted not having on sweats and gym shoes just in case she wanted to get gutter. I didn't know how white women fought but around my way we didn't fight fair.

"James Theodore Schultz IV, you better open this damn door right now!"

"What did she just say? Who did she just call him? That was my father's name . . ."

# Chapter Fifteen

## *James*

"I told you not to let your trifling ways rub off on that boy. Now you've ruined your family," my mother spoke into the phone. Ruthless to the day she'd take her last breath, she was never one to let me live down my mistakes.

"I don't know why I even called you in the first place. I've always been a disgrace to you, Mother." I spoke the truth. Had it not been for her controlling ways, I would've righted my wrongs a long time ago. But this family was all about cover-ups. "Just call Marie and try talking some sense into her. Beth is too drunk to do any good." As much as I wanted to handle the situation on my own, I needed at least one of them to help calm Marie. We knew what damage she could do to the Schultz name and lifestyle, so we were all supposed to act as one unit when it came down to it.

"I don't want not another thing to do with you all's mess. I'm on my last days anyway. Your father ran me into the ground. You've run Shawntay into the ground and Beth isn't far behind. But that spitfire Marie, she's gonna be the one woman to run y'all Schultz men into the ground. I hope my God lets me see the day!" This time my mother was the one who hung up in my ear.

Swerving into the parking lot of the casino, I jumped out heading toward the hotel entrance.

"Sir, where's your keycard? You can't go up to the rooms unless you are a guest of the hotel." Security stopped me in my tracks.

"There's a commotion upstairs involving my son; you have to let me through." I tried pushing past him.

"I can't, sir. But here's the manager to help you."

A scrawny white man with glasses approached us. "Is there a problem?"

"Yeah, I need to get to room 9139; my son is checked into a room there and is having a problem with his wife." Pulling out my phone, it was Shannon calling. "Hello, Shannon, please hold on; don't hang up. Sir, I need to get up to that room now!"

"I'll have to escort you to that room." The manager held down security, then led me to the elevators.

"Shannon, we seriously need to talk. I have some really bad news." Listening into the phone I heard nothing but screaming, fighting, and what sounded like gunshots.

"Shannon, are you there? Shannon?"

"A'ight, bitch, I said be quiet!"

"Gunshots have been reported in the hotel, take cover, code 911 on floor nine!" Voices loudly rang over the manager's walkie-talkie.

## Shannon

The unmistakable sounds of earsplitting gunfire were surely heard throughout the building.

"A'ight, bitch, I said be quiet!" I came out of the bathroom door, busting bullets to get their attention. I didn't care of the consequences or repercussions; I needed some immediate answers. My world was spinning, my equilibrium was off, wasn't nothing seeming right. Jay was on top of his wife holding her down and the plan was supposed to be for me to run past, down the stairwell, on with my business. But after hearing her call out my father's name, I completely snapped. I might've been a girl from the hood, a crackhead drunk's daughter who had the soul raped out of her, but a fool I ain't never been.

"Butter, what do you think you're doing?" Jay jumped up still holding Beth but behind him now. I couldn't see the image of my father I had glued to my membrane so maybe what I thought to be true actually wasn't.

"It's so over now, J.T. I swear to God when my daddy finds out about this your ass is going to be jobless and homeless!"

"I said shut up!" Shooting the gun into the ceiling again, I wanted the room to be completely silent when I asked my round of questions. "Now what did you say his name was again? And speak slowly." I aimed my gun toward Jay's wife so she'd know I was serious in wanting an answer. "His whole government name."

"James Theodore Schultz IV. That's your brother, Shannon."

"Daddy?" Looking up seeing my father standing in the doorway, my heart started beating a million pumps a second. Did he just say what I'd pieced together minutes ago? Oh my God, this couldn't be true! Staring between them both, I was trying to fight this ghastly truth. The only thing strikingly similar was that they're both white; Jay must've looked like his mother. I couldn't believe I'd been crushing with my own half brother, my own flesh and blood!

"Marie, come back! I had no idea I even had a half sister! Dad, are you fucking serious? You hid this from me? Does Mom know? I can't believe this shit; I've probably gotten my sister pregnant! I couldn't have even dreamed up nothing nastier."

James was speechless staring at us both. As we locked eyes for the first time in years, I felt myself grow even dizzier. It was like I was seeing a ghost. I was confused. I couldn't think. Falling to my knees, the ties I had with my past, present, and future collided at the same time. "I need my mommy." The room started to spin as my vision grew increasingly dark.

# Chapter Sixteen

## *Shannon*

"'If anybody asks you where I'm going to, I'm going up to yonder. I'm going up to yonder. I'm going up to yonder. I'm going to yonder to be with my Lord.'" The soloist was singing her heart out and there wasn't a dry eye in the church.

My heart skipped beats all morning as regret furled in the pit of my stomach. I couldn't believe my mother was dead. I clutched the obituary in my hand along with a box of Kleenex staring at Shawntay in disbelief. Resting peacefully in a shiny cream and gold casket with a yellow blouse, cream dress suit, and the Bible she grew to love in her hands, you couldn't tell Shawntay lived the hardcore life that she did. Through the years, I'd stored up a tremendous amount of hate for my mom. Even when she got right, I still turned her away. I'd never have another tomorrow, another chance, or another mother. My cries, sobs, screams, and breakdowns couldn't be contained.

"Momma, come back. I'm sorry, please we can talk. Wake up," I screamed, then sprung from my seat. The small crowd that was gathered to pay their respects for Shawntay gasped as I threw myself damn near into the casket with her. "Take me with you, Ma. Don't leave me here. I ain't got nobody." I was sure my screams could be heard miles away.

The pastor tried offering me prayer but I was too much of a lost soul. I pushed him off and continued to kiss and hug on the woman who birthed me. Damn, I fucked up. I needed her back. I needed to hit the reset button on life.

The entire congregation joined the soloist in singing "Goin' Up Yonder" and it stirred my emotions more. I was sure they knew about my mother's darkest sins, which meant they knew about mine. God's folks were always trying to save sinners by turning them into saints. And this was no different. They wanted me to feel the pain so maybe I could change. Shawntay's spirit was definitely in the room. I wanted to do something different. As sad as it was to say, I didn't want to end up like Shawntay.

"Come on, Shannon, it's going to be okay. Let your mother rest." James wrapped his arm around my waist and pulled me away. "You've got me now."

I got weak and collapsed into my father's arms. I didn't know if his words were true and if they were how he intended on sticking to them. But I was crossing my fingers like a kid praying he wasn't just pacifying me. I hadn't seen him since the embarrassing ordeal at the hotel when I found out my mom was dead and my lover was my brother. But none of that mattered at the moment because James was the only person giving me life. I wanted his lifeline to be real. I buried myself into him as they closed her casket and spoke the final words. My breathing was becoming sporadic as they prepared Shawntay for her final ride. I couldn't stand to watch her carried out so James rushed me outside.

"Listen, Shannon, there's so much to talk about and over twenty years of making up to do. But the first thing I want to help you with is mourning. I meant what I said back there; I'm here for you."

"I'd like to believe that. But with the crazy shit me and J.T. got ourselves into, I think that would be a little weird." I wiped at my tears then sifted through my purse for the rolled joint I had to calm my nerves. This was the second person I'd buried this week.

"That you guys have. But as brother and sister, the relationship must be mended. Beth and I are divorcing, Junior's begging his wife to come home, and you and I will be going to counseling.

This secret has torn our family apart, not you. If I would've been man enough from day one, neither of my children would be in this awful position. I'm sorry, Shannon. I truly am. Let's make the change together. You don't want to run out of time trying to right your wrongs."

Looking up as the church doors opened, I saw the pallbearers starting to proceed. "Naw, I guess not." I looked up into the heavens, smiling. "I guess you got what you wanted after all, Momma: peace, forgiveness, and for me to have my daddy back."

"That she did," James spoke up then ushered me into the car. "Shawntay always had a way of getting what she wanted."

**THE END**

# Outcast

by

*La'Tonya West*

# Chapter One

King was startled by the loud banging on the front door. He'd fallen asleep on the sofa watching TV after getting home from school. He looked around nervously, still half asleep, trying to figure out what was going on. He was trying to figure out if the loud banging had been part of his dream or if it was real. The loud banging started again confirming that it was indeed real. He could also hear a female voice that sounded like his friend Breezy, calling his name. He dropped the remote and jumped up from the sofa stumbling over his Timbs that were lying on the floor next to the sofa. He reached the door and snatched it open.

Breezy fell into his arms crying. "I can't take it anymore, King! I wish that I could just die! Why does she have to treat me this way?" She cried holding on to him with her face buried in his chest. Her frail body trembled in his arms as he held on to her. "Why does she hate me so much? How can a mother treat her own child this way?"

King let out a sigh as he tightened his arms around her. He felt bad for the things that she had to endure at home. He knew that her mama, Teresa, had been beating on her and talking shit to her like always. He'd never seen anyone treat their own flesh and blood the way that she did. He couldn't for the life of him understand it.

He and Breezy had been friends since they were in elementary school. They were in high school now and he'd always known her to be a sweet girl, the type who would give her last and do anything to help anyone in any way that she could. She'd always been a straight A student, well-mannered, and really quiet. She didn't bother anyone, just stayed to herself. When everybody else was out chillin' and running wild it was nothing to find her somewhere with her face stuck in a book or writing. That was what made it so hard to understand why Teresa was so damn hateful toward her and for as long as he could remember she'd always been that way.

The thing about the situation that bothered him most was how many times he'd begged Breezy to report her mother to child protective services. He'd lost count of the number of times that he'd begged her over the years. Her response was always the same each time: "I can't do my mama like that." And his reply was always the same to her response: "What about how yo' mama is doing you?" Each time she'd drop her head and shrug her shoulders.

King's biggest fear was hearing that one of Teresa's beatings had gone too far and she'd ended up killing Breezy. For years he'd lived with the fear of waking up one morning and hearing that his best friend had been killed at the hands of her crazy-ass mother. He'd tried his hardest to get Breezy to see how important it was that she do something to get herself out of the situation that she was in but none of his efforts seemed to register with her. He'd even thought about saying something to someone himself but she'd told him a long time ago that if he ever did she would never forgive him for it; because, when she'd first come to him about the situation, she'd made him promise to never say anything and he'd given her his word that he wouldn't. However, after seeing the numerous bruises and witnessing firsthand the emotional pain, it was hard to stand back and not do anything. To him that made him just as bad as her mama.

"Stop crying, Breezy," King said as he caressed her back, rocking her back and forth slowly in his arms. Hearing her sob and knowing that she was in pain caused him to hurt also. "And stop talking all of that nonsense about wanting to die. How do you think that would make me feel if something were to happen to you?" He hated it when she talked that way. After she didn't respond, he lifted her chin with his fingers so that she was looking up at him. "How do you think that would make me feel?" he repeated, looking down into her chocolate brown eyes. Her nose was bloodied and the right side of her face red and swollen.

"I'm tired. I'm just tired," she whispered with tears streaming down her cheeks. "You don't understand what it's like to have the woman who brought you into this world hate you and constantly tell you how much she regrets having you." She got choked up and couldn't continue.

"Shhhh. I know it's tough," he replied still rocking her back and forth in his arms.

She rested her head on his chest. This was the only place that she ever felt 100 percent safe, like nothing in the world could harm her. King was her safe haven away from her harsh reality. "She's just so hateful toward me. It's like I can't do anything right."

Before King could respond, Cheeks, the girl who lived in the apartment next door, came outside. "Heeeeey, Kiiiiinnngg." She sang the words, smiling and looking him up and down. She looked at Breezy and frowned her face up. "Uggggh I don't know why you waste yo' time with that ugly thang right there. Why don't you let me upgrade you, boo?" She switched her hot self in front of King so that he could get a real good look at the little yellow booty shorts that she was wearing.

King was one of the most popular guys in the neighborhood and there weren't too many girls who weren't trying to get with him. He was six feet one inch, with a brown paper bag complexion, jet-black wavy hair that he kept cut close, a thin mustache, thin lips, and a muscular build. The fact that he was one of the best basketball players on the school's team and was guaranteed a basketball scholarship was a plus.

"Last time I checked a ho wasn't an upgrade!" he barked giving her a nasty glare. "Now get the fuck out my face!" He was so sick of motherfuckers messing with Breezy. She didn't deserve that shit. Just because she was quiet and didn't bother anyone it made everyone feel like they could just treat her any kind of way and run all over her. They may have done it behind his back but there was no way in hell that it was going down in his presence.

"Well, fuck you too!" Cheeks snapped looking around to see if anyone had overheard the exchange of words between the two of them. A few guys standing a few feet away down the sidewalk let it be known they'd overheard it by laughing loudly and pointing at her.

"Damn, shawty, he just straight played you!" one of them called out as he held his stomach laughing.

Cheeks flipped him off. "Shut the fuck up. That shit wasn't even that damn funny." She was embarrassed by the way King had just shut her down. Feeling the need to try to save face, she looked back at King, placing her hand on her hip. "I heard your dick was little anyways."

"It's good that you heard because yo' ho ass will never get a chance in this lifetime to find out for yourself whether it's true," he shot back putting the finishing touches on her already-bruised ego.

The guys on the sidewalk laughed even harder. Now, completely humiliated, Cheeks smacked her lips. "Whatever." That was the only thing she could think of to say. Using her better judgment she decided to leave the situation alone. She walked off in the direction of her homegirl Sherita's house.

King turned his attention back to Breezy. "Come on in and let me help you get cleaned up." He led the way inside and she followed.

Inside, Breezy sat on the side of the tub while King wet a bath cloth and proceeded to clean her face up. "Ahhh," Breezy groaned in pain as the warm rag touched the swollen side of her face. Her hand went up, grabbing King's. "That hurts."

"I'm sorry," he apologized sincerely. "I'm not trying to hurt you. I'm doing it as gently as I can."

"I know." She let go of his hand so that he could continue.

A few minutes later, they heard the front door slam and shortly after Ms. Annette, King's mama, announced that she was home.

"We in here, Ma," King yelled.

"We who, boy? Who you got up in my house?" she asked making her way to the bathroom where the two of them were.

"Awww, man, I hate for your ma to see my face like this," Breezy mumbled just as Annette walked into the bathroom.

"Hey, Breezy . . ." Her words trailed off as her eyes landed on Breezy's face. "Child, what happened to your face?" Annette had a voice just like Loretta Devine but she was a little, petite brown-skinned woman with a short Jheri curl. She'd missed the memo that Jheri curls were no longer in style.

Breezy dropped her head embarrassed by her face. She fidgeted with her fingers as she told Annette what had happened. "My ma came in a little while ago drunk and started going off on me because I hadn't cooked." She fought back tears. "She'd been gone since last Thursday. How was I supposed to know that she was going to come home today?"

"You mean to tell me that Teresa be leaving you in that raggedy house 'round there by yourself for days?" Annette asked, feeling sorry for Breezy and personally wanting to go upside her mama's head.

"Yes, ma'am," Breezy responded, her eyes shifting to the floor. The way that her mama treated her bothered her more than anyone could've imagined. She was ashamed of her situation.

Annette shook her head. "That's a damn shame for her to treat you like she do. I would turn her in myself—"

Breezy jumped to her feet. "No, please don't. I don't want her to get in any trouble. Please, Ms. Annette, *please*." She was nearly jumping up and down begging.

"How do you expect for her to ever stop abusing you if you won't open your mouth and tell someone or allow anyone else to do it for you? As a grown woman knowing what is going on, I am supposed to do something about it. I am just as bad as your mama or worse if I keep sitting here allowing this to happen. For years, you walked around here and lied to me when I would ask you about the bruises and so I couldn't do nothing about it. I always suspected that she was beating on you; either her, or all them different mens she has running in and out of that house. But, I couldn't prove it. I know now, though, and you best believe I am not going to sit on my ass and allow this mess to go on any longer!"

Breezy started begging and pleading with Annette with everything in her. The thought of her mama getting arrested and going to jail frightened and hurt her all at the same time. Teresa may have treated her like shit but she was still her mama and she loved her. She just kept praying that one day she would love her too. A part of her believed that the reason her mama resented her so much was because her daddy had walked out on her, leaving her with all the responsibility of caring for her. She told herself that since she was there her mama took out on her what was really meant for her dad.

"Please, Ms. Annette, please," Breezy continued to beg, tears streaming down her face. All sorts of thoughts were running through her mind. She wasn't just afraid of her turning her mama in but also afraid of what was going to happen to her once her mama found out that she'd told someone about what she'd been doing to her. Her words were always, "Whatever happens in my damn house stays in my damn house. If I ever find out that you have been running your damn mouth, bitch, I will kill your ass."

Sadly, Breezy believed that she probably would. After fifteen years of abuse she had no other choice but to believe it. The things that she'd seen and been through in her short life, no human being should have to go through. Sometimes she felt as though God didn't love her because if He did He wouldn't allow her to go through those things.

Annette grabbed her firmly by her shoulders and shook her. Her eyes too were filled with tears. "Breezy, what the hell is wrong with you? Do you like being beat and dogged all the time? Don't you think you deserve to be treated better?"

"Yes, ma'am, but—"

"But, what? But, damn it, what? Why are you protecting her when it is obvious she don't give a damn about you?"

Even though she already knew that her mama didn't care about her, hearing it out loud was like a stab through the heart. Those words cut her deep and the expression on her face displayed her.

Annette's expression softened as she realized the impact her words must've had on Breezy. She turned her arms loose and then wrapped hers around her and hugged her tightly. "Baby, I didn't mean for that to come out the way that it did. I know that must've sounded really heartless. I'm sorry. I'm just tired of seeing you be treated this way. You need help, Breezy, but no one can help you unless you allow them to. I know that you love your mom but you deserve to be loved too."

"I know," was Breezy's reply.

They stood in the middle of the floor embracing for a while. Annette took that time to speak a few words of encouragement to Breezy, feeling really horrible inside for the comment that she'd made. Before releasing her, she made it clear that this would be the last time she saw a bruise on her and not report it. Breezy nodded her head letting her know that she understood.

Breezy looked around for King but didn't see him. She and Annette had been so wrapped up in their conversation that neither of them had even noticed he was no longer in the room. She went into the living room and saw him stretched out on the sofa watching TV. "I have to get back home. Will you walk with me halfway?" she asked standing next to the sofa.

"Yeah, you know that I ain't gon' let you walk home by yourself, girl." He smiled up at her before sitting up. He reached down and began putting on his shoes. "You sure that you don't want to stay here for a little while and chill? You could eat here and then go home. I'm sure my mama don't mind."

"Nah." She shook her head. "I need to be getting home."

King stood to his feet. "Ma, I'm going to walk Breezy halfway home," he yelled.

"Okay, but don't be gone long. I'm about to start dinner," she yelled back from down the hall.

"I won't." He looked at Breezy. "You ready?"

"Yeah." She walked out the door with him right behind her. She really didn't want to go home but she knew that she had to because she didn't want Teresa to come looking for her or have another reason to beat her ass when she got home.

For the first few minutes of their walk to Breezy's house, both of them were silent. Breezy was the first to speak sharing her thoughts. "I can't wait until I get grown. I am going to leave Boykins and never come back."

King reached over and ruffled her hair playfully. "As long as you let me know where you are then it's cool with me. You need to go somewhere and get away from your crazy-ass mama. I swear, I be wanting to run up on her and two piece her ass! Then she can see how it feels to have somebody beat on her for a change."

Breezy giggled and blushed because she knew that if nobody else in the world loved her, King did. He had never picked on or mistreated her. Whenever any of the other kids at school teased her he would always defend her. She looked at him and thought, *Yeah, God did love me because He placed you in my life.* "Boy, you is crazy. Of course I am going to tell you. You will be the only person who knows or even cares where I am. My mama won't care. She'll probably throw a party when I leave."

"Well me and you will throw an even bigger one in celebration of you being rid of her ass." They both laughed. "Don't sweat it though because in the end before it's all said and done she will need you. The same person she mistreated all of these years she will have to come to and ask for help. Not demand it but humble herself and ask you. That's when you tell her to kiss your ass!"

Breezy looked at him like he was crazy. She figured he must've been talking to somebody else because she was terrified of Teresa and there was no way in hell she would be crazy enough to stand in her face and tell her some shit like that. "Yeah, okay. Anyways have you done any studying for that history test that we are having tomorrow?"

"Nah, I'm just gon' copy off your paper like I always do." He laughed.

"You are just trifling," she joked.

"Whatever; call it what you want, just make sure we get an A." They reached Breezy's street and stopped at the stop sign like always. King leaned against the sign with his hands in the pockets of the hoodie that he was wearing. "Well I guess I'll get my butt on home but first I wanted to ask you what you had planned for your birthday."

Her birthday was that Saturday coming up and she honestly hadn't thought much about it. "Nothing, as usual," she replied truthfully.

"Well, if you can get away from your ma, I will borrow my mama's car and take you bowling or something. It is your sixteenth birthday so you have to celebrate."

"I don't have nothing to wear bowling." She looked down at the pair of old, dirty Nikes that she wore on her feet. They were done but she was still trying to hold on to them because they were all that she had, and her hair needed a perm in the worst way. Thinking about it made her feel embarrassed and she self-consciously reached up and ran her hand over her hair.

"You act like you trying to impress somebody. Just think about it, okay?" He gave her a hug like always. "All right, big head, see you tomorrow."

"Okay, I will. See you tomorrow," she told him, hating to leave him.

He walked off in the direction of his house and she continued down the street to her house.

# Chapter Two

When Breezy reached her house it was dark. There were no lights on at all so she assumed that her ma was inside passed out, or else gone. She opened the door and crept inside. Upon walking through the door, she tried to flip on the light switch in the living room but nothing happened. She tried flipping the switch off and then back on again but again nothing happened. She fumbled her way to the other side of the room to the lamp and tried to turn that on but that wouldn't come on either.

"They out. They cut the motherfuckers off about two hours ago." Terry's voice came out of nowhere, nearly scaring her to death and causing her to jump.

She looked around the dark room. There was a little bit of light coming through the window from the streetlight but not much. As her eyes adjusted to the dark some she was able to see his silhouette over on the long sofa.

"Where is my mama?"

"Down the hall in the bed drunk and asleep." He replied his words coming out slurred.

She could smell the stench of alcohol where she stood.

"Why don't you come over here and sit down and talk to me for a little while?" he suggested.

"I need to go on to bed so that I can get up a little earlier than normal and get myself right for school since the lights are off," she replied and started walking in the direction of the hallway. She walked slowly with her hands out in front of her.

Out of thin air she felt Terry's hand cover her mouth and with his other hand he grabbed her and pulled her back toward the sofa. She was trying to scream but his hand was clasped tightly over her mouth and all that was coming out was muffled sounds.

"Shut the fuck up you little nasty bitch before I snap your damn neck. If you wake up Resa, I'm going to tell her how your little ass be trying to come on to me when she ain't around." This wasn't the first time that one of her mama's men had raped her. She'd even been molested by a chick Teresa was seeing in the past. She already knew the routine. The last time that she tried telling her about one of her boyfriends touching her, Teresa beat her and told her that he wouldn't have touched her had she not been so fast and hot in her ass. She swore that Breezy wanted it. So Breezy knew without a doubt she would believe him over her.

*Hell she left me in this nasty-ass house with no food all weekend while she ran the streets with him. Obviously what happens to me is her last concern.*

"I'm going to take my hand off of your mouth but if you scream or try anything stupid I am going to fuck you up," he warned, his hot breath on the back of her neck. He removed his hand from over her mouth. "Now unbutton them pants and pull 'em halfway down. Then bend over the chair," he instructed from behind her.

She didn't budge. She stood there, her mind racing, trying to decide what she should do. She thought about trying to run but then thought about what might happen if she didn't make it out the door. Even if she did make it out the door, where would she go? She knew that she could go to King's house but she couldn't stay there forever.

Without warning she received a hard blow to the back of the head. Falling forward on the sofa, she reached back rubbing the spot where she'd been hit.

"I asked you to unbutton them pants! What in the fuck are you just standing there for? I don't have all gotdamn night! Now get the fuck up and do what I asked."

She did as he said. After pulling her pants along with her panties down to her knees, she leaned over the arm of the sofa. From behind her, she could hear him fumbling with his clothes. Then he grabbed her and pushed her over some more before she felt his penis trying to find her opening. When he found it, he shoved himself inside of her roughly and without mercy. She let out a loud yelp.

He hit her in the back of the head again. "Didn't I tell you to shut the fuck up?" he asked as he pumped in and out of her. She squeezed her eyes together and bit down on her lip as she prayed silently for him to hurry up so that the pain would go away. Thank God for small favors because it didn't last that long. After about four minutes he let out an animalistic growl and emptied himself inside of her. His flaccid penis slid out of her and he stood up stuffing it back inside of his pants. "Fix your clothes and get the fuck out of here."

She fixed her clothes and then felt her way down the hall to her room. She couldn't see anything so there was no way that she could go into the bathroom and clean herself up. Inside her room, she lay down on the bed and cried herself to sleep.

When she woke up the next morning the sun was barely up but it was light enough so that she could see. She got up and found some clothes to put on. She hardly had anything to choose from. Her private area was a little sore as she walked down the hall but the pain was bearable. It was the emotional pain that was killing her. She felt so nasty. She went into the bathroom and took off her clothes. When she took off her underwear, Terry's semen was dried on the insides of her thighs and underwear. What was even more messed up was the fact that there was no hot water being that the lights were off. After washing up in cold water she still felt dirty. She put on her clothes and then brushed her nappy hair back in the classic ponytail that she wore every day and put some Vaseline on her lips. She looked in the mirror and was ashamed of her reflection.

Grabbing her book bag she walked down to the bus stop. She was mad early but it didn't matter because she needed some time alone. She sat down on the sidewalk placing her stuff next to her. She took out her notebook and began to write a poem:

## Untitled

*As I lay here in the dark my face drenched in tears*

*I've been living in this world of intolerable pain for years.*

*A burden to everyone I feel so alone.*

*I pray for the day when my Father finally calls me home.*

*I'm ready to give up no need to go on.*

*This is a battle that can't be won.*

*You've stripped away all that I had.*

*Beaten me until my blood flowed like an endless river of red.*

*Raped me and taken away my dignity.*
*Scarring me both emotionally and psy-chologically.*
*Leaving me to drown in this misery.*
*For you it was over when you were done.*
*But for me the pain is never gone.*
*Neither is the sadness and fear.*
*Which is why I lie here in the dark with my face drenched in these tears.*

Breezy closed her notebook, looking up and down the street. She saw a few people headed in the direction of the bus stop, one of them being King with two of the guys he hung out with, Jalen and Sean. Sean was cool but Jalen always looked at her like she had a disease or something; but he knew better than to say something slick because King would be in his shit with the quickness.

When they reached her, they all spoke and so did she.

"Did you study for our test last night?" King asked as he took a bite of a bacon and egg sandwich that he had wrapped in a paper towel.

"Nah, I didn't get any studying done last night. I went to bed as soon as I got home but I pretty much already know everything that's going to be on the test."

"Good." He smiled showing off a mouthful of food.

Breezy frowned up her face. She hated when he talked with his mouth full.

"We gon' get an A today, buddy."

She just shook her head.

"King, Davita was asking about you yesterday," Jalen announced grinning and cutting his eyes at Breezy. He was more than sure that she had a thing for King so he assumed that his announcement would hurt her feelings because she was nowhere near on Davita's level. She couldn't dress, her hair was always nappy, and sometimes she even smelled. He couldn't understand why King hung around her dirty-looking ass but he wouldn't dare voice his opinion of her because he knew King would flip the script! "I think she want to holla."

"Who, Davita Newsome with the big ass?" King asked looking more than interested.

"Yeah, man, she bad as hell. If I was you I would be all over dat. All the niggas be sweating that ass but she want to holla at yo' ass. You ain't got no job and no car! I can't figure that shit out!" Jalen tried to clown.

"Shit, me either," Sean chimed in, laughing.

"Fuck both of y'all! I'm a fly-ass nigga; that's why she trying to give a nigga some play!"

*You ain't never lied,* Breezy thought, looking at her best friend as he laughed along with Sean and Jalen. He had the prettiest smile. She looked down at herself and cringed at how unattractive she appeared. She was skinny with no shape, small boobs, caramel-colored skin, and her chin-length hair had broken off all over. She knew that a guy like King wasn't trying to be seen with a chick like her on his arm. In her opinion all that she had going for herself was book sense.

"Whatever, nigga!" Jalen laughed. Again he cut his eye at Breezy picking up on how uncomfortable she looked. "You ain't all of that. I think she's just trying to give you some pity pussy."

"Y'all are just some haters." King stuck up his middle finger, flipping both Sean and Jalen off.

Breezy looked up the street and saw the bus approaching and walked a little closer to the edge of the sidewalk because she was tired of listening to the fellas' conversation. When the bus stopped, she stepped on and took the third seat from the front. She always stayed close to the front but this morning she had a lot on her mind with the incident that had taken place the night before between her and Terry. Most of the time she could pretty much block out all of the horrible things that happened to her; but not knowing if this would be something that he tried again had her worried, because she wasn't sure of what she should do. The worst part was she couldn't talk to King about this because she knew that he would confront Terry. She didn't need any extra problems and didn't want to cause him any either. She slid down in her seat and looked out the window as the bus pulled off.

"Kita, did you comb your hair this morning?" Breezy heard Angie Baker ask her cousin.

Kita burst into laughter. "Nah, girl, you know I don't be combing it. I just pull it back in that same ol' dusty ponytail every day. Most of the time I don't even wash my ass." She continued to laugh. Breezy knew they were talking about her but decided to do as she always did: ignore them.

"Yeah, I can smell the scent of fish coming through the seat." Angie continued to play along.

"Probably because I've been wearing these same drawers since last week," Kita replied and both girls giggled. The two of them continued to go back, unaware of the fact that Breezy was growing closer and closer to her breaking point.

Without warning Breezy jumped up on her knees in the seat, turning around she grabbed Kita by the front of her hair and started swinging. All of the pent-up anger and frustration that she'd been keeping bottled up inside she was now releasing on her.

Angie grabbed Breezy's hair trying to get her off of Kita but it wasn't working. She pulled harder on Breezy's hair. "Let go of her, you nasty bitch! Take your hands off of my cousin," Angie yelled but Breezy didn't let go nor did she stop swinging. Seeing that pulling her hair wasn't working, Angie started punching Breezy in her head and face. The blows were coming hard and fast, causing Breezy to finally let go and try to cover her face. No sooner than she let go of Kita's hair, both girls jumped on her.

King heard commotion coming from the front of the bus and then everyone started to yell, "Fight! Fight!" Everyone who was in the back including him started trying to get to the front. He could make out that one of the girls was Kita and then he saw Angie and realized that they were both fighting the same person, but couldn't see who because, whoever it was, they had her down in the seat.

The bus driver stopped the bus and got out of her seat. "That's enough! Break it up!" she yelled as she tried to make her way down the aisle but the students were blocking her path trying to see the fight. There was nothing like a good fight first thing in the morning and nobody was trying to have her ruin the excitement by breaking it up.

"Yo, who they fighting?" King asked Dre', a boy who lived down the street from him.

"I think its Breezy," he responded shrugging his shoulders and looking unsure. "I mean, I can't say it's her but it sure looked like her. Ain't she wearing a blue shirt?"

King didn't answer; he just started pushing motherfuckers out of the way trying to get to Breezy. Angie's cousin Marko stood in the middle of the aisle blocking the way so that he couldn't get through.

"Fall back li'l nigga; this ain't none of yo' business," Marko barked, sizing King up like he wanted to do something.

King had never been a talker so he simply stole him right in the jaw and the two of them began fighting. The next thing they all heard were sirens and police were coming onto the bus. The bus driver had called the police.

The police broke up the fights, cuffed everyone, and put them in separate police cars. King wasn't worried about himself at all; his only concern was Breezy and whether she was okay. When they got down to the juvenile center they called everyone's parents.

Within twenty minutes after getting the call, Annette showed up mad and raising hell. "Get them damn cuffs off of my son! Y'all act like he done killed somebody or something! He was in a little scuffle. That's what kids do! Why don't y'all get off of your lazy asses and go catch some real criminals? You know like some of them boys who's out there robbing people, raping people, and shooting people? Y'all gone bring some little schoolboys down here just because of a scuffle they had on the school bus!"

"Ma'am, we understand that but we had to put the cuffs on him. I am going to have to ask you to calm down," a young black officer told her.

"Don't tell me what I am going to have to do when I come down here and you have my son handcuffed like he's some damn criminal!" Annette continued with her hand on her hip. She was mad as hell seeing her son like that. Not only was she mad at the officers for cuffing him but also mad at him for being in that position. All the way down to the juvenile center she'd been thinking that he'd better have a damn good reason for why he was fighting in the first place. She didn't play when it came to him going to school and staying out of trouble. She was determined to see to it that he finished school, left Boykins, and became a successful man.

The officer walked over to where King sat on the bench, next to the other young men cuffed, and undid his cuffs. "We are going to allow you to go with just a warning this time but the next time you are involved in a fight or anything there will be consequences," the officer explained to King. "Do you understand?"

"Yes, sir," King replied nodding his head.

"Ma'am, I need you to sign a few papers and then you can take him home."

Annette looked at King and rolled her eyes. "What about Brionna?" she asked, calling Breezy by her government name. "Is there any way that I can take her home too? I mean, her mother has no transportation so it is going to be hard for her to get a way to come down here and pick her up."

"I understand that, ma'am, I really do but her legal guardian has to pick her up," he explained.

"I understand," Annette replied, hating to leave Breezy there but there was nothing she could do about it. She filled out the necessary paperwork required for King to be released and then the two of them left.

After leaving the detention center the two of them went up to the school so that King could be seen by the principal. The principal wanted to know what had happened on the bus so King told him.

"You do understand that I am going to have to suspend your son, don't you, Ms. Collins?" Principal Fenner asked peeking over the rim of his glasses.

"Yes, sir, I understand." Annette responded calmly but King knew on the inside she was pissed. He knew that she didn't play when it came to school and he also knew that she was going to let his ass have it when they got home.

"Okay then, King, I am giving you five days at home. I will not allow there to be any fighting on the buses or in this school. Do you understand me, son?"

"Yes, sir," King answered. He hated being suspended but he felt justified in his actions. It wasn't like he'd just been fighting for no reason. He'd been fighting for his friend. There was no way he could've sat back and allowed two girls to jump Breezy and not at least try to break it up, which was what he'd planned on doing before Marko got in his way.

After they were done in the principal's office, Annette got his schoolwork for the next five days from his teachers and they headed home.

They were sitting at the stoplight waiting for the light to change. Annette looked over at King, who was staring out the window looking as if he was in a trace. Without warning she drew back and back-handed him with every ounce of strength that she could muster. The sound of her hand connecting with his face echoed throughout the car.

"Oooooouuuch! What did you do that for?" King yelled holding his face and eyeing Annette like she'd lost her mind.

She slapped him again. The light changed to green before she could hit him again but that didn't stop her from giving him a piece of her mind. As they drove home she went in on him. "This don't make no damn sense! I gotta get off from work because your ass is on the bus fighting over Breezy! I am sick of this shit, King! Do you hear me? I'm sick!"

"But, ma—"

"But, ma, my ass! Shut up until I am done talking!" she demanded without taking her eyes off the road. "You can't save Breezy from everything.

You cannot fight all of her battles! Breezy has to start fighting for Breezy! I understand that they were jumping her but what were you going to do, fight some girls? Become a woman beater?"

"Nah, I was going to break it up. I wasn't going to fight them. I wasn't going to fight anybody until dude popped off at me!" he told her.

Annette let out a frustrated breath and shook her head. "Listen, I understand what you were trying to do but as your mother I have to do what is best for you and give you the best advice that I can. Right now my advice to you is step back some and allow Breezy to fight some of her own battles. I hate to see the way that she is being treated and I wish that there was something that I could do to help, but as you saw she doesn't want anyone to get involved. She keeps on protecting her mama and making excuses for the things that are being done to her in that house."

"Ma, I understand what you are saying but that has nothing to do with what happened on the bus. I am not completely sure why Breezy and those girls were fighting but I am going find out. Breezy couldn't have started it because she doesn't say a word on the bus and I am sure that she ain't hit nobody. I know they had to have hit her first. Those girls are always picking on somebody and bullying people."

"Look all I know is you better not get suspended no damn more," Annette told him as they pulled up in front of their apartment building. She parked, turned off the ignition, and the two of them got out of the car and went inside.

"Get started on that schoolwork and then I want you to clean your room, the bathroom, and the living room," Annette instructed. "I am going to go over to Teresa's house. Hopefully she's there and I can let her know what is going on with Breezy.

*Damn, all this because I was trying to do the right thing,* King thought as he walked to his room and put his book bag down. *Fuck it. As long as Breezy is good it was all worth it.* She'd always been a good friend to him and he swore to always be a good friend to her for as long as they both lived.

He heard the front door slam, telling him that Annette had left to go to Breezy's house. He got started on his chores and cleaned for most of the afternoon. When he was done he took a shower and lay down. A few hours later, he was awakened by the sound of his cell phone ringing. He looked around the room, realizing that it was now dark. He could smell the aroma of food, which told him that Annette was cooking dinner. He reached over and picked up his cell, which was lying next to him on the bed, and looked at the screen. The number flashing on the screen wasn't a familiar one. He pressed the send button to answer the call. "Yo, who is this?"

"Is that how you answer your phone?" a sexy voice asked on the other end.

"Yeah, I guess," he replied, confused because he couldn't place her voice. "Who is this?" he repeated.

"It's Davita," the female voice informed him, giggling. "I hope that you don't mind, Sean gave me your number."

"Nah, it's cool." He sat up some in bed, propping a few pillows behind him and getting little bit more comfortable. "So what's good with you, Ms. Davita?"

"Ain't nothing. I was trying to find out what is good with you," she replied trying to sound extra sexy and smiling like the Cheshire cat on the other end. She'd been trying to get King's attention for a minute and to finally be on the phone with him was a big deal. "I was hoping that I could get to know you better."

Before King could reply to her last statement, there was a soft knock at the door. "Hold on, Davita."

"Okay."

"Come in!" he yelled to whoever was at the door.

Breezy walked in and closed the door behind her. She flipped on the light switch because it was dark in the room and she couldn't see anything.

King was sitting propped up in bed, shirtless with his cell pressed against his ear. "Hey," she spoke.

"What's up?" he spoke, noticing that she had a few scratches on her face and her lip was swollen, but other than that she was straight. "Have a seat. I'm on the phone but I won't be long."

"Okay, take your time," she told him assuming that he was on the phone with Jalen or Sean or both. She sat on the edge of the bed, grabbed the remote, and turned on the TV and began watching the show that was on.

"Hello," he spoke into the phone.

"Yeah, I'm still here," Davita confirmed, wondering who the female was in the background.

"Good. So I heard you been asking about me."

"Yeah, I have."

"Did you find out everything that you were trying to or is there something else you want to know?"

"Well, I still don't know if you have a girl."

"Oh so, what you trying to be my girl or something?"

"Maybe."

Overhearing King's conversation was starting to make Breezy feel some kind of way. "Ummm, maybe I should go. I'll talk to you tomorrow." She stood up to leave.

"Nah, I want to talk to you before you go, hold up," King told her. "Hey, Vita, I'm going to holla at Breezy real quick and I'll hit you back before I go to bed."

"All right," she replied rolling her eyes up in her head. She knew Breezy really well; as a matter of fact the two of them had a class together. She knew that Breezy was King's best friend and that he would act a fool over her at the drop of a hat so she knew not to say anything out of the way about her, at least not until she got her hooks in him the way that she wanted.

King hung up and turned his attention to Breezy. "Dang why you rushing off?"

"I wasn't but I didn't want to sit around while you and Davita play kissy face on the phone," she said frowning up her face.

"Girl, won't nobody playing no kissy face." King laughed. "Now sit yo' little boney self down and tell me what happened this morning on the bus. Why was Angie and Kita fighting you?"

Breezy sat back down on the bed. "Because I slapped Angie." She admitted it like it was nothing.

"You what? Are you serious?" King couldn't believe his ears; she had to be joking.

"I just got fed up, King." She shrugged looking over at him and then redirected her eyes, trying not to stare at his chest. "They were sitting behind me talking crap about me and I just snapped. I'm tired of people messing with me all the time. I don't bother anybody but still people are always messing with me," she explained.

King smiled; he was proud of her. "Well it's about damn time, but next time how about you start out trying to fight one girl, not two."

She burst into laughter. He loved seeing her smile because she had a really pretty smile but it was something that he didn't get to see a lot of. He sat there looking at her; she was a really sweet girl and she wasn't ugly at all. All she needed was a nice hairdo and some cute clothes. She had pretty brown skin, almond-shaped brown eyes, the cutest dimples, and she was about five feet four inches and probably 110 pounds.

"Why are you staring at me like that?" Breezy asked after she noticed that she was the only one laughing and he was just staring at her. She felt a little uncomfortable.

He hadn't realized it but he was indeed staring at her. "My bad, I was just thinking about something. Anyways how did your ma act when you got home last night? Did she try to start with you again?"

The incident with Terry popped in her head. "Nah, she was 'sleep. Can we not talk about her please?"

"Sure. What do you want to talk about?" He picked up on how uneasy she'd become when he mentioned her ma. He figured that Teresa had probably hit on her some more and she didn't want to tell him because she knew that he would be upset. He decided to let it go.

"Let's just watch TV."

"Okay."

She picked up the remote and turned to an old Jennifer Lopez movie, *The Wedding Planner*. King got up and turned off the light. The two of them lay across the bed and started watching the movie. Twenty minutes into it, he heard soft snoring. He looked next to him and Breezy was knocked out. He wrapped her up, grabbed his pillow, and then went into the living room and called Davita back.

# Chapter Three

Breezy woke up the next morning to the smell of bacon and eggs and the sound of laughter. For a minute, she just laid there and listened to King, his mom, and her boyfriend Curtis interact with each other. They all seemed to get along so well. They were like a ghetto version of the Huxtables. They had problems too just like any other family but for the most part they all got along and were happy. Curtis and Annette had been together for over ten years and he was good to her and King. King had even admitted to Breezy that he looked at Curtis as his real dad versus his real own dad because Curtis had always been there for him.

Thinking about King and Curtis made her think about her own dad, who she'd never met. Sometimes she wished that he would come back for her and take her to live with him. She felt that would probably be the answer to all of her problems, too. *If he came back for me and I went to live with him my ma would probably miss me so bad that she would change her ways and beg me to come back,* she thought, figuring their situation was like most relationships, where a person never missed what they had until it's gone. *If I left I am sure my ma would miss all of the things that I do for her and realize how big of a mistake she's made throughout the years.* She lay there smiling at her thoughts. A tap on the door and then King pushing it open and walking in interrupted her train of thought.

"Dang you about to sleep all day ain't you?" he teased showing off that perfect smile of his.

She looked over at the clock, which read 7:22 a.m. "King, are you for real? You know, y'all get up at the crack of dawn around here," she joked.

"Nah, because once my ma leave I'm going back to sleep but I can't sleep with her keeping all of that noise in the kitchen, banging all of those pots and pans and mess like she's an Iron Chef or somebody."

Breezy laughed. King was always cracking jokes. "Give me a washcloth and a towel so that I can wash up," she told him while throwing back the covers and getting out of bed. "I need a shirt and a pair of sweats, too."

"Damn do you want a pair of boxers too?" he asked as he shuffled over to the dresser dragging his feet.

That got on her nerves. "Boy, pick your dang feet up!" she yelled tossing a pillow at him.

He turned around and tackled her down on the bed and started tickling her. She squealed and yelled at the top of her lungs begging him to stop.

"Nah, you bad, you bad! Say you're sorry! Say you're sorry or else I'm going to tickle you until you piss on yo'self!" he threatened.

"Sike!" She squealed. "I . . . ain't saying . . . jack!"

He continued tickling her and she accidentally kicked over the lamp that was on the nightstand.

They both froze. Then the door flew open.

Now to them it was all innocent but when Annette burst in and saw King sitting on top of Breezy, she wasn't sure of what to make of the situation. "What in the hell is going on in here? King, why are you on top of that girl? Breezy, get your ass up!" she said all of that in one breath.

King jumped up. "Ma, we were just playing," he said, sounding like a little kid instead of a sixteen-year-old nearly grown man.

"Yeah, we was just playing," Breezy chimed in.

"I'm sure y'all were but y'all ain't no little kids no more and he don't need to be all on top of you, tickling all over you." She gave both of them a skeptical look. "I ain't raising no babies!"

"Ma!" King yelled embarrassed that she would imply such a thing about him and Breezy.

"What? Tickling leads to other stuff!" Annette told him point blank. Something had been telling her for a while that there was something more between her son and Breezy. The way that he was over Breezy was more than just a friendship. She saw something more between the two of them, whether they realized it or not.

"Ma, Breezy is like my sister! I don't look at her like that!" he responded.

Breezy wasn't sure if it was the way that he said it or if she was just being sensitive but his words kind of stung.

"Yeah, well, I still don't like you tickling all over her so y'all cut it out," Annette told King and then turned her attention to Breezy. "Breezy, go on and get washed up so that you can eat something before you leave here." She looked back at King again. "I'm about to leave for work in a few. I don't want you leaving this house today. You are grounded for the next two weeks."

"Two weeks?"

"Yes, two weeks," she repeated. "Do you want to make it three?"

He smacked his lips and mumbled something before brushing past her and disappearing down the hall.

"A month damn it! Now smack your damn lips again in my damn house so I can take them off of your face!" she yelled after him before going behind him still talking trash.

Annette didn't play but it was clear that all her fussing came from a good place. She loved her son and there was nothing wrong with that.

Breezy looked in King's drawer and got her own tee and sweats. She had underwear in her pocketbook that she'd brought with her because she hadn't ever planned on going home the night before. She just didn't feel right staying there with the lights out and Terry there. She was afraid that he might try to touch her again.

She gathered the clothes and went into the bathroom, undressed, set the water in the shower, and then stepped inside under the warm water. It felt so good to be taking a nice, hot shower. She stayed in until the water started to turn cold and then got out and got dressed. King's clothes swallowed her and she had to draw the string really tight in the waist just to keep them on but it didn't matter, she wasn't trying to impress anybody. She went back into King's room and got her brush out of her pocketbook and brushed her hair back into a ponytail before going into the kitchen. It was quiet; she took it that Annette had already left for work. She looked on the stove and saw that there was a lot of food left from breakfast. She fixed her a plate and sat down at the table. After eating two plates of sausage, eggs, and biscuits, she washed her plate and then got something to drink. Feeling nice and stuffed she went back into the living room. King was laid back on the sofa with his eyes closed. "You asleep?" she asked.

"Nah, just resting my eyes," he responded still not opening them.

She took a seat down the other end of the sofa. "How many days did you get?"

"Five. How about you?"

"I got five too. Angie and Kita got ten, since they started everything and since it wasn't the first time that they had been in trouble for the same thing." Breezy looked around, her eyes landing on the clock that hung over the electric fireplace. It was a little after eight. She knew that she needed to be getting home but was in no rush to get there. "Do you have some paper?"

"Yeah, go look in my book bag."

She went down the hall and got some paper from his bag and then sat down on the floor and started to write. She wrote two poems and then folded them both and put them in her purse. She got up and gathered her things and went back down the hall. King had fallen asleep on the sofa. She tapped him. "I'm about to go."

"A'ight. Lock the door and holla at me later."

"Okay."

She left out locking the door behind her. When she got home nobody was in the front part of the house but she could hear laughter and talking coming from her ma's room down the hall. She walked down the hall to her room noticing on the way that her ma's door was half open. She didn't even bother looking in the room; instead she went in her room and started cleaning up.

Breezy was in her own world, humming and cleaning when she heard noises coming from Teresa's room. They were erotic noises, moaning and groaning. Then there was the sound of the bed springs and Terry moaning as well. She knew then that the two of them were having sex. Hearing the two of them made her sick to her stomach and she literally threw up a little in her mouth. She ran down the hall to the bathroom and threw up.

The commotion in Teresa's bedroom stopped and a few seconds later Breezy heard her yell. "Breezy, is that you?"

"Yes!" she managed to respond between puking up her breakfast.

"Oh, well get in the kitchen and wash them damn dishes! It better be done when I come in there, too," Teresa ordered with no shame that her daughter had overheard her having sex. She and Terry started right back up as if Breezy wasn't even there.

After getting herself together, she went down the hall and got started on the dishes. The water was cold because the lights were off and it was damn near impossible to remove the dirty food that was stuck on the dishes and the grease that was on them but she did. The entire time that she stood at the sink, Terry and Teresa were going at it like rabbits in the bedroom. She hummed louder in an attempt to drown them out but it didn't do much good because they were extremely loud.

When she was done with the dishes, she grabbed the book that she'd laid down on the coffee table the week before and sat down on the sofa. She was so wrapped up in the book that she didn't see Terry enter the room. She felt something wet and slimy on the side of her face and jumped. He was rubbing his nasty, wet penis on the side of her face. She tried to jump up but he grabbed her by the hair and pushed her back down. "Sit your ass down! It ain't nothing but your mama's pussy so stop acting like you ain't never smelled it before. Didn't she push you out of it?" He laughed while stroking himself.

"Please leave me alone," she whispered.

"Terry, bring me a cigarette!" Teresa yelled from the bathroom. "I don't know why but I can't take a good shit unless I have a Newport. Hurry up!"

Ignoring Teresa, Terry leaned down and fondled Breezy's left breast. "Your ma got some good pussy but yours is better," he said before going back down the hall. "I'm coming, baby," he yelled to Teresa.

Breezy got up and went in her room. She grabbed a shirt from the pile of clothes that lay in the corner of her room and wiped her face. She paced back and forth across her floor, with her arms wrapped around herself. She couldn't deal with this situation with Terry much longer. Something had to give. She had to try to tell her ma what was going on whether she believed her or not. She had to at least try. She sat on the edge of her bed and waited for Teresa to come out of the bathroom before she went where she was.

Breezy tapped on Teresa's door, which was still cracked open. Teresa was lying on the bed buck-naked along with Terry, who had slipped on a pair of boxers. The room smelled like sweaty ass but she ignored that and focused on the task at hand. She really needed to talk to her mama. "Ma, can I talk to you?" Breezy asked just above a whisper as she entered the room.

"About?" Teresa asked glancing in her daughter's direction. "Does it have to do with why your ass ain't in school? I'll tell you one thing, social services better not show up at my door asking why you ain't in school! I'll tell you that damn much! Now what is it that you want to talk to me about?"

After listening to all of that she wasn't sure if she still wanted to talk to her but she knew she had to at least try. "No, it's about Terry."

"Terry?" Teresa asked sitting up in the bed, her saggy breasts flopping as she sat up.

"About me?" Terry asked trying to sound like he had no idea what Breezy was in there for. He laughed and sat up as well. Reaching over on the nightstand he grabbed the pack of cigarettes and shook one out. After lighting it he took a long drag. "This should be interesting. Come on with it."

"Well spit it out," Teresa snapped, growing impatient. "You come in here talking about you have something that you want to tell me about my man so I want to hear it!"

"He raped me the other night!" Breezy blurted. "And when you were in the bathroom he put his thing in my face!"

Teresa's initial reaction was shock. Her mouth was open but nothing was coming out and her hand was over her chest like she was about to have a heart attack.

"That little bitch is lying, Teresa! I ain't touch that damn lying-ass bitch!" Terry roared jumping to his feet screaming.

Breezy didn't back down though. "Yes, you did! The other night when I came home and Ma was back here 'sleep. You did it to me on the sofa and you told me that if I told Ma, she wouldn't believe me and you also said that you would break my neck!"

"Why the fuck is you lying?" Terry asked like he couldn't believe what he was hearing. Breezy could see it in his eyes that he wanted to do some serious damage to her at that moment and even though she was scared she didn't let it show. "Teresa, I swear to you, baby, that I ain't touch her!"

"Yes, he did, Ma, he's lying!" Breezy yelled loud enough for the neighbors to hear.

"Shut up! Both of you!" Teresa jumped up off of the bed and started swinging on Terry.

Breezy stood in the middle of the floor paralyzed by shock, unable to believe what her eyes were witnessing. That was the happiest moment that she could remember in her entire life. Her mama was finally fighting for her, acting like a mother. All she could do was stand there in awe with tears streaming down her cheeks.

"You sorry motherfucker, you fucked my daughter? How could you do some shit like this to me? That's my child!"

"Baby, she is lying! I never touched her!" Terry stuck to his story, thinking what he was going to do to Breezy once all of this was over. He too was shocked by Teresa's reaction. Normally she acted as if she didn't give two fucks about Breezy but now she was acting like a totally different woman. Like she actually did give a damn about her daughter.

"Why would she lie on you?" Teresa questioned, swinging and connecting with the left side of his head. "Huh? Answer me that! What reason does she have to lie on you?"

"Because she's jealous! She probably wants me for herself! I keep telling you that she's hot in the ass! Spending the night down there at that boy's house. What do you think she is down there doing?" He was trying to manipulate Teresa into thinking that Breezy had been sleeping with King.

"I'll tell you what she's doing! Fucking that's what! Look at how she stood in the bathroom and listened to us fuck! That should tell you something right there!"

"I wasn't trying to listen to you. I was sick to my stomach!" Breezy screamed in her defense. "The door to the bedroom was open so I couldn't help but hear but I wasn't trying to."

"Yeah, I bet you weren't!" he yelled back.

"I want you out of my gotdamn house right now, nigga! Get your shit and get the fuck out!" Teresa screamed through tears. She was hurt and couldn't understand why every man who came into her life did something to hurt her. No matter how good she was to them, they always did her wrong in the end.

On the inside, Breezy was cheering and turning flips. She wanted to run over and hug her mama and tell her how much she loved her and how much she appreciated her taking up for her, but she didn't because, to be honest, she was afraid to, unsure of how Teresa might react.

"Fine then. I'll go but you are going to feel really damn stupid when you find out that her ass is lying!" Terry gathered his clothes and slipped them on and then brushed past Breezy nearly knocking her down. He slammed the front door hard on his way out.

# Chapter Four

Teresa sat on the side of the bed crying with her head in her hands. After standing there watching her for several minutes, unsure of what she should do, Breezy finally walked over and wrapped her arms around her mama. To her surprise, Teresa hugged her back.

"I can't believe that he would do some shit like this to me." Teresa cried on Breezy's shoulder. She felt so hurt and betrayed by Terry. "I have been damn good to that man . . . too damn good for him to do some shit like this right here."

Breezy sat there slightly confused; somehow it wasn't sounding like this was about her at all. It was sounding more so like it was about her mama and the fact that Terry had cheated on her rather than the fact that he'd raped her daughter.

She went on for more than an hour about Terry cheating on her. When she had calmed down some she stood up, picked her gown up off the floor that she'd been wearing before her and Terry's sex session, and slipped it on. She looked back at

Breezy who was still sitting on the edge of her bed fidgeting with her fingers, a habit that she also had. "I'll be right back. Going in the kitchen to get me something to drink."

"Okay," Breezy replied looking up at her mama briefly and then back down at her fingers. So many thoughts were running through her mind, along with mixed emotions. She couldn't remember the last time that she and her mama had sat and held a conversation; and although it felt good to be talked to for once instead of talked at, yelled at, or cursed at, this still wasn't about her like she'd initially believed. She looked up blinking back tears and let out a sigh. Her eyes were red and puffy from all of the crying that she'd done. "Well at least she didn't beat my ass and Terry is gone. Things could have turned out a lot worse so I won't complain."

Walking back into the room carrying a glass of water, Teresa looked around confused knowing that she'd just heard Breezy talking to someone. "Ummm, are you all right?"

"Huh?"

"I thought I heard you talking to someone."

"Nah, just thinking out loud."

Teresa crossed the room and sat back down on the bed. "Whew, I'll tell you the truth, Terry really did hurt me. I thought he was different," she started again, shaking her head.

Breezy decided to change the subject and ask her the one question that she'd been needing the answer to for years. She knew that they may never sit and talk like this again so she took this as her opportunity. "Ma, why do you hate me?" she blurted not beating around the bush at all. She wanted to know why things were the way that they were between them. "What did I do to make you treat me the way that you do? I am a straight A student. I've never been in any trouble until yesterday. I cook, clean, and do whatever it is that you ask of me but it's still not enough. I don't understand." She looked at Teresa, who was wearing an unreadable expression, and waited for her to answer.

Teresa smoothed her shoulder-length hair down and looked toward the window. "I don't hate you, Breezy. I could never hate you." She looked back at her daughter. Reaching over she tried to touch the side of her face and she jumped. Guilt ate at Teresa; she knew that Breezy was so jumpy due to the fact that she was afraid of her. She withdrew her hand and placed it in her lap. "I hate what you remind me of: your father." That was the honest truth. "I loved that man so much. I would've done anything for him all except for one thing: get rid of you."

Now that was a shocker, after hearing a million and one times how much she hated her and wished that she'd gotten rid of her. "He wanted you to have an abortion?"

"Yeah, he did. He wasn't ready for kids. See your father was captain of the basketball team and he was one of the best players anyone had seen in a while. He knew that he was going pro after high school. There was no doubt about that and he refused to let a baby hold him back. He sat me down and explained to me that he wasn't ready for a baby. He told me that he loved me but if I didn't have an abortion the two of us could no longer be. I was so hurt because I couldn't believe what he was asking me to do. I tried to reason with him by saying that I would take care of you by myself until he got established but he wasn't trying to hear that. He told me again to have an abortion because he wasn't ready for any babies. He said 'if you keep it, it's your responsibility. I want nothing to do with it and I mean that.' Well as you can see, I didn't get rid of you and as a result of that he broke up with me and wouldn't have anything to do with me."

"Did he ever go pro?" Breezy asked, thinking that was a dumb question. She knew that if her dad was a pro basketball player Teresa would have definitely taken his ass to court and had him up for child support.

"As a matter of fact he did. He used to play for Miami but he got hurt a few years ago and wasn't able to play anymore." She looked off into space as she thought about the man she'd been head over heels in love with fifteen years ago. "Dujaun . . ."

"Sinclair." Breezy finished her sentence in disbelief. She stood up and began pacing back and forth. This couldn't be true. Dujuan Sinclair was one of the best basketball players to ever play in the NBA and one of the richest. *She has to be lying,* Breezy thought before saying it aloud. "You can't be telling the truth."

"But I am." Teresa stood up and lifted her mattress. She rummaged around before putting it back down and handing Breezy an old picture.

Breezy took the picture from her hand and looked down at it. She nearly pissed herself. Sure as shit there was Teresa and a young Dujuan Sinclair. *Well I'll be damned.* Excited, she started jumping up down and yelling, "I'm rich! I'm rich!"

Teresa snatched the picture out of her hand. "No, you ain't! You didn't allow me to finish. Now sit down."

Breezy saw a glimpse of anger in her eyes so she sat down. She didn't want her to get upset because for the first time they were talking and she wanted it to last for as long as it could.

"His mother gave me a check for twenty thousand dollars when she found out that I was pregnant and had no plans of having an abortion. She said that money was to keep my mouth shut but not to expect another dime. I took the money and used it for as long as it lasted to take care of us but of course twenty thousand dollars doesn't last forever."

"Why did you take the money? You should have told her no and taken him to court. Then we wouldn't have to struggle like this and we would be happy!" Breezy exclaimed.

Teresa shook her head. "Y'all kids don't know nothing. I took the money because I loved him and I didn't want to hurt him by taking him to court."

To say that Breezy was confused was an understatement. She couldn't hurt him by taking him to court but she could hurt her by beating her ass every day. She sure had some crazy-ass logic going on. "Okay, so in that case, why didn't you have an abortion so that you could've still been with him?" She wanted to know. She needed to try to understand exactly what was going on in Teresa's head because at the moment none of the things that she had said were making a lot of sense to her.

"Because you were a part of him. You were what he and I had lain down and created. I felt like if I killed you, I would be killing a part of myself and him as well and I just couldn't do it."

The happy feeling and excitement of talking to her mama was dwindling by the second because nothing seemed to be about her at all. It was about her mama and the men in her life.

"I loved him so much and I still love him to this day. You look so much like him. Every time that I look at you, I see him and I become angry," Teresa explained. "Do you understand?"

"Yeah, I guess so," Breezy mumbled.

Teresa saw how sad and pitiful Breezy looked and felt bad. She decided to try to make things right between her and her daughter. "I'll tell you what though. I am going to try to control my anger from now on. I'm sorry for how I have treated you and I am sorry for what Terry did to you. Okay?"

Breezy couldn't even try to hold back the smile that took over her face. "Okay." They hugged and then stayed up most of the night in the dark talking.

The next morning they got up early and went down to social services. Teresa was able to get her light bill paid and food stamps. Over the next few days, she and Breezy laughed and talked nonstop. Breezy being suspended actually turned out to be a good thing because she and Teresa used that time to bond. Breezy had never been so happy.

# Chapter Five

Saturday rolled around fast. It was Breezy's birthday! Normally she wouldn't be excited but after having such a good week with her mama, she couldn't help but be excited. She jumped out of bed that morning, ran down the hall to Teresa's room, and peeked inside. Through the crack in the door she saw that she was still asleep. She pulled the door back closed and went to take her bath in hopes that Teresa would be awake by the time she was done.

She got in the tub and took a nice, hot bath, including washing her hair. When she was done she dried off and slipped into a pair of red sweats and a white tee that had some red writing on the front. She got an old toothbrush and took her time cleaning up her old Nikes. That didn't make them look too much better but better than they did before she'd cleaned them. She got her brush and styling gel and brushed her hair back into a ponytail. Then, she dipped her finger in the jar of Vaseline that was on the dresser and put a little on her lips. She looked in the mirror and though she wasn't thrilled with her appearance, she felt she looked okay.

She went back down the hall to Teresa's room again. She opened the door and saw that she was still in bed. "Hey, Ma," Breezy called.

"Hey, Breezy," Teresa replied from beneath the covers. "Happy birthday."

"Thanks, Ma!" Breezy squealed jumping onto the bed like a big kid.

Teresa removed the covers from her head. "I ain't got no money to get you nothing but I will get you something when I get my hands on some money," She promised.

"It's okay. I understand. I am just happy that the two of us have been getting along so great! That's gift enough." Breezy wrapped her arms around Teresa's neck the best she could with her lying down. "I love you," she whispered to her, meaning it from the bottom of her heart.

"Love you too."

Breezy smiled; hearing those words was better than any gift that money could buy. "I am going to go see King and Ms. Annette for a little while but I will be right back."

"A'ight. Lock the door on your way out."

"Okay." Breezy practically skipped up the street to King's house. When she got there she rang the doorbell. A few seconds later she heard someone unlocking the locks. The door opened and Annette was standing on the other side.

"Hey, Birthday girl! We were just about to come and get you."

"Hey. You were?" Breezy asked surprised.

"Yeah, I have a huge surprise planned for you. Well, King helped me think of it. So come on in and speak to him and then me and you have an appointment." Annette was more excited than Breezy as she stepped out of the way so that she could come in.

"An appointment?" Breezy grew excited. "What kind of appointment?"

"You'll see, nosey!" Annette teased, giving Breezy a hug. "Happy birthday again, baby," she told her.

"Thank you."

"King and his friend are in the kitchen; go ahead in there and speak. I know he can't wait to see you. You've been MIA on us all week."

"Yeah, I know but I was spending time with my mama. She has been so nice this past week. It's been like living in a dream world or something." Breezy giggled. "I sure hope that things remain this way."

"Yeah, me too. You are a good girl and you don't deserve to be treated the way that you have," Annette started but then stopped herself and smiled. "You know what? We ain't even gon' talk about that mess today."

Breezy smiled and made her way into the kitchen expecting to see Jalen or Sean since Annette had mentioned King was in the kitchen with his friend. She really hoped it was Sean because she really didn't want to be bothered with Jalen today. Her birthday was going great so far, she didn't need him and his slick remarks ruining it. She walked into the kitchen and was shocked to see Davita sitting at the table with King showing all thirty-two. He was all up in her face whispering something and she was giggling.

Breezy took a deep breath and cleared her throat. Both Davita and King looked over in her direction.

"Hey, big head! Happy birthday!" King jumped up and ran over to her with his arms open for a hug. On one hand she didn't want to hug him because she was a little jealous about seeing him with Davita, but at the same time she knew that she had no right to be, so she hugged him. "Where have you been the past few days?"

"Chillin' with my ma." Breezy blushed unable to reveal her good news without smiling.

"Really?" He sounded shocked, which was understandable.

"Yeah, I will tell you more about it later."

"Cool." With one of his arms still around her shoulder he turned and motioned toward Davita. "You already know Vita, right?"

"Yeah." Breezy smiled politely and waved as she eyed Vita. She envied the girl because she had a banging body, her hair was always laid, her gear was always on point, she was very popular, and all of the guys at school wanted her but most importantly King looked at her like she wished he'd look at her. "Hey, Vita."

"Hey, Breezy." Vita was all extra like the two of them were besties. "Girl, happy B-day!"

For as long as they'd known each other, Vita had never spoken a word to Breezy before so she knew that she was being fake but she just played along. "Thanks."

Annette came into the kitchen. "You ready, Breezy?"

"Where are we going?"

"Girl, just bring your little narrow behind on here. Ms. Annette got this girl! All you need to do is lie back and enjoy the ride, honey, because this is your day and we are going to make sure that you have the best birthday ever!" Annette smiled doing a goofy little dance, which caused everyone to burst into laughter. She stopped dancing and her demeanor became serious. Directing her attention to King, she waved a finger at him and Vita. "I don't want no mess out of y'all. Curtis is in the bedroom so he will be keeping an eye on you."

"Ma, what do you think that we are going to do?" King asked.

"I don't know what you might be thinking of doing."

"Nothing except talking like we are now."

"Good." She looked back at Breezy. "Come on."

"See y'all," Breezy told King and Davita, not liking the thought of leaving the two of them alone.

"I can't wait to see you later, Breezy!" King teased. "I might have to start calling you Ms. Breezy."

Breezy looked confused, trying to figure out what he was talking about. "Huh?"

"Don't pay him no mind." Annette grabbed her by the arm. "Come on here!" The two of them left.

During the drive Annette bragged about was how nice looking Vita was and how she was such a nice girl and how King seemed to really like her.

Breezy looked out the window trying her best to tune Annette out, though it was proving to be really hard since she kept asking her opinion. If she'd had an ink pen or something with a sharp tip she would've stabbed herself in both ears. She was beyond fed up with hearing about King and Vita. At this point she was ready to ask if she could just take her home but she was glad that she hadn't when they pulled up in front of Angel's Salon.

"Get out of the car," Annette told her. Breezy couldn't believe that she was about to get her hair done. She jumped out of the car and nearly ran inside. When they got inside, the receptionist greeted them and asked if she could help them with anything. Annette informed the woman that she'd scheduled an appointment for Breezy with Blue.

"Okay. I will let her know that you are here. You can have a seat." The receptionist disappeared toward the back of the salon and returned a few seconds later with a tall, curvy redbone sister with a blue weave.

"Hello, I'm Blue," she introduced herself flashing Breezy a smile that showed off the gold tooth in her mouth.

Breezy smiled politely and introduced herself, "I'm Breezy. It's nice to meet you."

"Is there any particular way that you want your hair done?"

"Just make it really pretty," Annette spoke up. "Today is her birthday and I want her to look stunning." She looked at Blue's hair and then added, "But no color for her."

"Oh okay, no problem," Blue assured her and then looked at Breezy. "Come on, birthday girl, follow me right this way."

Breezy followed her to her station. Blue got right to work on her hair, first giving her a much-needed perm, then sewing in some hair. She styled it in a doobie wrap that fell around Breezy's shoulders and framed her face. When she was done, she turned her around so that she could look in the mirror.

Breezy jumped up out of her seat. She was all in the mirror touching her hair. "Oh my goodness, I love it! Gosh it looks so good!"

Blue giggled at the girl's obvious satisfaction with her hair. "Sit back down so that I can do your eyebrows and makeup."

Breezy did as she asked and Blue worked her magic. When she was done, Breezy stood in the mirror with her mouth hung wide open. She couldn't believe that the reflection of the beautiful young woman standing in the mirror was actually her. Her eyes began to water.

Annette got up from the dryer and walked over to get a closer look at Breezy's hair. She saw the tears in Breezy's eyes from her reflection in the mirror. "Hey, hey now. There will be no tears today, young lady. Can't have you ruining your makeup."

Breezy turned around from the mirror to face Annette and couldn't hold back the tears that poured from her eyes. They were tears of happiness and appreciation. "Thank you so much, Ms. Annette." She cried, hugging her tightly. "No one has ever done anything like this for me before. I appreciate it so much."

"Awww, baby, don't cry." Annette rubbed Breezy's back, tearing up herself. Breezy felt almost like her own and, sometimes, she wished that she was her own so that she wouldn't have to go through the things that she did at home. "I am just glad that you like it."

"Okay, let me touch up your makeup," Blue told Breezy.

"I need to go and get my butt back under this dryer. I just walked over here to be nosey. When you are done over here, go over and let Samantha do your nails. This is your day and I want you to feel like the princess that you are." She smiled at Breezy, knowing that she was loving the birthday surprises that she'd put together for her.

"Okay," Breezy answered as Blue fixed her makeup. When Blue was done she went over to Samantha, like Annette had told her. By the time that Samantha was done with her nails, Annette had paid for everything and was ready to go.

"All right, we have one more stop," Annette informed Breezy once they were back in the car.

"Okay," Breezy replied unable to stop looking in the mirror at herself.

When they pulled up at the mall Breezy looked over at Annette. "Why are we here?"

"Well we can't have your hair and nails looking all cute and not get you a cute outfit and some shoes to go with it."

Breezy started screaming. "Oh gosh! Are you for real?"

"Yes, I'm for real!" Annette laughed. "Now come on here, girl."

Inside Annette bought her two outfits and two pairs of sneakers. She also bought her some new underwear and bras. Breezy felt like she was dreaming.

"Go into the bathroom and change into one of your new outfits and a pair of your sneakers," Annette instructed. "I will hold the rest of your bags while you change."

Breezy went into the bathroom and changed as quickly as she could, wondering what other surprises Annette could possibly have in store for her after all that she'd already done. She walked out of the bathroom and did a little twirl so that Annette could get a good look at her in her new clothes.

"You look gorgeous."

"Thank you, Ms. Annette. I really do appreciate everything. I can't thank you enough and I know that I certainly will never be able to repay you."

"Oh hush your mouth, child, talking about repaying me. That is just nonsense." Annette laughed waving her off. "And besides, I can't stand here and take all of the credit. King let me keep his allowance for the past few weeks to help pay for it, so he deserves some thanks too," she informed Breezy who just blushed at first.

"He did that for me?"

"Yep." She drove out of the parking lot and into traffic, headed to the final and biggest surprise. Ten minutes later, they turned into the parking lot of Golden Corral and got out. "I hope you're hungry."

"I sure am," Breezy told her, now missing her best friend and wishing that he was there with her. "I wish King's big head was here. Not that I don't like chillin' with you, Ms. Annette, but that's my buddy though."

"I understand," Annette replied smiling to herself.

They walked inside and Annette whispered something to the hostess.

"Follow me right this way," she told them. They did as she said. Before they made it all the way to the table, Breezy saw Mr. Curtis, King, and Vita seated at a table toward the back full of balloons, a cake, and a few gifts.

"Awwww, y'all, this is so sweet." She burst into tears for what seemed like the millionth time that day.

"Cry baby," King teased getting up to give her a big hug. He couldn't help but notice how beautiful she looked. She almost didn't look like his homegirl anymore. "Look at you, Ms. Thang, don't you look mighty fly. Dag, I'm going to have to kill them niggas at school if they see you looking like this. I can't have all of them hounds on my homegirl!"

"Whatever." Breezy hit him playfully. She wished that he would look at her like the guys he was referring to.

They sat down and ate and then Breezy opened her gifts. After thanking everyone for a wonderful birthday, Annette drove her home. She thanked Annette and King again before getting out of the car. She ran up to the door excited with her bags in her hand and what was left of her cake. She couldn't wait for her ma to see her new look and all of her gifts.

# Chapter Six

Breezy could hear music playing as she approached the door. She turned the doorknob, finding that the door was unlocked. She pushed it open and walked inside. The first thing she saw was Terry laid back on the sofa with a smirk on his face and Teresa up in front of him dancing with a bottle of Patrón in one hand and a blunt in the other.

Teresa noticed Terry looking past her instead of at her and turned to see what he was looking at. She looked back and saw Breezy all dolled up. She looked so good that she almost didn't recognize her. "Awwww, shit look at you. Happy motherfuckin' birthday, Breezy!" she yelled and threw her head back in laughter, like she was having the time of her life.

Breezy stood in the middle of the floor with the door still wide open, speechless and unable to move a muscle. It was like she was frozen in time. She was so angry, hurt, and disgusted. Everything all rolled up into one.

Teresa noticed that Terry's eyes were still fixated on Breezy. She stopped dancing and looked Breezy up and down real nice and slow, taking her entire makeover in. She walked over to her and touched her hair, taking a toke of the blunt that she was holding. "Damn look at you!" She coughed. "I almost didn't recognize your ass. Your little boy-friend down the street and his mama really did you up right nice!" She laughed. "Shit you must be fuckin him reeeeeaaaaal good huh?" The look on her face went from amused to disgusted in two seconds flat. Without warning she lifted the bottle of Patrón that she'd been holding and poured it in Breezy's hair and all over her clothes. It also got in her eyes and nose.

Breezy dropped everything that she'd been holding in her hands and started trying to wipe the alcohol out of her eyes. She screamed out in pain as she rubbed her eyes with her shirt. She felt a hard shove in her back and went tumbling onto the floor, hitting her head on the corner of the sofa on the way down.

"I bet you fucked him real good like you tried to do my man! You fast-ass little bitch! I should've never believed your nasty ass in the first place. Yeah, Terry told me what really happened about how your ass tried to get him to fuck you the other night." Teresa stood over Breezy who had sat up on the floor, still rubbing her eyes.

Terry sat on the sofa enjoying the show and the control that he had over Teresa. He knew that he now had access to Breezy anytime that he wanted a piece of her. "Hell yeah, with her fast ass. I been trying to tell you all along that she ain't doing all that hanging around that boy down the street for nothing. She down there fucking, plain and simple. Next thing you know her little ass will end up pregnant and she probably won't even know who the daddy is because you know that she probably fucking more than one."

Breezy finally spoke up in an attempt to defend herself against the things that the two of them were saying against her. "I haven't been sleeping around with anybody! He raped me!" She pointed at Terry.

Teresa drew back and slapped her hard across the face. "Shut up lying. My man ain't touched your lying ass. You're just jealous because you want him for your damn self but guess what, it ain't going to happen."

Breezy scrambled to her feet. She could see but everything was blurry. "I don't want him! He raped me!" she screamed at the top of her lungs. "How could you take his word over mines? What about all of the things that you told me the other night? You told me that you were going to change."

Terry jumped from the sofa and came charging toward her. She cowered against the wall, afraid of what he was about to do to her, but to her surprise

Teresa stopped him. "Nah, don't hit that little bitch! She might go running to the folks on you and have you locked up! I got this, baby!" Teresa told him and then looked at Breezy. "Get the fuck out of my house, and from now on when my man is here you can't be! I don't give a fuck where you go just as long as it ain't here!" Breezy didn't move because she didn't know what to do. Teresa reached down and grabbed her by her shirt, ripping it. "Get the fuck up! You gotta go."

Breezy got up and tried to gather her things but she wasn't moving fast enough for Teresa. She snatched the bags and ran to the door tossing everything out onto the ground. Breezy ran outside and began gathering her things. Her clothes had come out of the bag and had gotten dirty. She felt something hit her in her back.

"You forgot something, bitch!" Teresa yelled before slamming the door. Breezy looked down on the ground and saw that it was her cake and it had fallen out of the cake plate and was lying on the ground.

She'd cried so much that she just couldn't cry anymore. She finished gathering her clothes and held them in her arms trying to cover herself because of her ripped shirt. She walked down the street in the direction of the only place that she knew to go. When she arrived at the complex where King lived there were a lot of people outside as it always was on a Saturday night. She walked past the crowd not really paying them any attention but could hear the laughs and snickers. None of that mattered after what had just happened with Teresa and Terry. Someone from the crowd called her name but she kept going.

"Yo, Breezy. Breezy!" King called jogging after her with Vita right on his heels. She looked like shit. "Breezy, what happened?"

She just continued to walk.

He finally caught up to her and grabbed her by her arm. "What happened to you? Why are you wet? Why do you smell like liquor? Talk to me!" He looked at her and didn't see any visible scars but he could tell that she was hurt. Her eyes were bloodshot and she had a distant look in them like she wasn't even herself. She wouldn't even look at him. She just kept looking off into space.

"Breezy, talk to me, tell me what happened to you. I can't help unless you tell me what's wrong." He saw tears forming in her eyes and then start to roll down her cheeks. She'd been so happy when he, his mama, and Vita had dropped her off a little while ago. To see her in this condition now broke his heart. "Look, Vita, I'm going take her inside and then I will take you home. Wait for me out here. I will be right back."

"Okay," she replied.

"Come on, Breezy." He wrapped his arm around her and walked her inside ignoring the stares from the people who were outside. "Ma, come here!" he called once they were inside.

Annette came into the living room wearing her nightclothes with her hair wrapped up. "Boy, what . . . Oh my goodness!" She covered her mouth with her hand. "Baby, what happened?" she asked reaching out for Breezy.

Breezy was too ashamed to let them know that her ma had kicked her out because Terry had raped her. She felt embarrassed and nasty so she didn't respond. She just sat there and cried.

"Ma, I have to run Vita home but I will be right back," King told Annette. "Breezy, I'll be right, right back and when I get back I want to know what happened to you, okay?" His voice had a sternness in it that told her he wasn't playing and that he really wanted to know.

Breezy simply nodded her head but had no real intention of telling him the truth.


On the way to drop Vita off at home, she was full of questions. "Bae, what was wrong with Breezy? Did she get into a fight?"

"I don't know." King wasn't about to put Breezy's business out there like that. He knew how chicks got down. As soon as they found out some shit they was on the phone bumping their gums and adding in shit that ain't even happen. He wasn't saying that Vita would do that but he wasn't going to even give her the opportunity to, because if she did that would sure as hell earn her walking papers and he wasn't trying to send her on her way before he got a chance to hit that.

"I sure hope that she's all right. She didn't tell you anything?" She wasn't letting up. "I mean, I know that she is your best friend and all. I am just worried about her."

"Thanks but she'll be fine. Can we talk about something else?"

"Yeah, sure." She was a little disappointed about not finding out what she wanted to know. "I really do like you a lot, King. I'm hoping that this works out."

"I enjoy kickin' it with you too." He looked over to see her looking back at him smiling. He reached over resting his hand on her thigh. The rest of the drive they made small talk.

When they arrived at her house, King got out of the car and walked around to her side of the car to open the door for her.

"Ooh my boo is a gentleman." Vita got out of the car and wrapped her arms around his neck and pressed her soft, glossy lips against his. He wrapped his arms around her waist and slid his hands down to her round ass and gave it a squeeze while their tongues explored each other's mouths.

They stayed like that for at least two minutes but then he broke their embrace. As much as he would like to have stayed there and sucked face with her a little longer, Breezy was weighing heavily on his mind.

"Why you stop for?" Vita whined.

"I gotta get back to Breezy. I need to make sure she's good." He gave her another quick peck on the lips and smacked her on her ass. "I'm going to call you later okay?"

"Okay, boo." She walked up to the door switching as hard as she could, knowing without a doubt that he was watching. She looked back over her shoulder and smiled. His eyes were indeed locked on her ass. She opened the door and went inside.

After making sure that Vita had gotten inside safely, King jumped in the car and headed home. When he got back to the house, Breezy had taken a bath and changed clothes. Annette was blow-drying her hair and judging by the look on her face she was mad as hell! He didn't have to wonder long about whether she was mad because she let him know.

"This shit right here got me mad as hell! I don't care what Breezy says, I am going to be at Teresa's door bright and early like a damn Jehovah's Witness in the morning! I put a lot of money on this child to make her look beautiful and to feel special for her birthday and that trifling bitch gon' do some shit like this!" She paused and swiped some tears from her face that had been spilling down her cheeks. "This shit ain't right! You don't treat no child like this!" She cut off the dryer and slammed it down on the table and walked out of the room shaking her head.

King knew that she was really upset because she never cursed like that. He heard her bedroom door slam. He took a seat on the sofa and looked over at Breezy. Her eyes were puffy and she looked depressed.

She looked over at him. "King, I am so tired of living like this. I try so hard to make my ma happy but nothing is ever good enough." Her voice sounded strained as she sat and poured her heart out to him. "For the past few days the two of us have gotten along so well. We talked and she explained to me why she is the way that she is. I thought that we were getting somewhere." Tears fell on her nightshirt that Annette had given her but she didn't bother to wipe her eyes; she just continued. "You can't begin to imagine how I felt when I walked inside of my house tonight and saw Terry sitting there. I felt like someone had hit me in the stomach with a boulder and then on top of that she is going to take his word over mine! How could she do me like that? On my birthday, my ma put me out and treated me like nothing all because of him!"

King interrupted her for the first time. "I don't get it. Took his word about what?"

Breezy looked away and then dropped her head.

"Breezy, answer me! Why did she put you out?" No response. He felt his blood pressure start to rise. "Answer me, Breezy!" he demanded.

They heard Annette's bedroom door open and then she was coming down the hall. "What's going on? Why are you yelling, King?" she asked entering the living room.

King got up from where he was sitting and grabbed Breezy by her arm. "I am not my ma and you are not going to get by with only telling me a part of the story! I want to know what happened and I want to know right now! If you don't tell me then you may as well get your stuff and go right back to your ma's house because I don't want anything else to do with you!" Of course he was bluffing but he knew that would make her talk.

She started bawling. "Please, King. I don't want anyone to get in trouble."

Annette tugged at King's arm. She too was sick of playing this game with Breezy but she felt like he was going about getting answers the wrong way. "Okay, son, that's enough. Let her go!"

King ignored her and kept his eyes on Breezy. "Talk!" he barked. He wasn't prepared for what she said next.

"He raped me," she whispered as she looked at him in his eyes.

His temper exploded. This was his best friend since he was little. He'd always felt like God places people in your path for a reason and he knew that He'd placed her in his so that he could protect her. Why else had he always been drawn to her? Always wanting to take care of her and protect her? Breezy was the sweetest girl he knew. Hearing her say that she'd been violated in such a way made him want to kill Terry.

He turned Breezy loose and punched the wall. His fist went through it, leaving a large hole in the wall.

"Calm down, King!" Annette warned looking at the damage that he'd just done to her wall and knowing that she was going to have to pay for it.

King went down the hall to his room and got his aluminum bat out of the closet. He could hear Annette yelling for Curtis to get up because she knew that once he got upset there was no calming him down. By the time King made it down the hallway Curtis was in the living room. He was a big guy who kind of resembled Ving Rhames.

"Give me the bat, boy. I know that you are upset but this isn't the way to handle it. Come on now, give me the bat."

"Man, no disrespect but go ahead on, Curtis, this ain't got nothing to do with you." He wasn't trying to listen to reason at this moment even if he was right.

"Yeah, it is my concern. I love your ma and I know how it would make her feel if you go out here and get yourself in some trouble. I also love you as if you were my own son and so I refuse to allow you to do something crazy. Tomorrow morning we can get up early and Breezy can go down to the social services and the police station and file a report. That is the best way to handle it. Not only that but it is the right way to handle it."

"Please, son, listen to what Curtis is saying to you," Annette pleaded, standing next to Curtis wearing a worried expression on her face.

"King, I will press charges. I promise. But I don't want you to get in any trouble," Breezy spoke up.

He looked at her and then looked away. It bothered him to look at her. He gave Curtis the bat and then went into his room and locked the door. He turned on the radio and went over to his weight bench and started to work out.

He lifted until he was tired and had calmed down. He got up, grabbed some shorts, and went into the bathroom and took a shower. When he was done he went into the kitchen to get a bottled water.

On his way back through the living room, Breezy stopped him. "Are you okay?" she asked sitting up on the sofa.

"When did it happen?" King asked ignoring her question.

"It happened the night I left here when you walked me halfway home."

"Where was your ma?"

"Passed out drunk in her bedroom."

"Was that the first time?"

"Yeah."

"Has he done it again?"

"No, he just rubbed his penis on my face the other day and that's when I told my ma."

He got upset all over again but this time kept it under control. Through clenched teeth, he said, "If you don't do what you said that you were gonna do in the morning I am going to kill that motherfucka, or by the time I am done with him he will wish that he was dead."

She nodded her head.

"Go in my room and get in the bed. I will take the sofa."

She got up and hugged him. "I am going to do what needs to be done. I promise," she told him.

He hugged her back. "You'd better." Holding her he felt something, something that he couldn't describe or explain but something that he knew he shouldn't be.

He tried to break their embrace but she held him tighter. "Thank you for being a good friend and being willing to stand up for me when I don't have the guts to stand up for myself."

"Girl, stop it, you know that I'm gonna always have your back."

She stood on her tiptoes and kissed him on the cheek and went to bed.

Long after Breezy had gone to bed, King lay awake thinking about Terry and praying that the law dealt with him before he had to.

# **Chapter Seven**

The next morning when King woke up Annette and Breezy were already gone. He called Annette's cell but got no answer. He went down the hall to her room and saw Curtis sitting on the side of the bed watching TV.

"Hey, Curtis, where my ma at?"

"She and Breezy went down to social services."

"Oh okay." He felt like he needed to apologize for the way he'd spoken to him the night before. "Sorry about last night. I was upset. I didn't mean any disrespect."

"Oh you're good. I understand how you felt. Honestly, I was proud of you for being willing to stand up for Breezy like a man. She is lucky to have a friend like you." Curtis smiled proudly at King. He was proud to say that he'd had a hand in raising such a smart young man, who didn't hesitate to stand up for what he knew was right.

"Yeah, Breezy is good people."

"I agree. She's a good girl, son."

King left Curtis to finish watching his TV show and went outside. He stood on the sidewalk looking out across the parking lot of the apartment complex. It was the beginning of May, the weather was nice, and it was warm out. He stood staring off into space thinking about how he'd felt the night before when he and Breezy had hugged. For some reason, it kept crossing his mind. He was deep in thought when he heard a female voice ask, "Is Breezy here?"

He looked to the left and saw Teresa. "Nah, she ain't here." He looked out across the parking lot, feeling annoyed by her presence and her nerve to walk up in his face asking about Breezy after the way she'd treated her the night before.

"Well do you know where she is?" she snapped not trying to hide the fact that she had an attitude. She knew that the little young punk standing in front of her didn't care for her and neither did his folks but she didn't give a damn. Breezy was her daughter and she could do whatever she wanted to her.

"Didn't you put her out for that sorry-ass boyfriend of yours?" King asked matter-of-factly. Normally he didn't disrespect anyone older than him because he'd been raised better than that but to him she didn't deserve any respect.

"You need to watch your damn mouth and stay in a child's place!"

He looked past her and saw Annette's car pull up.

Teresa turned and looked in the direction he was looking in. She saw Breezy sitting on the passenger side of Annette's car. "Never mind, I found her my damn self," she snapped.

Annette and Breezy got out of the car. Breezy walked up the sidewalk behind Annette scared to death.

"Breezy, baby, take my pocketbook and go on inside," Annette told her. Breezy was frozen with fear and just stood there. She didn't know what was about to go down.

"Go ahead, baby, you don't have any reason to be scared. She ain't gon' do nothing." Annette looked at Teresa and rolled her eyes. She was waiting for her to get out of line.

Teresa rolled her eyes right back and smacked her lips. "I came to get Breezy. Thanks for allowing her to stay with you but—"

"You need to go home because there are some visitors on the way to your house as we speak, and until the investigation is over I have temporary custody of Breezy."

Annette's words nearly knocked the wind out of Teresa. She didn't know what to say. "What damn investigation?"

"Oh don't play stupid! You been abusing this child and on top of that, you let that sorry man you have lying up in your house rape her! Bitch, that shit stops today! I'm going to ask you nicely to go home before I lose my cool and show my ass out here!" Annette took a step closer to Teresa.

"You little bitch!" Teresa lunged for Breezy.

Without thinking twice, when King saw Teresa lunge for Breezy he grabbed her and slung her across the ground. "Nah, not today, bitch! Not this day and not any other day! What the fuck are you mad at her for, because you don't know how to be a mother?" he barked.

Annette grabbed King. "That's enough, son. She's still a woman and I'm not raising a woman beater. You step back and let me handle this."

By now people were gathering around and starting to come out of their apartments to try to see what was going on. Teresa jumped up off the ground and went charging toward King with her fist drawn back. "You put your hands on the wrong bitch!" she screamed. She swung and hit him. The blow landed in his chest. Annette swung and hit her in the head and they started getting it in. Teresa had Annette down and was getting the best of her. Cheeks, the girl from next door, came out of nowhere and started fighting Teresa.

"Get off of her!" Breezy yelled. Regardless of what Teresa had done to her, she was still her mama and there was no way she was about to stand back and watch two people fight her at once. She started pushing her way through the crowd trying to get to her mama.

King grabbed her by her arm. "Yo, what the fuck is you doing? Why are you trying to defend that bitch? She needs to get her ass dragged!"

She snatched away from him and looked him dead in his eyes and screamed, "She's still my ma! What would you do if that was your ma?"

"Let them beat her motherfuckin' ass! That's what the fuck I would do!" he replied truthfully, growing angry at how dumb Breezy seemed to be.

She didn't respond. She ran over and started trying to break up the fight.

Cheeks pushed her so hard that she slid across the ground on her ass. "Move the fuck back, Breezy!"

"No, that's my ma you fighting!" She jumped back up and went back over to where they were. She was trying to untangle Annette's fingers from Teresa's hair. "Stop, Ms. Annette! You are hurting her!"

"Bitch, I told you to move!" Cheeks yelled at Breezy before grabbing her by her shirt and pulling her out of the way.

Breezy reacted without thinking and slapped the piss out of Cheeks. The lick sounded off so loud that everyone who was watching let out a gasp and Cheeks looked stunned, but that was only momentary. She snapped out of the daze that she was in and punched Breezy in her face. Blood shot everywhere.

"Oh shit!" somebody yelled. Breezy shocked everyone because, instead of cowardly backing down like she normally did, she was actually fighting back; and she wasn't no slouch with her hand either. She was giving Cheeks a run for her money.

Curtis came out of the apartment and started pushing his way through the crowd. He'd looked out the window and seen Annette fighting. When he reached the fight he reached down and grabbed Annette and began dragging her toward the apartment. "Bring yo' ass on here, woman. You are too old to be out here showing your ass fighting in the damn parking lot like some damn teenager." He huffed as they headed toward the house.

"She had no business putting her damn hands on my son!"

"Bitch, this ain't over!" Teresa yelled to Annette. One of the guys in the complex was holding on to her to prevent her from going after her.

"I ain't moving nowhere no time soon! Trust me, I ain't hard to find," Annette yelled back as Curtis continued to pull her toward the house.

"Come on in here." Curtis was beyond pissed because he felt like there was always a mature way to handle any situation. He was completely against two grown-ass women out in the parking lot fighting. To him that shit was for kids.

King and another guy broke Breezy and Cheeks apart.

"What the hell is going on out here this morning?" Teresa overhead a bystander in the crowd ask.

"Motherfuckers want to try to tell people how to raise their fucking kids!" Teresa snapped. "That's what's going on."

"You ain't raising her! You beating the fuck out of her and letting niggas do foul shit to her!" King corrected her.

"You need to mind your damn business and stay in a child's place because you don't know what Teresa Lee be doing!" She stated her first and last name like she was somebody important. "You just want her down here so you can lie up with her whenever you want to. Thinking somebody stupid! Talkin' about some gotdamn best friends! Best friends my ass! Bet she is your best friend when she down on her knees sucking your little dick!"

"You know you ain't shit out here degrading your own daughter in front of all these people." King looked down at Breezy. "And then you have the nerve to defend her ass! I'm done! You got me and my ma out here fighting over you because of how her and her punk-ass boyfriend have been treating you and then you turn around and fight for her. You won't even fight for your damn self. I have to fight for you!" he said beating on his chest to emphasize his point.

"She is my mama, King! I can't just stand here and see two people fighting her and not do anything about it!" Breezy defended her actions. She understood that he was upset but felt he should understand that no matter what Teresa did she would always be her mama. Nothing could change that.

King wasn't trying to hear what she was saying because, to him, her defending Teresa was stupid as hell. "If she saw two people fighting you, she wouldn't do shit!"

Breezy dropped her head because she knew in her heart that he was right.

"You don't know what the fuck I would do!" Teresa spoke up.

Annette came back out on the sidewalk. She'd calmed down now. "Breezy, from here on out, I am done and my son is done. Whatever goes on with you and your mama that is you all's business! Situations like this is how people end up hurt and all for nothing. I hate it for you because what really makes this shit so sad is that you love her unconditionally while she couldn't care less about you. I hope and pray one day she can return the love that you have for her but, again, that is you all's problem. Come in and get your things because I can't continue to try to help someone who is obviously confused as to whether they really want help." She looked at King holding on to Breezy. "King, turn her loose and come on in the house."

He let go of Breezy and walked down the sidewalk and stood in front of his apartment. He didn't feel like going inside. Breezy walked past him and went inside to gather the few things that she had there. King shook his head unable to believe how messed up in the head his best friend was. She couldn't have good sense to stand up for someone who treated her the way that Teresa had and would no doubt continue to.

Teresa stood down the sidewalk smoking on a Newport while she waited for Breezy to get her things. Truth was she wasn't that concerned about Breezy; she just wanted her at home so that no one would notice that she wasn't there and report it to social services. She couldn't risk her assistance getting cut off.

Breezy came back outside carrying the bags with her birthday gifts in them. She felt like she had just lost her best friend. She stopped in front King and tried explaining one last time but he held his hand up to stop her.

"I don't even want to hear it. Save that shit because I am done with you and I mean that!"

"What do you mean you are done?"

He could hear the hurt in her voice but he didn't care anything about that because he was hurt too. "Breezy, get out of my face. Better yet I'll get out of yours!" He turned and walked inside the house, slamming the door behind him.

# Chapter Eight

*Seven months later . . .*

Breezy stood over the sink washing the dishes with tears streaming down her face falling onto her water. Her life had gone from bad to worse over the past few months and she only had herself to blame for it. After everything that Teresa had done to her, she'd lied for her when social services came out to their house to investigate the things that she'd told them. She told them that she'd lied about everything. Then, not even two weeks later, Terry raped her again. He knew that no one, not even her, was going to do anything about it. So he started taking it whenever he wanted.

She stood over the sink crying now because her period hadn't come that month and she'd been throwing up for the past three weeks. She was scared and alone with no one to turn to. King still wasn't talking to her. He wouldn't even look at her. He and Vita were walking around school like they were fuckin' Jay-Z and Beyoncé. Nothing hurt her more than not having King in her life because he'd always been there. She missed being able to talk to him and having him there to help her through the rough times. Sometimes he didn't have to say anything at all; just having him there made it all better. She dried her hands and grabbed a paper towel to wipe her face, but it was no use because the tears just kept coming.

Teresa walked into the kitchen carrying two grocery bags. She tossed them on the counter. "Cook those pork chops, and make some gravy and mashed potatoes and corn," she ordered, noticing that Breezy was crying. She rolled her eyes and smacked her lips, not bothering to ask her what was wrong because she really didn't care to know. "Hurry up because I'm hungry." With that she walked out of the kitchen.

Breezy went to her room and got the MP3 player that King had given her a few years back. She put her earbuds in, went back into the kitchen and started to cook. Jennifer Hudson's "Where You At" poured from her earbuds and the words tugged at her heart. All she could think about was King because he'd always been there for her and she'd pushed him away. With that song on repeat, she moved around the kitchen singing and wiping down the counter. When she was done wiping the counters, she scrubbed the floor and then went into the living room to wait for the floor to dry.

She flopped down on the sofa and picked up a magazine from the table and began thumbing through it looking at the pictures of all the celebrities dressed in the latest fashions. She came across an article written by a young female author, who'd recently published her first book of poetry. In the article the young woman spoke about a rough childhood that included being a victim of molestation and physical abuse. She said she was doing the article to encourage and give hope to other young women/men who may be in a similar situation. She wanted them to know that they didn't have to be victims forever and that it was up to them whether they chose to take control of their lives and not remain victims forever.

Breezy sat there reading the article with tears still rolling down her face. She didn't want to be a victim forever and she didn't want to continue to live this way. She knew in her heart that she was pregnant and she didn't want to bring a child into the hell that she lived in. She knew that she needed to do something about her situation but she didn't know how or where to begin. She closed the magazine and laid it back down on the coffee table, thinking that one day she would like to tell the story of how she overcame her horrible childhood.

"Lord, I need you to make a way," she mumbled before walking into the kitchen to check on the food. She opened the oven to peek inside and check the pork chops. The aroma of the food invaded her nostrils. She slammed the oven door and ran down the hallway to the bathroom nearly knocking Teresa down on her way.

"Watch where the fuck you are going!" Teresa yelled after her as she continued on her way down the hallway. "You almost knocked me down!"

Leaning over the toilet, Breezy continued to gag even after she had nothing left in her stomach to throw up. She stood over the toilet for a few extra minutes just to make sure that she wasn't going to throw up anymore before washing her hands and rinsing her mouth out. She turned off the bathroom light and went back into the kitchen to finish up dinner.

Teresa was sitting at the table. "You sure been throwing up a lot." She eyed Breezy, her nostrils flared.

"I think I may have a stomach virus," Breezy lied.

"Humph." Teresa let out a chuckle. "You'd better hope so because ain't no babies coming up in here. So whoever you been lying up with you'd better tell him to take yo' ass and that little motherfucker in."

Breezy didn't reply; she just continued what she was doing. She set a pot of water on the stove for the mashed potatoes.

"You can stand there and act like you don't hear me all you want, but you'd better hear me because ain't nobody had no stomach virus that damn long! Pass me a beer out the refrigerator."

Breezy opened the refrigerator and handed her a beer. She still felt a little bit nauseated and was beginning to sweat from the heat in the kitchen. She just felt bad and wanted to lie down but she knew that if she didn't finish cooking all hell would break loose.

Teresa continued as she sipped her beer. "I don't even want your ass here half of the fucking time! You know damn well I don't want some crying-ass baby in here!"

They heard the front door slam and then Terry yell, "Yo, yo, yo! Where everybody at?"

"In the kitchen, baby," Teresa replied, her eyes still locked on Breezy. She didn't like her around Terry at all and whenever they were all in the same room she kept a close eye on Breezy.

Terry walked into the kitchen with a bottle of Henny in one hand and a plastic red cup in the other. "Damn something sure smells good. I'm hungrier than a motherfucker."

"The food should be done in a little while," Teresa looked up at him and announced like she had cooked something. "I picked up your favorite, pork chops."

"Yeah, I'm going to fuck them mofo's up, too." He sat down at the table and poured Teresa a shot of Henny in the red cup that he'd been holding and handed it to her.

She took the cup from his hand, taking a sip before placing the cup on the table. "You will never guess what," she told him.

"Woman, I'm too fucked up to guess. What is it?"

"I think hot ass done went and got herself pregnant. I told her that she had better take that little motherfucker and her own ass wherever she got pregnant at."

Terry laughed, knowing that if Breezy was pregnant it was his. He laughed because he had Teresa right where he wanted her, believing whatever he told her. "Humph, I know that's right. I told you that she was hot in the ass. Out there slangin' pussy every which way."

Breezy had taken all that she could. Without turning around, she stated through clenched teeth, "Well I guess me and my baby will be staying right here then since this is where my hot ass got pregnant at! Ain't that right, Terry?"

"What?" he asked like he ain't hear what she'd said.

"What did you say?" Teresa asked.

Breezy gripped the handle of the pot of water that had been boiling on the stove and when she turned around she dashed all of it in Terry's face. "You heard what the fuck I said!" Terry fell from his chair onto the floor and yelled out in pain. His skin felt like it was on fire. Breezy wasn't done though.

Before Teresa had a chance to react she blessed her ass right in the temple with that same hot-ass pot. She fell back out of the chair, knocked out cold. Terry was still screaming and holding his face. Breezy grabbed the Henny bottle off the table and started wearing his ass out with it. After getting a few good licks in, she dropped the bottle and ran down the hall. She grabbed her book bag and then ran out of the house. She didn't stop running until she was at King's door.

She banged on the door. "Open the door, King! King . . . somebody . . . please open up!"

Annette heard all of the banging and screaming and ran to the door. She snatched it open with King right on her heels. Breezy stood there with blood all over her clothes. "What in the world is going on? Breezy, what are you doing here and where did all that blood come from? Are you hurt?" She started checking her over trying to see if she was okay.

Breezy was out of breath. "I . . . am . . . fine," she assured her, fighting to catch her breath. "Can I . . . come in?"

Annette helped her inside. "What happened, baby?"

"I just got tired. I hit my ma with a pot and I threw some hot water on Terry. I just couldn't take it no more, Ms. Annette," Breezy cried. "I'm tired. I can't do it anymore."

King sucked his teeth, unconvinced and not buying her whole "tired" act. "Man, take that drama right back down the street! Don't nobody want to hear that mess. You say that today and tomorrow you will be right back down there licking their wounds!" he snapped. "Why did you even come here?"

"Okay, King, that is enough! This is my house!" Annette set him straight. She didn't approve of him talking to Breezy the way that he was. She understood him not believing Breezy and not wanting to deal with her drama anymore but there was no way she would allow him to be cruel and disrespectful in front of her. The child looked like she'd been through enough. "You don't know what she will do tomorrow. Everybody has a breaking point and just maybe this time she has reached hers. Yes, I was upset with her also and I know that I said I wasn't getting involved again but there is no way I can just turn her away! You may be acting all hard and stubborn but you know just as well as I do that deep down you still love her to death and if something were to happen to her and we didn't try to help it would nearly kill you. You and Breezy have been friends for as long as I can remember so it's time to let the dumb shit go and be here for your friend. Our friends don't always make the decisions that we want them to and while we may get mad with them we are still supposed to have their back at the end of the day!"

"Man, whatever, I did have her back!" He stormed out, slamming the door.

"Lord, please keep me from putting my foot in that boy's ass!" Annette said after he was gone. She turned her attention back to Breezy. "Let's get you cleaned up and then you can tell me all about what happened and we can figure out what to do next." She went down the hall and got Breezy a shirt and a pair of shorts to sleep in. "Here you go. Take these and go into the bathroom and get cleaned up."

"Thank you." Breezy took the clothes from her hand and went into the bathroom. She took a quick shower, got out, and slipped on the clothes that Annette had given her. When she went back into the living room, Annette was sitting on the sofa waiting for her.

"I fixed you a plate; it's in the kitchen," she informed her. "Come on." They went into the kitchen. There was a plate with spaghetti, corn on the cob, and garlic bread sitting on the table.

"Thanks, Ms. Annette, I really appreciate this. It looks so good," Breezy told her, trying her best not to puke. The smell of the garlic was making her nauseated.

Annette looked at her strangely. "Baby, are you okay? You don't look so good."

Instead of responding, she made a dash for the bathroom and threw up. When she was done, she rinsed her mouth out and washed her face again before returning to the living room.

Annette looked really concerned. "What's the matter, Breezy? Do you have a virus or something?" Before Breezy could respond she added, "It could just be your nerves, you know, by you being upset and all. If you want we could just talk in the morning and I could let you get some rest."

"No, ma'am, I'm fine. We can talk tonight. Besides, this has been going on for the past three weeks and I haven't had a period so I am pretty sure it's not a virus or nerves." She was tired of keeping everything bottled up inside. She was ready to tell everything and stop carrying around the weight of so many secrets.

Annette's hand went up over her chest, across her heart. "Oh my goodness, Breezy. Baby, what have you done? I know that you know better than to be messing with these little boys without using protection."

"I wasn't out messing with any boys. Terry—"

Annette jumped to her feet, cutting her off. "No, that sorry motherfucker didn't! I am going to see to it that his ass is put underneath the fucking jail!"

"I will probably be the one going to jail," Breezy blurted.

Annette looked at her confused. Her hands were on her small hips. "What do you mean? No one is going to lock you up! His sorry ass raped you!"

"No, I'm not talking about for that." Breezy nervously fidgeted with the end of her shirt. "I threw a pot of boiling hot water in Terry's face, and I hit him a few times with a bottle of Hennessy."

Annette threw her head back and burst into laughter. "It's about damn time! Good enough for his ass! You should've killed him!" She continued to laugh.

"There's more. I hit my ma with the pot. I think that I knocked her out because she fell to the floor and just lay there."

"Humph, good you didn't leave that ho out. Baby, I know that's your mama but she deserves more than that. Don't you even worry about that mess; they ain't gone send no cops after you. You want to know why?"

"Why?" Breezy asked curious and anxious to hear.

"Because they know that if y'all have to go to court and you tell about how Terry has been raping you and she did nothing about it even after you told her, the both of them will be up shit creek without a paddle."

Breezy thought about what Annette was saying and she did have a point. They sat down and talked for a little while longer before Annette announced that she was going to bed. She also let Breezy know that she would be taking her to the clinic the next morning.

# Chapter Nine

When King pulled up in front of Vita's house, he parked on the side of the street and got out of the car. He'd called to let her know that he was coming. As he walked up the driveway he saw the front door open and her standing in it wearing a huge smile.

"Hey, boo," Vita greeted him once he made it to the door. She was wearing a little strapless dress that she'd put on just before he got there.

"Hey," he replied dryly.

"What's wrong, bae?" She took his hand and led him inside, over to the sofa. He sat down and she sat on his lap, caressing the side of his face with her small hand. She kissed him softly on the lips. "Tell me what the matter is."

"Nothing really, just some ol' bullshit." He wasn't sure if he could tell her Breezy's business, so he hesitated.

"Well what is nothing really? I'm your girl; you can tell me," Vita pressed already feeling that it must have something to do with Breezy judging by his hesitation to spit it out.

King let out a frustrated sigh and ran his hand over Vita's thigh. He needed to get out how he was feeling so he took a deep breath and began. "Breezy came over, before I left, crying and upset about something that her ma had done to her. Normally, I would be there for her but after the last time that me and my ma got involved and she went running right back, I am done with that shit! My ma over there falling for it all over again. I just can't. She ain't gon' do nothing but run right back!"

The jealousy that Vita felt toward King and Breezy's relationship wouldn't allow her to tell him that, regardless, he should be there for his friend. She'd been enjoying their separation because it made her feel secure. She'd seen the way that King looked at Breezy and vice versa; the two of them could deny it all they wanted but she knew that there was something more between them than friendship. She'd finally gotten King and there was no way she was about to lose him to some dirty, non-factor bitch like Breezy.

"Don't let that mess upset you. Just continue to do what you have been doing; ignore her." She paused and then continued. "I mean I'm not trying to be all up in you all's business but I have heard a few things about her being abused by her mama and her mama's boyfriend. I just be thinking that Breezy might be putting on a little bit because if her ma was so mean to her then why don't she tell somebody and get herself some help?"

He didn't have an answer to that question because that was something that he didn't understand himself. "I don't know," he replied, not wanting to discuss Breezy anymore. He had something else in mind. "Come on; let's go upstairs to your room."

A big grin spread across Vita's lips as she hopped to her feet. They went upstairs to her room. Within seconds they were both naked underneath the covers and King was sucking on her big, juicy titties. "Damn, I ain't got no latex. You got one?"

"Nah, but I'm on the shot so you are good," she told him.

He stopped giving her breasts a tongue bath for a second and looked up at her. "Vita, I ain't trying to have no babies," he warned seriously.

"Boy, ain't nobody trying to baby-trap you! I don't want no babies either," she said with an attitude.

"I'm going to ask you to calm your ass down!" he said referring to her attitude before he climbed on top of her positioning himself between her legs and entering her.

Vita smiled inwardly as he moved in and out of her moaning and groaning telling her how good she felt. *That's right, baby, enjoy this pussy because you ain't going nowhere.* She wrapped her legs around his waist and began to move in sync with his movements.

When they were done, King got dressed and kissed Vita, telling her that he would holla at her later.

When he got home he saw a cover on the sofa but didn't see Breezy. He prayed that she wasn't in his room in his bed because she was most definitely going to get up out of there. He went in his room and checked but he didn't see her. "Her ass probably done snuck back down the street to her ma's house," he mumbled shaking his head. He'd worked up an appetite with Vita so he went into the kitchen to get a plate of spaghetti. When he walked into the kitchen, Breezy was at the table writing something and listening to her MP3 player. He walked over to the stove and fixed his plate. After heating his food he went into the living room so that he could watch TV while he ate his food and because he didn't want to sit in the kitchen with Breezy.

The entire time that King was in the kitchen, Breezy intentionally kept her head down writing. She knew that he didn't want to be bothered with her and she understood.

King was getting into a rerun of *Martin* when he heard, "'You said that when the storm came you'd be there with your umbrella to block the rain. And you said you'd protect me from heartache pain lies loneliness and misery. You said you'd tear down the walls that were in the way you promised things would be okay. And I stood there in the freezing cold and I waited for you but you never showed. Where you at? Ooh, where you at? Boy, you said you would be here for me . . .'"

His food got stuck in his throat and wouldn't move. Breezy had the voice of an angel and he'd always loved hearing her sing. For some reason this time it felt like she was singing directly to him though. He got up to carry his plate in the kitchen because his appetite was gone. Breezy had stopped writing and her head was resting in her hands as she sang the words of Jennifer Hudson's "Where You At." He saw the tears hitting the table and could hear the pain in her voice as she sang.

As much as he wanted to give in at that moment, he just couldn't allow himself to get wrapped up in her bullshit again. He left out of the kitchen and went into his room, locking the door. He lay back on the bed in the dark and tried to go to sleep but kept hearing Breezy sing the words to that song over and over in his head.

# Chapter Ten

Annette and Breezy got up bright and early the next morning. Annette called in to work and let them know that she wouldn't be in. After getting dressed, Breezy helped Annette fix breakfast so that they could hurry up and get going. She had a lot of things planned to get taken care of that day and wanted to get them all done. She needed to cram everything into this day because she didn't want to be missing any more days out of school.

"Breezy, fix some scrambled eggs," Annette told her.

"No prob." She walked over to the refrigerator and took out the eggs. When she turned around, King was standing in the doorway of the kitchen dressed in all black, looking good enough to eat. She noticed that he'd put on a few pounds in the past seven months and in all the right places. The eggs slipped from her fingers and crashed onto the floor. She hurriedly bent down and picked up the carton and checked to see if any of them were broken. Only one was.

"Are you okay, Breezy?" Annette asked worried that she may be getting sick to her stomach from the smell of the food.

"Yes, ma'am," Breezy answered glancing at King once more before looking over at Annette.

"Good morning, ma." King walked over to Annette and kissed her on her cheek.

"Morning, baby," she responded.

Curtis walked into the kitchen and spoke, "Good morning."

Everybody spoke it back. Breezy went over to the stove and got started on the eggs. When everything was done, she and Annette served breakfast. She didn't even attempt to fix herself a plate. She just grabbed a glass of juice.

"Ummm, Ms. Thang, get a plate and fix you something to eat. You are already walking around here looking like a bag of bones," Annette told Breezy, after taking notice of the fact that she didn't have a plate.

"I don't want anything."

"I didn't ask you if *you* wanted anything. You need to eat," she said sternly giving her a knowing look.

Breezy got a plate and put some eggs on it. She looked across the table and Annette was looking like she might slap her so she put a piece of turkey sausage on the plate also. She hadn't even taken four bites when she felt it start to come back up.

She jumped from the table but didn't make it to the bathroom. All of what she had eaten came back up all over the kitchen floor.

Annette jumped up, grabbed some paper towels and wet them and handed them to her to wipe her face.

"I'm gonna get that up. I'm sorry," Breezy apologized still bent at the waist waiting to see if her food was done coming back up.

"I'll get it, baby. You go and get yourself together. You need some crackers or something to nibble on. Remind me while we are out to get you some." Annette now felt bad for forcing her to eat.

Breezy went into the living room and lay on the sofa. She heard Curtis tell Annette not to worry about cleaning up my vomit, that he would get it and for her to just make sure that she was okay. She was so thankful for them.

"Yo, ma, what's up with Breezy?" King asked.

"She's just a little sick that's all," Annette replied. "Why don't you stop acting foolish and ask her yourself? She has been through a lot and could really use her best friend right now."

"Ma, don't start."

"Don't start what? Telling you to act your age and not your shoe size? You are mad because she went back and I can understand that but now she is here asking for our help and you are still upset. Why?"

"Yeah, you right, she is here asking for help just like the last time when she made us both look stupid. Well this time she'll only be making you look stupid."

"First of all, watch your damn mouth! Secondly, she won't be making me look like anything. That child needs somebody and I am going to do whatever I can for her! Third, no one has to make your ass look stupid; you are doing a great job of that on your own running around here behind that fast-ass girl Vita. You need to open your eyes and see that her little hot ass ain't all over you for nothing. You have a chance of playing pro basketball when you finish school. She's seeing dollar signs! If you are having sex, which I believe that you are, you'd better be using protection!" After saying what she had to say, she walked out of the kitchen and went into the living room to check on Breezy. "Get up and go brush your teeth so I can get you to the doctor."

On her way to the bathroom, Breezy passed King. He gave her an evil look and kept it moving. She heard the front door slam a few seconds later as she entered the bathroom to brush her teeth.

At the clinic they confirmed what Breezy already knew. She was seven weeks pregnant. She didn't cry when she received the news because she'd done enough crying. Tears weren't gonna help her situation. She needed to get on some grown-woman type shit.

After leaving the clinic, Annette asked, "So do you know what you want to do? This is your decision. Curtis and I will help you in any way that we can."

"I am going to keep my baby and be the mother my mother never was. I know that it won't be easy but life isn't easy and so with that being said I am going to do what I have to do. Starting right now. Will you take me back to that salon that you took me to for my birthday?'

Annette looked confused. "Sure. Why are we going there?"

"I have some business that I need to take care of."

"Okay." They drove to Angel's Salon in silence, both consumed by their own thoughts.

When they arrived, Breezy got out of the car and went inside. The same receptionist was at the front desk. "Good morning and welcome to Angel's. How can I help you?"

"Hello, um, I was looking for Blue."

"I apologize but she's not working this week. She's on vacation. Is there something that I could help you with?" She offered her hand and Breezy shook it. "My name is Kendra Felton and I am co-owner of this salon."

Breezy took a deep breath. "Yes, ma'am, actually I was wondering if you all needed a shampoo girl?" She prayed silently for her to say yes.

"Well to be honest we really don't at the moment," Kendra replied giving her a sympathetic look. "Sorry."

Breezy couldn't hide her disappointment. "I understand." She turned to leave with her head hung low.

Something inside of Kendra urged her to stop the girl. She knew that it had to have taken a lot of courage for her to walk in and ask her for a job. "Hold up, ummm . . ."

"Brionna." Breezy turned back around. "My name is Brionna."

"Brionna, let me go and talk to my business partner Tamara and see what she says. Wait right here." Kendra disappeared for a few minutes and then returned with another woman.

"Hello, Brionna, I hear that you are looking for a job. I am Tamara Byrd," the woman introduced herself, offering her hand for Breezy to shake. Breezy accepted it and shook her hand. "Now to be honest, we really don't need anyone but Kendra told me that you looked like you really needed this job."

Breezy interrupted her. "Yes, ma'am, I really do." She decided to just lay all of her cards out on the table. "I've had it hard all my life and I have never had anything given to me except for a hard time. I need this job more than you know. This job is the first step to me bettering myself, and no longer being anyone's victim." She felt like she may have said too much but she thought, *oh well I need them to know just how bad I need this.*

Kendra had tears in her eyes. "Baby girl, do you go to school?"

"Yes, ma'am."

"Okay well, can you work from four to nine?"

"Yes, ma'am!" Breezy replied, unable to hide her excitement.

"Tamara, is that cool with you?" Kendra looked at her business partner and asked.

"It sure is but only under one condition."

"Anything," Breezy replied excitedly.

"Well actually two conditions. The first being that you report to work on time every day."

"Absolutely."

"The second being that you sit your little butt in one of those chairs and let me do something to that hair. You have to look like an angel to work in here, honey!" she said snapping her fingers.

Kendra and Breezy both laughed. "Okay, let me go tell my ride."

Breezy ran outside to the car. Annette rolled down her window. "Child, what are you so happy about and why are you not getting your butt in this car?"

Breezy was so excited that she was nearly scream-ing. "I got a job!" She jumped up and down.

"What? You go, girl!" She got out of the car and wrapped her arms around her. "I am so proud of you!"

"Thank you. Ms. Tamara is about to do my hair. She says I have to look like an angel to work here!" Breezy laughed.

"Awww snap. Well, I have to run in Walmart and you know that could possibly take hours. How much is she charging for your hair?"

"I think it's free."

"Well here take this." Annette handed Breezy three twenty dollar bills. "Just in case."

"Thank you."

She turned to get in the car and then stopped. "I'm really proud of you and just so you'll know, you are already a better mother than Teresa." She hugged her again before getting in the car and leaving.

Breezy went back inside and Tamara hooked her hair up. She gave her a perm and then sewed some deep wave hair in. Breezy looked in the mirror and was very pleased with her look. For the second time in her life, she felt beautiful.

She sat and talked with the ladies until Annette returned. When she got in the car it looked like Annette had bought the entire store. "Dag, Ms. Annette, you went crazy didn't you?" Breezy asked looking in the back seat at all of the bags.

"Nah, but I knew that you were going to need some clothes and so I bought you some things. I also see that you love to write so I got you some notebooks and pens. Just trying to help all that I can."

"Thank you so much."

"I also got you some prenatal vitamins and those crackers." She reached over and touched Breezy's stomach. "We are going to get through this together. I will be right here by your side, I promise."

"Thank you, Ms. Annette. I could never thank you enough."

"There's no need to. I am just doing what God has put in my heart for me to do. That is all."

# Chapter Eleven

After putting away everything that Annette had bought, Breezy lay down on the sofa to take a nap. A few hours later, she was awakened by King shaking her roughly. "Breezy, wake up! Wake up!" She opened her eyes but closed them back. "Breezy!"

"What?" she whined feeling completely drained. The pregnancy was draining all of her energy.

"What the hell are these?" He was shaking the bottle of prenatal vitamins that he'd found lying in the hallway. They'd fallen out of the bag when Breezy and Annette had put the stuff away but neither of them had noticed. Those pills were telling him something that he didn't want to believe and something that he didn't think he could ever accept.

Breezy looked up at him still half asleep. He reached down and pulled her up by her arms. "Answer me, gotdamn! What the fuck are these?" He held them so that she could see.

She wiped sleep from her eyes and focused on the bottle. When she realized what he was holding, her eyes got big as saucers. She hadn't wanted him to find out so soon. She'd known that she couldn't hide it forever but things were already bad between them and she knew this information would only make it worse. "T . . . they are p . . . prenatal vitamins," she stuttered.

King lost it and pushed her back on the sofa. "Are you telling me that you are fucking pregnant?" he screamed down at her. He was so mad he could have literally killed her with his bare hands. There were indescribable emotions running throughout his body at that moment. Emotions that he didn't even understand. The only thing going through his mind was that this shit could've been prevented.

"Calm down, King," Breezy pleaded. Her eyes filled with tears as she cowered back against the sofa as far as she could go. She'd never seen him this way before and feared that he might hit her. "Please don't do this."

He threw the bottle of pills across the room. The bottle crashed against the wall. The top popped off and pills spilled everywhere. Breezy had her head down with her arms covering her head. "Breezy, I am going to ask you one more time before I tear this whole entire room down with your ass! Are you pregnant?"

Annette heard King yelling and came to see what was going on. *Lord, if it isn't one thing, it's another.* She made her way into the living room.

She saw Breezy crouched down with her arms over her head and King standing over her. "What in the world is going on in here?" She wiped sleep from her eyes; she'd been taking a nap as well. Curtis was right behind her.

"Well? I'm waiting," he told Breezy not paying Annette or Curtis any attention. He needed to hear the words from Breezy's lips to believe what he already knew to be true.

"King, why are you asking me a question that you already know the answer to?"

"Answer me."

"Yes. Yes, I'm pregnant, King, but it isn't my—"

He snatched her up off the sofa by her boney arms and began shaking the shit out of her. "Yes, it is your fault! It is, Breezy! You were the one who chose to go back after he'd already raped you once! You made that decision! You! Not your ma! Not Terry but you!"

Curtis grabbed him. "That's enough! Now take your hands off of her. I'm not playing with you, King."

Without thinking King snatched away and pushed him causing Curtis to stumble back into the wall. "Get your hands off of me, nigga!"

Curtis got his balance and charged toward King. He was about to put an ass whooping on him that he felt was long overdue. King's attitude and temper had become too much and there was no way he was going to allow a child he'd raised to disrespect him and be putting his hands on him. He'd done way too much for King to accept that type of treatment.

Annette saw what was about to take place and rushed between them. "Curtis . . ." She placed her hand on his chest. "Baby, calm down, let me handle this."

"Nah, fuck that." Curtis knocked her hand off of his. "He got me fucked up. I will beat the brakes off of his little punk ass! Ain't no child that I raised gon' be putting their damn hands on me."

"I understand that but please let me handle this."

Curtis passed Annette and said to King. "You are lucky that I love your mama as much as I do because if I didn't somebody would be calling the paramedics in here for your ass today."

"Man—"

That was the only word that King was able to get out of his mouth before Annette turned around and smacked the rest of them from his memory. She slapped him so hard that it took him a few seconds to realize what had happened.

"Ma!"

She slapped him again and then walked up closer in his face.

"What are you going to do?" she asked, her eyes locked on his daring him to say the wrong thing.

"Huh? What are you going to do?" she repeated not giving him the chance to reply. "Boy, have you lost your mind? After all that this man has done for you and me. You have the audacity to stand here and dis-respect him?" King looked the other way and Annette reached up and jerked his face back around so that he was looking at her. "No, you look at me when I am talking to you. I don't know what your problem is and I don't care but that will never happen again. Do you understand me?

"Yes, ma'am," he mumbled.

"Now tell Curtis that you are sorry."

He looked at Curtis. "I apologize."

"You and I need to talk man to man and then you can apologize. I'll be outside when you are ready to talk." He turned to walk away but then stopped. "Let me just say this before I go. I don't care how upset you get; don't you ever let me see you put your hands on another woman, because you weren't raised that way! You have never seen me put my hands on your mother. Do you know why? Because a real man knows that his hands don't belong on a woman." He was so upset and disappointed with King that he could barely stand the sight of him. He walked outside to try to cool down some. He felt that the fresh air might help to clear his head some before he spoke to him.

\*\*\*

Curtis was sitting on the sidewalk watching two little boys wrestle when King walked outside. King took a seat next to him but didn't say anything. For a few minutes they were both silent just watching the kids play. Both of their minds were in overdrive. King was trying to think of what to say and also thinking about Breezy. Curtis was remembering when King was the size of the two little boys. He realized that he wasn't a baby anymore and that he'd grown up. He tried to place himself in his shoes and remember how hotheaded he'd been at his age, dealing with puberty, girls, and becoming a man. He knew that a lot of King's behavior came from the fact that his hormones were all over the place as he made the transition from a boy to a man. He also knew that there were a lot of different emotions consuming him when it came to Breezy. Emotions that he didn't understand, which caused him to react the way that he did when it came to her. He loved that girl so much that it was nearly driving him crazy and he didn't even realize it.

Curtis chuckled at his thoughts.

Hearing Curtis chuckle and seeing a slight smirk on his lips confused King but it also gave him the green light to speak. "Listen, Pops, I apologize for pushing you and disrespecting you."

Just that quickly the smirk disappeared. "Just don't let that shit happen again because next time I'm busting your ass," Curtis stated in a tone that told King that he meant business.

"I understand, Pops." King shook his head and ran his hand over his head. "I don't know what got into me. I just lost it when Breezy confirmed that she was pregnant."

"You love her," Curtis stated, still watching the kids.

King looked at him because he wasn't sure if he'd just heard him correctly. "Come again?"

Curtis looked at him for the first time since he'd been sitting next to him. "I said you love her. You always have but now it's different. You may not realize how much you love her but an old head like myself can see it bright as day. As a matter of fact I saw it years ago."

"Pops, you trippin'. I mean, yes, I do love her, I guess because we were friends for so long; but it's not like girlfriend-boyfriend type of love."

Curtis started to laugh.

"What's so funny?"

"You. A blind man could see that what you feel for that girl is more than some best friend shit. Look at how you are over her. You will rip somebody's head off over her, even now when you claim that you can't stand her. The anger that I saw in you just now isn't what you see in someone who only loves someone as a best friend."

"Yes, it is. I mean how else was I supposed to react?"

"You should definitely be mad but not like how you were."

"I have a girl, Pops, in case you haven't noticed."

"Humph. Yeah, one that I hope you are using protection with." Curtis raised an eyebrow at him and King dropped his head. "Son, girls like Vita come and go but girls like Breezy will be there when the world turns its back on you. Vita is one of those people who are only in your life for a season."

"Huh?"

"I mean that she ain't the type a man would settle down with but at your age that doesn't matter. You are only seventeen. You have awhile before you even think about settling down." He stood up and brushed the dirt from his pants. "Word of advice. Put your pride to the side and be there for Breezy. She needs you and if you don't stop acting like an ass you may push her away. I mean, imagine how she feels having to carry a child by a man who sexually abused her. This baby will be a daily reminder of what she has been through. If you ask me she is a strong-ass woman already and is going to make some man very happy one day." He winked his eye at King and patted him on the head. "If you play your cards right it could be you."

After Curtis had gone inside, King sat outside for a while just thinking. He wasn't ready to go back in yet. His phone rang; it was Vita. He ignored it because he didn't feel like talking at the moment.

When he finally did decide to go inside the house it had gotten dark outside. He didn't see Breezy on the sofa so he walked down the hall toward his room. She was coming out of the bathroom drying her hands. When she saw him she jumped. That made him feel like shit.

"I ain't gonna hit you. I'm sorry about earlier. I just need some time that's all. I'm hurt, Breezy," he admitted. "I've always been protective over you. When no one else was there I was. Holding you when you cry, fighting anybody who looked at you wrong. Your problems have always been mine because I made them mine."

"When you left that day with your ma that cut me deep because I was thinking that you were going to stay here so that you wouldn't have to go through that stuff no more. Then you went back and look what happens. You are carrying his child. I can't describe to you how that makes me feel knowing that nigga was touching you, hurting you, and taking advantage of you. Not only that but that sorry-ass faggot had the nerve to plant his seed inside of you." He was mad all over again. "I just need time, Breezy." He walked off shaking his head.

He went in his room and lay down on the bed in the dark. As he lay there, Breezy's voice started to play in his head again singing that song and only one part kept playing over and over. *"Boy, you said you would be here for me . . ."*

He jumped to his feet and turned on the light, walking over to the dresser. He rummaged through his drawers and pulled out a dark pair of sweats and a dark shirt. He hurriedly changed and left his room. He needed to take care of something. As he passed through the living room, he looked at Breezy who was sitting on the sofa eating some crackers. "You're right. I did say that and I meant it."

She looked at him confused but he didn't bother to give her any explanation. He pulled his hoodie over his head and walked out the door. Every step he took toward his destination his anger grew. When he reached the house the porch light was on. He walked up to the door and knocked.

Teresa was laid back on the sofa when she heard a knock at the door. "Who is it?" she yelled.

"It's King."

*What in the fuck does he want?* she wondered, making her way to the door. She snatched it open. "Hey, Breezy ain't—"

King pushed her so hard that she went sliding across the floor and he stepped over her. "I'm not here to see you," he growled and headed down the hallway in search of Terry.

"Yo, who that at the door, Teresa?" Terry yelled, laid back on the bed propped up on a pillow in only a pair of boxers.

"I'm who was at the door, you nasty-ass piece of shit!" King announced as he barged into the room.

Terry tried to get up off the bed but he wasn't quick enough. King jumped on the bed and started wearing his ass out. He beat him until he was unconscious. The next thing he knew two police officers were there dragging him off of Terry and cuffing him.

# Chapter Twelve

Breezy was curled up under the covers, knocked out when a sharp pain in her stomach woke her up. She tried to get up but the pain was nearly unbearable. She waited for a few minutes and then tried to stand again. This time she stood up but the cramping was so bad that she couldn't walk. She screamed for Annette and kept screaming until she heard her coming down the hallway.

"What is it?" Annette asked, her heart beating rapidly in her chest.

"My stomach hurts really bad."

Annette saw dark liquid running down Breezy's legs. A strange look covered her face. "Is that blood running down your leg? Oh my goodness, we have to get you to the hospital." She ran to her room and threw on some clothes.

Breezy grabbed the blanket from the sofa and wrapped it around herself. She felt sort of embarrassed but was in so much pain that the embarrassment quickly disappeared.

Annette came back with the phone pressed against her ear. "Yes, sir, apartment 117G. Please get someone out here as quickly as possible, please."

Curtis came down the hall carrying a foldout chair. "Here you go. Keep that blanket wrapped around you and sit down right here," he told Breezy.

"Thank you." She was scared to death. She'd never been through anything like this and didn't know what to expect. She knew that bleeding couldn't be a sign of anything good. So she began to pray silently. *Lord, I have a feeling that I am about to lose my baby or I already have. I know that you don't make any mistakes and so I won't question why. All I ask is that you help to ease the pain that I am feeling for losing someone I never had a chance to meet. I know that I should probably be happy right now because it was Terry's baby but I'm not because it was also my baby. I know that if no one else understands how I feel you do. So as you have helped me through so many things before, I ask that you will please wrap your loving arms around me and also bring me through this. Oh and please take care of my baby until I join him or her in your Kingdom. In Jesus' name, I pray, amen.*

The phone rang. "Maybe that's the ambulance, baby." Annette told Breezy, touching her on her leg. She pressed the send button to answer the phone. On the other end, an officer explained to her that they had King in custody for assault and battery. She went down the hall and checked King's bedroom to be sure that they had the right person because to her understanding King was in his room asleep. She opened the door and turned on the light. Hurt was what she felt as she stood there staring at her son's empty bed. "I will be there as soon as I can," she told the officer, feeling defeated. She felt like between Breezy and King she couldn't catch a break for nothing.

Breezy was in a lot of pain but she could tell by the sound of Annette's voice that something was really wrong. Annette walked back into the room with tears in her eyes. "Lord, I don't know how much more of this I can take."

"What's wrong with King?" Breezy fought through her pain to ask.

"Lord, have mercy; help me." Annette paced back and forth. "Lord, I can't handle all of this at once. I am only one person."

Curtis stood up and crossed the room to where Annette was. He stopped her from pacing and held on to her. "Baby, what's going on?"

"I just got a call that King is in jail for assault and battery!"

"What in the hell?" Curtis was shocked to hear the news about King, especially after he'd just talked to him earlier. "Listen, I'll go with Breezy; you go and take care of King."

"I don't even know if I have the money to get him out with." Annette ran her fingers through her hair.

"How much is his bond?"

"I don't know."

"Well it doesn't matter what it is. Get it from our joint account."

"I'll pay—"

"Annette, that's my son too. Now go and get our baby and bring him home." He kissed her. "Calm down, baby. Everything is going to be okay. I got you, like always."

Annette kissed him again. "I love you."

"I love you too. Now go and get our boy."

Annette couldn't describe how thankful she was to have Curtis. He was a good man. She let Breezy know that she would come to check on her as soon as she got King, and then left.

A few minutes later the ambulance arrived. Curtis was right by Breezy's side. When they arrived at the hospital the doctors asked a million questions. They tried to reach Teresa but no one was answering the house phone. They went ahead and gave Breezy the medical attention that she needed. She had to have a D&C done and they admitted her.

***

Two days later, Annette picked Breezy up from the hospital. She was more than glad to be out of there. "Where is King?" she asked as soon as they were inside the car.

"His ass is at the house after costing me fifteen hundred dollars to get him out of jail. Damn fool went over there and beat the hell out of Terry!" She cut her eyes at Breezy. "Tell me the truth; did you know he was going over there?"

"No, ma'am, I sure didn't. Right before he left he said something about him saying something and meaning it. I didn't know what he was talking about and he left before I could ask."

"I just hope that when they go to court Terry's sorry ass will drop the charges." She looked worried.

"Yeah, I hope so too. I sure hate that he did that. I just want to move on and forget about my ma and Terry. They have caused me enough pain to last a lifetime."

"I know what you mean."

The two of them continued to talk until they got home. When they walked through the door, Vita and King were hugged up on the sofa.

"Hey, Ms. Annette," Vita spoke.

"Hey," Annette replied before going into the kitchen. She wasn't crazy about Vita at all and to be honest she was getting quite sick of looking at her.

Breezy noticed that Vita hadn't spoken to her but didn't care. She was tired and all she wanted to do was rest. Her body had been through a lot. She sat down on the loveseat since they were on the long sofa where she slept.

"Hey, Breezy, how are you feeling?" King asked taking her completely by surprise.

"Hey. I'm feeling okay, just a little bit tired." She let out a sigh and tried to get comfortable on the loveseat.

"If you want, you can go back there and get in my bed."

"Huh?" She lifted her head and looked over at him, taking notice of what he was wearing.

Today he had on a pair of red Nike sweats and a black tee with a red/black durag. The diamond in his left ear shined like a miniature light bulb. He sat next to Vita looking like a young Memphis Hitz.

"I said that you can go back there and get in my bed if you want," he repeated.

"Yeah, I think that I will." She accepted his offer knowing that she'd rest a lot better in his bed versus the sofa. She glanced at Vita, who rolled her eyes. She ignored her and got up to leave the room.

On her way out she heard Vita tell King, "I love you, bae."

"I love you too, li'l mama," he responded.

Breezy went ahead in the room, changed her clothes, took her pain medicine, and then crawled into bed. Before she knew it, she was out like a light. King invaded her dreams.

*He was standing over the bed shirtless staring down at her. "Why are you looking at me like that?" she asked.*

*He leaned down and covered her lips with his. Getting in bed with her, he positioned himself between her legs never breaking their kiss. She wrapped her legs around his waist as his kisses continued down her neck and then back up to her lips again. "I love you, Breezy. I always have."*

*"King, I love you too."*

"Breezy, Breezy! Wake up!"

She opened her eyes and looked around. It had gotten dark outside. King had turned on the lamp next to the bed. "Are you okay?"

His eyes were glued to her chest, which caused her to look down too. Her nipples were hard as little pebbles straining against the thin fabric of the shirt that she wore. Feeling embarrassed, she crossed her arms over her chest. "I'm okay. How long have I been asleep?"

"Just a couple of hours," he said with a smirk and decided to mess with her. "That must've been some dream that you were having. You were moaning 'I love you' and shit. Let me find out you lying in my bed having freaky dreams about some nigga."

"Huh? Boy, be quiet. You just making up stuff." She knew that she'd said his name in her dream and was praying that she hadn't said it aloud.

"I ain't making nothing up. When I walked in you were saying 'I love you too.' I wish Ma had told me to come wake you up a few minutes earlier. I probably would've heard more than that." He laughed.

"Shut up!" She picked up a pillow and threw it at him. "What does your ma want?"

"For you and your dream man to come and eat!" he continued to tease.

She got up from the bed and pushed him. "You make me sick."

"Is that any way to talk to your best friend who just caught a charge for you?"

The mood changed some. "About that . . . King, I really wish that you hadn't done that. I don't want you in any trouble."

"He deserved more than what I did to him. He deserved to die! You just concentrate on getting yourself right and not going back there. Don't worry about me." He pulled her to him and gave her a big hug.

She melted against his chest and in those strong arms. He smelled so good.

"And for the answer to your question: I'm right here and that's where I'll always be."

She was confused. "What question?"

"When you was singing the other night."

She thought back to the other night when she was singing Jennifer Hudson's "Where You At" and smiled enjoying the feel of his arms around her.

# Chapter Thirteen

*Two months later . . .*

Breezy kept her word and didn't go back home and things in her life were finally looking up. She was holding down her job at Angel's Salon, after school and on the weekends. Her appearance had changed drastically as well. She now kept her hair and nails done and her gear stayed fresh. All of a sudden every nigga in school was trying to holla at her. Even Sean and Jalen were seeing her differently. She'd also put on a few pounds, which made her look a lot healthier. She still didn't have a banging body like Vita's but she was holding her own. The thing that made her even more beautiful than she'd become over the past few months, was that with all the attention she was getting now she still stayed to herself. The only two people she dealt with were King and her new boyfriend, Montez.

Montez went to school with them. He was a nice-looking guy, five feet nine inches, about 198 pounds, brown skin, with dreads and an iced-out grill. He drove a money green Range Rover with twenty-sixes on it and played football for their school. He was one of the starting quarterbacks.

King didn't care for Breezy dealing with Montez because he felt like Montez wouldn't have taken a second look at her a few months ago and he was right. Montez only noticed Breezy now because she looked different but he really was feeling her and she was feeling him as well.

As for King, he'd recently gotten a job working at McDonald's after school and Vita and him were still together. She'd dropped a bomb on him a little over a week ago, informing him that she was four and a half weeks pregnant. He'd been pissed but had no one to blame but himself for believing that she was on the shot.

Annette was so upset when he told her that she hadn't had much to say to him since then. Curtis had seen it coming a mile away. Instead of fussing, getting upset, or not speaking to him, he simply sat him down and talked to him, letting him know that he needed to work and save up his money so that he could take care of his responsibility once the baby was born.

King walked in the house around three-thirty on Tuesday to get something to eat before it was time for him to head to work. Breezy was sitting at the table eating a bowl of Lucky Charms and talking on the phone. "Are you gonna take me to work . . . I ain't gonna give you nothing . . . Oh it's like that? I gotta pay you to take me to work now?" She giggled into the phone. King could tell that she was talking to Montez by all the giggling she was doing. "Tez, you are so silly." Giggle. "Bae, stop playing." Giggle.

"Ain't shit that damn funny," King mumbled as he took a bowl from the cabinet to make some cereal and then walked over and got the milk out of the refrigerator.

Breezy didn't hear him because she was too busy giggling at everything Montez said. "I have to be there by four. You know if I'm late Kendra and Tamara are gon' get in my ass. They cool but they don't be playing that late shit."

King sat down at the table to eat his cereal. There was a magazine lying on the table. It was an *Urban Lit* magazine. He picked it up and started flipping through it. There were a bunch of authors in it and poets. He knew that Breezy loved that magazine so much because she wanted to be an author one day. For the past two months, she'd been writing short stories sending them into the magazine hoping that one of them would get picked to be featured in the magazine. He thumbed through the pages and could imagine flipping through it and seeing an article written by her one day or one of her short stories, or even her face gracing the cover as the featured author of the month. He smiled as he envisioned her on the front of the magazine. He placed the magazine back down on the table and noticed the notebook that she wrote in lying next to it. He slid it over and began reading a poem that she'd been working on:

### To My Soul Mate

*I wish that I could tell you how I feel.*
*Tell you what's been in my heart for years.*
*Tell you how I fall asleep each night with you on my mind.*
*Tell you how patiently I've waited for the day when you will be all mines.*
*I look at you and somehow I believe that you feel the same way too.*
*It doesn't only show in the things that you say but more so in the things that you do.*
*Like how you always come to my rescue.*
*Even if it means catching a charge. Yeah, you'd do that too.*
*You're my knight in shining armor.*
*With me and you it will always be death before dishonor.*
*A bond that will forever remain unbreakable.*
*Though I'm with him and you with her we both know there's no denying what's obviously out of our control.*

King sat staring down at the notebook in shock. It didn't take a rocket scientist to figure out that the poem was about him but seeing it in writing and the words that she'd chosen to express her feelings was indescribable. He looked over at Breezy, who was still giggling like a damn airhead at Montez and totally oblivious to the fact that he'd just read her poem. He slid the notebook back to where it previously sat and said, "Nice poem."

That got her attention. "Huh?" She looked at the notebook and then back at King. Her heart fell to her stomach at the realization of what he'd just said. "Hold on, Tez," she said covering the phone and looking at King through squinted eyes. "King, did you read my poem?"

"Yes, I did and it was really sweet." He laughed while putting his bowl in the sink and then walked out of the kitchen feeling himself.

Breezy hurriedly picked up the phone and told Montez she'd see him when he arrived to pick her up for work. She didn't know how to feel about King reading her poem; there was a mixture of emotions flowing through her at that moment. She was upset because he'd read her personal thoughts and feelings without her permission and embarrassed because she wasn't sure of how he'd taken it. Seeing him laugh made her feel as if he'd taken her feelings as a joke; that hurt and made her feel silly. She stomped down the hall to King's room, pushed his door open and walked in. He was in the middle of changing his clothes for work and had already taken off his shirt.

"Why did you read what was in my notebook?" Breezy asked with her hands on her hips.

King laughed because it was funny to him how she was trying to act like she was so upset. He'd already heard her say she loved him in her sleep a couple of months ago. He decided to mess with her. "Breezy, what's the big deal? Why does it matter if I read it or not?"

"Because you shouldn't be reading my stuff!" she snapped.

He realized that she really was upset but what he couldn't understand was why. If that was truly how she felt he couldn't understand what the big deal was. "Damn are you seriously mad?"

"Yes, I am because you have no right reading my stuff!"

"Stop trippin'. I've read your stuff before and you ain't trip like that." He continued to laugh. "You're only trippin' because you're afraid that I will guess who it is about and your secret obsession will be out in the open."

"Obsession?" Breezy asked offended by his choice of words and the fact that he was still laughing like her feelings were a joke. "Boy, bye. There is nothing to guess about; that poem is about Montez. Remember him? My boyfriend! So please tell me where the obsession comes in at when I've already bagged that?"

It was King's turn to catch an attitude. "That bitch-ass nigga ain't gone catch no fucking charge for you! Get real! And besides that, if I remember correctly the poem said, 'Though I'm with him and you with her, we both know there's no denying what's obviously out of our control.' Like you just said, you've already bagged that so that wouldn't make sense. The entire thing doesn't make sense if it's to him."

"How do you know what he will and won't do? He would catch a charge for me." Breezy defended her man, purposely ignoring the last part of what he'd said because she didn't have an explanation. "And why are you so worried about who it's to? You act like you are jealous!"

Her last statement had been a blow to his pride. "Bit . . . Breezy, get the fuck out of my room!" he roared, trying to catch himself because he knew that he was about to say something he may regret later. "King Collins isn't jealous of any nigga walking, believe that. I been fuckin' bad bitches and can get more bitches than Montez lame ass will ever get in his lifetime. Please. I'm supposed to be jealous because he's fucking with you? Are you serious? We are talking about the same nigga who didn't even know your ass existed until just recently! I was the only nigga who was kickin it with you when your hair was nappy and your gear was all fucked up! Don't let a perm and some weave blow yo' fuckin head up!"

The look that covered her face reflected the hurt but he didn't care because he felt like she shouldn't have come out of her mouth like that, accusing him of being jealous of Montez.

"You know what? Forget you, King. And for the record you been fuckin' nasty bitches! FYI Vita ain't the definition of bad because she got a fat ass and she will open her legs for any nigga who buys her ho ass a ninety-nine cent hamburger. A bad bitch don't need no nigga to do for them because they will do for themselves. Every time I turn around she begging you to get her nails done or her hair done and in return she lying on her back. Not to mention her thirsty ass lied so that she could baby-trap you. A bad bitch don't do shit like that because they don't have to. It seems more like she's a needy, insecure bitch."

"Man, whatever." He smacked his lips, waving her off.

She wasn't done yet though. "And, another thing, Montez may not have noticed me before but at least I ain't gotta lie on my back and trick off my pussy to keep him and to get him to do shit for me." She waved her wrist and showed off the gold bracelet that Montez had given her for their one month anniversary. "And no, I still haven't slept with him. I don't know what your definition of a bad bitch is but, hmmm, if you ask me I am way more deserving of that title than that trick you dealing with! Look at the things I have been through and the way that I have refused to allow those things to keep me down! I don't need you to throw in my face what I used to be or what I used to look like because, trust me, I haven't forgotten. The fact that I haven't forgotten is what motivates me every day to continue to strive to become better and not go back to that."

"Breezy, if you don't take your ass down the hall and out of my face, you are going to be wearing that cheap-ass bracelet around your neck."

"Whatever!" She stormed out of his room, slamming the door behind her.

King stood in the middle of his floor after she'd walked out, confused as to how things had taken such a messed-up turn just because he'd read a poem in her notebook. She could lie all she wanted but he knew in his heart that poem was for him.

No sooner had Breezy walked into the living room than the doorbell rang. She walked over and answered the door. When she opened it Vita was standing on the other side. "Hey."

Vita looked Breezy up and down and then tried to brush past her to walk in but Breezy blocked her.

"Ummm, excuse you, rudeness, but you don't just be busting up in people's house. Not only that but is something wrong with your mouth?"

Vita smacked her lips and held her hand up in Breezy's face. "Girl, please! You better move the hell outta my way!" She tried brushing past Breezy again and again she blocked her.

"I said you don't be—"

The palm of Vita's right hand connected with the right side of Breezy's face as she smacked her.

Without hesitation Breezy drew back and returned the favor. From there the two of them went at it.

King came running from the back. He couldn't believe what his eyes were seeing. Breezy and Vita were on the living room floor going at it. Vita was on top of Breezy so he snatched her up. "Both of y'all chill the fuck out!" he shouted at them both.

Just as he got that out of his mouth Annette came through the door. She looked from Breezy to Vita and then at King standing in between them. "What the hell is going on? Are y'all fighting in my house?"

"Yes, ma'am, and I apologize but she ain't got no respect. She just gone bust up in here like her name is on the lease or something. I told her when you come to the door, you speak and ask for somebody or something. You just don't brush past me with your nasty attitude and walk on through the house! Then she gon' slap me!" Breezy rattled off without taking a breath.

"Vita, do you have anything to say? It's two sides to every story." Even though Annette was playing it cool she looked like she was about to explode at any second.

Vita began being extra animated, waving her arms and popping her mouth as she told her side of the story. "Ms. Annette, she's right I didn't speak to her but I don't like her so why be fake and grin all up in her face? She knew that I was here to see King so why make a big deal about it like she pay bills or something up in here! This ain't her house! This is your house!" She clapped her hands together with each word. "She is lucky that King broke it up when he did because I was about to choke her ass out! These little broads gon' get enough of running up on me like I am to be played with or something! They better stop letting the cute face fool them."

Breezy rolled her eyes.

"Are you both finished?" Annette asked becoming more annoyed after listening to Vita's side of the story. Both girls nodded their heads. "Okay, first of all, Vita, chill out with all that extra mess that you are doing because I am home now and there will be no more fighting in my house. Number one, I don't appreciate y'all fighting in my house because it's very disrespectful. Number two, Vita, whether or not Breezy pays bills here is irrelevant. She lives here so she is at home and you should respect her like this is her home. If she came to your house she should give you that same respect. Number three, you are pregnant with my grandchild and so that means that you will be around for a very long time. Which also means that even if you don't like Breezy, you are going to have to deal with her because she ain't going nowhere. She's family. If you don't mind me asking, why don't you like her?"

"I don't like her because her helpless used and abused ass was the cause of King getting locked up. He is always feeling sorry for her, why I don't know." She rolled her eyes at Breezy.

"You are pathetic and insecure. That is why you don't like me," Breezy spat. "You feel threatened by me. It's funny how you are supposed to be such a bad chick but at the same time is threatened by little nappy-headed, dirty, no-clothes-having Breezy. I guess y'all shook because I ain't the underdog no more. Y'all chicks see me climbing that ladder and realize that it's only a matter of time before I reach the top. Gotcha shook, don't I?" She laughed while winking at Vita, further pissing her off. "That just goes to show that a fat ass and a hot coochie will only get you but so far!"

She turned her attention to Annette because she truly felt bad about disrespecting her home. Especially since she'd been good enough to give her a place to stay. "I apologize for the disrespect. I never want to disrespect you in any way because you have been more than good to me, better than my own mama; but there was no way I was going to allow her to put her hands in my face and not defend myself. I have been beat on, walked over, and disrespected enough to last a lifetime. I can't live like that anymore. People will treat me like I treat them or I guess I will go through the rest of my life fighting. I was a victim but not anymore."

Annette looked at Breezy through proud eyes. Words couldn't express how she felt to hear the strength that she now possessed. Breezy had come a long way and all she could see was her growing even stronger as time passed. "No need for apologies, baby. I can't tell you how good it felt sitting here listening to you. You are becoming such a beautiful woman inside and out." She looked at Vita. "Vita, I'm not taking sides but it is what it is. You were wrong. Breezy didn't make King do anything. They have been friends forever and he has always been very protective over her and I doubt that will ever change. The decision that he made to do what he did to Terry was his choice. I thank God that Terry had the charges dropped, probably because he knew that the truth would come out about his sorry butt. Anyways let this be the end of this mess, okay?"

"Yes, ma'am." Vita didn't look happy at all but she didn't say anything else.

\*\*\*

That night at work, Breezy couldn't stop thinking about the argument that she and King had
earlier that day. She felt bad because she hated it
when the two of them argued. Everyone at work
noticed her sad and gloomy mood as well. They
kept asking her all evening what was wrong but she
kept lying and telling them nothing. She was glad
when she finally made it back home. The first thing
she noticed when she got there was that King's
car wasn't parked in front of the apartment in its
usual spot. Normally Montez would come in for a
few minutes when he dropped her off but tonight
he told her he didn't feel like it and she was glad
because she didn't feel like entertaining company.
All she wanted to do was take a bath and lie down.

After taking a shower, she went in King's room
and got in bed. She was so tired that she fell asleep
as soon as her head touched the pillow. King came
in at around 2:00 a.m., waking her by slamming
drawers and moving around the room.

He had a lot on his mind as he moved about
searching for a change of clothes. He too had
been thinking about their argument the entire
afternoon and the fight between her and Vita. He
felt like he was caught between a rock and a hard
place, dealing with his feelings for her and Vita's
pregnancy. He turned on the lamp and that woke
her completely up.

Breezy sat up and looked at the clock. *Is he serious?* she thought, lying back down and putting the pillow over her head. She heard him turn the lamp back off and was happy so that she could she could try to go back to sleep. Next thing she knew, the pillow was being snatched from over her head.

"Wake up; we need to talk," King said, lying next to her.

"Why can't we talk in the morning?" she whined sleepily as she fixed her scarf on her head and attempted to turn back over.

King grabbed her shoulder and flipped her back over. "Stop playing, Breezy, before my mama wakes up and starts tripping because I am in here with you at this time of the morning with the lights off. You know how her mind works."

"Well then go into the living room and we can talk in the morning."

"I heard you tell me that you loved me in your sleep two months ago," he blurted knowing that would get her up and he was right.

Her eyes popped open. "Huh?"

"Breezy, before you deny it, I don't feel like dealing with the games tonight. Just keep it one hundred, please." She didn't say anything so he continued. "You were asleep and when I walked in, I heard you say 'King, I love you too.' What was that about?"

She propped her head up on her hand. "I don't know. I was asleep so I don't know why I said it."

"Okay, fair enough, but what about the poem?"

She let out a sigh. "What about it?"

"You know what I am asking and you also know that I know it wasn't about Montez. Is that really how you feel? Like I'm your soul mate?" There was light coming in through the blinds from the streetlights. He looked at her and waited for a reply. Her eyes dropped to the bed as she fidgeted with the edge of the pillowcase.

"Honestly, yeah," she admitted as she lifted her eyes in time to see a smile spread over his lips. Butterflies filled her stomach. Her nerves got the best of her and she lay back on the bed, covering her face with the pillow.

"Why are you covering your face?" He laughed at her shyness.

"Because . . ." she answered from beneath the pillow.

"Because what?"

She didn't respond. After a few seconds, she felt him tugging at the pillow. She let go of it but didn't bother opening her eyes until she felt his lips cover hers. They sent electricity throughout her entire body. She'd kissed Montez a lot and it had never felt like that. Her hands unconsciously went up around his neck and they kissed like two long-lost lovers. His hand found her thigh and began caressing it. Her lips were like two soft pillows. He'd never experienced anything like the kiss that they were sharing. It took every ounce of strength within them both to pull back.

King didn't move for over a minute. He just lay there staring at her.

"What are you thinking about?" Breezy asked, beginning to feel uncomfortable under his gaze.

He reached over and took her hand, placing it up to his lips. He kissed it and then held on to it. "I'm just thinking of how I've made such a huge mistake."

"What do you mean?"

"Pops told me awhile ago to be careful with Vita but I didn't listen. He also told me about these feelings that I have for you and I denied them, knowing all the while that he was right and that I truly do love you." Breezy blushed as she listened to him confess his love for her. "Now, I've gotten her pregnant . . ." He paused and then got up grabbing the other pillow. "Good night."

"You're going to bed?" she asked confused, thinking that they weren't finished talking.

"Yeah, I'll talk to you in the morning." With that he left the room.

After he was gone she couldn't get to sleep so she lay awake staring up at the ceiling thinking about what had just happened. She felt more confused now than she had been before he'd told her how he felt. At the same time she felt bad because Montez deserved a girl who cared about him and only him, not someone who was in love with her best friend and only using him as a fill-in.

# Chapter Fourteen

The rest of the week dragged by slowly. King and Breezy tried to act normal like nothing had happened between them but the kiss they'd shared was present on both their minds throughout the entire week. Every time that they made eye contact, they'd blush but neither of them brought it up.

Saturday finally rolled around and King was more than happy because he had the day off. It was the first Saturday that he'd had off in quite a while. When he woke up that morning Breezy and Annette were already gone, leaving him and Curtis alone. After taking a bath and getting dressed, he went into the kitchen and found Curtis at the table eating. Annette and Breezy had cooked breakfast before leaving. There were pancakes, eggs, turkey bacon, and grits. King fixed a plate and heated it in the microwave.

"Morning, Pops." He greeted Curtis as he moved around the kitchen.

"What's good, son?" Curtis asked as he chewed on a slice of bacon. He glanced at the TV that sat on the counter and then at King.

"Ain't nothing. How long ma and Breezy been gone?"

"They left about forty-five minutes ago. This food was so good, I'm on round two." He laughed. "To my understanding Breezy has the day off so her and your ma decided to turn it into a girl's day out."

King chuckled as he placed his food on the table and took a seat. "Ma thinks that Breezy is her daughter. I'm glad that they get along so well."

"Well daughter, daughter-in-law, same difference." Curtis laughed giving him a knowing look.

King tried to play like he didn't know what Curtis was getting at. "Pops, what are you talking about?"

"Boy, don't play dumb. You know exactly what I am talking about. We are both men here. Don't get me wrong, I like Vita but we both know she ain't the one. Breezy on the other hand . . ." He nodded his head. "That right there is a keeper. I am so proud of that girl I don't know what to do! She is gonna be somebody. That girl is gonna go places. You watch and see what I tell you. Son, Breezy is destined to do amazing things.

"Look at what that child has been through and look out how far she has come. Yes, we helped her but look at the moves that she has made on her own. She is a straight A student, works, and she has a gift when it comes to writing. Last but not least she has the voice of an angel. I walked through the house the other day and heard her singing." He shook his head remembering how good Breezy had sounded. "That girl is going to be somebody! Makes an old man like me so proud to see a young person do good things."

The way Curtis spoke about Breezy brought a proud smile to King's lips. "Yeah, she is special."

"Yep, so special that one day she is going to be Mrs. Collins."

"Dang, Pops, you done planned a wedding and everything!" King laughed.

"Shit if you know like I know you'll be planning one." Curtis leaned over and playfully hit him in the shoulder. "I sure hate that you went and got Vita pregnant but we make mistakes, son."

"Yeah, I care about Vita a lot though. Even if she did lie to me about being on the shot, I am going to take care of my child and do what I have to do to make sure that she is straight. I told her that I still plan to play ball though. I feel like I can be a father and live out my dreams."

"You sure can. I know that I ain't your real daddy but you feel like mine and you know that there ain't nothing that I won't do for you. I want you to play ball because you are extremely good and I can definitely see you going pro. Your mother and I will make sure that baby is taken care of until you get on your feet."

King felt tears sting the back of his eyes because Curtis's words touched him. "Pops, get outta here with that 'you ain't my real daddy' mess. You the only daddy I know! Thanks for everything." He got up and gave Curtis a hug and he hugged him back.

"You don't have to thank me, son. I would do it all over again with no hesitation."

King smiled. "That's what's up, Pops. Enough of this mushy stuff now."

They both laughed. With the women out of the house, the two men decided to kick it and watch sports. Something that they hadn't done in a while. Vita came over around three-thirty. She wanted to go out to eat.

"We can go later on. I'm chillin' right now. You welcome to chill too," King offered.

"I guess I have to since you don't want to go out." She smacked her lips and flopped down on the sofa next to King. She had on a pair of skin-tight jeans.

"Vita, why do you have on those tight jeans? I know that you ain't big yet but you still don't need to have those pants so tight on your stomach, I don't think."

"Chill out, King, they ain't even that tight. I'm not going to hurt our baby." She kissed him on the cheek. "Okay?"

"Yeah, okay but don't come back over here in no more tight jeans because if you do we are going to have problems."

"Okay, daddy." Vita pouted.

They both turned their attention to the TV. A few hours later, Annette and Breezy came in. They had so many bags that it was ridiculous. They'd even bought food. King and Curtis helped them get the bags out of the car. They looked so happy, talking and laughing nonstop. Vita looked like she was a little jealous of how Annette was so into Breezy.

"Dang y'all bought everything you saw didn't you?" King teased.

Annette walked over and gave Curtis a peck on the lips and then gave King a peck on the cheek. "We found some sales."

"Sure did. Don't worry we didn't forget about you. I got you something and I bought the baby some stuff. I know it's early but I couldn't resist!" Breezy squealed.

"Yeah, we really outdone ourselves," Annette added. "Oh and some girls from the shop are coming over later. Kendra and Tamara coming over to play spades."

"Is that why y'all bought so much food?" Curtis teased.

"Yeah, I don't want nobody at my house getting hungry."

Annette and Breezy started putting their stuff away. After they were done Breezy walked back in the living room and handed King two Rocawear shirts and a little mint green baby Rocawear shirt. "I figured a girl or boy could wear mint green. It was just so cute; and I got this too." She handed Vita a navy blue Old Navy diaper bag. "I hope y'all like it."

"Yeah, thanks," Vita said dryly, taking the diaper bag from Breezy and placing it down on the floor next to the sofa by her feet. She didn't want anything from Breezy except for her to get the hell out of her face.

Breezy ignored Vita's obvious attitude and the fact that she'd sat the diaper bag down on the floor. "I can't wait until Kendra and Tamara get here! They were talking mad smack about how they were going to whip us in spades!"

"Child, they can quit that yapping because ain't none of that popping off in here. All I know is we are fixin' to get our nails done for free for the next four months," Annette bragged and high-fived Breezy. "See they bet us that if we win we could get our nails done for free for the next four months but if we lost their lunch was on us for the next four months."

"Dang y'all done got real tight with those women down at the salon haven't you?" King asked.

"I guess you could say that." Annette laughed.

The doorbell rang and Breezy all but ran to get it. "I'll get it," she announced already on her way to the door. She opened the door and started screaming. King jumped up to see what was wrong and so did everyone else. He snatched the door open only to see four women. He looked at Breezy, who was still screaming, confused.

"Girl, what in the hell is wrong with you?" Annette snapped trying to figure out what the problem was.

Breezy finally spoke. "Oh my God, it's Judy Richwood and LaToya Jones; they're the owners of *Urban Lit* magazine! Oh my God!" she squealed jumping up and down.

"Yes, it's them!" Kendra laughed at Breezy's excitement. It had been her idea to surprise Breezy because she knew how much she loved their magazine and how much she wanted to be a writer. "Now let us in! It ain't hot out here!"

Breezy was star struck! She backed out of the way with her eyes still glued to the ladies.

"Y'all come on in," Annette told everyone. "Y'all done nearly gave my baby a heart attack." Everyone came in and Annette made the introductions.

"Breezy, we ain't nobody special, honey," Judy told Breezy as she took off her jacket and sat down getting comfortable. She was a really beautiful older woman. The grey hair around the edges of her hairline hinted her age but didn't take away from her beauty at all. "I am flattered by your reaction though." She laughed.

Breezy was done. She felt like she was dreaming. She couldn't believe that she was actually standing in the same room with Judy and LaToya. "I just don't know what to say. I have every issue of your magazine. I love your magazine."

"Thank you." LaToya spoke for the first time. "We read over one of your submissions that you sent in not too long ago. We were both very impressed. We're going to have to see what we can do about getting you a feature."

"Really? Please don't play with me like that." Breezy looked like she might pass out. She was holding her chest like she really might have a heart attack.

"I am not playing. Not only are you a great writer but I have heard great things about you from Tamara and Kendra. I am always willing to help someone who is trying to help themselves. We need more young people like you."

"Oh my goodness! Thank you so much." She turned to Kendra and Tamara. "I don't know what to say to y'all. Thank you so much."

"That's good enough," Kendra told her.

"I am about to release my next book and I was thinking that it would be cool to give the readers a little treat by featuring a short story from you at the end of the book." LaToya smiled at Breezy. "How does that sound?"

Breezy couldn't hold it together any longer and broke right down. "Are y'all serious? I mean for real? Please tell me I ain't dreaming." She looked up at the ceiling. "Lord, you are truly good. All those times that I have cried myself to sleep praying for a break, a way out. I can't thank you enough, Lord. After all of the pain and suffering. I guess my storm is finally over."

There wasn't a dry eye in the room after witnessing her breakdown and give thanks like that.

King looked at her and thought, *My pops is right. She is definitely a keeper.* He knew what he needed to do and he made up his mind that he wouldn't allow another day to go by without doing it.

Breezy finally pulled herself together so that they could get the card game started.

Around twelve-thirty, Vita started to complain about being tired and sleepy. "King, can you drive me home?" she asked. "My ma dropped me off earlier. I didn't drive."

"Yeah, I'll take you," King said rising from the sofa and helping her up. He walked into the kitchen. "Hey, Ma, I'm going to use your car to take Vita home."

"All right, be careful and don't be gone long," she said, not taking her eyes off of the card game.

"All right." He grabbed the keys off of the counter and he and Vita left.

As soon as they pulled out of the complex, Vita reached over and ran her hand up his thigh. "Baby, let's go to the park before you take me home." She never was sleepy in the first place. She was just tired of sitting at King's house watching everybody play cards. "I know you didn't really believe that I was sleepy did you?" She giggled.

"Yeah, because that's what you said," King snapped. "Damn all you do is lie, ain't it?"

Vita looked at him puzzled by his attitude. He'd never gotten upset with her before when she'd suggested they go to the park and have sex. "What's your problem?"

"You are my problem," he stated. It wasn't just that she'd lied to leave his house but it was everything. The fact that she'd lied about being on the shot, her attitude, and most importantly the fact that she wasn't Breezy. He glanced over at her. "This thing between us isn't working out—"

"What in the fuck do you mean this isn't working out?" Vita yelled in disbelief. "Oh so you trying to be one of those deadbeat niggas? Is that it? You fuck with me, get me pregnant, and then roll on to the next bitch? Is that what this is?"

"Are you done yet?" King asked calmly. He wasn't about to waste energy arguing with her.

"No, I ain't done yet! You need to explain to me what in the hell brought on this sudden change of heart? Is there another bitch? Is it Breezy?"

"If you would shut up then I could explain but you keep yapping so I can't."

Vita sat in the passenger seat glaring at him through anger-filled eyes. She was more hurt at the thought of missing out on being a baller's wife than she actually was about losing King. She cared for him but it wasn't love. It was the dream of sitting courtside wearing all of the latest fashions, walking the red carpet at different events, living in a big-ass house, driving the flyest whips, going out shopping, flying first class all over the world and vacationing in exotic locations. She knew without a doubt that King was going to be a professional ball player and she wanted to be right by his side reaping the benefits.

"No problem, I'll be quiet."

"Truth is, I haven't felt the same about you since you lied to me about being on the shot—"

"I didn't lie to you," she cut him off.

"Yes, you did, Vita. You and I both know that you lied so cut the antics."

"I did not lie. You can ask my mama."

He ignored her continuing to lie. "Not only that but I've never been in love with you. I've always been in lust with you. I know that isn't right and it may sound fucked up but it's the truth." By now they'd reached her house. He pulled up in front and put the car in park.

"So you are going to leave me while I am pregnant with your baby?" Her eyes filled with tears. "King, don't do this," she pleaded.

Seeing her cry bothered him but not enough for him to change his mind. He was ending their relationship before she got out of that car. "I am still going to be here for you and my baby. As a matter of fact, I still want to take you to all of your doctor's appointments and anything that you ever need I will try to provide."

"Fuck you!" She grabbed the latch on the door and opened it. Before getting out she turned to King and said, "I am going to make your life a living hell. I am going to put your ass up for child support the same day that me and the baby come home from the hospital! Don't no nigga try to play Davita and get away with it."

Her ignorance was pissing him off but he remained calm. "Cool."

"Oh that's cool?" His calmness only pissed her off even more. "You'd better watch your back, motherfucker, because I am going to get my cousins Mookie and Earl to beat your punk ass! We'll see if that's cool, too," she said getting out of the car and slamming the door behind her.

King rolled down the window. "Tell your bitch-ass cousins that they can both suck my dick! I ain't scared of either one of them niggas and I ain't hard to find so whenever they get ready to do something tell them to holla at me." He didn't wait for her response. Instead he rolled up the window, put the car in drive, and left her on the sidewalk yelling after him.

When King got home, the house was empty, all of the guests had left, and Breezy was cleaning up the kitchen. "Where did everyone go?" he asked her walking into the kitchen and hanging his coat on back of one of the chairs so that he could help her with the mess in the kitchen.

"The ladies went home and your ma and Mr. Curtis are gone to bed. I told them that I would clean the kitchen for them," she answered. She stopped washing the dishes for a second and looked over at King. "Wow can you believe what happened here today? LaToya and Judy were here and LaToya wants to use one of my stories in her book." She smiled at the thought and shook her head. "God is amazing."

"Yeah, He is, but you deserve it." Something crossed his mind. "I bet your ma will be knocking down doors to get to you now. She'll probably want to be nice."

She looked at him and laughed because the same thing had crossed her mind. "Oh well, she is going to be in for a big surprise. That chapter of my life is closed. I am looking forward to my future and she is nowhere in it."

"Is that right?" King asked. "Well, I hope I'm in that future."

"Stop trying to play me. You already know what time it is."

He smiled at her. "Nah, I don't. Why don't you tell me?"

"It's time for you to go and get my slippers out of the room because these heels are killing my feet." She laughed.

"You know you ain't right." He swooped her up in his arms surprising her and carried her in his room and sat her down on the bed. He could tell she was wondering what he was about to do. She looked nervous. "Relax." He told her and then reached down and unzipped her boots and took them off. He sat down on the floor and massaged her feet.

She looked down at him and thought about all of the years that she'd harbored a secret crush on him and how she'd always loved him but was too afraid to say anything. To know that he loved her back was a wonderful feeling. "I broke up with Montez," she blurted.

King stopped what he was doing and looked up at her. "What do you mean? I mean, when?"

"After you kissed me the other night. I couldn't continue being with him knowing how I felt about you. He deserves someone who only loves him and is not using him as a fill-in. I'm not the type of girl to use someone and I realized that is exactly what I was doing. So I broke it off."

King was speechless. "Wow."

"Yeah, well he took it pretty well. He told me that he respected my honesty and hoped that we could remain friends."

"You told him we kissed?"

"Nah, I just told him that I had feelings for someone else and that I couldn't continue a relationship with him knowing that I had these feelings for someone else."

"Oh," was King's reply. "Well, I broke up with Vita tonight."

"What?" Breezy laughed.

"Damn don't look so sad," King teased.

"Nah, I'm not laughing because you broke up with her. It's just crazy how I tell you that I broke up with Montez and then you turn right around and tell me that you gave Vita her walking papers."

"Yeah, well she wasn't as nice as Montez," he admitted. "She went in on my ass. Even threatened to get her cousins to jump me."

Breezy's hands went up over her mouth. "What?" she exclaimed becoming afraid for his safety. "What are you going to do?"

"Nothing." He waved his hand. "I ain't thinking about them niggas. She is just blowing hot air because I don't want to be with her."

Breezy let out a sigh. "I sure hope so." She didn't like the sound of that at all. King started back massaging her feet. "Oooh that feels so good." She leaned back like she was in heaven with her eyes closed.

"Breezy, please don't say things like that because I can't take it right now. I can't promise you how much longer I will be able to practice self-control."

Her eyes popped open. "Boy, stop it!"

He laughed and continued to massage her feet for a little while longer before rising to his feet. "Well, I am going to go on and finish cleaning up and then hit the sofa." He kissed her on her forehead. "Good night."

"Why are you going to bed so early?" she asked looking disappointed. "I wanted to talk for a while before we went to sleep."

"Actually, I just need to get away from you for a while because my hormones are going crazy and it's obvious that I need to try to keep them under control. Look at the mess that they already got me in with Vita."

"True." Breezy laughed, appreciating the respect that he had for her. "Good night, big head."

King left the room and she got undressed and crawled into bed.

# Chapter Fifteen

*Two weeks later . . .*

Breezy walked into the gymnasium humming, oblivious to the three girls standing in a group watching her with angry glares. She walked past them and went into the locker room to get changed. As she walked over to her gym locker she sang the hook to Ja Rule's "Always on Time" and a few of the other girls joined in. She turned the dial on the combination lock. "'Baby, I'm not always there when you call, but I'm always on time. And I gave you my all, now baby be mine.'"

Vita and her two cousins, Rachael and Michelle, entered the locker room and walked directly over to Breezy, who was rummaging through her locker singing. Vita nodded to Michelle and Rachael. One of the other girls who had been singing with Breezy knew that the three girls were up to no good by the way that they all had come in and walked up behind Breezy. She opened her mouth to warn her but was too late. Michelle punched Breezy in

the back of the head as hard as she could and then
she and Rachael both proceeded to beat her. The
attack had caught her totally off-guard. She fell to
the floor and balled up into a fetal position with her
arms up over her face.

Vita stood off to the side laughing and egging
her cousins on. "That's right, beat that bitch's ass!
Stomp that ho!"

The same girl who'd attempted to warn Breezy
jumped in the fight and tried to break it up because
everyone else was just standing around watching.
"Somebody help me!" she yelled as she tugged on
Michelle. Two other girls started to help her break
it up and someone else ran out and got the gym
teachers.

Ten minutes later all four girls sat in the principal's office, with two of the school's security guards
standing between them. Vita looked over at Breezy.
"How's your head feeling, bitch?" She laughed.

Before Breezy could respond, Principal Fenner
intervened. "Ms. Newsome, you are already in
enough trouble. I am going to ask that you shut
your mouth."

"For what? I didn't touch anybody," Vita snapped.

"No, but you instigated the entire thing. Several
of the girls in the locker room said that they saw
you tell Michelle and Rachael to attack Brionna
while she had her back turned."

"They're lying." Michelle smacked her lips.

"So why did you all attack Brionna then?"

Michelle looked over at Breezy being sure to make eyes contact with her. "Because she like going around messing with things that don't belong to her."

"Oh my God, are you serious?" Breezy jumped to her feet but was immediately asked to sit back down by one of the guards. "Y'all jumped me over a boy who don't even want her. The fact that y'all would jump me over a dude says a lot about every one of you!"

"And the fact that you go around fucking other people's men says a lot about you." Vita shot back. "I bet you will think twice the next time that you think about fucking with somebody's man!" Vita and her cousins all laughed.

"Laugh now but I bet I'll be laughing last because I plan to press charges against every one of you!" The girls got quiet because they hadn't expected that. Breezy looked back and forth between Michelle and Rachael. "I bet you two pit bulls will think twice before putting your hands on someone."

Principal Fenner nodded his head. "I don't blame you one bit. This violence has to stop!" he began and then pointed to Breezy. "Look at those scratches on her face and that knot on her head. It could've been worse."

"It should've," Vita mumbled not wanting to hear the mess that he was talking.

"You have a lot to learn, Ms. Newsome. Violence is never the answer to any problem. You are sitting here in front of me in a world of trouble, about to be suspended from school and have charges pressed against you, all over a boy. Did you ever stop to think that you don't have to fight for someone who loves and wants to be with you? Now you are in all of this trouble and he is still going to be living his life, doing what it is that he needs and wants to do. While you, on the other hand, are suffering the consequences for your action."

"So? And?" She shrugged her shoulders.

Principal Fenner let out a sigh and decided he wouldn't say anything else until the parents arrived. He realized that the young lady in front of him was headed down the wrong road if someone didn't step in and do something fast. When the parents arrived they were informed of what had taken place.

DaVita's mother, Dianne, was so disappointed to find out what she'd done. "DaVita, you know better than to do some mess like that! Michelle and Rachael, you two know better as well." She scolded all three girls but mainly her daughter. "You cannot make anyone want you and fighting surely isn't going to make him want you."

"I agree," Annette spoke. "I'm not trying to be mean or nasty but you girls are going to pay for what you did to this child. She is under my guardianship now and I refuse to let this go. When we leave here, I am taking her down to the police station so that she can file charges on every one of you. You need to learn that there are consequences for your actions and you are about to learn starting today.

"Vita, I halfway want to sympathize with you because you are the mother of my grandchild but I realize that I have to treat you the same as these two in order for you to learn before it's too late. Maybe this will help shape and mold you into a more mature young woman, which in turn will make you a better mother for that baby you are carrying in your stomach. You can't be running around like this, doing mess like this once that baby is born. What kind of example would you be setting for your child? I know that you want the best for that baby, don't you?"

Vita rolled her eyes and tears fell. Annette's speech had gotten to her. "Of course I want what's best for my child," she snapped still trying to act tough.

"In that case you need to get your act together and stop doing mess like this."

Vita didn't say anything; she just sat there with her head down crying.

Principal Fenner suspended Vita, Michelle, and Rachael for fifteen days apiece. Breezy didn't get suspended because she never hit anyone and they all attacked her. She still decided to take the rest of the day off from school.

"I'm not going to press charges," Breezy told Annette as they walked to the car. Her lips were swollen, which caused her words to come out distorted.

Annette looked at her. "What do you mean? Those girls need to pay for what they did to you. If you let them get by with this, they will do it again to someone else."

"I can't because Vita is pregnant and I don't want to put her through any unnecessary stress. I think she knows what she did was wrong. I could tell by how she broke down in there."

Annette hit the unlock button on her keychain remote to unlock the car doors. They both got in and she turned to Breezy. "Are you sure?"

"Yes, ma'am. I'm sure." She nodded her head. "I just want to go home, take something for this headache, and lie down."

"All right," Annette agreed. "I swear you are better than me because I would be pressing charges on all of them with the quickness."

"Yeah, well I've learned that sometimes you have to sit back and allow God to handle things. They will get theirs. If you ask me they are already getting theirs because while I will be at school getting my education so that I can graduate and better myself, they will all be at home and may possibly fail for missing so much work. I am about to have one of my short stories featured in a book and one of my poems featured in my favorite magazine. I have a job, I am surrounded by people who love me, and I refuse to stop until I reach the top. I'm winning and the best payback that you can ever get on anyone is to continue winning. Those girls hate me because they ain't me. I saw jealousy in all of their eyes and to be honest I felt sorry for them. They'd rather see me being beat and dogged to secure some type of popularity among their peers because with me in the game they feel threatened." She shook her head unable to understand. "Those girls scream all day how they are the baddest bitches when really they are the most insecure bitches."

Annette laughed as she started the car and put it in reverse. "Baby, you are a mess, with yo' old soul." She continued to laugh, feeling blessed and proud of the gift that God had given her in Breezy. She was a good kid and she felt blessed to be a part of her life.

When they got home, Breezy took a shower and lay down.

King couldn't wait to get home after hearing what had happened to Breezy. He'd called her phone to check on her but hadn't gotten an answer because she'd turned her ringer off before lying down. He rushed through the door and was greeted by Annette who was sitting on the sofa watching TV.

"Hey, Ma," he spoke dropping his book bag down at the door.

"Hey, son." She noticed his urgency to get down the hall as he speed walked past the sofa. "She's asleep," she called after him as he headed down the hall.

He didn't reply; he just continued down the hall and pushed the door open to his room. Breezy was knocked out with her mouth opened snoring. He could see that her face was swollen and bruised. That angered him because he felt partially to blame. What bothered him the most was that he couldn't do anything about what had taken place. He let out a sigh. Not wanting to wake her, he kicked off his shoes and got on the bed behind her. He kissed her on her cheek and wrapped his arm around her, causing her to stir in her sleep. Her eyes fluttered open and she turned and looked behind her.

"Hey, what are you doing here?" she asked unaware of the time.

"School is out." King replied enjoying how she felt in his arms.

"Don't you have to work?"

"I took the day off."

"Why?"

"To be with you. Now hush up and go back to sleep. You sound like you're high."

"I'm fine, you can go to work. I took some Tylenol for my head and it made me groggy."

"I know you're fine but I'm still not leaving you so hush up and go back to sleep."

"Okay," she mumbled and closed her eyes. A few seconds passed before she added, "I love you, King."

"I love you too, Brionna Lee." He wrapped his arm around her a little bit tighter and they both drifted off to sleep.


"I don't know what we are going to do with those two." Annette shook her head as she and Curtis stood side by side in King's doorway watching him and Breezy sleep so peacefully.

"Plan their wedding," Curtis replied and they both laughed before closing the door and leaving the two lovebirds to rest.

# Down 4 Whatever

by

*T.C. Littles*

# Prologue

"Hey, Mike, man, ya might wanna go in there. I heard a few shots." Spook walked across the street seeing his niece burn rubber on two wheels around the corner.

Not wasting another second, Mike grabbed the pistol from his waistband, busting the window out. Shattering glass everywhere, knocking the remaining pieces of broken glass from around the frame, the fact that no one from inside screamed at him entering the house like a madman sent an eerie sensation up his spine. "Keep a lookout, Spook."

Climbing in, Mike wasn't prepared for what he saw. Running to her side, he grabbed up his only flesh and blood cousin, holding her dead body. "I'ma send her your way," he whispered and closed her eyes knowing exactly who was responsible. Not giving a ghetto fuck about the one other body laid out only a few inches from them, he kicked ol' boy out of pride knowing he had to have been the reason behind all of this.

# Chapter One

## *Corielle aka Cori*

"Could you please shut up and drink this damn bottle?"

The young mother next to me shoved a plastic bottle with a dirty nipple into her infant child's mouth despite the milk streaming out onto the baby girl's chubby cheeks, which had rash red chubby cheeks. More like a rhetorical question, irritated that the baby wouldn't stop screaming and crying, the young, inexperienced mother flipped her daughter over onto her lap in an attempt to rock her to sleep.

"Sorry, she got a fever and shit but my petty-ass caseworker cut her Medicaid off. Otherwise, we'd be at the hospital."

Looking at me for pity, I was too busy holding my breath at the pissy smell of the obviously soiled diaper. "Oh, you cool, it's nothing," I lied, making sure my Textgram posted letting people know I'd be doing check stubs today on special. Looking up, hoping to see another seat in the overcrowded

Department of Human Services office, I wanted to be anywhere but near this musty broad and her crying kid. "I'll save your seat if you want to go change her." I came up with a quick alternative for getting a break from the strong, offensive smell.

"Oh naw, she got two more times to pee in this diaper. Until my cash gets cut back on we struggling," she explained as she continued to shake her knee, not making the little girl any less cranky. "I ain't got it like that." She laughed.

"Damn, that's all bad." I shook my head but not feeling sorry for her. In my life, emotions were reserved for the weak and I was far from that. "I know somebody who gets down with Walmart cards if you need to get a case of diapers or whatever when your worker gets your case right." Seeing an opportunity to get money, I knew the ghetto girl was just as wrapped tight in getting a hood scheme as I was into pulling one off.

"Oh straight up? That's what I'm talking about! Hell to the yeah. I need one of those bitches like right now!" Sitting the whining child into the filthy stroller, she pulled out her refurbished Android to input the number she thought I was about to give her.

"How much you trying to spend on a card? Double that to spend." I put her down on the scheme, knowing I was ready to deliver.

"You got the hookup like that?" Her eyes brightened. "I've got twenty-five dollars on me now, so what's up?"

Normally people who got down with scams didn't dabble in petty amounts, but I took it all. You could come to me with ten bucks looking for a hookup and I'd find you one. "Then you'll have a card worth fifty dollars that you better get to as soon as you leave this dungeon."

"Let me get your number, too. I can keep in contact and spread the word. This was a real good look."

"Yeah, lock me in. I gets down but this is not the place for me to run down my resume." Cutting our conversation short I really wasn't interested in her smelly, germ-infested kid or if her woes were worked out. I'd gotten her money and a person to refer me to others; she could peace be gone for all I cared. I was like a vulture when it came to hustling. And by it being the first of the month, I was scoping for money spenders in all forms: big bank, little bank, or borrowed bank. I wanted it all.

"Tandalaya Jenkins!" The door opened as a big-bellied black woman popped out with a manila folder in hand. "Tandalaya Jenkins!" Shouting with crumbs falling from her mouth, the alleged "better than us" social worker tapped her foot with little patience.

"Here I go, I'm coming," she yelled, jumping up, struggling with her grimy belongings and reeking daughter.

I blatantly held my nose, catching a whiff of her musk and funk as she moved around. *I hope her trifling ass gets some soap and deodorant off that card, too.*

"Thanks, girl. I'm about to jump fly tonight." She looked over her shoulder, continuing to huff toward the door like she could read my mind.

"Uh, uh, okay," I half replied, finally able to breathe since she was out of nose reach. Watching the young girl waddle to her worker and behind the closing door, I glanced at the wall clock hoping my worker would be appearing next. Sitting back in the orange plastic waiting chair, I didn't know how much more of this poor-people place I could stomach. Even though it was only eight-fifteen in the morning, as usual the DHS was turned up live with scallywags, loud snot-nosed kids, lazy bums, and even a few homeless people waiting to get turned down for not having an address. Dressed in pajama pants, a pair of Ugg boots I'd lifted out of Nordstrom, and a North Face fleece jacket, I smacked loudly on my chewing gum, agitated that I had to be here. *My worker be on that straight bullshit with these early appointments. I can't take it with her! I could've dropped this shit in the drop box and been back in my bed by now.* Continuing to watch the scene, shaking my head at the rainbow of ratchetness that was flooding through the doors, I couldn't wait to turn these papers in and get up out of here. For some reason or another, even though we were all from the same hood, cut from the same cloth, I considered myself to be too good for this.

"Corielle Greene!"

"It's about time," I mumbled under my breath, seeing my assigned caseworker swing the door open scanning the crowd. "Yup." I jumped up not missing a beat. Rushing over with my paperwork out in hand, I was hoping she'd just take it like times before, letting me be on my merry way. But something about her tight lips, twisted face, and rolling eyes told me I was in for a war this go-around.

"Good morning, Ms. Donahue," I intentionally greeted her, playing the role but not knowing what her problem was.

"Good morning, Miss Greene." She kept it formal, holding the door open for me to walk through. "Right this way." Leaving me behind to trail her, I instantly caught an attitude at how arrogant and snobbish she was coming across.

*I ain't in the mood for this paper-pushing bitch today. Please, Lord, don't let her try me this morning.* Wishing I would've hit the blunt a little harder or longer before getting out of the car with Nique, I held my head low, trying to get my game face right for front game ahead of me. *Be cool, don't let her funky attitude get you rowdy. Be easy and be out.*

Going into her cubicle as usual, she offered me a seat before sitting down on the other side of her desk, typing into her computer. Plopping down in the chair, I unfolded the paperwork I had Nique fill out and forge so the handwriting wouldn't come close to mine, along with the generic check stubs I made, and placed them onto her desk. "Here's the stuff you wanted completed and returned. You can keep the original; I've already made a copy." From here my shit looked top-of-the-line official. Knowing I was testing the system, running the same game I'd been winning at for years, I tried playing her by having all my forms prepped for easy acceptance. With every line complete, each signature present, and no scratch-outs for her to verify and have me initial off on, once again my fraud game was on point . . . or so I thought.

Looking down at the papers then back up at me, she laughed under her breath, instantly pissing me off. "I'm not going to be able to use those forms, Miss Greene."

"Excuse me? What you mean you can't use these forms? Why the hell not?" Losing my cool, before I knew it my voice was carrying throughout the back area. Even ol' musty Tandy turned around at my outburst.

"All recipients receiving cash and food benefits must recertify, Miss Greene. Part of my job is to verify all information submitted to me, which I did." Hitting the print button, her grin grew wide. "And from taking a quick glance at what you've presenting, they're not legit."

*Oh hell naw.* She had me in a trick bag. *Think quick, Cori, think quick!* "Ain't nothing about this right here fake. You got me fucked up." I decided there was no other choice but continue with my lie.

"I'm gonna have to ask you to calm down. If not, I'll call security to have them escort you out of the building." Cool and collected, she wasn't the one getting ready to go down for welfare fraud.

"Yeah, whatever. Like I said, ain't nothing about these papers fake or fraudulent so get your life."

Sliding her proof across the desk, her slick, government-working behind had clearly gotten one up on me. "Come on now, Miss Greene, cut out the shenanigans already. We both know what's going on, and that you've been illegally getting food stamps in addition to cash assistance for probably your entire time on record."

Snatching them up with attitude, intentionally knocking over the picture frame of her and some mangy mutt, I began to scan over the shelter verification form that was much different from the one my girl Ta'Nique hooked up. My landlord unknowingly snitched me out to this white bread–

acting caseworker about my subsidized rent and included utilities. Milking the system as I knew it was coming to an end. "Well no wonder you acting all funky and shit. You done pulled a whammy so you feeling yourself."

"I'm just doing my job. So you know I'll be calling your place of employment to verify hours worked, et cetera. I must be very thorough in detail as to why I'm closing your case; just following protocol." She picked up my fake stubs already knowing the real deal.

I couldn't take her being happy at my expense. I'd never been the type of broad to let other girls get ego or big feelings at the cost of my reputation. Never that. *I see she wants it with me.*

"Fuck you think? You ain't calling shit. You can shove that punk-ass two hundred dollars in food stamps and two hundred dollars in cash once a month up your tight asshole." Snatching my stubs from her now shivering hands, I was in rare form ready to turn up. "I oughta punch you dead in the face for fucking with me, lady." Pushing her chair back, standing up, on point with my reflexes, I snatched off my Cartier hoop earrings ready to scrap it out on government property. "You want it, bitch, what?"

"Security," she yelled, backed up against the file cabinet, shook up. "I need immediate help."

"Yeah, security, come save this ho." Knocking over a few more trinkets on her desk, I hawked up a big glob of saliva and spit right on top of her computer keyboard. "I'll catch your scary ass on the flip side, trust."

By the time the slow, fat security guard showed up to her rescue, I'd gathered my falsified papers up and was passing him up the walkway. No way in hell was I getting ready to face charges behind clowning at DHS. Ms. Donahue was going to be forced to meet me on my turf.

"Damn, girl, it's about time." Nique started the car as I slid into the passenger seat, fuming.

"That slick bitch had the nerve to call me out on having bogus paperwork," I yelled, grabbing the tail of Kush from the car's ashtray. Hyperventilating, pissed to be caught off my square, I needed to get some weed in me quick.

"Whoa. Slow down . . . What?" Nique was just as caught off-guard as me. "What in the hell happened in there?"

"She had one up on me, that's what," I yelled, aggravated to the point of wanting to ram my fist through the windshield. "You know I can't stand a bitch playing me for a fool, Nique. And she got down on ya girl real good." Pulling on the blunt hard, I felt my lungs almost collapse at the impact of the thick smoke. I needed the downer bad. Blowing out the leftover smoke into Nique's beat-up Taurus, I continued with the story, giving my girl a play-by-play of what went down.

"Wow. Mr. Goldstein foul for that anyway. If he can call for some head in exchange to take money off the rent, he could've called for that."

"That's what I'm saying. But she's dirty for even taking it that far. It ain't like it's her money that's loading on my bridge card ever' ninth. I hate heffas who overdo their job."

"Girl, that's why I ain't even tried messing with they ass; I don't see how you did it for this long," she said as she shook her head.

"Don't even start. It is what it is. But I'm ready to get with her ass for busting me out like that. That was uncalled for."

"True that. So why you over here being all irri like she can't get handled? That heffa on every social network just like everybody else. You better do your research so we can creep on her."

Nique had a point. I had to give my girl props. We were a pair of criminally minded chicks who only knew how to handle our beefs and vendettas in the street.

"Besides, Mr. Goldstein will go back on whatever it was he sent with, probably just a hand job," she continued, knowing that was the last thing I wanted to do.

"You think that didn't cross my mind? I thought about that first; that's why I went plum nigga nuts up in there." The mere mention of his name had me getting excited all over again.

"Well, slow down, boxer." She laughed, pulling out of the tight parking spot. "Don't forget we've gotta hit this beauty supply right quick so you've gotta have your game face on."

"Aw, man, that totally slipped my mind. Ms. Donahue's hating behind has gotten me all twisted up."

"Um, then get up out of those knots, boo. You know my first client is at eleven, Cori. We need to get my products stocked more than ever now. So shake whatever voodoo hex that lady put on your morning so we can get to work."

"Oh no doubt, let's be there. I've gotta stock up on some makeup anyway. Your cousin's party is tonight so I've gotta be cute for him." Grabbing my phone to send him my usual good morning text, I hoped he was up on the early worm chase so he could start a private convo with me.

"Before you start your morning cake and bake session with his bogus behind, why don't you get at Wally about getting some work? With your case-worker tripping, I'm assuming we won't be eligible to get emergency state assistance for shutoffs or evictions. We need to make another guaranteed line on money."

"I feel you, but the way we smoke, we'd be blowing through our whole supply. Wouldn't be any product to profit off of. You know how we do." I was being honest with her and myself. We were both fiends for marijuana and that could be a problem when trying to sell it.

"Bitch, please, we need to flip this cash making sure we keep some money in our pockets. I'm tired of being broke so if we gotta drop this habit cold turkey, then so be it."

Nique was talking out of the side of her neck. I had no intention of giving up weed, point blank period, and neither did she.

"You gonna be blazing 'til the day you die, so spare me the sponsor speech," I said, rolling my eyes and making her laugh. "But you're right about being broke. It's played out and I'm surely ready for a change. But Wally ain't the one I'm trying to get a come up through. As soon as I call that nigga he gonna be on some old 'fuck me' type shit and it ain't even about that. Me and Mike about to be exclusive so I'm about to take my pussy off the market."

"You must be smoking more than this Kush Cookie if you think Mike is about to come up off the streets to settle down right now. You might as well hook up with Wally to see what he's really talking about."

"Easy for you to say." Despite truly wanting to, I sent Wally a text message letting him know I needed to speak to him on business. *I hope this shit doesn't go south on me.*

After a few seconds he responded; then we began to exchange casual conversation about this, that, and the third. I tried to keep it strictly business so he knew this wasn't me trying to get a tricking session on. I'd gotten down with him in the past when I needed a few dollars, but I was so far past being on that tip with him. However, I knew the game and, with girls like me, dudes never think you can change. My street senses were telling me that I'd have to let Wally at least bang to get him to be my connect. *Oh well, that's what this pussy is for: work, work, work.* Finally setting up a time to see him when me and Nique came from running the streets, I deleted all the texts so there wouldn't be any evidence for Mike to possibly find. Nique might've said some slick shit I let slide about him not being that into me, but he'd prove otherwise on the regular going through my phone, marking his territory.

# Chapter Two

## *Ta'Nique aka Nique*

Cori and I came from the same type of family up-bringing. Hell, our moms were childhood friends since the age of ten. They were the original Thelma and Louise of Detroit. Mama and Auntie Faye shot dope together, smoked crack together, and even seemed to have overdosed together. So Cori and I were forced to fend for ourselves, and naturally gravitated to one another even as kids, because our moms stayed high. And now we out here on some new breed, second-generation dynamic duo–type shit, robbing and boosting in makeup and heels. Times had surely changed.

I needed my ride or die buddy to get it together. Cori knew Wally the weed man had a thing for her we could use to our advantage to getting some weight, so I didn't know why she's sitting up over there caught up in her feelings like she didn't know the game. Sometimes you had to be down for what-ever to get a come up; it's called life. And this bitch

right here was trying to win. If Wally was into me,
I'd be doing splits on his dick for a few ounces to
sell. Looking over seeing her texting, I hoped it was
to get the ball in motion with him and not checking
in with my cousin. I wasn't hating that they were an
item; I was just more concerned about us getting
that bread.

Eager to get to the beauty supply store, I was
wasting no time. Not only did I need to jump right
for my cousin's party just in case my boyfriend
Vic's groupies were lurking, but a few of my loyal
customers had been blowing up my cell looking for
a deal on bundles. Forget cutting the next man in
when I could hit the lick myself. I would have much
rather been in bed because my stomach was doing
cartwheels, but I needed this quick lick badly!
Taking a sip from the Vernors pop I was nursing, I
was willing to try anything to feel better.

Since shade was already thrown at basement
beauticians, I tried to have my hustle run like a true
business. I wasn't about to get a bag tag for having
my clients bring needles, thread, spritz, glue, or
whatever else needed to get the job done. Besides,
that was less money I could charge. By me and Cori
lifting my product, everything made was profit.
Sure we took the risk of being caught; but them
coco puff Koreans weren't equipped to handle our
swipe skills.

Pulling into the parking lot of one of the hottest beauty supplies in the city, I made sure to position my car pointing toward the alley for a quick get-away. Back to school time, the first of September, kids were posted at all four surrounding bus stops in their crisp new uniforms. Me and Cori had gotten down right before Labor Day with Walmart cards for back-to-school supplies; so I was sure some of them were rocking stolen apparel and book bags.

"Black folk know they be out early." Cori finally looked up from her phone, peeping more than just the school kids but stragglers walking around with no destination in mind. "We better hope the car is still here when we come out."

"I know right. Ain't no telling on the Mile. Cats over here don't sleep, take naps, doze off, or nothing." It was a joke but thinking twice I didn't want to burn bread on us. I said a quick prayer to make sure our outlaw ways weren't getting ready to catch up with us now. This wasn't the time to get caught up trying to be slick.

Ding. Ding. The door had chimes that sounded as I pulled it open for Cori to walk through first.

"If you not see, we not sale. If you break you buy." A small-framed Korean lady greeted us, cheesing from ear to ear, obviously proud of her stained yellow teeth. Walking in automatically being watched, neither one of us twitched knowing this store's cameras were there for show.

We'd been in here a dozen times stealing their high-priced merchandise they bought for dirt cheap at wholesale prices, so this was regular routine for us. Splitting up, I knew Cori had her own thing to do. She already knew to snatch me up some combs, grease, and sheen. Having her grab the smaller items, while I hassled them about hair textures, worked more than well. The black girl who used to work here got fired for giving everyone the hookup, so we preyed on their inability to speak English.

"Can I get some help with the hair?"

Watching both the young Korean girls look back and forth between me and Cori with their slanted eyes, Cori was too crafty for them. Within seconds of them watching to see what move I was going to make, Cori had pulled the plug on their metal detector and swiped both bottles of O.P.I nail polish she'd been clutching in the palms of her hands. *Bet girl, do ya' thang 'cause I'm for damn sure about to do mine!*

"Uh uh, can I help you?" Dragging each vowel like a true Korean would, one of the employees finally opened her mouth to help me. "Yes, your sign outside says you have one hundred percent human hair on sale; what kind specifically?" Not talking like the true-bred hood girl I was, I wanted to throw her off.

"Um, yes, Outre collection is on sale, ten to twenty-five percent off depending on style. You want see?"

Acting confused, this was all part of the plan. Not only did I not care about what so-called sale they were offering, I was starting to get irritated by her strong accent. These little pale-skin munch-kins always set up shop in the heart of hoods but couldn't speak a lick of English, let along the Ebonics everyone around here spoke. "Let me see the Remi Velvet eighteen inch if you have it, 1B."

Watching her scurry off, I went back to scoping the scene at hot-handed Cori. She was moving up and down the aisles, watching over her shoulder as she tossed shampoo, hair color, perms, oil sheen, and combs into her purse. My eyes widened, sig-naling her it was time to dump that merchandise and come back for a second round. *What is she doing? That greed shit is gonna get us caught. Get smart, Cori!* We'd been robbing for years, but as of late, Corielle was starting to get more reckless.

"Here go hair. Ring up now?"

"Um naw, I gotta check y'all product out first. I brought some weave out of here a few weeks ago and it napped up on me super quick." I shook my head playing off disappointment. Reaching for the pack of hair, she eyed me suspiciously before handing it over.

"No problem. No problem." Opening the package so I could feel the hair a little, I ran my fingers from the wefts down knowing I was already planning on snatching it up.

Almost having to snatch it from her hands, I held it up in the mirror trying to see if it would match my hair color. Once again none of this mattered. "I'll need three more eighteen inches of these please. Do you have any hair that's already dyed blond?" I was going to send her back and forth as many times as it took for me to snatch up at least ten packs of hair.

"We have, yes, let me get." Scurrying back off like I hoped, she was about to get ran until her feet hurt.

After reaching down discreetly to snatch up a few of the miniature bottles of oil, I turned to see Cori coming back in the door, this time headed toward the clothes and knock-off jewelry section. *She's supposed to be over here helping me distract this chink chick, not wandering off for that cheap trash. She knows this hair goes quick, fast, and for top dollar.* Not before I finished my thought, the chimes went off, signaling a customer had entered. *A'ight, game changer but definitely not a spoiler.* I wasn't leaving up out of here without this weave; and that was that.

"Here you hair. You ready to buy?"

"What's your name?" Putting on my best inno-cent girl voice, I was trying to make this Korean lady feel at ease.

"Sue. You buy yet?"

"Listen, Sue, I own a shop and I offer my clients the option of picking up the hair I need for their style. Here's my list. I ain't here to waste your time, trust." I had to do something for dramatics. Reaching into my pocket I pulled a wad of bills out to flash for imitation only. I saw her little slanted eyes force themselves wide, seeing the greenbacks of hundreds she'd never touch.

"Tell me list. I get hair so you buy." Sue wasn't budging with her attitude.

It was starting to piss me off. I could've easily yoked her from behind that counter smushing her face into the ground, but I was trying to do this with ease so me and Cori could frequent this spot. I was getting tired of driving deep east.

Running down a few different brands and col-ors, she hurriedly got to work, fooled by the hopes of making this off-limits cash. Each time she left to get me a new selection to feel, compare, and cross off the list I made sure she saw, I stole a whole bun-dle. I had her twisted, confused, and losing count. Finally having Remi Velvet, Indian Remy, a few packs of Malaysian wet and wavy packs, and a few Milky Way bundles for those needing to spend less, I'd crossed everything off my list and was ready to go. Once the customer approached the same hair counter as me, it wasn't a second thought on my mind other than getting up out of here. "This will be all, Sue. You can take them to the register and help this lady. I have to pick up a few more things."

"Come on, girl, *let's go.*"

Hearing Corielle shout, seeing her run up the aisle way toward me with a gang of merchandise in hand, I didn't know what had happened or what tip she was on but blowing up the spot was what she had done.

"I said run, bitch, run."

Close on her heels, a Korean man wearing a short ponytail was almost close enough to snatch her back. "Stop her, Sue, stop her," he yelled, running full speed but not fast enough for crafty Cori.

"She not steal from here." Turning into only something I'd seen on television, the old bob-wearing sunk-face chink I'd just gotten down on jumped over the hair counter, knocking over the Styrofoam mannequin heads.

"Naw, Sue, she will." Tripping her as she landed before she could get a head start on Cori, I kicked her in the back of her head making sure she stayed put before making my getaway. Hearing the middle-aged black lady screaming at the hair counter made me run faster knowing the police would get called faster. *Damn this ain't our day.* Now, behind the Korean man, who was two steps from grabbing the door to trail Cori to the car, I picked up one of the pressing combs they had on display, running full force and slapping him as hard as I could on the side of his head.

"Ahhh," he screamed out in agony, grabbing the side of his face and hitting the floor.

I hammered on him a few more times and blood started to pour out down the side of his face onto the comb and floor. Then I kicked him in the back of the head like Sue; I couldn't take the chance of being stuck up in here with two against one—hell, maybe three if the spectator wanted to get it on it.

"Y'all chink suckas never give anybody a break in the hood anyway!" Grabbing a few hair magazines, lip glosses, and the sunglasses I'd eyed when we first walked in, part of me wanted to hold ol' girl hostage and steal more stuff up out of here.

Cori was laying on the horn as she pulled up to the front door and signaled me to catch a clue and get out of here.

The greed was real though. Doing a double take almost running back to snatch a few more packs of hair, I thought twice about doing too much, especially seeing the middle-aged woman with her phone out filming me. There was no way I could leave this place without that phone in my possession.

"Hey yo, bitch, give me that cell," I shouted, running toward the now-shrilling woman. She wasn't going to go down easy after seeing me nut up on ol' boy and Kung Fu Sue. I couldn't blame her but that didn't mean I was giving her a pass. Taking off full speed up the opposite aisle kneeled down, I cut her off at the end, ramming her into a rack of cheap costume jewelry.

"Who the fuck you thought I was?" Snatching the iPhone from her trembling hands, I punched her in the face, drawing blood from her nose instantly. "This is what you get for wanting to be a snitch." Shaking my head over her as she held her face wailing, I was disgusted at any- and everyone who had a snitching mentality. Hearing Cori honking the horn outside, I knew that was my cue to get out up out of here fast.

Hearing the door chimes ring again, if this was another customer, I for sure was busted. Seeing ol' boy's limp body in the doorway would be an alarm for anyone to run out screaming. *Damn this ain't supposed to be going like this.* Afraid to turn around, I bent down not wanting the person to see me.

"I don't know what you're in here doing, girl, but bring your ass," Cori shouted.

It brought a sigh of relief over my body. "Girl, bye, I thought you were another customer." I popped up automatically, back in the game. "Wait 'til I tell you what went down." Glad to see my girl and not another eyewitness, I thought quick on my toes, searching little miss lady for a wallet then snatching her purse. She never put up a fight but with prime examples laid out, I dared her to. "I'll be at your door if you ID me or my girl, trust that, Mrs. Tandy." I pulled the identification card from her wallet making sure the faces matched.

Whimpering, she nodded in agreement. I didn't have the need or time to torture her anymore. With this being 7 Mile and Wyoming, time was ticking before another actual customer did come in looking for weave deals. Me and Cori had to be out. Now being petty and trying my luck, I ran to snatch some more bundles of wet and wavy. Hell, you can't blame a girl for seizing the opportunity.

"You not steal from us, black girl." Sue lifted her hand in protest trying to drag herself across the floor. Squinting through her eyes, even half delirious she managed to degrade me.

"I can, will, and did, ya little cat-eating cunt." I swiftly kicked her in the head, harder this time. Seeing her head bounce off of the commercial-carpeted cement floor like a basketball, I knew she wouldn't be rising up to disrespect me again. I didn't feel the least bit of regret for knocking her skull loose. It served her right for making this about race when this was clearly about the haves and the have-nots.

"Come on, girlie, let's go. Somebody just pulled up," Cori said, starting to panic. "Now who's the greedy one?"

Throwing the lady customer's purse over my head, swooping up the bags of weave I'd dropped plus grabbed up in gluttony, I ran out with Cori holding the store's door open. Thankfully, I was able to quickly toss everything into the opened trunk, slam it shut, and hop in the driver's seat ready to burn rubber. "Thanks, my baby, let's be out," I yelled, breathing hard, trying to get my composure. I didn't want to chance anyone catching a glimpse of my plate or a description of my car. If so, me and my ride or die would make breaking news. Nobody in the city had a silver Taurus with a red hood, blue passenger side door, and silver spray-painted fender but me. Don't judge me; I got where I needed to go, and we coasted up the side streets, making our way back to the hood.

"No doubt, I got you all day every day. But um, what in hell really went down back there? I walked in almost tripping over Sam Lee's body, Sue a few feet away, and the customer I ran past laid out in the aisle."

"It's a long story, Cori. Let me just calm down so we can get home. We can blow through a fat one while I tell you all about it." Checking my rearview, making sure to stop at all stop signs, I didn't need any lurking police to flick me seeing the stolen stuff linking me to Hair City. I didn't plan on driving past that corner let alone shopping in that beauty supply ever again in life.

"I got you on that. But real talk as ya girl I gotta keep it one hundred, and from what I saw with Sue, you couldn't be contained. You went crazy up in there and we both got an eyewitness in this Kelly Tandy woman." Cori pulled the woman's ID out her purse holding it up to read it.

"Please, Cori, let me get back on the block first at least," I screamed at her needing to focus. My heart was still racing from taking down two Koreans and one black lady, plus stealing enough stock to fill my pockets. This getaway was a must so I needed my girl to lay low, text Mike, and be cool until I was at least a safe enough distance from Hair City for comfort.

"Damn the block; you better pull into the first gas station you see so we can start burning through these cards." Looking over into Cori's lap, she was pulling out Visas, Master Cards, and Discovers, multiples of each. "I wonder if they all work?"

## Corielle

Ta'Nique did her thang in the hair weave section; but I had makeup, knock-off jewelry, undergarments, countless boxes and bottles of hair care products, a tray of eye contacts, plus a few pairs of ceramic flat irons. I wasn't even done taking inventory of the stolen goods I'd personally lifted and had already made up for what Ms. Donahue had taken out of my pocket. It was the eye contacts that got me red flagged ending up with chink boy Sam chasing behind me. I couldn't help myself though; girls and now the flame-throwing guys out here were starting to rock them dry. Of course the hustler in me saw potential money being flipped and couldn't resist the risk. Once she told me all of what went down, how my greed had her slightly caught up, I felt a tinge of regret for not thinking twice about going behind the roped-off counter to snatch the tray.

There was no doubt in my mind this story would get light press, but nothing major. No way in hell these two chinks could go down in the heart of the city without anyone blinking an eye, especially with the mayoral election around the corner. Nique and I both decided to lay low from hitting beauty supplies for a while. But that didn't mean we couldn't clean up in other territories.

# Chapter Three

## *Cori*

"Hey, what up, Sam," I said, walking into the gas station nearest our house. Nique might've been shook up but stupid she was not. Seeing the cards in my lap made her drive like she had some sense, flooring the pedal so we could make this unexpected opportunity lucrative. This gas station was so ghetto and trifling, down for whatever; you could fill up your whip with your government assistance card if you gave them a few extra dollars on top. They got robbed so much for fifty cent bags of chips and juice that they put a fence over the entrance to the first two aisles. All about making smash-and-grabs less convenient, but all about scamming the system and those who spent money on a daily basis with them.

After grabbing a few snacks, juices, and crackers for Nique's upset stomach, I was back out the door right as she swiped one of Kelly's cards for the first two fill-ups: ours and some young chick dressed in medical scrubs, on her way to school or work.

"What up, Cori? Let me get a dollar or two," I heard my junkie neighbor begging me. "I can pump your gas." A fiend could be tricky; she was included in the pact. Having the option to have the nozzle hold itself on, there's no need to pay someone like back in the day. No work, no gain; I didn't care what come up I'd just gotten down on.

"Damn, woman." I lied with a straight face like it was nothing. "You caught me at a bad time. I just spent my last on this. I ain't got shit on me but a bridge card and you already know I sell my stamps as soon as they post." Keeping it real by giving her real-life circumstances she was familiar with, hopefully she'd get back to digging through the trash for cans or possibly tossed food.

"Yeah, yeah, yeah, if you say so. You young girls nowadays is always holding out on a li'l something." Walking away with much attitude and deflation, it was clear the old head was hip to my lies.

*Oh who the hell cares? As long as my pockets are tight, then the next female can continue to struggle!*

Sitting in the car, I broke the seal of my Pepsi, gulping it down fast. Nique had gotten another fill-up request and was taking care of business in spite of the on-looking gas station attendant. He wasn't new to serving customers around the way, so seeing a gas scam going down shouldn't have had him on the phone dialing for help. "Get your half and let's go, Nique." I rolled the window down, alerting my girl of the attendant's move.

"Fuck his 'rab ass. He wasn't talking about giving me no job to run the lottery machine, so whatever. I've gotta get all of mines and not a penny less." Looking at the attendant dead on, she gave him nothing but the meanest ripped mug. Not caring that she was flat-out stealing the gas, she wanted him to react to her with the upmost respect.

"It's too many stations out here for your greedy ass to burn a card out already on this one or possibly get caught, come on." As I rolled the window back up manually, I was now the one beyond anxious to get out of dodge. Getting caught wasn't worth it.

"Wow, look who wants to flip the script and play the momma now. Bitch, you already know I ain't about to slow my cash flow down for his pig-faced ass. Get your scary ass out and start seeing if they want fill-ups. You could be swiping too!"

Knowing she was right, especially since this was my idea, I got on the grind, jumping out, getting two sales instantly. Gas was at an all-time high at almost four dollars a gallon in Detroit, so people were overjoyed to see me at the pump charging half for whatever amount their fill-up came up to. Trucks were the best profit for us of course but I took any amount from a person down to their last five bucks. After I inserted the card into the pump on one side starting a transaction, I moved around to the other side to get two sales going at once. With four pumps going at one time, I had an assembly line of cars pulling in and out, all cash-paying customers. When I saw the same bum from earlier still hovering around for work, I called her over and promised her a handful of spare change if she could help pump gas until this well ran dry. She was more than eager to oblige and helped the entire process move faster. I was able to clear twice as many cars.

"I call the police on you three! They take you to jail for stealing gas." Sam's square-shaped head popped out of the gas station's door. That was a dumb move. He never should've warned us about his plan to alert the boys in blue. When I saw my impromptu worker's eyes light up when I tossed her a crisp ten dollar bill, I knew every bum within the city limits of Detroit was going to be knocking on my door looking for work.

"Leave my girls alone, Sam, damn," she yelled over to him, shoving the single bill into her worn pocket. "You always fucking with somebody over this rat infested–ass gas station." Just a few min-utes ago she was attacking my head. I couldn't help it. I had to laugh at the bum to myself as I watched her walk away strutting with much swag like George Jefferson. It was easy to tell she felt like a million bucks, able to fund her own morning package: black coffee and blow.

"Get away from here, shoo," he said, throwing his hands up, waving her away; then he walked back inside.

I collected the last of my money from the fill-ups currently going down before running back to Nique's car. I knew Sam was serious as a heart attack about calling the boys on us because every fraudulent dollar made during any of our transactions would actually turn into a loss for him. When Kelly reported these cards stolen, none of this gas could be paid for, or recovered. We were a thorn in his side in the worst way.

Both jumping into the car at the same time, Nique started the ignition and watched the notch glide from below E all the way to full. "Fuck that, I'm about to rush you to your car so we can hit a double whammy before these cards get cancelled."

"Say no more. You already know I'm down with it."

Me and Nique split up going separate ways but with similar things on our minds: burning these cards dead. She was going to hit the strip of gas stations up and down Livernois Avenue while I planned on hitting a lick all around east Davison. Ms. Donahue thought she'd put an axe in me but that prissy-acting bitch hadn't stopped nothing, and that's fa'sho.

As Drake's song "All Me" played as my ringtone, I threw my hands up, having a party in the car by my damn self. Hype and not wanting to answer, I didn't have a choice since it was Wally calling.

"Hello," I answered nonchalantly.

"What's up, beautiful? You and ya girl still out in the streets?" His voice was deep and raspy.

"You know we stay on a paper chase. We are in separate cars though."

"I feel that, baby girl. You coming through here in a few or what? I've got business on the east but wanted to hook up with you first." Wally was a busy man but he probably didn't really have anywhere to go. He thought with his dick the majority of the time, so he probably wanted some.

"I've got a few more stops before I make it over there, babe. Can you please wait on me? I'm trying to burn these cards out before they get cancelled. If you've got some people trying to get some gas, I'm over here off East Davison near the housing projects." Wally wasn't about to get on with this good-good right now; him and whatever he secretly had planned for me would have to wait.

"I'll put the word out for you, ma. Hit me up when you're on the way. I'll be here." He'd tested his luck coming up short. Too bad the tables would be flipped on me later. I needed something from him so he for sure was gonna demand what I was equipped with between my legs.

The BP gas station was small but known to usually have lots of traffic. Not having any eighty-seven octane, their fill-up spots were empty. Since I wasn't using my money anyway, I treated my old beat-up Grand Am with premium today. With a gang of teenagers being turned around for not being allowed to skip on the premises, I pulled them to the side offering to buy their products for them. I could use every dollar, especially since this place was super slow; and that was a quick twenty dollars made. While inside, I managed to sway away two paying customers but otherwise the station was dead. Not wanting the attendant to flag me for suspicious behavior, after making a simple fifteen dollars from one person and twenty from the other, it was time to be out.

"Ay, li'l ma, let me get the hookup," one dude said, approaching me as I got ready to get into my car.

"Well, you're going to have to follow me to another gas station because I think I've just about burned this motherfucker out."

"I'm down for that, baby. I'll follow you off the earth with yo' fine ass." He eye fucked me in slow motion.

"Well, that's not called for. You can just follow me to another gas station."

After I jumped in my car, I hightailed it a few blocks down to a Speedway. Ol' boy was on my bumper each time I came to a stop sign. Acting desperate for some gas, something told me he was only about to get a few dollars and it probably wasn't my time to even stop. And I should have followed my first mind. He only got ten dollars in gas with his broke ass so that was only five bucks for me, and he wanted a deal on that. I sent him on his merry way. This gas station was turning out to be a way worse bust than the other one. Mixed in with a few grannies that refused to be a part of my illegal activities and the corner boys with their own burned out debit cards, I'd only lucked up on one middle-aged woman gripping her man's truck willing to pay forty dollars for an eighty dollar fill-up. I checked my phone once I got back into the car and saw that Nique was blowing me up. I wondered what the urgency was since we both had two cards apiece. Hopefully there hadn't been a glitch in the plan and neither of hers had stop working. "You better be making money, ho." I laughed when she picked up.

"Most definitely but I've got a client about to meet me at the house, so I'm about to head back on the block."

"Oh okay, I feel you. I'm about to drive around to see where it's some stations popping. It was slow over here today, not even worth my time for real." The disappointment was clearly noticeable in my voice.

"Damn for real? Well go to the ones downtown. You should have more luck down there since the prices are spiked toward the wealthier parts of town. That's where I would go if I were you."

"You're right; I should've went down there first. Not only can I catch a few taxpaying workers on their lunch breaks looking for a deal, but the high school teens skipping as well. My pockets are about to be fat." I turned my car around and headed in the direction toward the most affluent part of the city.

"Make sure you answer your phone, chick. Did you get in touch with Wally yet about what we talked about?" Nique wasn't letting the issue die down.

"Yeah, we're supposed to be hooking up later so you can take a quick chill pill. Ya girl is on it."

"That's what's up. I knew you weren't gonna leave us hanging. We need this come up badly." She spoke into the phone with urgency.

Nique was highly anticipating what I was dreading but I was used to taking sluggers for the team. Hell, let me not be selfish; we both were.

"After you get us right, you can start focusing on being faithful to Mike since that's your main goal."

"Girl, bye, let you tell it. He ain't checking for me like that." I nonchalantly played her comments off, knowing that regardless of what she really thought to be true, Mike was feeling me. Each time his toes curled in bed, I was moving closer up to his heart.

"I know better, Cori. I just wanted you to get your mind wrapped around doing business with Wally. Mike probably really is into you; he don't run around giving dick to just any hood ho so you better feel honored it was you who got blessed since you feeling him so tough. But, back to business, answer your phone like I said. Peace," she yelled out before finally hanging up the phone.

Damn, she was rude as fuck. Nique was playing like my pimp, but in the back of my mind, I knew her greed for the money was right. It was gravy though because I was in money mode also. Seeing a lot of police changed my mind about following Nique's advice about pulling a gas scam on one of the hottest streets in the city of Detroit. But they weren't about to send me back to my neck of the woods without trying my luck with at least one. I parked my car on the side street in an attempt to remain discreet then jogged over to my destination. If anything was to go south, I'd be able to get out of the overcrowded lot with quickness and ease.

I walked up on a few patrons as they were exiting their vehicles letting them know the deal I was bringing. Only one snobbish white man turned his pointy nose up at me thinking he was either too good for what I was offering or I was too low to be in his presence. Either way, I was sure I heard him mumble something about me being a degenerate thief but I let the harsh truth roll off my back. The other two men gave fifty dollars without question for their SUV fill-up. Come to find out, some white people loved a hookup too. After getting over the initial point of being scared and not seeing a dangling fiend around to help me, I got into an easy rotation like earlier having cars move in and out. I had to start the transaction, load and unload the nozzle, and get my cash but things were moving like clockwork. If caught though, we'd all go down. Making it my business to keep my eyes on both the attendant and my surroundings, if anyone seemed like they were on to me, I'd dip in a heartbeat.

I'd made close to $1,000 before the card burned out. I had to send willing customers away.

I shot Nique a text message back in the car letting her smart-mouth ass know that the first card crapped out; but not before I took off $200 for my own pocket. I knew she was probably out in these Detroit streets taking off the top too, so fuck it. It was an unspoken mutual understanding. *So, I'ma do me, you better believe it.*

Going in the direction of home, I wasn't in the mood to meet up with Wally. I needed some down time after all the drama that had taken place this morning; plus I needed to get Mr. Goldstein on board with recanting the paperwork he'd sent to Ms. Donahue. I'd catch up with Wally before Mike's party. Both him and Ta'Nique would have to understand.

## Nique

I gathered all the stuff that I'd stolen from the beauty supply stashing it into my padlocked bedroom. Cori and I shared a three-bedroom flat on the west side in a run-down neighborhood of abandoned homes. On any given day you could catch a copper bandit running from the half-standing house next to your home with plumbing pipes on their back. Or a catalytic converter thief under your only car. Yeah, we were Detroit born and raised to the bottom of our motherfucking hearts. Neither one of us had jobs but that didn't matter; we had hustle about ourselves, so the bills always got paid. Hook or hustle, Cori and I handled our business. Word to the empty purse sluts out here giving ya goodies away: wise up. As long as you have a pussy, aka a rent box, you're never really broke. If a bitch wakes up broke, she had no business taking her raggedy ass to sleep. But times were getting hard, and by it being a drought our pockets were looking light 'cause niggas weren't out here generating funds like they normally did. That's why we needed the link with Wally badly.

Waiting on the porch for my first morning client, I was also waiting on Cori to pull back up. She was still out using ol' girl's credit cards and, if I was lucky, hooking up with Wally. That was the link we needed, plus Vic would have a reason to come back to me full time. It had been a hella busy morning with no slow down in future with heads to do back to back. Against my better judgment, I dialed my boyfriend's number hoping he'd answer. Vic had put me out of his apartment last night after I told him my period was late, and hadn't bothered to call to see if I'd made it home safely.

"What up, doe?" he answered groggily, obviously sleeping well not knowing if I was alive or not.

"Damn, nigga, so you wasn't gonna call to see if I made in last night or nothing? You ain't shit." Not wasting any time, I began cutting into him instantly. I was partially upset with myself for thinking he was going to take the news easily. Vic wasn't the type of man who women fished for when looking to get wifed, but I thought my pussy had kryptonite in it. Now all I had was a crumb snatcher in my uterus.

"Kill that noise, Nique. Did you find out about that situation you called yourself bringing to my table last night?" Breathing hard and grumbling, he still didn't seem thrilled about the mere mention of the subject.

"Not yet. I've been running around with Cori all morning taking care of business. I plan to though." Seeing my client pull up, I waved that I'd seen her and to come on in before rushing to disappear into the house.

"You should've checked your piss before you called yourself checking me. What type of dumb shit are you are on, Nique?" Vic called himself checking me. I could hear it in his voice that he was waking up ready to go hard like last night. The bass and hostility in his voice took me back to being manhandled then tossed onto my ass.

"I'm not on no dumb shit as you like to call it, babe. That was me keeping it real and preparing you for our future. But your reaction was harsh and bold. I didn't expect for you to clown me like you did. You don't want to stress me out do you? I could be carrying your seed." My intentions were to lay it on thick so I put on the soft girl voice that got me the long stroke on many days. I needed for Vic's mood to lighten up. He was too tense over nothing. Having a baby, a small family, and committing to what we've been doing for months wasn't so bad . . . at least in my opinion.

"Bitch, please. Piss on a stick then get back at me." Swiftly dismissing everything I'd just told him, Vic hung up the phone not giving me a second thought.

# Chapter Four

## *Cori*

Safely back at home, Nique was in the dining room with a client while I was snuggling up with my pillow watching *The Game* reruns on Netflix. When I first got home from sliding through the gas stations, I went online to order a few credit cards with the information found in her wallet. When the instant application was approved, I had them overnight the card and provide the sixteen-digit number for instant online shopping. Everything was mailed to abandoned houses throughout the neighborhood so it couldn't be traced back to me. The UPS man was an undercover junkie I'd pay twenty dollars to forget it ever happened. Since he wanted his drug habit to stay under wraps to keep his good-benefits job, he never gave me a problem. Once done burning through all other cards ordering a few laptops, cameras, and video games for Mike, I cut the cards up, but anticipated new ones coming bright and early in the morning.

Everyone came to me for legitimate-looking paperwork like insurance, identification cards, check stubs, and even bills. I was a mastermind when it came to crafting replicas and had been getting down on the system for years. Tax time was my best time. You didn't have to work daily and pay taxes to get a refund at my establishment. All I needed to hook you up was a social security number, state-issued ID number, birth date, and the checking or savings account information with routing numbers so the returns could be direct deposited. Knowing all the drop dates, it was customary for me to stalk like a hulk and make sure those who owed me paid the fee. I'd wait on doorsteps or usher to banks if necessary. I made sure me and Nique ate like kings from January to April. It was hit and miss every month after that. Identity theft should have been a major in school; I would've never dropped out.

A single day hadn't gone by in the last year I hadn't been on the streets grinding. Rain, sleet, snow, or blazing hot rays of sun, you could catch me trying to turn what little I had into something more. When I called dry-snitching Mr. Goldstein and told him to recant his form and send a new one to Ms. Donahue, he agreed but not before requesting a hand job at least. My rest was about to end shortly. I knew from past experience he was quite punctual when it came to getting his nut off. Getting bored with the made-for-TV saga between

Melanie, Jenay, and Derwin, I decided to do some social surfing to see what people had up for the day. Mike was too busy getting everything ready for the weekly gambling party to text or talk to me so there was nothing but spare time to kill.

As usual, my Facebook feed had the same long, drawn out sob-story posts. I wasn't trying to scroll through all that nonsense having my own woe-is-me book to write so I quickly logged off to log into my Instagram account. Now on here it was popping. Laughing at all the joke photos and videos until my stomach ached, my drama-filled morning had turned back around. I didn't know how people lived before the invention of social media. Continuing to kill time, I took a few snapshots of myself making a collage and hash tagged them selfie before posting for likes. Slightly ratchet with my purple bonnet on, I didn't care 'cause my brows were crispy and even on my worst day I was cute. Waiting on the picture to load, I damn near dropped my phone at what popped up in my feed.

"Really, Mike? So you're out getting liquor? This looks like a light brunch date to me." Sitting up from comfortably lying across the bed, I spoke out loud as I intently studied the picture of him and some random female. I was looking for details that told a definite when and where the picture was taken. *Where'd this flunky come from? Who is she? And why is she cutting in on our morning wake and bake sessions?*

As bad as I wanted to jump crazy on his phone, me and Mike weren't official so I didn't have that privilege. Instead, I studied the picture so hard I could imagine myself at the same table with them going upside his head. My mind was psychotic over this good-looking man but he refused to give me sincerity, commitment, or even the hood label of wifey. How we got down was more between us but having the side title of his side chick was better than anything. Not being able to contain myself, I doubled tapped the picture and joined the other ten people who liked it so far. I was sure I wasn't the only thirsty side piece in desperation for his attention. *Oh well, guess he'll catch up with me when he's done caking with her less-than-pretty ass. He's gotta drop those gift cards off anyway.*

With my attitude now sour, my stress reliever quickly turned into an even worse stressor. Once I hit refresh, the newsfeed reloaded itself and the first post had me more choked up than the picture of Mike and his mistress. *Is this a joke? Already? It ain't even been but a couple of hours.* CrimeIn-TheD, a social networking site that gives almost real ticker time brief details of crimes that take place in Detroit, just posted a picture three minutes ago of the beauty supply Nique and I robbed. The headline read LOCAL COMPANY BURGLARIZED WITH OWNERS LEFT FOR DEAD. My soul nearly jumped out of my body, scared shitless if the only real witness we knowingly left behind was currently singing like a canary. My hands momentarily went numb as the phone fell to the floor.

"Nique," I shouted, swinging my bedroom door open, running into the front room.

"Girl, what's wrong?" She turned around holding up a smoking hot pressing comb. "I almost sizzled her scalp."

"Bring ya ass to the back right quick. It's important." Once I noticed her client staring me up and down, I calmed down almost instantly. Because females always found a reason to keep my name in their mouth, I didn't feed them with tidbits of my business. I'd never been too fond of females.

"It better be, girl. I'm trying to stay on schedule." Nique placed the hot comb on the already burned-up towel then tapped her client on the shoulder. "I'll be right back, boo." She must've read the seriousness in my face and caught on to what I was doing then played right along with it. Nique was always good with picking up on my vibe. The customer looked on pissed with a half head of weave, probably more so because she couldn't be privy to what was going on. Not paying it any mind, Nique followed me back to my room.

"Someone already reported the break-in," I whispered low enough so the nosey client up front couldn't hear. I handed my cell phone over for her to see the same post that had me on ten.

Her eyes immediately bulged out. "Already? This is crazy."

"Yeah, it is. Which makes me think one of those three are talking." Taking my phone back, sitting down onto the bed, I was ready to take action and roll out.

"I don't think so, Corielle. We already knew the Koreans had to report everything that happened. But half-English-speaking Sue and Sam won't be able to tell them anything specific other than "black girl, medium hair and short hair." Nique imitated Ms. Swan from *MADtv* perfectly.

"If you're that comfortable, then I guess I should just cool out." I shook my head while checking the ashtray for a long-enough tail to smoke. "But if I hear a description even close to one that matches yours or mine, we're on Kelly Tandy's head!" I was ready to go take her out now. What was the point of leaving someone the opportunity to talk?

"No doubt, no doubt. You already know how we get down so if the time presents itself, it can be whatever." Taking a few puffs of the stinky Mary Jane it was easy to tell Nique had something else heavy on her mind. Knowing she wasn't the one to vent about her business, easily able to mask her emotions, I didn't probe for answers. Whatever it was, though, had her better judgment clouded. We were a ghetto force to be reckoned with but I wasn't comfortable with leaving my fate in some stranger's hand. This bell might have to be rung with me on the solo tip. Kelly Tandy wasn't going to be my downfall.

After a few more times of passing the blunt back and forth, Nique left without even bringing up Wally. That was a definite red flag that something was up with my girl. I couldn't be the monkey on her back, though, 'cause I had my own issues with Mike. Not seeing him respond to my text had me feeling some type of way. It was hard not to let what he was doing faze me since in my mind we were working on a future. Hood girl or not, I had a heart that he was way too crafty at manipulating.

Hearing my stomach grumble, the big girl in me was starving. I hadn't eaten since last night's weed-induced munchies attack. It was time to get down in the kitchen before the landlord arrived. I was bound to regurgitate tricking with him on an empty stomach for sure, so this was a precautionary measure, too. In the short time I had, I prepared a pot of extra cheesy grits, pork link sausages, and wheat toast, topping it off with an ice-cold glass of tropical fruit punch Kool-Aid Cori made last night. My plate could barely cool down before I was scarfing the food down my throat. I was hungrier than two fat starved hostages. Once I swallowed the last bite, my phone rang. Mr. Goldstein must've sensed I was close to falling into a food-induced coma. My head was more than ready to hit the pillow.

\*\*\*

"You better sign where necessary and fax these papers before end of business today, old man." I shoved in his face a copy of the illegitimate forms my caseworker shut down earlier. "And next time you get something about me from them, you better make me your first call." Repulsed that I had to jack him off, I wiped his thick, sticky goo from my hand onto the rag I'd brought out. It was so nasty and disgusting but what other choice did I have? With a case pending for welfare fraud, the only thing that mattered to me was preventing the charges. I didn't care nor expect my assistance case to be reopened.

"I'm gonna be calling your sweet brown self all right. With all that goodness, I'd like to call you first for a lot of things. How about we go by our spot for a few hours? Make ya'self a little change? Let me taste that black sweetness?" Mr. Goldstein reached over and rubbed my thigh thinking the proposition of money could make me wet. But money can't make you cum in all situations. For a middle-aged businessman he should've turned me on. Instead, everything about him grossed me out.

"Naw, I ain't late on my rent and don't plan to be. Just make sure you sign those papers." Sticking to the most important matter at hand, I didn't want him to get deflected nor feeling some type of way at being dismissed.

"You'll be calling by the fifth." He squeezed my thigh again, this time trying to slide his hand up farther. He was an old, dirty bastard.

I cringed and moved over in an attempt to let him know his plan wasn't about to go down.

"I hope you're late so I can charge a fee. Them slob jobs you're so good at have me sleeping like a baby." He winked before hitting the unlock button, signaling me to get out.

"I plan on having your cash on time this go-around, Mr. Goldstein. But please make sure to keep your word and fax those papers. If they lock me up for welfare fraud you won't be getting none of this."

"A deal is a deal. Plus I've been counting on you to get me off at least once a week for the last year. I wouldn't dare ruin a good thing. I'll have them faxed with a recant by tonight."

"Thanks, babe." I gritted my teeth then leaned over to give him a quick peck on the cheek. At this point I was working hard by laying it on thick. I could feel his dirty old man eyes fixated on my curves as I sashayed up the walkway so I made sure to put an extra pep in my step and switch to my plump behind with confidence to keep his mouth watering. Once he honked the horn and pulled off, I knew his clammy hand was wrapped tightly around his pink peckerwood.

"Cori. Hey, niece," Uncle Spook called, coming from across the street. It wasn't even noon and he was already sipping on a beer, a cheap one at that. Not really my uncle, but the oldest dopefiend from around the way, everyone from the neighborhood gave him the handle as way of showing him a little respect.

"Nothing much, Unc, about to go crash. My worker was on the tip this morning at my appointment and sucked the life out of me. You know how that goes."

"Shit, I can't stand them cock suckers down there," he slurred, smelling like straight Paul Mason. "Did you hear me and my boys steal that big heavy-ass awning off of the porch last night from that corner house?" Spook kept talking, dismissing the fact that I'd just said I was tired. "That scrap paid out big time for us, so we're about to hit all of these abandoned houses around here." Seeing the hood at its best, Spook should have felt a little guilt for tearing his community down. He should've been preaching to the youth to have brighter days, rallying against the thieves, drug dealers, and common criminals who peddled to the poor, and pumping hope into his hometown. Instead, Uncle Spook was contributing to the failed black man statistic. His whole purpose in life was to hustle the next man in his ploy to get high.

"Naw, for real? That shit is crazy. I don't see how y'all pulled that off without getting the cops called 'cause that shit was big. It had to be loud, too." Biting my tongue, catching myself from clowning Spook too hard, my real question was how his skinny, crack-rock-hunting ass lifted anything over a few pounds. I guessed with a rock being involved, Superman strength was possible.

"Yeah, but we wasn't playing, niece. I'm for real. Tonight at like four a.m. we're gonna hit up the house next door to you. So don't be alarmed coming out to shoot ol' Uncle Spook." Even though he was laughing, Spook knew that under the right circumstances, which would be the wrong for him, I'd do him in. When it came to my safety, no one's well-being mattered.

"Spook, you crazy. Don't come down this way fucking up my sleep. G'on around the corner to those duplexes or go steal everything down to the paint chips somewhere else." I laughed at him, still trying to make my way up the porch stairs into the house.

"If you're going to Mike's gambling party later, we can hit it then. Everyone worth it will be over there so they won't know me and my boys working."

I wasn't comfortable with Spook probing me for my night plans. No matter how cool he was or how friendly the exchange seemed between us, he was still a fiend and in street rules that meant not to be trusted. I wasn't getting ready to let him know my exact schedule of when my house was going to be empty. Spook was a lurker from the outside who never deserved to know what was on the other side of my door's threshold. "I can't call what I'm doing yet, but one of us will probably go. But the way I feel, I'll probably be posted while Nique goes to show face." This way he wouldn't know if my house was empty or not, unless he saw us with his own two eyes. We could trust Spook enough not to be distrusted, but where I'm from, giving a person the opportunity to be disloyal was sometimes a legitimate reason enough to get played.

"Let's blow one, niece. I know that old Goldstein dude set you right." Spook was relentless, always looking for a handout or a freebie. I had to give the old man credit for persistently trying.

"Naw, I'm straight, Unc. I've gotta stay focused for the rest of the day. You know I have to keep a clear head when I make my runs." I turned down the offer to smoke with him as usual. Me and Spook weren't about to share a blunt, no way, no how. We weren't on the same level no matter what he thought. "I've got this bag of shake that might equate to a nickel bag," I said, tossing it to him on the humble. Spook was a clear reminder of what I'd be in for if Wally could put me on with some work: niggas coming at me for credit.

# Chapter Five

## *Nique*

All I could think about, stretching the thick black stocking cap over my client Tasha's big head for a quick weave, was that I couldn't wait to be done. I wanted to clear house, get off my feet, then rest up for my cousin Mike's party. It had been an exhausting week with my boyfriend Vic pulling dodge moves on me. I knew that nigga was freezing up getting scared at the possibility of having a permanent responsibility with me, but I wasn't about to walk this line alone. Me and him had been inseparable for the past six months so I thought he was about to wife me up. Silly me for thinking with my heart and not my coochie. If I would've kept it ratchet like the no-class-having heifers he liked to run up in did, my woes would be nonexistent. I couldn't wait until I was around my family so I could unwind. Between Vic and today's traumatic events, everything in my world seemed to be flipped upside down. As I stared out of the taped-up broken window, my mind drifted down memory lane.

Doing hair has been my main hustle since I was a young girl on the block. It came second nature to me. In our shallow-pocket home, I was the basement beautician. I learned how to grease my momma's scalp, lay her with a press and curl, and even knot up some tied zillions like the Africans. The more time my mom spent in the streets party-ing, the more women came knocking on our door looking to get hair appointments. Neither one of us were into turning money down so she allowed me to service the entire neighborhood from the washroom in our basement. I brought more cash into the house than she did. My trade was nothing but an asset for her and I did it all: twenty-seven pieces, weave coloring jobs, sew-ins, blow-and-go's, and I even specialized in natural hair care. Please believe I was a beast with the scissors and could leave your hair flawlessly laid.

"Hey, Nique, I'm about to take a quick nap. Wake me up when you're done with this hot and ready." Cori laughed, purposely putting my client on blast. Her bluntness snapped me back to reality quick.

"Hot and ready? What's that supposed to mean?" Tasha played dumb with Cori, already knowing what it meant.

"Don't front boo-boo. You already know that means you're quick, fast, and cheap." Cori was cutting into Tasha with no remorse.

"Quit playing, Corielle. I ain't got time for your jokes and shit today." You could tell Tasha was annoyed by the way she smacked her lips. However, she never denied the allegations on the table. "G'on and take your troublemaking behind back to forging documents, or whatever it was you were about to do," Tasha said, shooing Cori away. I knew Cori didn't care about the low blow. She lived by the hustle; therefore she gave it much respect.

"Me leaving won't change your truth. But sure, I'll go." Cori continued mocking Tasha until she completely disappeared back into her bedroom. All I could do was laugh. As always, Cori had my back. She knew my motives with Tasha weren't good. I was on some sneaky, vindictive, payback type shit. Tasha could probably sense my mood. I could feel her intentionally jerking her head around and making smart comments about me and my roommate underneath her breath. It was easy to let the remarks roll off of my back. There were bigger deceitful plots brewing. It was time to get to work. Carefully spreading the black bonding glue across the thick weft of her Milky Way weave track, I couldn't help but smirk knowing it was mixed with super glue. I was about to go down as Tasha's number one enemy in life. After aggressively laying it horizontally onto her head, I pushed down onto the sides extra hard making sure the adhesive stuck.

"Dang, Nique, between you and your girl, I don't know which one of you is worse. What's wrong with you?" Tasha was responding to me squeezing her temples with no remorse.

"I can't speak for Cori but I'm good." I laughed, playing it off. "Just sit still so I can get you right. You know I gotta make sure this shit holds." Only half of the plan was completed. Unbeknownst to Tasha, because this was normal routine, I sprayed a generous amount of spritz across the same super-bonded weft then blow-dried the area until she cringed from the excessive amount of heat. It was pure bliss to watch her in so much discomfort. She had no idea I could be this ruthless.

"You're right. I'm not trying to have my tracks slipping while I'm on the pole. Plus I've got a date lined up that's planned to get a little hot and heavy; my shit has to be whipped." Hearing Tasha's voice was making my skin crawl. This trick better be happy I was about my bread. Too bad for her I was a sneak like Cori was a fraud and was all about getting revenge on the sly. Rumor had it she'd been tricking for my dude getting hers while I kept her looking A1 for him. Well it was timeout for that. Since I was the one lucky enough to have trapped his seed in my womb, I was looking to knock any and all other chicks off his radar. What potential baby momma wouldn't? I wanted my full sixty dollars and couldn't wait for her to come looking to cash in on an ass kicking once she realized I'd purposely made her baldheaded. Jesus Christ Himself was gonna have to lay hands on her head to get this quick weave out.

"Oh I got you. It'll be tight so you can make that the least of your worries." Putting extra glue and spritz on first the stocking cap then the weft, I watched with a grin growing on my face as it bled through onto her natural hair. This trick was gonna learn her lesson about creeping with any taken nigga of mine.

Tasha sat back playing on her phone while I worked hard at getting retaliation. It took me no time to clip her layers, wand her curls, and pocket her cash. These three twenties were going straight to the "get rid of it" fund, if a collection was even necessary.

"Girl, you're a beast at doing hair." Tasha complimented me while checking her reflection in the mirror. "You always get me together."

"No doubt, girl, that's what I do." Playing it off, now sweeping into a pile the hair I'd cut, I was ready for her to poof and disappear. With more serious matters at hand in addition to being preggo, I couldn't give her the proper ass whopping she had coming.

"Let me get up out of here before your cranky-ass roommate comes back up here ready to pop off." She now was the one trying to perp. "Pen me in the schedule for next week, same time."

"Cool. I got you. Tell my old dude I'll be waiting up if you see him down at the club." I couldn't help but throw hints that I knew she checked for Vic.

"Oh fa'sho, no doubt." Tasha hurriedly scattered toward the door. "That's if I see him." The dumb look on her face told me she was cold busted and the rumors were true.

"Girl, bye, I ain't stupid. You already know the hood been talking. Just tell him to get at me. It ain't nothing."

"Whoa, wait up. First, Corielle cuts into me about being a hot and ready then you snap out the side of your neck about me having sidebars with your dude. If you got something to say, then say it."

"From what you're playing back to me, you've already heard where me and my girl are coming from. I don't know how many ways to spell h-o to you." My pregnancy hormones couldn't be contained.

"Ho? That ain't right, Ta'Nique. Me and you go back to elementary school. I'd never cross the line with your dude. We're better than that." Tasha tried to get emotional but she was using the oldest line in the book. I wasn't falling for it.

I couldn't believe this fake, cheap-weave-wearing broad had the balls to be lying through her teeth straight to my face. The hood hadn't lied and the innuendo Facebook statuses hadn't either. Tasha was checking for Vic and bold enough to slither her snake ass around me. "I don't put nothing past nobody, you included. Let's not make this about no Barbie doll bullshit, Tasha, we're way too grown for that now. You've been tricking with my dude, you thought I was dumb, but you're gonna be looking like a clown in the end." Clapping my hands at each point made, I was getting hype ready to tear a mud hole off into her ass. I wanted Cori to hear the commotion so she could swoop in to help tag team Tasha. With the cash pocketed and the underhanded dirty deed done, all hell could break lose for all I cared. The beef was wide out in the open now.

"On that note, I'm about to bounce." She slung over her shoulder the stolen Michael Kors purse Corielle sold her a few weeks back. "I'll pass ya nigga the word but please, baby girl, any beef you got with him, take it up with him. I ain't the one. Despite what these broke-back bitches around here speak up on me, I ain't no foul friend!" Turning to march out the house, Tasha could've spared me the loyal friend speech. She was as low-down and grimy as I was a vindictive sneak. Gluing her bald was enough payback for me, for now.

"Bitch, be gone. I've got bigger fish to fry. I'll catch up with you on the flip side," I spoke out loud into the now-empty dining room, tossing the mixed tainted glue into the trash. I paid no mind to Tasha revving her engine, or burning rubber out of my driveway. I sent Vic a quick message that I just got at his slut bucket so the score had been leveled. I knew his low-down dirty behind was too much of a coward to admit to being busted, or even question me on what I meant. So instead of holding the phone waiting like a fool, I turned the ringer off, promising myself not to sweat his little stack-having ass. Besides, if he was running up in ol' trife-life Tasha, condom or not, he was marked for a future shot of antibiotics with a dose pack of pills. *Ugh, he makes me sick.*

Warming up a bowl of grits and the one spare sausage Cori was barely nice enough to leave me, I could barely get it out of the kitchen before I was smacking on a mouthful. This right here was on point! Out of nowhere I started to feel lightheaded, nauseated, and repulsed by the food I was swallowing.

*Oh shit, say it ain't so.* I covered my mouth quickly as I gagged hard, almost letting it rip all over the floor. *Run to the bathroom, stupid!* I couldn't get over the fact this was actually happening. I took off at full speed and barely made it to the toilet before all of the grits, cheese, and sausage was right back in front of me.

*I guess it's so. I'm pregnant.*

# Chapter Six

## *Corielle*

Ta'Nique and I lay back in her bed watching a scorned woman saga on Lifetime while blowing through a blunt. We both needed this downer as today thus far had been long. As we sat in silence I tried to read her mind. We'd been friends for so long; I could tell something was wrong. Her whole aura and disposition was off and I thought it had to do with Tasha and Vic. If the rumors were true, Nique had every right to be offended and pissed. Whatever the case, I had to play the friend card so she could start feeling better. My girl simply wasn't herself. It felt good to be totally still and relaxed. All that came to an end once my phone vibrated and disturbed my sleep. I snatched it up with the quickness hoping I could send the call to voicemail but it was Wally who'd sent the text message. So much for resting.

No excuses. Why you hit me up to bullshit? Come thru, Wally's text read.

"Nique, wake up a sec. I'm about to meet up with Wally so I'll be back." I didn't get much of a response from her as she groggily rolled over getting more comfortable. I shrugged my shoulders walking out. Her mood would improve once she realized things were in motion with Wally.

After I let him know I'd be on my way in a few, I got prepared for what might go down. Even though this wasn't planned to be a sex thing, if needed I had to manipulate him with pussy. Rummaging through my panty drawer for a cute set to wear, I then headed to the bathroom to wash the monkey extra good with Summer's Eve. Nothing turned a guy off more than fishy-smelling coochie so I needed it extra fresh if he went to lick the cat. Not putting too much emphasis on my attire, I slid on a pair of too-tight leggings that accentuated my plump behind with a wife beater and jean jacket. After I laced up my retro Jays and grabbed my car keys, I was out the door. I'd have much rather been on my way to get dicked down by Mike but from the looks of his feed, I was still an afterthought. I couldn't wait to question him about that light, bright broad. Maybe Nique was right after all.

"Yeah, Wally, open the door," I shouted up to him as I arrived at his four-family flat. I wasn't in the mood for long, drawn-out procrastination 'cause I had to put my cards on the table.

"What up, girl, hit this purple. Ain't no nigga in town got weed hitting like this." He eagerly grinned as I walked in the door. The aroma in the air made my eyes tear up. It could only be described as downright stomach curdling. Wally was the type of dude you'd describe as foul to his very soul. Dude smelled like he took a long bath in straight vodka with no chaser in addition to at least a whole pack of stale Newport cigarettes. *Ugh. You can tell his ass been trapping.*

"Oh shit." I choked and coughed, feeling my lungs expand as they filled up with the potent Purp that had Wally's eyes bloodshot. My body instantly felt stuck. The only good thing was that I wasn't feeling nerved about cutting into him about doing business. Coughing hysterically, surely waking one of three attached-unit neighbors, no doubt his product was indeed fire. I passed it back, not even needing a second puff. It was too strong for my blood. Besides, it was time for me to talk business and get out of here.

"Naw, girl, don't tell me that you're a rookie out here." He laughed loudly. "Got you over here choking out and shit." Animated, Wally imitated the face I made once tasting his purple power.

"Boy, stop it. You already know ain't nothing about C-Money rookie." I was playing it off. His one hit had me on cloud nine. Me and Nique could make a killing easily off this killer Mary Jane.

"Damn, your legs looking tight right in those leggings, ma." Wally paid me a hood compliment as I leaned back onto the couch. I knew I didn't want to lead him on but the buzz had me feeling heavy.

"Thanks, boss. You got the whole building smelling nasty with your eyes hung low." I smirked and slid closer beside him on the cracked leather couch. I hadn't come for a sex session but my pussy was starting to tingle needing some attention. The game plan had just been changed. I didn't know if this was Wally's game plan or not but I was all in. I was about to smoke this nigga's shit, fuck him extra good, get some weight and be back home in no time. The new blueprint had just been set.

"You already know how I do, girl. So what's up? Chop it up with a nigga."

"Me and Nique trying to get a zip. We can lock up our hood with that strong shit you're puffing on." I stared at him dead on in all seriousness trying to read what he was thinking before the reply left his mouth.

"Straight? You and ol' girl trying to take me and my game over, with me leading y'all straight to the honey pot huh?" He tapped the ash from the rolled Mary Jane blunt into an empty beer bottle and got up stretching and blowing the strong thick smoke into the air. "I don't know about all that." Wally's jaw line had tightened, which meant he was in deep thought.

"Don't cut into me like that. You already know I ain't into no shady biz when it comes to you. We hold each other down." I refused to give up without a good fight. "You have to give me credit for at least that." It was then that I started to talk a little more seductively.

"Yeah, I hold your ass down after you come up out of those panties." He winked, passing the blunt back. "So what will I get out of this deal?"

I decided to work my magic, taking off my clothes leaving just my thong and bra on. Wally, with his criminally ugly ass, was like a mouse on cheese as his hands moved up and down my curves as his dick grew in size. He wasn't the best I'd had but truth be told he wasn't the worst. And since Mike was on a hiatus with the mystery girl, I owed him a payback nut. I took a sip of Wally's purple then took a few more puffs of his product. There was no turning back.

I bounced my ass up and down on his thick black dick as he fucked me like an inmate fresh out the joint making me bust nuts all over his living room couch. I kept picturing that girl on Mike's arm and it made me grind harder on Wally. This had become more than me working on a percentage off a zip. It was making me feel slightly better. Even with a condom on, Wally pulled out when he came. That didn't make me feel no type of way 'cause I wasn't the mothering type. After we both got our clothes back on, he smacked me on the ass and told me to holla at him when we were out. I didn't question him or take my time getting out of the family flat. I knew I didn't have kryptonite in my pussy even though I bounced my ass like my life depended on it. Doing grams on consignment was common in trustworthy relationships. What was odd was that we hadn't even discussed the terms on this deal. That had even my swindle-minded-ass confused.

*Oh well! I'll tell Nique he couldn't take a loss and charged me for the whole zip. That way, I can keep her half of the money in my pocket.* 'Cause, don't get me wrong, she was my girl, but she hadn't just been bust wide open either.

Once back at home I found Nique was up and halfway out of her funk, trying to find something to wear for the party. I set the Ziploc bag and scale onto her dresser then immediately made a dash for the shower. Wally had put the pipe down, giving him credit, but I wanted his scent off of me. Before getting into the shower for a complete redo, I tracked my packages from UPS to assure they were on their way. I had to make sure the ball was rolling from each end. "So, how are we going to split the money?" Nique asked, throwing a few outfits onto the bed for me to look through for my opinion.

"How about we pay DTE first so our lights and gas services aren't shut off, then we split everything else we make evenly down the middle."

"Yeah, that's a good idea. We need Mr. Goldstein to work there," Nique joked, but I agreed with her. We'd be set straight for life.

"Me and Wally still gotta talk about the re-up situation so let's just deal with profiting on this zip. This is just a trial so if we do good with this then there's more to come."

"How much did this zip cost?"

I was quick on my feet deciding to charge her for "back minutes" since I had to put my pussy on the line to get us product in the first place. "Two hundred fifty dollars; he couldn't take a loss giving me a percentage off," I lied. There was no way of her knowing otherwise so that was the story I was going to rock with.

"Damn, Cori, he charged you the whole ticket? I thought for sure he'd come down a bit since y'all got down." She went into her nightstand drawer and started counting out the quote.

"Yeah, I'm just as surprised as you because I put my all into that dick. But you know how stingy niggas get when it comes to their chedda."

"Well, trick, you better try harder next time so we can keep more cash in our pocket. God gave us vaginas for a reason." She handed me the money then went back to searching for something to wear.

"No doubt or we can just make it a threesome next time. God also made me who love vaginas." I tossed the idea of me not doing all the work onto the floor. And by the change in her facial expression, I thought she got the hint.

# Chapter Seven

## *Corielle*

"Come on, Cori, let's be out."

"No doubt, here I come." Once I made sure the makeup I'd stolen earlier was flawlessly laid onto my honey brown skin, I slid on my earrings, bracelet, and imitation Rolex before meeting her walking out of the front door. We'd already bagged up a few grams to slip sale to a few people at the party so we'd always be making money. The truce has always been made for us not to smoke up our entire supply.

Mike owned more than a couple of houses in the neighborhood. A few were occupied by small low-income families he allowed to stay rent free, no upkeep included but reinforced, and others were reserved for his drug cook-ups, transactions, or like tonight's gambling party. He made money and spent money in the hood. But when it came to calling it a night and laying his head down, he drove more than forty-five minutes outside of the city knowing the D was too gritty for even a hustler of his caliber. I'd only been there twice.

Even though me and Nique walked the few blocks to the party, we had no intentions of getting back home the same way. I didn't know what my girl had up her sleeve for slick Vic, who I hadn't seen around the house lately, but I was planning on throwing it so heavy on Mike that he wouldn't let me out of his sight. That was my game plan and I was sticking to it. Dressed in a blue sleeveless crop top, stonewashed high-waist jeans, and matching blue studded sandals, everything about my style tonight was cute and simple. Nique had revamped both of our hairstyles so let me tell you I was rocking the hell out of this jet-black layered bob. Looking over at my girl, we both had our A games on. Neither one of us had a worry . . . well, from the looks of it. Nique was rocking a pair of galaxy leggings, magenta crop top, jean vest, and custom studded Chucks. I loved her punk rock look and the fact she could truly pull it off.

The block was crowded. Everyone was out in numbers trying to floss and be seen. Old-school Monte Carlos, Grand Prix, and Cutlass classics decked out with rims, TVs, and custom paint jobs were lined up the street like a car show was going on. Wasn't nothing like a black man being boss. Mike knew a lot of cats getting money in the streets, east and west, and tonight it seemed like they were all in attendance. Switching up on the porch so I could clearly peep the scene, I was looking for Mike's truck but a cherry red Benz stood out amid all the outdated revamped vehicles. *Damn, somebody in here working with a big bank!*

Inside of the house was no different than outside. As always Mike's gambling party was shutting even the club down. The speakers were blasting Young Jeezy's "Lose My Mind" and automatically, I started gigging getting hype. "Been at it all week, time to unwind." Jeezy's verses blared out as everyone sang along. I sang, dancing, throwing my hands up letting the crowd know the party had entered the building. I got everyone's attention, even Mike's. He gave me a low-key smile and nod and I kept doing my thang knowing he was caught up in watching my body move. "I'm out my mind; I just blew a thousand swisher sweets!" Dudes were starting to flock toward me for dances or to simply feed off of my energy. I was soaking it all up, enjoying even the hating-ass chicks who thought I was trying to pull cards with their men. Caught up in myself and the chase I had going for Moneymaking Mike, their lowball niggas weren't on my mind at all, not one bit.

"Let's grab a table so we can get to work. I'm seeing money drizzling all over the place," Ta'Nique screamed over the music then snatched at my arm leading the way.

Mike was watching everything go down. I blew a kiss and winked at him letting him know he was heavy on my mind. The party was slapping. For a neighborhood festivity, no one came slacking without a bottle or bag of Kush to contribute. Cups were overflowing, blunts were in full rotation, and guys pulling out large rubber banded wads of cash to bet against the next man in an attempt to triple their pockets' worth were all over the place. Me and Nique worked the crowd as usual. It was a lot of people who needed their bills paid, hookups on gift cards, or my daily moneymaker: no-fault insurance certificates. People who knew us for getting down with every hood scheme connected us with more people who wanted the luxury of scamming the system. Word of mouth went a long way with the type of business we were in; and since our hookups always worked, people didn't have a problem highly referring us. I'd passed out my minute cell phone number to over twenty people in twenty minutes. Business was about to be major and I was more than ready.

Never losing eyes with my main focus, I watched Mike's every movement with a keen eye. Standing firm in his Jordan Retro '89s, denim Levi shorts, and matching green glow Nike shirt, I loved everything about his style and swagger. My wannabe wife eye was lurking. You couldn't tell me this sexy brown man wasn't mine. He had juicy lips, deep dimples, and a killer smile. My panties were getting moist just looking at him. Up from the table now cleaning up in a dice game, he was scooping piles of money off the floor, ripping niggas a new asshole with his pop off the wall technique. *Yeah, baby, get that chedda.* I was his number one fan.

"I peep you all up Mike's ass and all, but can you get your head in the game to get this bread?" Nique was annoyed but it wasn't because of me. I might've been watching Vic and his entourage of groupies staring hard, but Vic ignoring Nique stood out amid everything else. Her secret wasn't safe. Actually, it had been exposed.

As I continued to sip from my own personal bottle of Coca-Cola mixed with Hennessy, the liquor had me feeling myself. I turned back to the game, tossing out my play, winning the book. "And I peep Vic." Blast for blast. If she wanted to call me out for Mike, she had hers coming of course.

Tossing her own cards onto the table, she automatically lost the game, costing us the twenty dollars it took to sit down. "Yup, you're right, Cori, and he ain't shit." Marching straight over to Vic, my girl was like a Tasmanian devil going nuts on him. Pushing him into the pool table, exaggerating each point with her hands, yelling and crying; I didn't know what was up between them but that was my best friend cue to get my girl up out of here or at least from causing any more of a scene. Usually we stayed out of each other's personal affairs, but Vic was playing her mad low by shaking his head no, giving her the dumb boy expression. He had no reply to her rants and to me he seemed colder when she fell to her knees in tears. Vic was an antagonist who got off on Nique being weak for him obviously.

"Whoa, get the fuck up, Ta'Nique. This ain't even about to go down like this." Mike got to his cousin before I did and roughly snatched her up by the arm.

I put more fire under my feet wanting to be close to him and I jogged over letting Nique know I had her back, too. "You okay?" I whispered.

"Naw, I ain't okay," she yelled. "I hope you die in your sleep for what you said to me, Vic."

A hush fell over the room. Those who weren't aware of the yelling match between them were definitely on alert now.

"Let's go, babe. Whatever he did, fuck him. Let's just go so you can get yourself together." I was trying to be a good friend. Plus I didn't want her to make more of a fool of herself than she'd already done.

"Yeah, cuz, g'on and cool out. This clown was about to bounce out of here anyway." Mike grimed Vic up and down letting him know his pocket money and presence was no longer necessary or wanted. It was family over foe this way.

"Yo, Mike man, your cuz is crazy tripping on some other shit. I'm trying to flip these dollars." Pulling out a wad of bills, Vic was stunting hard, or at least trying to.

"Go ahead and drizzle on us you ol' broke-ass bum," Nique shouted with bitterness. "Still staying in ya mom's basement with a house full of lowlife–ass nigga." Each word she shouted was laced with venom and hate. My girl was going hard in the paint.

"That's why you trying to trap me huh? Get the fuck up out my face, li'l girl," Vic spat, shooing Nique away with his wad.

Single dollar bills flew everywhere as Nique knocked his money from his hands. "You ain't working with shit," she screamed, twisting her lips up giving him much attitude.

"You ol' thirsty, nothing-having-ass trick." Vic degraded her and me too with each low-down word. Within a blink of the eye, he grabbed Nique by the throat and leaned her across the pool table. From the look of it, he was attempting to choke the life out of my best friend in front of everywhere here. Letting go but still leaning his weight over her, his cold, callous threats could be heard clearly. "Like I said, I'll abort the bastard myself."

*Wow, what? Pregnant? My girl was holding out on telling me? I hope she ain't planning on keeping his kid.*

"Hey, man, get your hands the fuck up off my cuz." Mike yoked Vic up from on top of Nique with one swift motion. "Get up out my spot, dude; I ain't even trying to repeat myself." By now Mike's goons had popped up ready to reinforce anything he was demanding. He worked efficiently alone but his team was always willing to step in to handle his light work.

"Shit, bro, fuck ya cuz with her dehydrated rat ass. I should've worn a rubber," Vic spat, looking Nique directly in the eyes. I saw her feelings go numb. Ol' boy was doing too much.

Mike's eyes widened as they looked from me, to Nique, to Vic acting cocky. "You doing some real big shit talking for me to already have dismissed ya ass." I could tell it was about to be trouble. Mike landed his fist directly into Vic's nose twice, completely catching him off-guard. "Get this chump-ass nigga the fuck up out of here."

Screaming threats as they dragged him out, Vic made sure he let Nique know she'd see him again. She stared at him with tears in her eyes but trying to play the big girl role. The party was starting to continue as the crowd moved on. Arguments around here happened twenty-four-seven. Everyone was a prime candidate for World Star.

"Oh my God, baby, are you okay?" Running up to Mike with the concerned voice only a mother could have, my face immediately ripped. *Yeah, it's my turn to clown now, if it ain't the breakfast broad.*

Mike turned my way to see if I was watching. Indeed I was. I twisted my mouth up raising my brow questioning him every nonverbal way I could. He knew I wanted to know who this girl was. He'd already ignored me all day for her and now she was on my territory. I felt the blood in my veins boiling. Smiling, throwing me for a loop, he grabbed her arm and started marching her my way.

"What is he doing?" Nique questioned, out of her trance now that Vic was gone. Still with a face of dried-up tears, she was still on guard for me.

"I don't know, but we're about to see." I had to keep my fronts up. If nothing else, I was looking good. In the short time of watching ol' girl, she wasn't much to look at. She was bone thin and unexciting—no competition for the thickness Mike loved to grab on with me.

"Corielle, this is Alyssa. Alyssa, this is my ride or die chick Cori." He let her hand go.

She had the nerve to raise it up to shake mine. Nique giggled.

"Nice meeting you, Cori." She smiled, not knowing I'd knock her head from off her shoulders. Obviously she didn't know any better so this would be her pass.

"Yeah, whatever, same to you. Mike, can I holla at you please?" Cutting my eyes hard, I was letting him know that no wasn't an answer he could give.

"Sure. Alyssa, baby, g'on and get up out of here. I'll meet you back at your crib when I shut the trap down." He then smacked her on the ass making me want to smack him across the face. The blatant disrespect was uncalled for. I saw a lot of that was going down around here tonight.

"Okay, Mike baby, whatever you say. Nice to meet you again, Cori." Not waiting for a reply, she walked away with confidence not knowing a cold-hearted bitch who wanted revenge off rip was watching her with evil intentions.

"So who is homegirl? And since when do you call the girl you're sleeping with a ride or die chick? You've got some nerve nigga." I wasted no time going in on him. We might've not had a title to what we were doing but he wasn't about to flaunt girls in my face either. I might've liked Mike but he was trying my tolerance like I was some type of lightweight powder puff girl.

"Chill out, C. You and my cousin are both amped up tonight." He laughed then took a swig from his Corona like it was nothing. "That's Alyssa, like I said. I introduced y'all so you should've asked her when you had the chance." Mike was talking with a smirk. He wasn't taking my anger serious enough.

"I'll go stop her and see for myself then." I turned around quickly, ready to go chase Alyssa down and make good on my word, but he grabbed me back.

"Your ass stays feisty unless you blowing. That's just a shorty I've been hooking up with; you know a nigga be down for whatever. Ain't nothing serious like wedding bells, Cori, so calm your hype ass out. The turn up ain't needed. It's been enough heat surrounded around me for one night."

"Boy, bye, whatever nonsense you talking, I ain't trying to hear it. You keep that stank-breath bitch out of my face or else. You've got a lot of nerve to come at me about keeping the heat off of you when you invited her here. This is my turf."

"Don't threaten me, baby girl. You know I don't take well to threats." Mike's dimples disappeared. He was all the way serious.

"And I don't take well to people tempting me. So we're even."

"Get your ass to the back, Cori, now."

I wasted no time doing as I was told. Moments later I was in the back bedroom with Mike's tongue stuffed down my throat. As his hands roamed my body, rubbing on my exposed stomach, up my spine and unclipping my bra, he lifted my shirt then sucked each nipple like a starved child. I was moaning loudly in pure bliss and heat. I didn't care who heard plus hoped Alyssa had crept back in and was listening outside of the door. I was serving Mike my milkshake and he was loving every drop.

"Now that you've calmed that little attitude of yours down, let's talk business."

# Chapter Eight

## *Nique*

Not supposed to drink because I was carrying Vic's child, I sipped from Cori's cup needing the liquor to help numb the hurt I was going through. I knew he wasn't going to be thrilled about knocking me up, but I didn't expect him to go as crazy as he did. Let that be a lesson to all men claiming not to want babies: strap up with a Magnum or get ready to help strap shorty up. He was acting like having a child with me was a death sentence or at least twenty-one years to life. True, I was a thief twenty-four hours of the day with the temper of a bull; but he was my bad boy and I thought together we'd be the new power couple like Bey and Jay. I hadn't even gotten a chance to tell him I'd gotten some grams to flip from Wally. Here I was trying to get him back on in the streets but he was kicking me to the curb.

As I thought back on how the whole fiasco played out, I took a few more sips feeling it start to get me buzzed but nauseated at the same time. Images of the expression on Vic's face as he yoked me up over the pool table wouldn't go away. I thought Mike was gonna let him kill me. That nigga so tight with his money, he probably could rationalize a good reason and understand Vic set-tripping for me knocking his money from his hands. The only thing I could think of when I was trying to rip his chubby fingers from around my throat was how good it felt when we were together. Nothing in my life was going down the way it was supposed to. *I've never been dealt the best hand of cards to play with so I guess karma ain't done kicking my ass.*

"Tell ya girl Tasha she can still run up." I rubbed my big belly mean mugging the two chicks who were known to run with her who were staring off to the side. "Pregnant or not, her fake ass will still get the business." Vic and his dick had caused nothing but problems for me.

"So how much did he give you?"

"Twenty-one hundred-dollar bills." Cori waved the counterfeit money in the air. "That's ten each."

"What does he want on the come back?"

"I've got his list, don't worry. He would've charged you two hundred dollars cash but wanted to contribute to helping you out of a tough situation." Cori didn't hold me up by blatantly pointing to my midsection.

"What the fuck? So instead of getting sexually pleasured, y'all were back there running down me getting the vacuum hooked up to my coochie?" Mike and Cori had me twisted.

"Girl, chill out. Please believe we weren't back there sweating you getting knocked up by Slick Dick Vic. Your name came up as a sidebar when he ran down how to spend the cash at hand. Please don't overplay your position."

"Oh shit, that's my bad. I just had to check two of Tasha's friends for staring at me before you came from the backroom with Mike," I apologized to Cori. I thought my hormones might've been getting the best of me, too.

"I ain't trying to get cursed out for caring, Ta'Nique, but please just think long and hard about what's best for you. If you keep that baby though, I'm gonna have to find me a place to stay. Between your hormones and Vic practicing for Wrestle Mania, I ain't got time."

"Girl, whatever. You owe me big for keeping chink boy Sam from snatching your ass up this morning. He was on you like white on rice, and you know they love them some rice." Sharing laughs with my girl felt good. Me and Cori had been so caught up in drama, trying to survive, and the daily bullshit that surrounded us in the hood, that we'd forgotten how to just chill being two twenty-one-year-olds doing careless things.

It was totally time out for young-minded foolish-ness as we pulled into the parking lot of Walmart. It was time to do what made us most comfortable: being sneaky. Mike had given us $2,000 in coun-terfeit bills that we were getting ready to pass off as legitimate. If all went well, he'd promised to produce more. Almost three in the morning, the stores were close to empty as expected. Besides a few vamping strangers getting late-night snacks or odds and ends, it was just me, Cori, and the underpaid workers. It could've been high noon with a store full of shoppers and we still would've done it big. I didn't know about Cori but I felt real boss-like with a pocketful of money, knock-off Ben Franks or not. Both grabbing separate buggies, we each intended on filling them with miscellaneous items while scoping the scene. Even though the main goal was to get gift cards, we always shopped for other items to blend in and not seem too suspicious.

I strolled down the aisles with a watcher's eye trying to see what everyone was doing. As always, Cori was already in motion not caring who or what could've been two steps ahead. *The more I try to steal smart, the more reckless she becomes.* Mov-ing a little faster so I didn't have to see what she was doing, something far more distracting caught my eye. Overwhelmed by the tiny clothes, bottles, and decorations in the baby section of Walmart, I couldn't help myself from becoming emotional. If I were to have this baby, I'd be in sections like these day in and out. I went into a fantasy land as I ran my hands over the clothes gently trying to connect to the idea of possibly having a son or daughter. The idea didn't seem too bad. It would finally give me the opportunity to be a better mother to my child than my mother had been to me. I decided to purchase the cutest unisex outfit that I could find. Tears were welling in each eye. My decision wasn't made yet but, just in case, my preparation had begun.

Finally meeting back up with C, we knew the routine when dealing with self-checkout. Any items that passed the register without being scanned would trigger the register to stop scanning, alerting both the cashier and customer the item needed to be scanned. And neither of us wanted that glitch in our plan. I picked up five gift cards and was planning on loading $200 on each to flip for half. I started scanning items and hurriedly stuffing the baby clothes into a bag. I didn't want to hear Cori's opinions and judgments.

"Baby clothes, Nique? Are you truly serious? Hell naw, did Vic cut the oxygen off from your brain when he was choking you?"

"This ain't the time or place." I cut my eyes in her direction, refusing to look at her dead on. I knew what I was doing seemed half crazy and in no way could she relate but I wasn't the type of girl who backed down from dudes who threw her shade. As much as we were alike in setting it off with a scheme, we were like night and day when it came to wearing our hearts on our sleeves. I didn't think Corielle could understand even if she wanted to.

"Chick, whatever, but you're doing the most."

"I know you're not judging me with a buggy full of men's products. You're all up Mike's ass." I rolled my neck at Nique giving her just as much judgment as she'd just given me.

"Bitch, bye, this is business right here. You know everything I do is tied to getting down." I watched Cori insert each fake bill into the machine and not one shot back out. As her total balance due decreased to zero, at the end her change and receipt shot out. "Hurry your slow ass up, baby momma. Toss me the keys; I'll have the car curbside." She winked.

I watched Cori for a minute as she rolled her cart out of Walmart. She was already on her phone texting people we were on deck with gift cards.

# Chapter Nine

## *Corielle*

The sun peeked through my blinds as I awoke to the same usual gunshots, screeching tires of a speeding car doing at least seventy-five miles per hour up the block, and the wails of some innocent bystander caught up in the middle witnessing the whole ordeal. It was a different day, same shit; good morning. What just went down was nothing in my ratchet neighborhood. Only the few neighbors who still cared about the property value of our neighborhood still bothered to call 911 but if a squad car bothered to show up, it would only be one and they'd barely take pictures or an accurate report.

I rolled over trying to get my droopy eyes to focus on the digital numbers on the DirecTV box. It was only seven-nineteen in the morning. *Shit, I'm dizzy tired. I need about couple more hours of sleep to get right.* Closing my eyes back, wishing I could really stay that way, I had to get up and get busy making all of the orders I'd gotten last night at the party. Four people paid me up front for insurance paperwork, so they had to be ready by nine o'clock at least. Running a ghetto business didn't mean you had to adopt trifling tactics. My word was bond because my reputation meant everything.

Looking over at Nique, she was cuddled up with her blanket on the opposite couch. Comatose sleep, she didn't even blink or budge to the gunshots. My girl was going through the motions in a bad way. We'd barely made it in the door last night after going through a whirlwind of drama at Mike's spot and Walmart afterward. But it felt good to crash with her like kids having girl talk about ol' girl Alyssa but most importantly the situation between her and Vic. It was hard to stay quiet about how I felt since this really wasn't my situation to have a say in, but I didn't know what the holdup was on Nique's end. Going to the abortion clinic should've been the second step after confirming the pregnancy. I would've stuck a hanger up my own twat if I were in her situation. Not a second thought about it. Not only did Vic not want the baby, but he was a jerk as well. Nique should've been running from his coward ass instead of trying to breed with him. But again, that's just my opinion.

Once I got to my room, I peeled my clothes off as my mind drifted off to the impromptu sex session with Mike. He hadn't texted or called back from me letting him know all went well and the cards were on deck. He was probably knee deep in Alyssa. *Oh well, when it's my turn, it'll be mine.* I put off taking a shower, left on my cum-stained panties and bra, and slid on one of the shirts he left over here a while ago. I wanted to smell like him longer. Powering up my computer and sitting down with the spiral notebook I kept my customer's information in, I diligently got to work. I was a mastermind when it came to creating illegitimate seven-day insurance policies. Mimicking an actual policy issued by these knock-off places like LA Insurance, who charged over $250 for seven worthless days of insurance, you could pay me a lowball fifty dollars for the same thing. My desk had all the necessary supplies to make each form look certifiable; and never once had my knock-offs not worked. I'd charged seventy-five dollars for each one last night: a twenty-five buck increase because I knew the big spenders in attendance had it. Instead of putting the $300 into my bill stash, I set it aside for the Ta'Nique abortion fund. After getting all four of them printed out and slid inside a stamped manila envelope to appear extra official, with no hesitation I hit up each one of their cells letting them know their forms were ready for pickup. I didn't play when it came to getting my customers in and out. The quicker they got their product, the quicker they'd be out of my hair and hopefully referring my services to others. I wasn't a friendly type chick but I was infatuated with making love to the money.

It was just after eight-thirty. No one had responded to my text as of yet but I promised myself they weren't about to hold me up. Today was going to be a moneymaking day for sure. Macy's had a sale going on today so I had to get to my hands on the good stuff only the early bird risers were privy to. Making sure my scarf secured my weave, I hopped into the shower using the Dove body wash I stole from Target to wash and moisturize my skin. Rubbing the loofa over my breasts and stomach, thoughts of Mike flooded my mind, this time mixed with those of Alyssa. Whoever this chick was she was getting major time. He'd fed me some bullshit about it not being that serious, but if that was truly the case, why was she getting so much press? Breakfast photo ops, public affection, and getting to drive his truck; she was more than just the jump off he classified me as. I'd heard him tell Alyssa he'd be there after the party last night and since I played sleepover with Nique last night, I obviously wasn't the chosen one. He'd pacified me with a nut at his party. I'd gotten played. Letting the water soothe me, I washed up a few more times then stood there talking to God. I was in desperate need for Him to get my life right. He had to guide me to a path much better than this one. I was tired of the struggle.

As I rummaged through my closet for something relaxed to wear for the day, I decided to keep it simple with a pair of lightweight cotton Abercrombie and Fitch jogging pants, T-shirt, and no-brand boat shoes. Standing in front of the mirror, I was trying to decide on what type of accessories I should rock and if the nerd glasses would be doing too much. I wanted to blend in with the preppy girls who would be spending money since I'd be swiping everything that caught my eye. My closet was needing a makeover plus the people I usually boosted were calling to spend money. Who was I not to deliver on demand? As I applied my makeup, I was yawning out of control but I refused to turn down the opportunity to shop when someone else was treating.

"Good morning, sissy, I see you're up and at it." Nique was standing in my doorway with sleep caked up in the corners of her eyes. The long wand curls that were flowing down her back last night were now pulled up into a ponytail, limp and dry. Fighting, crying, and getting tipsy while pregnant wasn't ending up being a good look for her.

"Hey, good morning, boo. How do you feel?"

"Like shit, but I'll be good after I blow through this blunt and take a long shower. What's up on your agenda for today?"

"I'm about to hit that Macy's sale, clean a few racks off." I laughed, acting like I was popping my collar.

"Oh, why didn't you wake me up? I'm trying to ride out too. We can hit a few stores up and make a killing real quick." Nique was already making a move for the bathroom. "Roll up since you're already looking like a doll. I won't be long."

"If it weren't for me wanting to give my customers a little more time, you'd be ass out. Make sure you hurry up in there please," I shouted behind Nique as she slammed the door before my words were finished.

"Cool it, Cori, I'll be right out. Do not rush me." Nique's hormones were more than kicking in. They were flat out annoying me. *She'd better direct that feistiness to Vic's nut-busting behind.*

Picking up my ringing cell, the first of the four people I was waiting on had just pulled up. I grabbed their paperwork and headed outdoors so I could hurry to finalize the transaction. After meeting them on the curb, they pulled off, quickly headed toward the Secretary of State a few miles away from here. It took no time for the other three to follow suit, which meant that was quick money made. *Tell ya friends about me.*

The sun was shining bright, the assumed crime scene from earlier had cleared, and the hood was coming all the way alive. Bright and early, already dedicated fiends were out tapping on windows trying to get their rise and shine early morning blows on. Some of my neighbors were already outside sitting on the porch gossiping, some still up from last night high off the flow of cheap alcohol and their drug preference. That's one thing I liked and couldn't deny about the hood, especially mine: there was never a dull moment. On the dullest Michigan winter storm night, cats in the D could make even the simplest task like making grape-flavored Kool-Aid into a federal case. After witnessing crazed shit like seeing crackheads slug it out over whose eyes got bigger after a blast, or being snatched out of my slumber by fence-stealing thieves leaving the elementary school unprotected from carless drivers and random wanders, I'd seen it all and was probably actually part of even more.

I decided to post up on the porch looking cute until Nique got ready so to kill the time I pulled out my phone to check the CrimeInTheD post. Not seeing any leads to suspects or information, I was right about today being good 'cause ol' girl hadn't snitched after all. I tried to keep myself from checking Mike's page but I couldn't fight the temptation. I wanted to do a search down on this Alyssa chick who was so worthy of his time. Seeing her name linked to one of the pictures because she'd commented on with only a kissy face emoticon, I clicked on her page but as suspected it was private. With no other choice, I logged on to the fake page all of us girls kept to stalk and lurk our niggas and was quick to request her. Once she accepted, I'd be checking for her from the inside. Everything I did was well plotted out.

"What up, C-Money baby?" I heard Uncle Spooky greeting me by my nickname but I didn't know where the voice was coming from.

"Spooky-Spook, my fam Where you at, Spook? Come out already." Surveying each abandoned house to see which one he was chillin' near, it was nothing for dudes to post up on porches of vacant cribs that once housed working families. See, no lie, Spook was so dark that you couldn't see him but in the daytime. No shade, 'cause black is definitely beautiful, but real talk he'd be a perfect Instagram joke for a "dark-skinned niggas be like" joke. Before I knew it, Spook crept up on me quick, fast, and in a hurry. With a stained white T-shirt on, reeking of gin and cigarettes, masked with bloodshot eyes, you could easily tell he'd been getting his early morning wake and bake on for sure.

"What up, niece?" Every girl was his niece and every boy was his nephew. Old heads in the hood felt they were related to everyone.

"Nothing much, Spook. You cooling?"

"Slow motion, you know how I do it." He laughed, trying to pimp swag but tripped on his own two feet.

*Damn, this joker right here is high as a kite.* "Be easy, Spook." I laughed watching him stumble back up the stairs to finish getting high. He sat on the same milk crate day in and out smoking from the same burnt-up pipe. Uncle Spook was cool though 'cause he kept his ear to the streets and whenever me and Nique had scams we needed the word spread on he was the mouth to do so. Spook knew everyone in, out, and around the neighborhood. He was the man in his day and could've been the boss running the whole city if his addiction wasn't more powerful. Hearing him coughing and choking, I knew that crack monster was on his back in the worst way.

"I hope you've rolled up 'cause I'm ready to roll out." Coming out the house with her purse in hand, you couldn't tell Nique had fallen off her square last night. Dressed in a long, flowing green sundress, a jean jacket vest, and wife beater sunglasses to mask her puffy cried-out eyes, she looked like she was truly dressed to shop.

"Yup, I sure am. I was born ready."

## Nique

Me and Cori rode to rap while we burned through the pre-rolled blunt on our way to the mall. As pitiful as it was for me to say this, my mind was still wrapped around Vic even though my body was moving toward making money. My emotions were in shambles. Last night was mad crazy. Not only had I embarrassed myself in front of the whole hood, everyone out here knew my business to talk about and judge. If nothing else, I had to get my reputation back on point. In the hood that's all we had to thrive for. Pulling into the closest parking spot I could find, we both jumped out of my beat-up ride ready to steal 'til our hearts were content.

"Have you talked to Vic?" Cori questioned with her mug ripped. She'd never been a Vic fan.

"His trifling ass sent me a few threatening text messages in the wee hours of the morning talking about getting some of Tasha's friends to kick this baby from my stomach, but I ain't worried." I secretly wished one of Tasha's friends, or her for that matter, would come to bust bows with me. I'd box anybody out over Vic if they wanted to try me.

"So tell me again what you plan on doing? I don't see how you're putting up with him," Cori finally said what she'd being thinking all along. "Am I going to be an auntie or designated driver after the twilight procedure?"

"Girl, I'm not trying to be Vic's baby momma. You saw how that nigga went ham on me last night. I ain't trying to live my life with no nutty-ass baby daddy." I was masking my emotions and glad I had sunglasses on to shade the tears that were starting to draw up in the corners of my eyes. I hated admitting the truth; more than likely, I'd have to kill the only child I'd ever conceived. *I hate you, Victor Jamison. I hate you to the depth of me!*

"I'm glad you're talking some sense, Nique, 'cause that buster definitely is not the one you need to breed with."

Cori didn't have a lot of room to talk. Chasing my cousin down like he was going to wife her tricking ass was the dumbest thing I'd ever witnessed her do. But who was I to judge? She was grown and could see just like the rest of Mike's jump offs that he was messy, down for himself, and loved women hanging from his nut sac too much to settle down. I listened to her degrade and talk down about Vic for the first five minutes of our shopping trip. I never said a word but let her think she was giving me great sisterly advice. The only thing on my mind though was getting to the bathroom to pee. Being pregnant had me pissing waterfalls!

## Cori

Vic might've had Ta'Nique on a rollercoaster of emotions, but you couldn't tell by the way she was cleaning up at the mall. She was a self-healing go-getter for sure. Quick on her boost game, going in and out of Macy's with bags of merchandise unnoticed more than once, Nique was easy on the eyes. A flawlessly laid weave, soft brown complexion, and a room-stopping smile made it easy for her to blend in with any crowd. Dressing like a dainty girl when hitting the shopping districts of suburbia made it easy for her to swipe petty items like Victoria's Secret sprays, lingerie sets, kids' clothes, and knick-knacks she'd ultimately keep for herself, too. The fact that she looked like some rich man's wife I was sure had to help. She'd stolen bottles of perfume, Michael Kors swimsuits and dresses, 7 For All Mankind Jeans, Polo shirts, belts, and a few Sean outfits for both Mike and Vic. Macy's never saw her coming. On any given day my girl was a star at stealing. She could boost almost anything the hood ordered: food, clothes, shoes, phones, and even self-care products.

I, on the other hand, was coming out of a whole different box when it came to style. I guessed you could call it gangsta because I kept it wild at all times. From snatching Tom Ford shades off a chick's face, to grabbing purses in those same shopping plazas to help distract from Nique's scheme, I didn't care who got caught in my whirl-wind of illegal activity. I had to get mines. Who did I have to fall back on? Faye? Shit, a bitch wasn't about to end up like her. Whenever I saw a lucrative opportunity for financial advancement, even at an innocent person's expense, I was all over it. Truth be told, that's when I got down best. By the time we left the upscale department store, their security team was on high alert.

After Macy's, we hit Westland Mall, Target, and Toys"R"Us making sure we looked out for the things we needed around our house and some of the neglected crack babies we looked out for on the block. Store after store, counterfeit bill after bill, every transaction went through without any problem, working like a charm. The car was filled to capacity with clothes, shoes, household supplies, personal care products, baby dolls, and plush toys for the kids.

"I've gotta drop two cards off before we go home. Do you have some stops to make?" Nique went down onto the free going opposite from our house.

"Not really. Just swing me past Coney Island when you're done. All this swiping we just got down with has worked up a major appetite."

"Came up that's all me, stay true that's all me." My phone was ringing again but I didn't want to answer to Wally. I didn't want to answer my phone seeing it was Wally. We hadn't talked since that day so I didn't know how he was getting ready to come out the box.

"What up, doe?" I answered the phone like nothing was up. Maybe he had meant to give me some work in exchange for a little loving.

"Shit, you, Cori. What time this evening?"

"Straight to the point I see. I thought we were straight since we got down." I twirled my hair like a dumb girl but knowing better.

"I ain't for the games, baby. This ain't the time."

"It's cool, we cool. I'll have the cash over there. Two hundred fifty dollars, right?" Straitening up in the seat, I could see this conversation wasn't going in my favor.

"Naw, that right there is top strain. $325 and that's with me giving you a little off for a taste of that twat."

I guess I wasn't going to get out of this deal without paying. "All right, I'll call you once we're done in the streets."

"Naw, that ain't gonna work. I'll be your way in an hour. Have my money or I'm beating your motherfucking ass, C. You should have known better not to leave without tossing my cash, high or not, you know the rules. Play me and get played." Wally had flipped the script on me and hung up in my face. I expected him to have a certain demeanor about himself but this was a tad bit much.

I stared at my phone watching the duration time of the call blinking, signaling the call was over. I was in total disbelief that he'd clowned so hard so quickly. I didn't know who that "can't eat pussy right" faggot thought he was dealing with. Free weed or no weed, I wasn't into being beat on or told what the fuck to do. No nigga was going to run me or "beat my motherfucking ass." I was way past regretting even calling him against my better judgment in the first place. I should've never mixed this type of business with him. It was proving to be a huge mistake. I just went from having a reliable trick in Wally to a having foe.

# Chapter Ten

## *Corielle*

After stuffing my cheeseburger deluxe and card-board fries down my throat, I joined Nique on the front porch for the yard sale we were hosting. We'd kept the best products on reserve for ourselves but in a pinch of course everything would go. Each time we were lucky enough to get down in a major way, we set up shop right on our front grass selling it off to our neighbors. The whole lot was set out for them to rummage through: from stolen hair care products, Macy's highest tagged clothes, and toddler toys. And from previous experience, I knew it would sell. Of course we hung the best in our own closets, but if necessary we'd sell them too. Everything was priced ready to go. Girls were already spending money fast knowing our stock was 100 percent straight official.

"I figured you wanted to do the honors," Nique said and handed me the mail before walking into her house on the phone. My guess was that it was sorry-ass Vic on the other line. "Your ass owes me that twenty-five dollars he charges, too."

"Oh shit, with everything going on, I'd forgotten about even ordering these cards. And I got your cash even though he got down on you for an extra five. Everybody gotta have a hustle I guess." Ripping the envelopes open of both a Visa and Master Card in Kelly Tandy's name, I'd just come up on another card to pay bills with.

Hearing the subwoofers of a car rattling, I looked up in just enough time to see Mike bending the corner in his cocaine white F-150 on chrome rims. *Speaking of the devil, his ass must be coming for the money.* As he illegally parked his truck in the vacant lot next to our house and got out, my eyes were fixated on him mixed with lust and hate. *Shouldn't he be with Alyssa since he dissed me for her last night?* I was trying to be mad but Mike's presence made me soft. Yeah, a trick like me wanted more than just the long pipe he'd lay off in me weekly.

"What up my nigga, Mike?" Uncle Spook yelled, leaning over the porch banister. I swore Spook could sense a person with money a mile the fuck away.

Mike, gold bracelet sparkling in the sunlight, stopped in his tracks waiting on Spook to get up the street before he spoke back doing a quick dap and hug. "Shit, Spook. Money is up with me, guy, you feel it," Mike replied, looking the old G up and down.

"Naw, dude, I don't feel it." Spook shook his head laughing as he went in his pocket to pull out a stale half-smoked Newport, asking for a light. "My money ain't been up in a long time, playa."

Mike pulled out a red lighter handing it to Spook before informing him that he'd catch up with him later once he finished handling his business.

"Yeah, holla at me, moneymaker. I'm out here bad so I need you to look out for me. I can't front, boss," Spook negotiated, ducking back down to continue getting high.

Mike couldn't catch a break. Between Spook, other old heads in the hood, and the young girls on our front grass, he was getting an overload of attention.

"What up, beautiful? How are you?" Mike smiled walking up on the porch.

Leaning back in the white plastic chair playing nonchalant, if it weren't for me wanting some more counterfeit bills Mike would've been getting thrown moonlight shade. "Shit, I can't call it. I see you answered to the money."

"Of course, you already know how I get down."

"I thought I did, until I saw that saddity bitch all up on your arm. You jerked me around at the party last night, Mike, but I ain't with that shit this morning." Not being able to let his Unforgivable cologne persuade me to keep quiet, Alyssa's scent stood out more. I hated this girl I didn't even now 'cause obviously she was taking the place I wanted, which was right next to him.

"Alyssa ain't did shit to you, girl. So quit acting all jealous."

"Don't take what I said to the head, nigga. I'm not nearly jealous of that watermelon-head broad."

"I might be a street nigga, C, but a fool I am not. But let's not talk about Alyssa right now. I'd rather get to feeling on that good-looking body of yours. Get up, girl." I didn't try to resist him.

Letting him hug me tightly, I whispered softly into his ear that he felt too good as he hugged me tightly. I loved being this close to his body even though ol' girl's smell still lingered. Even though it didn't work I closed my eyes in an effort to block the scent out. Instead I got lost in my mind wishing I were his girl. When he placed his face into my neck, I was sure he could smell the soft-smelling Flowerbomb body oil he was known to love. Running his hands from my back, finally landing on my soft booty, moans escaped my lips. *Damn this nigga always throws me off my square. I couldn't shake him if I wanted.* "You like what you feel?" My intentions were to entice him.

"Yeah, girl, don't ask stupid questions. This dick is waking up for you. I've gotta finish that kitten off." Still embracing me, both of us rocking side to side, we were both reacting off the other's sexual energy. Not bothering to be discreet, I slid my hands down and grabbed at his manhood. He was long, strong, and ready to go to work on me. "You've got favors to return to daddy."

"I know," I cooed back in such a low tone I could barely hear myself. I couldn't wait to drop it low working for a permanent spot.

"Why don't you two just get a room?" Nique swung the steel security door open. "Not everybody wants to see all that lovey-dovey crap." She was pulling at a blunt even though she wasn't supposed to. Me and Nique were homegirls, aces, and BFFs in short terms, but I swore sometimes she just didn't know when to shut up. She could've easily backed down until me and Mike got down having our kissy face session or at least kept quiet. As of lately, all I saw was a hater in Ta'Nique 'cause her situation was messy with Vic and that li'l bastard she was unsure of. She didn't have to rain on my parade 'cause her life was in shambles though. We might've been ride or dies but I wasn't riding for that. Mike broke the embrace we were sharing then went for the blunt Nique was passing. Unfortunately for me, he never made a comment on what she'd said about us getting a room. Once they started talking about family business, I'd definitely become old news and a third wheel. Not liking the feeling, I excused myself into the house to get his stuff from Walmart. My phone was blowing up with text messages for orders, so with the unexpected free time I grabbed my notebook to write them down. Since Mike was here and everything went good last night, I'd have the counterfeit bills to get everyone's requests. Two people wanted a gift card to Best Buy for at least $500, a few people wanted to know if either me or Nique had a hookup for the PlayStation 4, one person had returned my message about the $200 Walmart cards, and three people needed a bill paid. I responded back to each text accordingly, letting them know I'd be in touch within a few hours. These were my regular customers, so they didn't doubt my reliability.

"I don't think we were done for you to just up and walk away like that." Mike pushed my bedroom door open and invited himself in. I was so caught up in calculating the money I'd premade in my mind that I hadn't even heard his heavy footsteps making thuds across our raggedy wooden floors.

"Naw, it wasn't like that, Mike. I just thought I'd let family business be just that." I smiled leaning back onto my bed, letting him know by the look in my eyes I was interested in picking up right where we'd left off.

"Don't play games with me, Cori baby, that camel toe looking like love to a nigga." He licked his lips, easing his way near me after shutting my bedroom door.

"You just don't know how bad I've been wanting to get with you," I revealed as I uncrossed my caramel legs inviting him toward my needing body.

I began to feel slightly uncomfortable about myself as he stood in front of my bed staring at my frame from head to toe. Mike didn't know, but he had a hold over me and I was starting to fall in love. "Stop thinking," he demanded, as if he'd read my mind. "I like to see what I'm about to do and study my prey."

Thrown off by his ego but turned on by his attempt to let me in on his so-called stamina, I was yearning for him inside of my walls even more. He knelt down onto my purple Target comforter and began kissing my feet and rubbing on my thighs. The slightest touch was sending tingles through my mind. I tilted my head back and enjoyed as he massaged my legs, inner thigh, and belly button with his tongue. As his finger reached my clitoris, it was a repeat like last night: an Aquafina flow. "I see you're wet for me," he said, before plunging his tongue into my pussy as he still managed to finger fuck me. I was grinding myself into his face as he reached up and spread my legs into the butterfly position. My moans got louder as he continued to eat me out, dining like this was his last meal. "Damn you taste so sweet," he murmured, then wiped the mouthful of cream I'd left him with over my comforter. Unzipping his pants, I jumped up eager to return the favor but was flipped over with the quickness. "Naw, not just yet."

Mike brought orgasm after orgasm ramming his black monster inside of me with no holding back. He was relentlessly fucking me like a beast; and I was loving it. I continuously screamed his name over and over again until he finally decided to release his cum all over my back. I felt it run down my ass and crack but didn't care. He could have me however and whenever he liked. I flipped over and spread-eagle out on my back while resuscitating his dick back to life with an infamous jack job. It took no time to get him back up. This time I rode him for what seemed like a lifetime until he tossed me over nutting all over my stomach. Mike had that work and that's why I was sprung over him. Once done I knew the drill so I got up and put on my robe to get washed up and get him a warm, soapy washcloth.

When I went back into the room Mike was on the phone making plans to "be through there in a minute," which deflated me more than I hoped my faced showed 'cause I wanted another session with him. I hated our dynamic, always a "hit it quick" type of thing.

"Come here, baby girl." He motioned for me to come into his arms realizing I was in the room looking salty. Either that or he was busted treating me like a trick. Regardless I rushed over to him, giving him the warm, wet cloth. As he washed himself off and dried the moistness with my sheets, he pulled me by the waist over to him pushing my face toward his dick. "Now it's time for you to return the favor."

I guessed I had no choice but to give him the mouth, so I obliged and swallowed every drop of semen he let out, salty and all.

"So was that Alyssa on the phone? Was I just filling in while she was getting her braces tightened or something?" Taking a shot at her, I was sure Mike no longer speculated about me being jealous. It was written all over my face.

"You're crazy than a motherfucker, Cori, you know that?" Wiping the saliva and cum from his semi-hard dick, he stood up putting on his boxers.

"Don't leave this room or send me on no duck chase, Mike. You did this same slick shit last night." Right now I was showing my whole hand but didn't care. He had to know that my swag could match his swag, if only he'd be the one to wife and upgrade me. "Why have you been dissing me for Alyssa?"

"You really need to do something about your self-esteem. If every piece of ass I stick my meat into is gonna bother you, fucking with me might not be the way you want to keep going." Mike's words were brutal as he cut up the relationship my small mind thought we were building on.

"You and I both know I ain't going nowhere. So the question still stands, was that Alyssa or not?" Falling back onto the pillow, I was exasperated with trying to get the truth out of him.

"You drive a hard bargain with your ghetto ass. Not like it's any of your business real talk, but yeah, that was her."

"Straight up? That's how you gonna keep playing me? You're treating me like an appetizer but that ho like an entrée." Now sitting up pulling the sheet over my naked body, for the first time I was starting to feel less than inferior. Thinking back on the pictures from Instagram, then seeing her live and in person at the party, Alyssa modeled everything I hated: a preppy, had-it-all, tailored female who once again had it better than me.

"Yeah, that was her but that ain't nothing for you to be worrying about, Cori. Like I told you last night, me and her get down with business. Ain't no thang that I stick my rod up in her from time to time, so don't go all gangster on me blowing my spot up." Now getting fully dressed, I could tell Mike knew he'd fucked up by telling the truth. But nothing said could be undone.

"What type of work she doing for you that I can't?" Instantly getting defensive, I jumped up ready to prove my point. Grabbing the bags of personal items including drawers, undershirts, socks, soap, deodorant, lotion, and even toothpaste, I dumped them onto the bed folding my arms like a little kid. "And here's your money from the gift cards I've already sold plus a few outfits from Macy's. That high-class-looking Alyssa broad ain't out here rough hauling in the streets like me. I ain't got a single bill left." Mike needed to see that I was on his level enough to play my role efficiently. How dare he continue to dog me when we could be getting down together?

Picking up the few items, he threw them back down onto the bed showing me they were meaning-less. "You think this is some top-notch queen shit to do, C? I mean, don't get me wrong, I appreciate you looking out for ya mans so no disrespect, but this is toddler-level shit compared to what Alyssa's been putting me down with."

"Then why are you here, nigga? If I can't do no real big girl shit for you, then bang the door down on your way out." Hotter than fish grease, I swiped everything from on top of my bed onto the floor. I was in rare form about to throw a massive tantrum. "I can't wait to see that trick again though. I'm gonna cut into her like I should have at the party. You can't have your cake and eat it, too, nah."

Yoking me up, he shoved me up against the wall. "Me and you get down with what we do but you ain't about to back me into the corner about no chick I'm banging. Any girl I get down with is off-limits, especially Alyssa. Let me find out you went at her and I'm on your head in a major way. Play your role, baby girl. Do you understand?"

The writing was on the wall. Maybe Nique had a point about him not coming off the streets for me. *Damn, maybe I'm just as naïve as her*. I hated feeling like a basic bitch.

"Yeah, I got it, Money Mike. Have it your way, I understand."

"Cori. Corielle."

My eyes got wide hearing my girl scream. I grimed Mike one last time letting him know I was highly disgusted then ran out of the room to see what Nique was screaming about.

# Chapter Eleven

## *Ta'Nique*

My phone hadn't stopped getting messages from Vic since Mike put him out of the gambling party. They ranged from him asking for us to be able to sit and talk things out to promising to crack my cranium open. Not knowing what field he was playing in from one minute to the next, I kept any response I had to myself. It was a new day so that meant trapping to get new money. Almost everything from Macy's had been sold plus the credit cards Cori ordered had arrived. Once Mike left I was sure we'd be back hitting the streets. I was more than happy to stay busy with hustles so I wouldn't have to worry about the baby in my stomach.

Hood traffic was deep but everyone was posted up shooting dice, on the porch in pointless conversations, or sleeping their afternoon buzzes off. I took pictures of the merchandise we had left then put them up on Facebook for anyone interested to inbox me. In just one hour we'd made nearly $300 on stuff we didn't spend one dollar on. No matter how much we made, the greed imbedded in my soul wanted to make more.

Sipping on an ice-cold lemonade with my shades down blocking the sun, I was trying to map out my next plan. Things had been so hectic over the last few days that I hadn't been able to put anything into a clear perspective. One thing was for sure, though, I needed money badly so I couldn't take a rest on grinding. Making a Textgram that I'd be doing all hairstyles for ten dollars off starting Monday, my notifications were already blowing up with potential appointments. I jumped up quickly to grab my appointment book but swung around at the commotion that had just pulled up.

"Cori. Corielle." Yelling as loud as I could for my girl to get out here, I wasn't a coward by far but knew for sure I couldn't handle the gang of girls jumping out of Tasha's car.

"What up, Nique? I heard you had a message for me." Now out of the driver's seat walking toward the porch, Tasha was tough and cocky, totally different from yesterday.

"Yeah, the same message I had when you ran up out of here on that BFF bullshit yesterday," I snapped, turning around fronting her off. "But fuck the past 'cause I see you're here now." Letting her know I wasn't about to back down, she could've brought an additional carload of three more bat-carrying girls and still have a battle on her hands.

Tasha was dressed in tight black leggings, a spaghetti-string baby tee, and gym shoes with her super-glue weave wrapped up in a pink scarf. I snatched off my earrings and Chanel shades then, slipping off my sandals, I was ready to square up with my ex knock-off best friend. "Bring it, bitch, let's box."

"It's whatever. I'm about to box that bastard baby up out ya ass."

That's all I needed to hear before I went bat shit crazy, running off the porch and into the girl who was standing in between Vic's and my happy family. She'd probably been the one in his ear getting him to flip on me in the first place. Tasha had come to fight but ended up getting her ass whopped instead. Punching her dead in the nose, I instantly drew blood but continued lay haymakers disfiguring her otherwise cute face. "I bet you won't pop up over here again. I'll kill you, Tash." My fist was stinging so I switched hands and in the process took a few blows to the jaw myself. Tasha wasn't going down easy, but trust her ass had no other choice but to get knocked out. Her team must've known Tasha wasn't coming back from the beating I was putting on her. They jumped in pulling my hair and arms. It was hard trying to fight one on three as Tasha wildly kicked toward my midsection. *Where in the fuck is my team?*

"Get up off my girl. Mike, grab the pistol, it's crazy out here."

I finally heard Cori run out of the house. And that's when one of Tasha's friends took her last and final chance to knock me upside the head before Cori snatched her to the ground. Stomping blood from her mouth, I took my chance at revenge kicking her head like a Nerf ball. The other girl took off running up the block screaming for help when Mike bust shots into the air. "G'on and take Tasha out; I'm on that runner's head." Cori jumped in Tasha's car and took up flying up the street.

"Bring that motherfucking car back, yamp," Tasha yelled trying to run toward her car but was slowed down to a limp. Cori had bent the corner and you could hear screams piercing through the air of the girl who had come with Tasha. Ol' girl had it coming for coming to jump me.

Tasha fell to the pavement after I knocked her in the back of the head twice. Me and Cori weren't playing but all three of them deserved what they had coming for popping up on our territory. I swooped my sundress up between my legs like a lady and sat down on top of Tasha. I was getting ready to enjoy every moment of this twisted retaliation. The fight had turned into a massacre and the point I was about to prove was gonna be brutal. Her hair was matted and covered in blood as I continued to slam her cranium into the ground.

"So you came to do what? Box what baby out of me, bitch? You better tell Vic to send some real goons."

"Get the fuck up off that tramp, Nique." Mike aggressively snatched me off of Tasha.

Getting up was nothing, I'd already beat her limp. There was nothing else to but hawk up a big glob of saliva on her. "This is from my unborn." Smiling in a few of the cameras, every fight in the hood went viral so this would be no different. I didn't care though 'cause I wanted everyone to see why I wasn't to be tested. Something told me Tasha wasn't going to be the only girl Vic sent this way or who wanted to try me because I was nesting his seed. I saw that Cori had just bent the corner on foot once I looked up the street. She was walking like she had no worries, her shirt had been ripped and her hair was a mess. I hoped she hadn't gotten dealt with helping to fight my battles. "You straight, my baby?"

"Hell yeah, that bitch begged me to back down."

Mike was clearing the scene of nosey neighbors who had crowded around with their camera phones out. Some had gotten away with merchandise that was already stolen but with the focus on the brawl going on, no one even noticed. Holding our ground, we propped up on the porch daring them to cross the line again.

"Come back on this block again and I'm gonna do more than kick your head into the sewer, bitch. You ain't got no business around here from today forward," Cori yelled up the street to the girl she chased around the corner.

The girl had gotten into the driver's seat of Tasha's car and was pulling back up the block to get her girls up off the ground. A few of the young boys on the block helped drag them into the car per Mike's orders. They had the block hot no doubt so our illegal yard sale had to shut down. I couldn't help but send Vic a few pictures of Tasha as the obvious losers of the battle me and him should have been fighting.

*Let that bitch Tasha know if anything happens to our baby, I'll kill her dead.* I meant that to the depth of my soul and I hope Vic sensed that once the message went through.

"Hey, Nique, tell ya girl Cori I'm outside."

Mike looked Wally up and down before getting into his truck pulling off in the same direction as Tasha just went in.

# Chapter Twelve

## *Cori*

Not seeing my phone plugged up to the charger how I left it, I scrambled fast looking for it. I cherished my phone like my child so I kept up with it better than I did myself at times. Mike must've gotten to it. That wasn't good 'cause I knew there were messages in there from Wally. He might've been up front and out in the open about him being a whore with chicks and females; but I didn't want my personal sex life out there, especially when it wasn't even like that. Finally finding it tossed on the floor in the corner, I swiped it up instantly hot pissed 'cause that nigga had cracked my screen probably throwing it there. *Really? But I can't go hard about Alyssa?*

"Hey, girl, Wally is outside," Nique said, standing in the doorway.

"What the fuck? Are you serious?" With all that just went down, I totally forgot about him saying he'd be through here. "And where's Mike?"

"Whoa, slow down. Yes, I'm serious. And Mike is gone."

Rolling my eyes into the back of my head, I knew for sure he'd been through my phone and saw the messages between me and Wally. Just my luck this nigga popping up while he was here. I should've gone to pay him before trying to pig out on some Coney Island. "Thanks, boo. Let him know I'll be out in a minute."

"No problem. And thanks for helping me scrap with them bitches. I can't believe they blew up our spot like that."

"Girl, we're one hundred, I'm always gonna have your back. But that nigga Vic is bad news. He sent that trick Tasha here and no doubt they'll probably be trying to retaliation. Or at last a round two."

"I feel you, but it's bittersweet for me 'cause I ain't trying to be like my momma getting back-to-back abortions like my body or babies ain't worth shit." Nique dropped her head finally exposing her dilemma.

"That's real admirable of you, Ta'Nique, but are you seriously debating bringing a baby into all of this chaos? I mean come on, what we gonna do, train the kid up to be hot-headed thief? Are you gonna send invites for your baby shower out on CrimeInTheD?" I knew I was being cutthroat and harsh but me and Nique shared too much for me to keep giving her space to make this dumb decision.

"Bitches can change. But I ain't for you, Mike, Vic, Tasha, or whoever else who is full opinions about me killing this baby." Nique actually had the audacity to look hurt.

"I ain't trying to leave you out here like a wounded dog; it really ain't like that, friend." Sliding on my shirt, I walked over and gave her a tight hug. I hated seeing her going through all of this, especially knowing the emotional ties were pulling at her heart 'cause she only wanted to outsmart, outlive, and be a better person than her momma had been.

"I'm gonna be straight," Nique said and pulled back, making sure she didn't get caught up in the moment crying. "Wally didn't look too happy so you better get outside."

"Oh shit, yeah, his ass." Grabbing the money I owed him, I ran out the door to take care of our debt so me and him wouldn't have problems. Too late; he had taken the liberty of getting out of his car and was coming into our door quicker than I could tell him hold off.


Me, Wally, and Nique went through a whole pack of ninety-nine cent Zig Zag Cigarillos before it was all said and done. After I gave him the cash, he'd lightened up tremendously. It was a lesson learned though for me not to plan on a re-up with him.

Wally was smelling like Gucci Guilty, dressed in a pair of light blue True Religion jeans, red and blue striped Polo button up, and wheat-colored Timbs. *Damn this nigga looking kinda good. If he wouldn't have tripped so hard off that little stack of hundreds, maybe I could give his ass another taste. It wasn't that bad.*

Wally bossed up and took two bags of Kush from the pocket of his grey hoodie and placed them on the table. "I know one of y'all choo-choo train smokers got a blunt. Roll up real quick," he joked but knowing it was the truth.

I took the privilege of grabbing his stash up first. He was my boy and my side dick so it was obvious I called myself weighing in. "I got it, babe." Bending over letting my C cups hang in his face, he licked his lips staring, not caring that Nique's eyes were locked on us.

"Damn, take that shit to the back after we get done getting blazed."

"Whoa, ma, why are you throwing salt in my game?" Wally didn't know what was up with Nique or why she seemed so uncomfortable with both of us outright flirting.

"I ain't trying to throw salt in your game. I'm just in a bad spot with my dude so I don't want any reminders." Nique began telling him all about how Vic was dissing her and then sent Tasha to our house. Keeping it real, I was shocked she opened up to Wally like that.

"Sounds like you need to get out the hood for a while to teach that nigga you're not so accessible," Wally said, playing the concerned role.

"Who you telling? Do you know of a spot that's slapping tonight?"

"Y'all should slide through that spot inside Ignite Lounge inside of MGM. I've never been but the line is always wrapped long to the roulette table I be playing at."

"Sounds like a plan," I cut into the conversation, seeing Nique outright flirting with Wally. He might not have been my dude and I might have been banging her cousin, but she was way out of place right about now. Call me crazy but with Vic and that bastard baby brewing in her stomach, she had enough to be bothered with to be sneaking smiles to my side piece.

## Nique

Wally was looking good to me, probably 'cause I hadn't had a good dicking down in a minute. Vic was freezing me out of course but even when I was getting it on the regular, he'd only last for a few minutes. And yeah, Mr. Goldstein climbed on top of me every other month pumping so hard his old heart almost stopped. But I'm talking about getting it from a young goon who would have me speaking in tongues. Catching Cori giving me the side eye, I tried to calm my dick-dehydrated ass down. Hell for all I knew, this might have been my pregnancy hormones working overtime. Not only was she like a sister to me, there was money on the table with Wally that I didn't want to jeopardize. I first wanted him to be our connect so I could secretly get Vic back on. That was a dead plan however, since he'd sent Tasha to kick our baby out of my stomach. Vic could rot in the gritty streets of Detroit broke and struggling like the rest.

Scrolling up and down Facebook, people from the neighborhood were still posting videos clips from the fight me and Tasha had. I couldn't front, had I not been going toe to toe with the lightweight mob Tasha brought with her, I would've been taping it too. Rolling over putting the television on mute, I could hear Cori and Wally going at it. She was moaning loudly as the headboard kept banging against the wall. I'd never been jealous of my best friend until now. She'd been getting dick all day while my pussy was sitting stale and dried up. Feeling my hormones taking over, I slid my hand down inside of my panties to handle my business wishing Wally was in here banging my insides out. *Cori is having all the fun! Maybe I'll find a nigga to please me tonight.*

# Chapter Thirteen

## *Cori*

Mike hadn't been responding to any of my phone calls. I'd tried everything from begging to sending him naked pictures but he still hadn't reached back out. I'd racked my brain hard, surfing through my own phone trying to see how much he could've seen before joining me and Nique during the fight. I couldn't believe I'd slipped not deleting the messages. To make matters worse, I know that nigga wanted to ram my head through the wall seeing Wally pull up. I knew Mike better than he thought I did and his ego was hurt. As much as he boasted about controlling women putting us in our place, that nigga couldn't handle me dipping out doing the same thing.

I got dressed against my will; what I really wanted to do was get in touch with Mike so I could tell him why I really was hooking up with Wally. There was a need to explain myself. But trying to be a good friend, I slid on the sexiest black dress and pumps I'd stolen from Macy's making sure my appearance was on point before joining Nique at Ignite. She'd left an hour early having to drop off a few more cards so I'd promised to meet her there. I swore myself not to say anything until I got more evidence but the vibes Nique was throwing off toward Wally told me she was feeling him. Low key that's why I took him into my room letting him fuck my walls raw. Yeah, it made me seem like a ho 'cause I'd just gotten down with Mike not an hour ago, but that's what chicks in the hood did to mark their territory.

I'd never partied at Ignite before because it wasn't my type of crowd but since my girl needed a break from the roughhouse drama we were into on a daily, to hell with it, I was down. Mostly drunk Caucasian people looking to drink even more beers, listen to loud rock music, and dance off beat were flooded into the casino's nightclub partying their asses off. As much as I kept trying to, I couldn't get into groove even though the later it got the more folks like us poured in. Nique ordered a bottle of wine and hadn't slowed up one bit. Pregnant or not she was still getting it in. We had a spread at our table, doing it real big since I was paying with the Tandy's credit card.

The DJ started to play some hip hop in the mix. I finally started to get into my element. I stood up starting to dance, letting go all of the frustration today brought. We both were partying hard. The waitress kept chilled bottles coming to our table and the tab kept growing. If this place didn't cost an arm and leg to party at, this would've been my new spot. Making our way to the dance floor, the strobe lights made me seem even drunker than I already was. Dancing, grinding, and feeling myself, I dared anyone tonight to tell me I wasn't the baddest chick in the club. Nique was sandwiched between a group of guys but was holding her own. Each with a bottle in hand, we were living the high life on someone else's pocket. This was the American dream.

"I know I've been tipping back these bottles, Cori, so excuse me if I'm wrong, but ain't that Mike's girl? You know, what's her name, Amy, Anna, Alyssa?" She was slurring a little.

I took the wine glass from her hand not wanting to clean up a drunk's mess, or have the guys thinking she was easy to go. Looking up from grinding to Rocko's "Goin' Steady" song in the direction Nique was staring in, I saw Alyssa walking in with a large group of people. "Yeah, that's her."

*If this ain't some bullshit. Why she ain't booed up with Captain Defendo with her stank ass?* Hurrying to get back to the booth and sitting down to not draw attention to myself, I continued to gawk seeing her flash her badge to gain access to a roped-off section. "Hey, Nique, it's time to sober the fuck up, chick. Looks like your cousin is fucking a cop." I watched Alyssa, the girl I was jealous over, mix and mingle with a few other narcotic cops I knew for a fact worked the streets of our neighborhood as shifty cops. These were the same dudes who ran in on Mike and his crew a few times before, stealing his stash several times in the process. They bought her drinks, freaked her out on the dance floor, but what caught my eye the most disappeared once people from the same hood they worked in showed up. When she took a large wad of cash from one of the cops I knew stole drug money, I knew for sure she was foul. She was making cash on top of her measly salary but disturbing my life in the process. Alyssa was just a prop, probably to get closer to Mike. Too bad for her, I was Mike's secret weapon and was going to make sure he stayed untouchable.

# Chapter Fourteen

## *Down 4 Whatever*

Making sure my Smith & Wesson was fully loaded before placing it onto my lap, I flexed my fingers outward ready to put in that work. I was thirsty in the worst sense of the word. Discreetly following the F-150 me and Nique had been trailing since downtown Detroit, we turned into a subdivision of mini-mansions with football stadium front yards. *I can't believe Mike been banging a sneak snake all this time.* My mind started to race as my fingers began to itch. From the looks of it, we'd hit the jackpot and were about to get on in a major way. The payout on top of her salary had Alyssa living quite swell. I was impressed. We crept on Alyssa by watching her every move in the club until she left the club pissy drunk. In the time it took her to make it to her car, we'd slid on clothes we kept in Nique's trunk for moments just in case.

"You ready for this lick, Cori? I see Mike's slick ass has been sliding up in public enemy number one." Nique kept a safe distance behind the car as it slowed down and turned into the driveway of an unlit house. We kept past the house a few feet then turned the ignition off. Skilled at our trade we both simultaneously slid our black face masks down, only leaving our eager eyes exposed.

"Come on now, you know I been couldn't stand her. Just this confirms why." Putting the Kush tail of weed out into my empty can of Red Bull, my body was starting to fidget with anticipation on what was about to go down. I had a personal vendetta with this redbone yellow bitch.

"I feel ya with ya bitter ass. So let's do this!"

Jumping out the raggedy Taurus I was riding shotgun in, I was beyond reckless with my intent. I watched for any nosey neighbors who might call the law as me and Nique ran up the dimly lit block to our victim's house dressed in all black, with the core goal of getting money. Anyone or anything that had other intentions, false purpose, or a plan on stopping our endeavors would certainly end up a casualty in the war. That was the game in these cold, harsh streets of Detroit; we were just living by the rules. We moved fast and deliberate, ducking behind bushes and creeping along the side of the brick wall in order to gain unnoticed access. Right on time we slid underneath the closing garage door, catching Alyssa Anderson off-guard. She didn't have a chance to react before I grabbed and wrapped one hand around her long, fluffy ponytail muffling her horrific screams with my other. "Is someone waiting on the other side of that door for you?" I whispered into her ear coldly.

She shook her head. I shoved my chrome-plated pistol into her side making her grunt, "No."

Keeping one hand over her mouth, I patted her down quickly to see if she was packing any heat. Off duty or not, her career was to carry a concealed weapon so I had to be sure. Miss High and Mighty didn't know what hit her but I was sure coming to grips real quick that today wasn't her lucky day.

As I ran my gloved hands up and down Alyssa's curvy-framed body, the terrified off-duty Detroit police officer's hands trembled by her sides as her eyes grew big. Usually armed, ready to bust bullets at common criminals like us, she was now at our mercy.

Ta'Nique wasted no time pushing in the cracked door Alyssa was only moments from entering when we crept up. "Oh yeah, we hit a bankroll bitch this time. This right here is what I call lifestyle of the lavish living." She laughed, going all the way in Alyssa's unsecured home.

"Is that so?" I gritted my teeth, feeling my bitterness grow. "Well you already know what we came to do, my baby!"

Alyssa jerked trying to get free from my grip but was no match for the gangster that ran through my veins. Eventually she had no other choice but to bow. "Please don't try me." I raised my Smith & Wesson to the back of her temple ready to unite her with her Maker. "I swear I ain't leaving this house in cuffs without you in a body bag." Clicking one into the chamber to let her know I meant business, ol' girl's best bet was to fall in line and play her role right. Me and Nique had come too far from our shady, decrepit hood to go back empty-handed, especially with it being Mike's girl as our mark. I had a personal interest in all of this.

With tears streaming down her face, the prissy cop seemed to say a silent prayer that she'd make it through the night alive. By morning she could have the whole unit out like hound dogs for this duo. "Please, you can take everything I've got. I'm just begging you not to hurt me."

She was shaking and crying obsessively as I flung her down onto the ceramic-tiled kitchen floor, her once thick-coated makeup was smeared across her pale rock-cratered face.

"Please shut her the fuck up. I really can't stand all that crying and begging." Nique grimed the powerless woman before hawking a big gob of spit onto her floor. "Please believe me, Alyssa, we out here on some straight hooligan-type shit. We ain't come to talk or negotiate." Nique wasn't fazed by the heartfelt pleas for us to have mercy on her well-being as she moved on from us to close the curtains and ensure the three of us were alone.

Not having any type of sympathy or empathy for the trick, I roughly yoked her up by the collar of her blouse then shoved my gun into the lower spine of her back. "Shhh, don't say another motherfucking word or I swear on everything I love, I'll put a bullet straight through the back of your skull." Seething with a purpose, I vowed to the crooked cop who was cowering at my feet, if she didn't cooperate, shut her mouth, and act like she had some common sense, this ordeal had the potential to turn all the way up real, real quick. "Don't make your night worse than it's already planned to be."

Alyssa Alexander grew nauseated, frightened half out her mind. With a face full of tears, she was trembling like a homeless man sleeping underneath the freeway overpass on a bone-chilling Michigan winter night; and here it was middle of July, almost eighty-one degrees to be exact. Did I give a shit when she pissed on herself like a newborn? Hell naw, not me. Being a veteran in the streets, her cries only pissed me off more. I was not the least bit moved by her begs for God to have mercy on her soul and for me not to take her life.

My blood ran cold on the regular and tonight was no different. See, I had that arrogant west side of Detroit pumping through my veins. That "bitch, I'll kill you and not give a fuck about going to the funeral and smile all up in your mama's face" type of pedigree. I was a female who stayed thirsty for a scheme, scam, or hookup. My struggle to live and survive out in these miserable streets was real no matter who got hurt. The only time I was privy to the luxury life was during my reality show television watching time.

High as hell off the two blunts we'd smoked on the ride over, my adrenaline was still pumping as I glanced around amazed at the large suburban magazine-styled house. No wonder Mike had been licking her cat down; the wealth seemed endless. This was some shit I'd dreamed about living in as a kid. Each room was overcrowded with large, posh-looking furniture, oil portraits hung neatly on the custom-painted walls, and plush area rugs covering portions of the shiny pine-colored wood floors. The only things out of place were me and Nique. Getting caught in my feelings, starting to feel inferior in my scuffed, worn-soled gym shoes, my hate for this middle-class working woman grew. Alyssa was living good as a motherfucka having my man as her side piece while I was caught up in the struggle. *Now that's where I'm gonna have to call bullshit.*

Dizzy with envy, hearing this "ain't got no worries" bitch sniffle even after I told her to shut the fuck up twice made me want to permanently silence her. "Didn't I already warn you about all that crying and shit? You must think I'm a joke." I snapped back to reality and the true reason as to why we were here. "Get back onto your knees with your hands behind your back. Move slow; one flinch with ya knock-off Snow White ass and I'll blast your motherfucking head off." Cold and callous, gritting my teeth, right about now wasn't a chick walking this green earth more serious about getting this paper than me. Any false moves, a sneeze, or even the rolling of her eyes, and I was going to bang that big head of hers through the glass coffee table. Don't get it twisted, I wasn't a murderer. I was a thief. But tonight I planned to be the most vicious at my craft.

"I'm sorry," she panted, gagging for air. "Please don't hurt me. I swear we can work something out."

Hearing her continue to beg against my orders not to, I felt like once again she wasn't taking my gangster seriously. I smacked the officer of the law across her face with my bare hand and a long red welt immediately spread across her cheekbone and jaw. "Shut the fuck up means exactly that!"

As I watched Mike's love interest's slender lips twist up as she almost hyperventilated from holding in her cries, instant gratification surged through my body. Mike had been flaunting her in my face, making sure I knew she was untouchable but here she was a cop, a pig, the type he hated on a sunny day. And not only that, with rent due and welfare fraud charges pending over my head, I needed this bump badly to get right with old Mr.

Goldstein by cash only. I hadn't forgotten about my obligation to him.

"We're all clear. Time to tie ol' girl up and get to work." Nique stepped back into the room grinning ear to ear. Not hating Alyssa with a passion, it was easy for her to work efficiently and with ease.

"Damn, it's about time. Ol' girl over here fidgeting, screaming, and pissing me off. I was just getting ready to splatter her blood all over this nice white carpet."

The woman turned beet red at every word coming out of my mouth.

"Toss me those handcuffs, tape, and cords." I couldn't let my emotions get the best of me. From birth Nique and I were trained to be about our dollars and cents; this summer breeze night would just be another notch under our belts.

"Fa'sho, let's see what's in bag number one." Nique winked her eye then dropped the black duffel bag down in front of Alyssa's shivering body. I found humor in Nique taunting her. She unzipped the bag slowly then dangled the handcuffs, duct tape, extension cords, and the roll of Home Depot Husky contractor clean-up bags back and forth across her face.

Bending back over, Alyssa puked almost instantaneously.

"Aww come on now, chick, don't tell me your prude ass wasn't expecting this. They ain't train you better than that, rookie?" At each turn Nique kept letting her know this occurrence wasn't by coincidence and she was chosen to get tortured.

"Listen up, lady. You need to get your shit together real quick." I waited a few seconds before continuing. "I'm going to need you to lead me to where you stash your cash."

Slobbering, wiping vomit and snot across her face, the lady who was only accustomed to answering 911 calls to break-ins wept pitifully. She looked across her family room at Nique and seemed to get angered at her clearing the entertainment center of DVDs, CDs, speakers, radios, and video gaming systems.

"Hey, stay focused. Don't worry about her. I'm your main concern. Get up and move, bitch. I ain't got all night." Moving closer to her, I was ready to strike again.

"Wait. Okay, okay, please just don't hit me again," she screamed, just as vain as the first day of her introducing herself at Mike's gambling party.

She was barely standing barefoot; I'd literally knocked her out of her Jimmy Choos.

"It's in my top dresser drawer in my bedroom, upstairs to the left," she confessed in between sniffles.

Exasperated and drained, it was clear she'd given me the true placement of her most valuable possessions when she hung and shook her head in defeat.

"See, now that wasn't so hard." Antagonizing Alyssa, I knew she was hotter than fish grease.

"Here's your bag. Tie her up already and let's get this on and popping. We don't have all night." Nique handed me a contractor bag, walking behind Alyssa, tying a blue bandana tightly around her eyes so she couldn't ID me or her once we took off our black masks. "Get that rock off her finger, my baby."

"I can't be smoking before licks . . . got me tripping." Slipping the nice-sized diamond ring from her finger, she shook with overwhelming fear and probably anger. When I bent it back to hear her shrill, that was just an added bonus.

The look was written all over Alyssa's face. I know she regretted spending her free time out of this protected suburban lifestyle she had. Maybe this lesson would teach her to leave dudes from the hood alone. It hadn't been said Mike was the relating link but I was sure the thought had crossed her educated mind. *Wow, this shit is crystal clear. I'm hitting her jewelry stash fa'sho.* Alyssa's shrills almost made even me want to cry as I carelessly ripped a pair of gold hoops from her ears then ripped her necklace and pendant from around her neck.

"Why are you doing this to me? Why? You're not gonna get away with this. I swear you're going to regret everything you've done thus far."

"Here the fuck we go." I raised my sneaker and stumped her in the small of her back. "I knew you'd give me a reason to stomp throw down on that ass," I hissed before grabbing her by the rear of her neck squeezing tightly. All I could see was her hugged up with Mike and I lost it. I couldn't hold my temper any longer, jealous of the wealth surrounding me along with her now-bold attitude. So there you had it: a shoe to the back with a bruised-up neck, exactly what she deserved.

"You people always taking things that don't belong to you. Get a job for Christ's sake." She was struggling to break free, wheezing for air but still talking shit the whole time. "Taking my stuff ain't right."

"You people? Ain't that about nothing, you flat-booty, no-courage-having tramp. You ain't nothing more than a dirty cop who loves long dick. So fuck you and your across-the-board judgments," I shouted, spontaneously beating her several times across her face with the barrel of my burner. *Fuck*. I was mad as hell. As I went to work on the face I hated to see on Mike's arm, her screams made my anger boil even more.

"What the fuck?" Nique rushed over grabbing me by the forearm. Catching me deviating from the game plan and whipping ol' girl's ass, she hurriedly tried to get me back on track. "What you doing? Damn, stay on point so we can get the hell up out of here."

"Fall back, Nique. I'm slow teaching her a little lesson about talking down to me." I mocked Alyssa's proper, valley girl voice. "Let her see how the fuck it feel to be down and out." At that moment I was high off an adrenaline rush from beating her face until blood oozed onto the carpet. Staining my knock-off scuffed sneakers, Miss Thang was bucking frantically but my stomps to her stomach calmed her wild ass down quickly. I was getting the best of the one-sided battle until Nique, fed up with my over-the-top antics, pulled me all the way off her.

"Yo, listen up and get back into role. Enough of her; let's clean this house out." Grabbing another bag for herself, we both stood over a limp, beat-down officer of the law knowing she was knocked out cold. "Damn, you went to town on Alyssa. Mike ain't gonna recognize her ass."

"That was the point. Now let's get to work."

Ta'Nique was happy to hear that since she'd already started getting down. I finally took the time to look around Alyssa's house. I had to give ol' girl props, it was decked out no doubt. I ain't fronting, please believe I was keeping it one hundred. This wasn't the hood-style living me and Nique had grown numb to closing our eyes to nightly. It suddenly become more than me just wanting some dollars, diamonds, shoes, clothes, and furs. I wanted Alyssa's easy life. This was bigger than her though. Up until encountering the greedy, jealous faces before her, she'd probably never been so unlucky. She had the life my moms couldn't give me because she was too caught up on the pipe. I'd fantasized about most of this stuff as a kid and here before me was my chance to finally have it. If it was possible to back a U-Haul up in the driveway in broad daylight and empty this entire spot, I would in a heartbeat.

I was about to leave this whore bare and really afraid to visit Detroit. I wanted her to feel all the pain, anguish, and humiliation me and my friends from around the way were forced to feel every time we'd take our last to survive and government state emergency relief programs failed to help us.

Not needing to hear her voice just in case she woke up, I duct taped Alyssa's mouth closed, leaving enough room for her to breathe out of her nostrils. Pulling her up and onto one of her barstools, I used the extension cords to secure her down. Fuck getting away or screaming for help. "This should keep you out of trouble. And I'll be taking all of what you've got in those pockets." I cleared and put the few dollars, cell phone, and stick of gum I found into my own. Now out of energy and spunk, she refused to fight back.

Me and Nique ransacked the house taking practically everything we could load into her Taurus and Mike's F-150, hatchback included. Not forgetting about the stash in her dresser drawer of jewels, cash, credit cards, and even a few bank statements I could forge later, my girl and I had hit a nice little lick thanks to my side boo I desired to be my man. No doubt this was going to be our meal ticket for the next few weeks.

Ta'Nique, who was always laidback and collected, pulled off first heading back to the nest. Making sure the coast was still clear I ran past the woman on my way out of the door callously kicking her in the back of the head giving her some words of wisdom and some small but free bit of advice. "Money makes mischief, and with real thirst out in the streets, ain't no telling who gonna be down for whatever." Still moaning, trying to break free, I giggled at her being so persistent. "I've gotta give you credit though, you can sure enough take a beat down. You just might be equipped for the hood after all."

I turned the lights off and closed the door behind myself, quickly scanning for early bird neighbors before making my way to Mike's fully loaded truck. Quickly jumping in, I felt unstoppable. *Yeah, now who is the bad bitch behind the wheel? I'm about to be the new queen on Moneymaking Mike's arm, believe it.* Once I adjusted the seat and turned the air conditioner on blast, I threw the car into reverse then backed out of the driveway. It was time to make my escape just how'd we'd made our entrance: slow, calm, and unsuspecting.

# Chapter Fifteen

## *Nique*

Back in the grimy zone I'd survived in since a young sprout playing freeze tag outside of my mother's crack-infested shack, I was instantly depressed again. Being in Alyssa's reminded me of my situation. Even with a carload of stolen merchandise guaranteed to go for top dollar on the street, upgrade my appearance, or even get an abortion, having seen better at her well-to-do community made my life seem much worse. Sharply pulling into our pothole driveway, I popped the trunk to begin unloading the ill-gotten goods. Not too long after that Cori pulled up.

"I'm glad you made it, my baby." I set down the bag I was carrying onto the porch then embraced her in a tight hug. "You lost it in there, so I'm glad you were able to drive with some sense." Cori and I had been more like sisters than enemies, comrades than opponents, and companions when it came to hustling to maintain. She had really been a true friend through all this drama with Vic so I appreciated her.

"Shit me too. And I'm glad you were there to hold me down. I wanted to kill that trick."

We pulled back from the emotion hurriedly getting back to work. Not asking for any help from the next man, full of greed and refusing to share, this was a two-way split and there wasn't enough for an extra hand in the pot. Once Mike found out about everything, I was sure he'd be coming for his cut to make this a three-way split. In my neighborhood if you asked a person for so much as a slice of bread at the end of the month they felt like you owed them your first born in repayment. It took us a good twenty minutes of breaking a sweat going back and forth up and down a flight of stairs but the aftermath was gonna be gravy for us, and us only.

"I ain't gonna lie, we got down this time for sure." Cori smiled locking all three deadbolts on the front door and the security gate. "I mean like damn, she had some high-priced shit stashed everywhere. If there were more time, we would've left that house high, dry, and empty. Once I got my temper in check and hit that upstairs drawer, I felt like a kid in a candy store."

"Who the fuck you telling? I was stealing petty stuff just for the fuck of it."

"I know right, but that's exactly what her snake in the grass ass deserved for trying to play Mike like a sucker. And to think, he was dissing me for her. That shit has me livid. Matter of fact, I'm going to swing by his crib in his truck and break the news face to face since he won't answer my calls." She was grinning from ear to ear.

"Girl, g'on and get your man. After he finds out you saved him from going down with a dirty cop, he gonna be all up your ass for sure." I was geeking Cori up but was right back up in the dumps. Here she was going to get more dick but I was going to bed alone. This was not how I expected this night to go. Running out of the door, Corielle left me with my thoughts.

# Chapter Sixteen

## *Cori*

Getting to Mike's house, I saw the lights were on and Alyssa's red Benz parked in the driveway. I didn't waste any time getting out banging on his living room window.

"What in the fuck?" he mouthed, looking out seeing me and his F-150.

"I tried calling so I could tell you," I blurted out. "You should try answering the phone."

Mike pulled me into his house where I began to run down everything that had played out over the past few days, starting with my stamps getting cut off. I didn't leave any parts out, not even the ones concerning Alyssa being a Detroit police officer. All Mike could do was stand before me with a dropped jaw once I finally gave him word to how me and Nique had robbed Alyssa, leaving her tied up in her mini-mansion.

"Damn, a cop? Are you sure?"

I continued to run everything down to him, even told him how Wally suggested we go down to Club Ignite where I ran into her. "You were playing me for a dirty cop, ain't that some shit?"

"Looks like you took care of that though." Mike pulled me into him kissing me deeply, the most passionate he ever had. He took my clothes off piece by piece as I allowed him to devour my body. For the first time, I was sure: I was being fucked by my man.

# Chapter Seventeen

## *When Being Down for Whatever Goes Wrong*

Me and Mike were finally going to make it official. I couldn't wipe the cheesy smile from my face as I drove back to the hood in his truck to pack and wait for him. I'd never been out of this broken-down city before; and now the love of my life was getting ready to be the one to escort me out of here. Stopping by Meijer to get a new swimsuit and a few new outfits for our impromptu trip to Miami, I had to get right to floss on his arm. Calling Nique to let her know me and her were officially going to be family, she seemed to be a little occupied. Chalking it up to her still being stressed over Vic, I hung up but promised to bring her something nice back.

I pranced up and down aisles at last feeling good about myself. I tossed a few different swimsuits, colorful wife beaters, pajamas, panty and bra sets, and mesh booty shorts into the shopping cart then headed to check out. Mike was in the process of packing and taking care of a few loose ends with the streets; then he was gonna meet me on the block. And I wanted to make sure I was all set, ready to go. All of the self-checkouts were closed for servicing so I walked up to the attendant. I wasn't worried about there being a problem since I'd been using the card freely since the day it arrived in the mail. But for some reason, my nerves were getting the best of me.

"$219.25," she said, smiling and waiting for my form of payment.

Without thinking twice, I reached into my purse then handed the card I'd ordered in Kelly Tandy's name. For some reasons my palms were starting to sweat and I couldn't get my game face on.

"Excuse me, umm Ms. Tandy, but, ma'am, can you please wait right here a moment? A manager has to sign off on all of credit card purchases because my machine is down."

I was instantly on alert. The cashier might've been trying to play it off, but it was obvious something was wrong. She tried not to seem obvious as she looked back and forth between me and the register's screen before heading toward the customer service desk, but it didn't work.

Flashing alarms went off in my head. *Shit! That card is burnt out. That bitch thinks I'm dumb.* No way in hell was I about to get carted off to jail after finally winning big with Mike. Nope, not me. I might've been making a rash decision, but with too little time it was the best one I had. I flew like a bat out of hell out toward the car.

I could hear security yelling behind me as I ran like lightning speed. I was scared as fuck because I couldn't go down. With all the prints I'd left behind during robberies, they'd bury my young, beautiful ass underneath the jail cell. Hopping in the car quickly, I pulled off without a second glance. I heard a loud thud before rolling over what seemed to be a speed bump.

"Oh my God. Call the ambulance. She's run over Security Officer Baldwin," I heard one employee scream.

Looking back in my rearview mirror but definitely not stopping or going back, I pushed my foot all the way down onto the gas pedal and sped off. Once on the freeway, I started calling Nique nonstop. I was pretty sure the hit and run was reported to the police by now. Not only had I given them a bad credit card, still stealing the merchandise I'd shopped for, I now had a hit and run to be held accountable for.

"Fuck, fuck, fuck." I hated my life. I truly hated my life. Now Mike's car was involved with a hit and run. His plates, if anyone saw, would be run then plastered on the news for sure. Oh well for that new relationship.

I rapped to Jeezy *President is Black* rap as I floated to the house. I'd been calling Nique the entire time to get her advice before calling her cousin but was having no luck. As I cautiously pulled up in front of our house parking next to Nique's ride, my nerves were still on edge. I pulled a bag of weed from my purse to roll up quick. Since I'd made it safely back on the block without sirens trailing, it was safe to assume I'd gotten away. After a few puffs, I was in the zone on the strong Purp we'd gotten from Wally. I didn't want to call Mike but I didn't have a choice. What other option did I have? He was going to nut all the way up once he saw the damage I'd created. Spook walked up as I was getting out the car. "Cori, let me get five dollars so I can something to eat." He walked over with his hand out.

"Damn, Spook, I ain't even got it," I replied, slightly agitated and caught up in my own drama. For once I thought things were looking up for me then right back like that, shit had gone back south.

"Well run in the house and tell Wally to come out for a second. I know he'll give his boy Spook a few bucks. I know fa'sho his ass got it," he sarcastically said.

"What the fuck, Spook? Ain't no damn Wally around these parts. That was earlier," I replied surveying the block for his Caddy.

"Damn, niece, you ain't gotta lie. I might be a crackhead but a fool I am not." He turned around and walked away seeming pissed and insulted.

And that's when I spotted Wally's car parked a little farther down the street like it was an attempt to be hidden. Running up the concrete stairs, I was too worked up and anxious to see what was really going on. Why had Wally parked his car up the street and why hadn't Nique been answering? I reached for the gold-plated doorknob on the security door; it was locked. *What the fuck?* The door was never locked and that was a dead giveaway that something wasn't right. On my toes as always, I went around to the back of the house careful not to trip on anything or make any noise.

Initially I felt Nique was in some sort of trouble but that was me being naive not wanting my one and only friend to turn out shady. My bedroom window was still open in an attempt to let the smell of raw sex from me and Wally or Mike out, whichever one had my room so fresh of ass. I used the garbage can to climb up on then lifted the window up far enough for me to climb in quietly.

"Deeper, bitch. Deeper," I heard Wally grunt.

*Ain't this about a bitch. The devil is a lie.* As I crept through the doorway of my room peeping into the living room, I could see Wally's back as Nique sat on her knees deep throating. *Oh hell naw.* It was time to go to the sock drawer on these bastards. I was quiet as a church mouse, and tip-toed to grab my gun for the gunfight me and Wally were about to have. I couldn't believe the nerve of them. I'd been holding Nique's knocked-up ass down even with Vic treating her like the last man's trash and this was what I got in return? I could expect Wally's ass to be disloyal but Nique, that bitch should've been first in line to take a bullet for me, not stab me in the back.

"Oh yeah, Nique, your head game is way better than that slick bitch Cori's," I heard him say. "I knew you wanted to swallow this big dick monster up when you were watching me earlier," I heard Wally scream assuming he was cumming in her mouth. "You couldn't wait to call me up."

*Damn, I can't wait to put a bullet in this nigga. He's taking too many liberties. First sexing me, then her.* Shaking my head, I'd had enough of being picked over. I'd taught Alyssa a lesson and these two were about to be next. In a rush I almost dropped the entire box of bullets onto the floor trying to load my pistol.

"So she called herself trying to get the weed for free? That sneak charged me up front. She's such a lying bitch."

I heard Nique speak badly about me. The cat was out of the bag but after all the shit I'd done for her these last two days, how dare she put me on blaze?

"Yeah, well that's your ride or die, so you say. But both of y'all obviously on some sneaky, shady-type shit. Hell, I just made both of y'all whores suck on this cock."

"I can keep sucking on that cock on the low if you want me to. Now that I know Cori don't really be on my side, I can start the process of getting rid of her. That bitch we robbed earlier was a cop; I could put the whole robbery on her. Plus that beauty supply robbery I know she didn't tell you about." Nique was telling it all.

*Oh no, this stank bitch just didn't say she'll put it all on me. Boy have I been fooled. I see dick has her flopping like a fish out of water.* I was enraged.

"Well you know better than me what you gotta do. I ain't in the middle of that shit." I watched him zip up his pants. "You'd be weak though if you didn't front her off about trying to get down on you, especially if y'all supposed to be in the streets together."

Wally had some nerve trying to give her advice.

"Unless you're into getting your card pulled."

"Nigga, please, she ain't pulling no card this way. Don't get me wrong, me and her have been cool since our childhood years but I never been with a bitch trying to get over on me. If it weren't for you coming through here to talk business about a possible re-up with some different ganja, I never would've known."

Dropping her head, Nique had the nerve to play like I'd done something so horrible to her. I was sure she'd gotten hers off top before too.

"It's cool, boo. Now that you know, handle it." Wally was giving her advice he didn't know she wouldn't be able to play out.

"I'm going to for sure let Cori know I ain't the one." She picked up her cell phone. "And once Mike gets confirmation that she's been raw dog—" Nique stopped talking in midsentence.

Her face turned pale as her eyes bulged out catching sight of me walking into the living room. My Smith & Wesson was out, fully loaded and aimed directly at them. The look on Wally's expression was cocky as he sported a cocky grin that matched mine. "Oh my God, not this bitch. That's what you want to say right?" Nodding my head, I knew I was the only one with the real power in this room. Wrong or not for having my way with Mike, fucking Wally, or taking any other liberty that I felt entitled to, how dare Ta'Nique, my supposed comrade in life, be so cool with sharing dick? I ain't play those games and was feeling real betrayed right about now.

"Damn, I see y'all whores are crazy for real. Fuck the loyalty around here." He laughed, pulling on his cigarette. "G'on and put that pistol down, C. You know I'm packing hella heat, baby girl so this ain't the way you wanna go out." Wally still thought it was him with the upper hand.

"Shut up, Wally, don't test her 'cause you gonna make it worse. Just get your shit and go so me and her can kick it." Nique needed a reminder that she no longer could call the shots.

I fired a single shot into the air. I wanted silence. "Both of y'all can shut the fuck up. I ain't down for talking about nothing with your trife-life ass, Nique, we ain't cool." My whole body was trembling as I stared at the girl I'd shared my fears, joys, and friendship with over the last twenty years of my life. "See, this ain't no easy shit to get over." I waved the gun in the air feeling myself start to get emotional. Wally was starting to get uneasy, shifting around in his seat. Ta'Nique stared back at me stiff, recognizing the same anger in herself about Vic and Tasha.

"Ay yo, C, this shit you pulling getting a rise out of ol' girl but I ain't the one. All I know is that if you pop a bullet to kill, ya ass bests be killing me," Wally vowed, speaking his final words.

I'd had enough of Wally trying to punk me around. I'd taken enough blows for the day. His words meant absolutely nothing.

I shot at Wally, landing one bullet in his throat and one to his chest. I heard Nique screaming bloody murder and if she didn't shut the fuck up quick I'd land two inside her also.

"Bitch, be quiet," I screamed at her pointing the gun directly to her face.

She was smart, following my orders instantly.

"Get the fuck up and give me all your money, cards, everything; and move fast," I demanded realizing that I had almost zero time to get out of dodge.

She didn't want to end up like Wally, so she did as she was told. "Please don't kill me, sissy, please." Nique's words were pissing me off.

"Bitch, kill it with that sissy shit. I thought we were better than that, Nique, but you had to go fuck my leftovers. If it wasn't for me climbing up on garbage cans crawling through windows to see what was up, I would've been snuck by your dirty ass. You were in here swallowing nut then talking about me like a dog. I blame myself though. You're carrying my godchild, we're supposed to be aces for the rest of our lives then ball out in heaven like true ghetto bosses do, but I guess I was wrong. Faye told me about trusting hoes."

Nique was silent, refusing to respond. How could she? I'd caught her red-handed. She just threw the money down to my feet, rolled her eyes, and tried to make a dash to the door. I couldn't let the ho live; it was the point and principle. "I'm gonna go ahead and take care of Vic's situation. Fuck you and that li'l bastard!"

I left off a single shot then a single tear of remorse rolled down my cheek. She was the only one real friend I had, or so I thought. We did everything together but today she'd die alone. I watched her body slump over the armrest of the beat-up recliner that sat in our living room. The same place she was just getting dick from Wally at.

*Damn, what the hell have I done?* I'd robbed a Detroit police officer, done a double murder . . . This day was just going down all wrong. I ran to both of our stashes grabbing all of the money not leaving one cent. Then I packed a few duffel bags of clothes so I could keep myself together once I got to wherever my destination was going to be. I needed somewhere new to call home. This place just turned into a murder scene and I would surely be the prime suspect. A bitch wasn't going to jail, trust that.

"Came up that's all me, stay true that's all me." Looking down at my phone ringing it was Mike. *Damn.* Peeking out of the blinds, I saw that he'd just pulled up in Alyssa's Benz. "Fuck, this can't be happening." I wanted to walk out of the door, get into the car, and live the rest of my life happily ever after. But that would never be my reality. I'd killed his blood cousin Ta'Nique, so to him, we were now enemies.

I took Wally's keys off of the coffee table, stuffed my phone deep into my pocket, then grabbed the few bags I'd packed. It was time to make a break for it.

"Came up that's all me, stay true that's all me."
Mike was calling back but I had to go. I left out the
same way I'd come in. I ran up the alley cutting out
where Wally's Cadillac was parked and jumped in.
I drove past the house discreetly watching Mike
knock on the door.

"A'ight, niece, I'll be seeing you around, Cori."

All I saw was Mike in my rearview waving for
me to stop. "Came up that's all me, stay true that's
all me."

"Naw, nigga, it's a wrap for that. I'm out."

# Chapter Eighteen

## *And Then There Was One*

"Hey, Mike man, ya might wanna go in there. I heard a few shots." Spook walked across the street, seeing his niece burn rubber on two wheels around the corner.

Not wasting another second, Mike grabbed the pistol from his waistband and began busting the window out. Shattering glass everywhere, he knocked the remaining pieces of broken glass from around the frame to climb in. The fact that no one from inside screamed at him entering the house like a madman sent an eerie sensation up his spine. "Keep a lookout Spook." Mike wasn't prepared for what he saw. He ran to Nique's side, grabbing up his only flesh and blood cousin, not being able to come to grips she was dead. "I'ma send her your way," he said, closing her eyes, knowing Corielle was responsible. Not giving a ghetto fuck about the one other body laid out only a few inches from them, he kicked Wally out of pride knowing he had to have been the reason behind all of this.

# Chapter Nineteen

## *What Will Be, Will Be . . .*

Shit, it had been one long fucking complicated day. Matter of fact, it had been one of the longest weekends of my life and I was more than ready to put a close to this chapter. Now I know what you're thinking, at this point in the game I should be gassing up my ride hitting the freeway to parts unknown. But I just didn't give a damn no more. Whatever is meant to be will be. I'd been down for whatever for years and what the fuck had it gotten me?

I pulled my beat-up doom buggy into the parking spot closest to the door and jumped out with confidence like I was Superwoman. I only needed one or two drinks to soothe my mood. After that, I'd be hitting the road to never return. As I sat brazen and bold in the rear section of the downtown club sulking about today's events and my two ex-friends dead on my living room floor murdered by my hand, I got chills up and down my spine. I needed to finish this drink so I could head South before Mike got the city on my head. It'd always been family first with him so he'd never listen to reason. It was no love lost for the D. I'd worn out my welcome and burned this city dry with all the robberies, shoplifting, hustles, schemes, fake insurance papers, tricking, and now murders. I had to go somewhere that no one knew me; and what the hell, the South had been a lot of people's fresh restart.

I took my last shot of Patrón then downed the final drop of my Blue Motherfucker before catching a glimpse of what I knew had to be a dream. At the worst time ever, a fucking nightmare had come back to me. I knew for sure my homegirl was smiling down seeing irony play out. Tasha and her crew of girls walked in like celebrities. After we locked eyes with one another, I shook my head knowing the beef was on. Since Nique wasn't here to settle the score, it was now me against the three-woman crew.

"Karma is surely a bitch. What up, Tasha? I see we meet again."